# Annie's
# Second
# Wind

A NOVEL BY **WALLY CARLSON**

BOOK PUBLISHERS NETWORK

Book Publishers Network
P.O. Box 2256
Bothell • WA • 98041
PH • 425-483-3040
www.bookpublishersnetwork.com

10 9 8 7 6 5 4 3 2 1

Printed in the United States of America

LCCN  2008932131
ISBN10  1-887542-86-8
ISBN13  978-1-887542-86-9

Editor: Vicki McCown
Proofreader: Julie Scandora
Cover Artist: Colleen Carlson
Typographer: Stephanie Martindale

# SEVEN SISTERS ISLAND

A n island is a touchstone of the human heart.

Twelve thousand years ago the grinding crush of glaciers plowed the earth rough and sterile. In time, the icy tentacles retreated, leaving in their milky wake an island: the edges chiseled and raw, the uplands barren and rocky, and the shoreline protected by seven sentinel rocks. Only the healing rain and the power of the tidal moons could once again make the land fertile.

The land lured stouthearted men and wildcat women onto its protective shores. Their lives, patiently lacquered layer upon layer on the crust, changed the texture of the land forever.

To belong to an island is to grasp the satin edge of immortality.

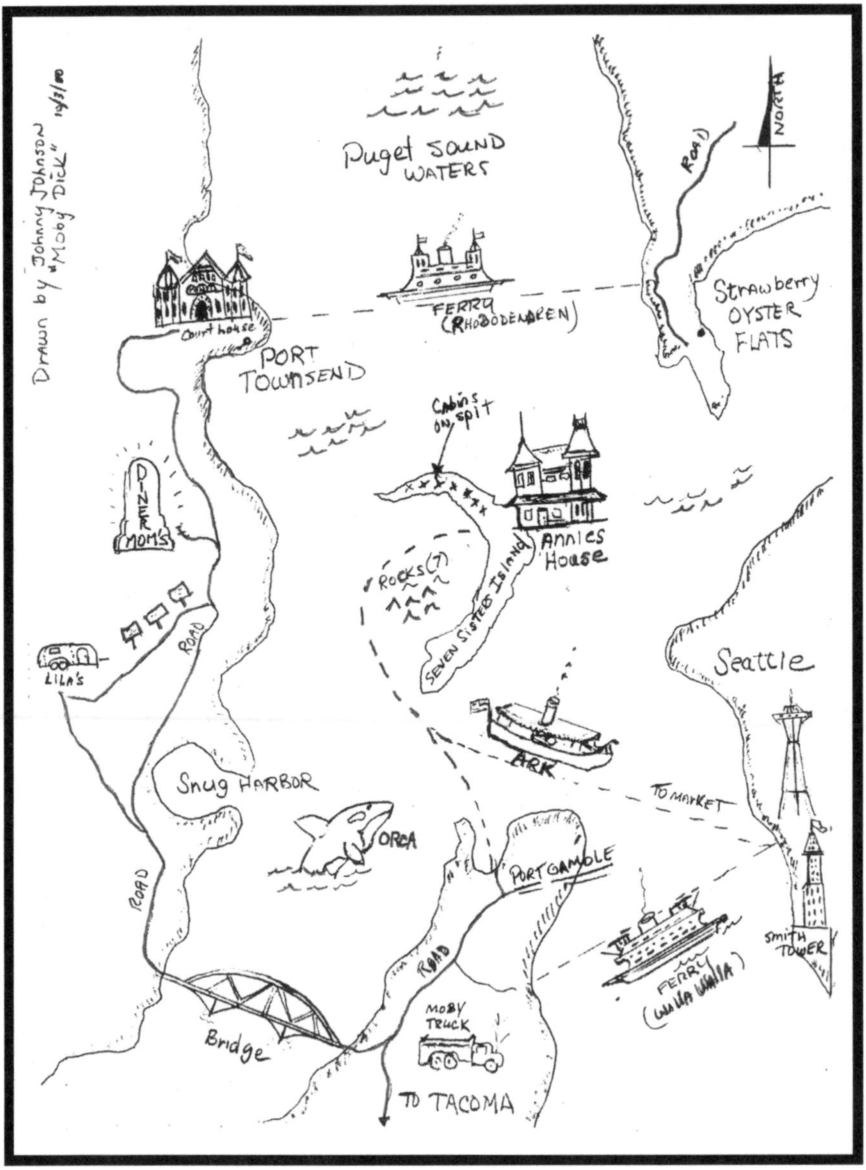
Drawn by Johnny Johnson "Moby Dick" 10/3/80
Puget SOUND WATERS
NORTH
ROAD
Strawberry OYSTER FLATS
FERRY (RHODODENDREN)
Court house
PORT TOWNSEND
Cabins on spit
Annies House
DINER MOM'S
ROCKS (7)
SEVEN SISTERS ISLAND
Seattle
LILA'S
ROAD
ARK
TO MARKET
Snug HARBOR
ORCA
PORT GAMBLE
ROAD
ROAD
SMITH TOWER
FERRY (WALLA WALLA)
MOBY TRUCK
Bridge
TO TACOMA

# PROLOGUE

The telegram had chased Annie across four continents. It caught up with her high in the Peruvian Andes.

*Aunt Amelia in coma, near death.*

*Come home as soon as possible.*

*Calypso*

Annie pursed her lips and gave a deep sigh. *Calypso*, the sea nymph, Jacques Cousteau's boat, Annie's self-named wayward daughter…her only child.

Annie went into her canvas tent to let the bad news settle. She knew Amelia, her closest sister, had been very sick. It wasn't surprising; after all, she was in her seventy-seventh year. The sixth of seven sisters was about to fulfill the legacy of death. A legacy some called a blessing and others a curse. It had started as mere coincidence and now it had taken on a life of its own. Nevertheless, Annie called it damned inconvenient. There was still work to be done.

The Red Cross point-woman for calamity, Annie was directing the rescue operation of a village that had been swept into the valley by an 8.1 earthquake. Shell-shocked villagers and burros wandered aimlessly as rocks the size of Volkswagen beetles still tumbled through the village and down into the jungle below.

Annie hated to leave, but this was family.

Annie Perkins was going home.

She flew into Sea-Tac Airport and took a puddle-jumper to Port Townsend on the shores of Puget Sound. From there she phoned the three-lane bowling alley/laundry/pizzeria her daughter managed somewhere north of Seattle.

"Somewhere near Timbuktu," Annie grumbled as she dropped coins into the pay phone, trying to remember where the hell her daughter lived.

"Aloha Bowl," came the bored voice. "Can we help you make that spare?"

"It's me," said Annie, as though it had been four days, not four years, since she'd spoken to her daughter. "How is Aunt Amelia?"

"Glad you could make it, Mother," Calypso said sardonically. "She's still in a coma. She hasn't taken in any food or fluids for more than two weeks. They don't know how she's hanging in there. She's at Memorial Hospital, if you're interested."

Annie bit her tongue. Fifty-two years old and Calypso was still holding a grudge.

Well, Annie chastised herself for the ten millionth time, you should have never abandoned her. It was a mother's guilt she lived with everyday.

"Thanks," Annie said. "I'm on my way."

Annie hadn't been to the hospital since she was a child. New wings had been added, creating a maze of halls that finally led her to the basement information desk where she asked in which room she might find her sister, Amelia Perkins.

The woman at the desk didn't look up.

"Down the hall, turn left, Room 17."

Annie trailed her hand along the wainscoted wall as she slowly walked down the hall and turned the corner. Room 17 stood in front of her, the door closed. Annie involuntarily shivered as she turned the handle. Inside a scrum of white uniformed medical personnel surrounded what appeared to be an empty bed.

"She must be waiting for something," a nurse murmured. "It's a miracle she's still alive."

Annie peeked under the nurse's arm and saw the object of their attention: a frail, motionless, hospital-gowned skeleton. Abruptly the figure sat up and pointed a gnarled finger at the crowd. The doctors and nurses parted like the Red Sea, leaving Annie exposed.

Then she heard that distinctive gravely voice.

"Annie," Amelia's eyes burned brightly, "you've finally come." She paused, as if gathering together the last vestiges of strength hiding in her shell of a body. "Get the farm back on its feet. It's your legacy now. I entrust the island to you."

Annie winced. So many witnesses. But she nodded.

The figure in the bed convulsed backward and stared slack-jawed at the ceiling. Amelia Perkins lay lifeless, her mission complete.

Annie sighed. Gone forever the retirement bungalow in the tropics, the ninety-degree days tempered by the gentle trade winds. Hello to sixty-degree summer days and the incessant rain clouds of the Pacific Northwest.

That had been three years ago, and ever since, Annie had dedicated herself to saving the farm, tangled as it was in a web of taxes, rezoning, and unrelenting county officials wanting the island for development. There were only a few years left now before she would be the one turning the island over to her daughter or maybe even to her granddaughter.

"Thank God for the curse," Annie sometimes mumbled to herself.

And she yearned for a simpler time when her life had been filled with hurricanes and floods.

# Chapter ONE

"**S**top complaining, girl, and get up," Annie murmured to herself, waking up with a full bladder and the unpleasant thought of a long cold run to the outhouse.

She yawned, carefully stretched, and dangled her feet off the side of the bed, assessing the damage. The great toe on the left was stiff and sore. She wiggled it and grimaced. Right knee, left thumb: unbendable. One eye refused to open, and the other could not focus. Obviously, the body was not yet available for service. She lay back, dragged the quilt over her legs, and turned on her side, looking out the small panes of the wood-framed window.

Even the windows don't reflect clearly, she thought to herself as she stared at the imperfect hand-blown panes that gave an astigmatized view of a hawthorne tree, one of many planted by her great-grandfather.

Annie dozed off again, sprawled in a bed where four generations had been conceived and born, covered by the quilt she and her mother had made, in a house built by her great ancestors in an apple orchard planted long ago.

The second time Annie woke up, she grabbed a threadbare flannel robe and stuffed her feet into Amelia's hand-me-down fuzzy avocado green slippers. She eased herself down the squeaky wood stairs that protested as much as her joints then crossed to the wood-burning kitchen stove. The emblem on the oven door read, "Sensible"; the date, "1865," was stamped at the top. By the time Annie arrived on the scene—the last-born of seven girls—"sensible" had already been taken, along with "drama queen," "passionate," and "businesswoman." Annie didn't mind; she was all about adventure.

Annie tilted open the damper. She pushed in a handful of cedar kindling and gently blew on the coals from the night before. The crackle of the exploding resins woke up Buddy, the golden retriever snoozing under the stove.

Hopping from one foot to the other in agony, Annie dipped the ladle into the galvanized bucket and filled the coffee pot. Then spooning grounds into the strainer, she snapped on the lid with the glass knob. The satisfying metallic sound completed the first order of business, the same morning ritual her mother had performed faithfully in the exact sequence. Nothing much ever changed on the island.

Her bladder screamed for relief. Sprinting for the door, she halfheartedly bleated for Buddy to accompany her. He declined the offer and continued doing his best dead-dog imitation, his feet protruding from under the stove as he sucked the first of its radiant heat.

As she ran up the hill, Annie grabbed an alder branch to fend off the dreaded spider that lived in the outhouse. From the tropics to the Arctic, she had done battle with cousins of this eight-legged menace, once going head-to-head in Kenya with a spider the size of a dinner plate. Now, she threw open the door to expose a culprit she had fought to a draw all summer. Dusted with the September dew, his web shimmered in the morning sun like a thousand crystal chandeliers.

The spider, about the size of a quarter, sat exposed on the white lid. Annie began to flail away. No fool, it rappelled down to the floor and disappeared into a crack between the wall and the floor. Annie could have easily gassed the intruder, but she followed the dictates of the Geneva Convention, and anyway, she preferred to execute spiders personally. Annie still remembered vividly how, once in Indonesia, she had swatted a plump, melon-like arachnid from the bamboo rafters of her hut. It had produced a pleasing splat as it hit the dirt, as if it were a jar of applesauce hitting a tile floor.

She propped open the door of the outhouse and gave a begrudging, respectful grunt and a deep draining sigh.

To distract herself, she turned her attention to the outstretched sandy arm of the beach on which six dilapidated oyster-picker shacks were perched askew, fifty feet apart. Each one had been built from whatever the sea provided. No shack looked the same, with their different roof pitches, oddly shaped windows, and tilting porches. One included '57 Buick doors, complete with windows that cranked down and side-view mirrors. Another had a shingle roof over an old forty-foot yacht, with a hole punched in the hull for a door. The rest were built from, as her father called it, "tidal action." Whatever washed up on the beach was incorporated—rusted metal, street signs, fencing, driftwood—all compliments of the ebb and flow of the relentless seas.

Next, Annie rested her chin on the palm of her hand and studied the stone-facade root cellar dug into the side of the hill. Perishables were kept behind two massive wooden doors, holding the cold air that drifted somewhere from caves deep in the island core. The entire apple crop and vegetable crop were kept behind the wooden bulkheads till market day. There were still long, jagged scratches in the door where a black bear had tried to claw his way through to some hanging venison till her father crept up from behind and shot the bear through the ear.

Next to the cellar, water poured from an artesian spring into an old claw-foot tub. Gravity fed itself through a rusty pipe inside to the kitchen. Indoor plumbing, her mother called it. No one dared dispute her.

The coffee had begun to perk, filling the farmhouse with its fragrant aroma. Annie warmed her hands over the stovetop and put on wash water. Leaning against the stove rail, she fetched a brown, earthen bowl filled with apple crisp from the shelf above the stove and put it into the oven to warm.

Taking off her robe, she pulled on a pair of denim bib overalls that had been warming behind the stove. The heated rivets made her dance as they found bare skin. She slipped on a man's tee shirt. Grabbing a sage-green, cable-knit sweater from another peg, she pulled it over her head while her left hand liberated her thick, braided pigtail, now mostly gray flecked with burgundy. She avoided looking in the mirror. It was a face she'd studied a million times and with which she had always found fault. Annie still had the aura of a redhead, but to call her a redhead these days was a stretch. She hated her gray hair, but then a lot of things she didn't like had happened over her seventy-five years.

The porcelain skin showed the lines of age, but time had not given her a respite from the cursed genetic freckles. She had surrendered to the freckles years ago in an uneasy peace, after once spending two days lying in bed, her teenage face covered by a washrag soaked in lemon oil concentrate guaranteed to fade freckles forever. Instead they stood out even more in a field of yellowy-white skin, but people *had* complimented her on her citrus scent.

Enough musing, Annie chided herself. Time to get it in gear. Market day, time to make some money.

Half an hour later, Annie climbed into her cedar-planked boat in the boathouse. She pressed the electric start; the engine belched black smoke from the stack and settled to a deep-throated purr in neutral. Annie busied herself, checking the orange life jackets, tying one on Buddy, even though he was obviously embarrassed by the notion that he couldn't take care of himself. Annie had never worn a life preserver in all her years on the water. She taunted the gods to take her now, at this stage of the game. She slipped the lines and slammed the throttle to forward. The boat jetted out from the boathouse into open water.

She surveyed her cargo. She had packed the boat last night under a harvest moon. The apples, loaded in bushel baskets, were nestled under the kingfisher blue canvas awning of the open boat, along with the applesauce, candied applets, and aprons. The wizened faces of the apple dolls stared out at her from their safe haven under the covered bow. The oysters had rested in a sack in the water until the last moment and now joined the apple goods in the boat.

Christened *The Ark,* the forty-foot boat had been painted snow-white and outfitted with a thirty-horse diesel Wisconsin engine. A tall, black smokestack penetrated the center of the canopy. Distinct in a sea awash with fiberglass fishing boats, the wooden *Ark*—dubbed *The African Queen* by the locals—was revered throughout the Sound.

The fog was just beginning to lift as Buddy took his place on the bow. Notches had been cut along the gunwale to support the leg lengths of the island's various dog feet over the years. Buddy assumed the catbird position and proceeded to bark at every passing gull and seal. Annie stood holding the tiller and stared into the fog, keeping an eye out for other boats and the pesky deadhead logs that lurked just below the water's surface.

This time of morning was reserved for working boats. The recreational crowd still lingered over breakfast, and the yachtsmen busied themselves polishing their brass, winding their mooring lines into tight spirals, and consulting their GPS systems. *The Ark* would have none of that "nonsense."

A blast from an air horn startled her. A huge breaker thundered across the bow, knocking Buddy from his perch, spraying Annie with cold saltwater. The Bainbridge ferry steamed alongside. The captain tipped his hat from the bridge and gave a couple of quick toots in salute.

Annie wiped her face with her sleeve and felt the power of the huge ferry engines as they churned the water to a white froth. A short, bald-headed man leaned over the stern with a camera. Annie waved, thus providing him with a classic picture.

The waves played out, rolling *The Ark* from side to side. Then the seas calmed again. Annie slalomed her way to the edge of the Seattle waterfront, still encased in a dense fog. Only the tops of the tallest buildings penetrated the shroud, basking in the glorious sunshine.

The Seattle skyline had changed dramatically over the years, but Annie had eyes only for the Smith Tower to the south of town. Built by a typewriter magnate early in the century, the Smith Tower had been the tallest building west of the Mississippi for a time. Annie still remembered when her father had taken her up to the top of the building. She had gazed down and seen her own island in the distance, the mountains surrounding the city, the working tugs and gritty cargo ships on the water looking like toy boats floating on a flat pond. Her father had raised her up with his powerful arms and sat her on his shoulders so she could feel even taller.

On the way home that evening long ago, she had fallen asleep in the bow of the boat, covered with her father's scratchy wool jacket, smelling the rough chew of tobacco, and listening to the water rushing past her ear on the other side of the wood planks while she lay dry and warm and safe.

The harbor of her youth had given way to the tall erector-set skyline of a world port, a stark contrast from when she and her father ruled the world. Annie steered straight to the public dock and turned the tiller hard to the side at the last moment. The boat nestled perfectly into the slip. A young man hired by the port nodded his approval.

"Nice work, Captain."

Annie smiled, threw him the mooring line, and climbed over the side of the boat while Buddy stood guard.

Annie plodded up the gangplank to the street and flagged down a horse-drawn carriage that worked the waterfront. The driver slowly turned his horse around in the middle of the empty street. A slim black man with an engaging smile, he ordinarily would be trolling for tourists, but Annie figured correctly that he would take what he could get this early in the morning. He climbed down from his perch.

"Apple Annie," he said, recognizing her from her stand at the market. "Don't that beat all."

The driver loaded up as Annie went up to the big chestnt Clydesdale, patting his flank so he knew of her approach. The horse turned his head square to her, centering her between his blinders. His big, expressive eyes, rimmed with long eyelashes, were as liquid brown as a camel's. She rubbed his nose and fed him an apple.

Levering herself up into the coach, Annie stood surrounded by her apples, like a homecoming queen in a parade float. When they stopped at a light, the bald man from the ferry stepped out of a cab, jogged across the street, and squatted down to get a better camera angle.

"Where are you going?" he called up to Annie. "The Public Market?"

Annie nodded.

"Can I hitch a ride?"

Annie nodded again, and he clambered aboard, introducing himself as John Hunt, food editor for the *Seattle Times*. He motioned to one of the baskets.

"Can I have an apple?"

Annie handed him a red-and-green-striped Gravenstein. They headed north up the street, four blocks to the market.

As they entered the one-way alley, John exited the carriage first and shot more pictures. Annie greeted other vendors who were unloading their flowers and produce from assorted trucks and trailers.

A man charged from the doorway of the Russian piroshki bakeshop.

"Aunnie," he called, "you are a sight for hurting eye sockets. 'Stella . . . Stella . . . I coulda been a contender.' 'We're gonna need a bigger boat.' Go ahead, make my day.'"

Annie marveled at the range of the intense immigrant's Hollywood lingo, pried from the sound bites of video classics. She laughed and launched an apple overhand. He caught it handily and returned to rolling out his dough.

The Pike Place Market block was filled with colors, smells, and sounds of commerce. Giant bouquets boasted of a long summer's bounty. Scented roses joined with the smell of leather and diesel, and vibrant dahlias with the earthy colors of giant cabbages, carrots, and onions. Every nationality of shopkeeper held court—volatile Italian and Spanish truck gardeners shared spaces with polite Filipino and Japanese strawberry and raspberry farmers, each vying for space and customers.

The ground had already been littered with trampled lettuce leaves, culled flowers, and other debris of the trade. Across the alley, the warm smell of fresh-baked bread wafted from the Black Crow Bakery, commingling with the thick aroma of garlic and basil from That's a Some Italian Pasta Shoppe. Together, they created an aromatic confluence that made street people stop in the middle of the intersection and turn their noses to the wind.

The carriage came to a stop under a long overhead metal sign with black and white peeling paint that read "Seven Sisters Island Apples and Oysters, established 1868." The words were flanked by two giant red apples, looking good enough to eat.

John and the carriage driver helped to unload as Annie gingerly handed the baskets down. The two men worked briskly, and when they were finished, Annie gave the carriage driver a bushel of apples in payment and personally took a second apple to the horse.

Annie immediately launched into her routine for organizing her stall. The top apples in the basket were buffed with a cloth. The aprons, the dolls, the applets, and the applesauce in canning jars topped with gingham were all displayed within easy reach of the crowds that would soon stream by.

Annie next gave herself a grandmotherly appearance, donning a frilly white apron and a wide-brimmed red felt hat festooned with tall, wispy black feathers that curled at the ends, suitable for strawberries and cream at Wimbledon. Depending on the mood of the crowd, later in the day, she might switch to a Mariners' baseball cap worn backward, Griffey-style.

The baskets of apples received red-satin bows, a marketing strategy pioneered by her mother, which allowed her to sell the apples for a premium price. The oysters sat in soggy gunnysacks unadorned, ugly, and delicious. They sold themselves. You either loved them or you didn't.

John witnessed the shop set-up and Annie's transformation and realized he was watching a master at work.

"Annie, would it be all right if I hung around and watched for a while, took a few more pictures for a story? Maybe we could schedule an interview later?"

Annie had quickly sized up John. He seemed earnest and enthusiastic. She liked people with a passion.

"You buy lunch and you're on," she said.

When Annie hawked apples, she became the consummate showman. Spying two college girls with their boyfriends, she coyly extended her hand with an apple in it, saying, "Come my pretty, take a small bite." The girls laughed, each bought a basket, and Annie had her first sale of the day. Sometimes she would raise her voice and yell out, "An apple a day keeps the doctor away!" or "Apples keep you regular!" or "No one ever got in trouble eating an apple—except Adam and Eve!" If she saw a young, starry-eyed couple, she'd switch her pitch: "Oysters are the key to virility!"

By eleven, she had sold half her stock of apples and one of three gunnysacks of oysters.

"Like to give it a try?" she asked John.

With a smile, John exchanged places with Annie—and was promptly ignored. He picked up three apples and started to juggle. Annie raised her eyebrows in surprised admiration.

"The only talent I cultivated during my fraternity days," he explained.

When John dropped an apple moments later, Annie said, "You're paying for that one." He dropped two more, followed by the same admonition. Soon their giggles gave way to guffaws so hearty Annie almost fell off her stool.

"John, they can buy apples cheaper at a store. Ya gotta sell 'em, boy, ya gotta sell 'em!"

John grimaced and gave a determined growl. He grabbed Annie's feather hat, stood on the table overlooking the crowd, and declaimed an impromptu ode to an apple. "How do I compare thee?" he started.

At last, he began to sell apples. Forty-five minutes later, honest sweat pouring from his brow, he turned to Annie.

"Lunch break?"

Annie yelled over to the "Love Potion" booth across the aisle.

"Madeline, will you watch my apples?"

Madeline, who possessed the largest set of crimson lips Annie had ever seen outside of a Ubangi tribe, was decked out in a see-through blouse, a micro-mini skirt, and black fishnet stockings. Her to-die-for legs were poked into cowboy boots adorned with the out-line of two chrome-studded armadillos effecting a gymnastic Kama Sutra position. The composite seemed to charm her patrons. Madeline mixed her potions—available in squirt bottles, edible jellies, and the handy gallon size with optional pump—in her kitchen. She was a fellow huckster whose living depended on the fickle fortunes of free trade. She could be trusted.

Annie and John charged through the crowd together, weaving their way through pallets and traffic, but Annie's diminutive size and her experience in crowded third-world countries allowed her to slip ahead. John followed the red hat, catching a glimpse of the feathers crossing in front of the market's brass pig, just before he had to duck to miss being hit by a flying fish—a familiar hazard at the Pike Place Market. With a bravado born of repetition, fish mongers routinely threw salmon over the heads of amused bystanders to their cowork-ers at the counter, who caught the fish neatly in butcher paper to be wrapped and weighed.

"Everyone's in showbiz," John said.

He could see Annie homing in on the piroshki bakery, where the Russian immigrant stood in the front window, his powerful hairy arms rolling out dough in front of an appreciative crowd. The window was smeared with handprints, noseprints, and foggy circles where the bated breath of the people on the street met the warmth of Ivan's miniature meat pies. Ivan dolloped the fillings—cabbage, onions, carrots, and beef—in careful mounds. Waving a large, showy, curved knife with a wooden handle, he cut crisp squares around the stacks.

He folded the overlapping leading edge to cover each dumpling, and with a floured pinch of his thick forefinger and thumb, sealed the crust. He placed the pocket meals in neat rows on a flat sheet of steel then turned and popped them in the oven.

This Russian virtuoso had carved his own unique niche in the land of lattes and lutefisk.

Annie tapped on the glass to get the baker's attention, then led John inside. Looking up, Ivan gave them a big smile and came around the end of the counter, a fluffy cloud of flour trailing in his wake.

"Annie, I am missing you," he said, picking up Annie and squeezing her, imprinting two flour handprints on the back of her sweater. "And who is this one?" he asked. He pumped John's hand as Annie introduced them. "John, this is also name for bathroom, yes? Come, you wish to eat?" He dragged them both behind the counter of his shop, which was no bigger than a small walk-in closet. Installing them on two stools, he wrapped four of his latest creations in wax paper and placed them in front of John and Annie. He leaned down to open a blue plastic Coleman cooler, extracted two bottles of apple juice, and set them, dripping, on the counter.

"When I come to this country, I need job," Ivan said. "My church send me to market; Annie get me this wonderful place." He spread his arms wide, touching both sides of his shop. "I make good money and send home to family. Someday, my family all come here. Work with Ivan." He stopped to catch his breath. "You eat. I bake."

As they ate, Annie ladled out the survival problems of running a family farm in the middle of Puget Sound. John listened and took notes. The county had slowly eroded away tax shelters for subsistence farms like hers on Seven Sisters Island, which had no access to electricity or roads.

"The taxes go up every year; I could lose the island just from taxes alone. I have to prove I make enough money selling apples and oysters to maintain what's left of my subsistence farm status. That's a tall order. Forget paying back the money my sister's had to borrow. And the county assessor wants to rezone the island residential—or worse, commercial, to accommodate building a resort."

"My mother always said, 'The gold is in the apples.' But that was a simpler time." Annie concluded, "My sister passed it on to me, as it was passed on to her. The island must be kept in the family."

Annie repeated this mantra loudly and often, as if her dear departed sisters needed to know that their youngest sister—"Mama's little mistake," "hand-me-down Annie," "tail-end Charlie," and the only fertile one of the entire sisterhood—was still on duty, still trying to keep the island in the family.

Annie stopped talking and looked down. She had finished her two piroshkis and part of John's.

John could feel a growing excitement at a story that had begun to mushroom beyond his original idea.

"I may be just a food editor, but I know a human interest story when I see it. This is a great story of the trials and tribulations of a market farmer and the indomitable Northwest spirit. I would like to come visit you on your island, take more pictures, and interview you some more. I will bring my wife, Betsy—and a picnic lunch. What do you say?"

When Annie hesitated, he gave her his most earnest and engagingly look.

"Please—say 'yes.'"

Annie popped the last bit of John's piroshki in her mouth and washed it down with a swig of juice.

"Sure," she said. "Come on out anytime."

With a smile, John stood, stuffed his camera and notes in his pack, and flicked the leather strap over his shoulder. Pulling a wallet from a back pocket, he extracted a few bills and laid them on the counter.

"Thanks for lunch, Ivan," he called over his shoulder. With a wave he hurried out the door and disappeared behind a roving espresso wagon.

By mid-afternoon, Annie desperately needed a nap. She sat in a rickety rocker, holding her cash box, and catnapped, while sales continued on the honor system, watched over by the ever-vigilant Madeline. She awoke with a start at the sound of a serious Southern drawl.

"Why, these dolls are precious," the voice cooed. "I just love their little scrunched-up faces."

Annie barely raised her chin, hoping she could ignore the voice and catch a few more winks. She squinted open one eye to assess the customer. Her other eye flew open as she took in spiky pumps and slender, well-toned legs, topped off by a very tight mini-dress. Annie pretended to yawn—all the better to view the rest of the package—and spied one of the largest clumps of big, blonde, Texas hair this side of El Paso.

The woman held the doll at arm's length.

"How can you sell these dear creatures? They are just too darlin' for words! And this one looks just like you, with the same apron and the braid! Y'all have a gift." The woman flashed a mouthful of perfect white teeth at Annie. "How ever did you learn to do this?"

Not sure she wanted her face to be likened to that of a wizened apple doll, Annie decided to overlook the comment and court the customer, big hair or not.

"My grandmother made them for me, and I picked up the art from her," Annie said.

The woman stared at her.

"Me too! I mean, my nana used to make dolls like this for me when I was a little girl," she gushed. "But I never learned how to do it myself."

"Well, I live on a farm, and I build these dolls during winter when things are kind of slow. I dry them out above a wood stove, and then make the clothes and paint the faces."

The woman opened her purse and brought out her billfold, extracting a hundred-dollar bill, which she handed to Annie.

"I'll buy your whole stock."

Annie carefully wrapped each doll in a flurry of tissue paper.

"It's nice to know they're going to a good home," she told her benefactor—and winked.

At the end of the day, Calypso, her daughter, Sarah, and Sarah's husband, Peter, appeared from the thinning crowd.

"How are you, Mother?" said Calypso, who always managed to make the word "Mother" sound like some kind of affliction. She gave Annie a quick Hollywood air peck on the cheek as she flailed her lit cigarette in the air.

Calypso, Sarah, and Annie—three women, stepping-stone identical as if in a generational soap commercial: red hair, delicately turned-up noses, a generous dose of freckles, wide-set blue eyes, each, twenty years apart.

Looks aside, the empty space between them was formidable.

Annie had named her daughter Lynnette after her best friend in high school. Her daughter never knew her father, but then Annie had hardly known him herself.

And Calypso/Lynnette had never forgiven her mother for leaving her to molder away on the island in the care of her aunts and grandma. The tattoo on Calypso's arm portrayed a sailor mounted on the back of a mermaid with the words "Rowed Hard and Put Away Wet," which characterized Calypso's hardscrabble life since leaving the island. Her saving grace in Annie's eyes was that she had always kept Sarah close. Sarah, in turn, was devoted to her mother.

Annie felt the last few years had given her and her daughter a chance to know each other better, to begin to heal the rift between them. Even better, Sarah and Peter, after years of struggling to conceive, were expecting twins. Annie knew that Sarah would be the kind of mother that she had not been.

And she could not wait to be a great-grandma herself, ready to lavish on the twins all the attention she had been unable to give Sarah or her mother.

Annie loaded the few items she did not sell into the trunk of Sarah's little red Honda.

"I had a good day," she said. "Dinner's on me."

"Thanks anyway, Mother, but I've gotta go," Calypso said. She patted Sarah's stomach, gave Peter a kiss and Annie a dismissive wave, then disappeared into the crowd.

# Chapter TWO

Peter piloted the car through a maze of cobblestone streets left over from the pioneer days when a Seattle made mostly of wood had burned to the ground. They roller-coasted down the steep, white-knuckle hills toward the waterfront and, with well-earned karma, found a parking place right in front of their favorite fish bar overlooking the harbor.

As they drew nearer the restaurant, Annie saw children lying on their stomachs, noses pressed into cracks in the dock, peering into the water below. Annie recognized the art of pogy fishing—hand-held monofilament with the ruby-colored piling worms squirming provocatively on hooks. A nearby coffee can held the day's catch.

Sidestepping the young fishermen, the three headed toward the outdoor counter. They ordered fish and chips then sat with feet dangling over the pier, watching the ferry traffic. The scolding gulls in the water below pig-piled pell-mell on top of each other when Sarah threw her fries into the water.

As Annie licked the last of the tartar sauce off her fingers, Peter said, "I have something to show you," and pulled out of his side satchel several sketches. "This is my design of the Icicle River Sewage Recovery Plant. It's up for an award." He smiled broadly. "I'm starting at the bottom and working my way up. Sewer plants today, a nice little toilet paper factory tomorrow, and with any luck…"

Annie admired the drawings while Sarah put her arms around her husband and gave him a hug.

"It won't be long before you'll be doing airports and skyscrapers, honey. The company knows you're brilliant, and soon everyone will know it."

Back at the public wharf, Sarah and Peter unloaded the trunk while Annie called for Buddy. Barking, he came bounding out of the fire station near the ferry dock, followed by three firemen with wide grins. The retriever had a fireman's red baseball cap on, with his long ears flailing out the slots cut in the sides.

The men leaned over the rail.

"We've been watching the boat for you, Annie," yelled one, "except when we had to go out on a call. Buddy had come up to visit, so we took him with us up to The Spaghetti Factory to put out a car fire. He howled like a banshee when we turned on the siren." The man laughed. "He's a keeper."

With a cocky strut, Buddy trotted down the ramp, took his place in the bow, and barked at the indifferent street-wise gulls sitting on pilings.

Annie hugged Sarah, then Peter, and slowly climbed aboard while Sarah unhooked the lines for her. Peter towed the boat to the end of the pier, where the engine caught with a cough.

As she pulled away, Annie could see that Sarah was yelling something, but she could not hear over the motor. Finally, Sarah gave up and just waved.

Annie pushed the throttle forward as far as it would go, momentarily unsettling Buddy from his perch. If she had looked behind her, in the dusk she would have seen the lights of the city begin to twinkle, the freeways forming an endless chain of ruby-beaded taillights in one direction and sparkling diamonds in the other. She would have seen the skyline of a giant metropolis, a world player in airplanes and computer software, a town that reinvented coffee and exported it all over the world.

The sun had set over the Olympic Mountains, and the Pacific Northwest was scrambling to end a long weekend. The canvas snapped in the wind as Annie hunkered down in her flannel-lined jacket and pulled the watch cap over her ears.

The throb of the engine, the splashing waves, the surge of the water passing under the tiller created a harmonic rhythm. Annie's mind wandered, thinking how her life had come full circle. When she had left the island at the age of fifteen to join the Red Cross and save the world, she had vowed she would never come back. As an evacuation nurse, she vagabonded around continents, chasing earthquakes, volcanic eruptions, hurricanes, tornadoes, and typhoons. She had come to a tacit understanding that nature toyed with the hopes and dreams of men.

And then there was the war in Europe, World War II.

The brutality of war had overwhelmed Annie. The disruption of an entire generation, the lives of so many people extinguished, and the millions of families displaced. Her only lifeline had been an Army Ranger, a parachutist from Ohio named Tom, whom she'd met in a dance club basement during an air raid. The nights they spent together in a rented room above the Iron Maiden Pub were the only thing that made sense in the midst of the nightmare.

She had often been startled awake during those days by the banging of the louvered shutters. She would lie in the dark, staring at the ceiling fan, listening to sirens screeching, the buzz of the V-2 rockets, the scurrying footsteps in the alley below. Yet she had felt safe in Tom's arms. Being with him seemed real; the rest hadn't mattered.

Then one morning, mumbling something about an invasion, Tom had given her a long, soulful kiss and walked out the door. A week later the Allied Forces invaded Normandy. When Annie never heard from Tom again, she wondered if he had been among the thousands and thousands of casualties on that beach. She used all of her resources to track him, but she hit a stone wall of security silence.

She had wanted to tell him he was to be a father.

The pregnancy filled Annie with a new maternal resolve, not for motherhood, but a rededication to rejoining families shredded by an uncaring war.

For a while after her daughter was born, Annie tried a series of nannies in different countries. Finally, she figured her baby girl would be in better hands among loving relatives than being dragged from one dangerous place to another. Annie had brought her to Seven Sisters Island and asked her mother and aunts to take care of the child during the several months at a time Annie would be away.

Annie sighed.

"If only I had stayed home more. If only her father hadn't disappeared."

If only.

The boat shuddered against the white-capped waves, spraying Annie with the cold saltwater of present reality. A bitter north wind made her eyes water as the rural shoreline changed to reveal large black voids between the houses, illuminated like jack o' lanterns. Abruptly, she turned the bow south into the darkness till the black shadow of the island blotted out civilization. The outline of the island had always reminded her of a surfacing whale.

Annie rounded the south end of the island, passing by the seven large rocks that stood just offshore for which the island was named by the natives. She steered into the oyster cove where the sea calmed, buffered by the long hook of land that divided the water into moods: the wild side and the mild side.

Like a workhorse headed back to the barn after a hard day's work, the boat seemed to pick up speed of its own accord, heaving an audible sigh as Annie turned off the engine and coasted into the boathouse. Quiet reigned with only the occasional call of a loon. Annie looked up through a hole in the boathouse roof to see stars. She left everything in the boat, walked slowly up the trail, onto the porch steps, and into the house.

Annie spent the next day cooking and preserving, stockpiling for the cold months ahead. She made applesauce on top of the stove and canned mushrooms in sturdy glass jars. She felt sorry for people who didn't enjoy mushrooms. She thought they were God's gift to mankind.

The days slid by rapidly as Annie attacked the many chores that came with fall. With Buddy in tow, she trundled down into the pasture with a ladder and picked the remaining king apples, made two batches of applesauce from Gravensteins, and gathered four gunny sacks of oysters, which she tied to the piling so the tides could keep them fresh till market day. Near the old schoolhouse, she checked a new crop of chanterelle mushrooms. She'd save them for later.

She headed back up toward the house through the middle of the orchard. After fruitlessly bounding after a deer, Buddy followed.

The long walk through the tall, wet, orchard grass soaked her pants and made them cling to her knees. She set down her burden and leaned against a gnarled orchard tree. It felt good to lean her back against something growing, something that had prevailed over a hundred winters, something older than herself.

While catching her breath, she appraised the weather-beaten, gray farmhouse. In its glory days, the entire body of the house had been painted a no-nonsense, stark white.

What made it a landmark on the water was the three-story rounded tower on the waterside, wrapped with wood-framed glass windows and stained glass transoms. Before the advent of sonar and radar, a kerosene lamp in each tier at night gave the water traffic a comforting landmark in the black darkness.

Cedar from the island provided the lap siding, and the steep-pitched, wood-shingled roof had been replaced periodically over the last 140 years. Like an aging beauty, the house had good bone structure, but the façade cried out for an infusion of time and money that Annie could ill afford.

Although the week had seen a fair amount of blustery weather, Saturday held out promise with a thick blanket of fog—a sure sign of afternoon sun. The foghorns honked like lost goslings searching for their mother. The pervasive grayness surrounding the rocky reefs and jetties seemed as insular as a cocoon. By mid-morning, the circling moths of wind and sun had eaten holes in the gray cloak, and the fog gave way to the beautiful autumn day.

Watching from her window, Annie saw an anchor splash down from the stern of a boat with the name *Bon Appetit* on the side. Three flags snapped in the wind: an American flag, a yellow triangular banner from the Shilshole Marina, and a bright red one with black lettering, celebrating "John's Spaghetti Sauce."

A man and a woman climbed into a small rowboat, *Appetizer II*, and headed toward the beach.

Annie made it down the trail and to the shore as the dinghy landed. She stabilized the bow with one hand and accepted a picnic basket in the other as the crew of two stepped over the bow onto the beach.

"Welcome to the island, John," Annie said.

"Annie, this is Betsy, my wife.

Betsy smiled and put out her arms as if to embrace the island.

"I can't believe this place! It's like *Fantasy Island*. A Victorian farmhouse with a view of mountains in one-two-three-*four* directions," she said as she spun in a circle, identifying Mt. Baker, the Cascades, Mt. Rainier, and the Olympics to the north, east, south, and west.

"No wonder the tax man loves this place," said John.

"Don't even go there," Annie threatened. "Come on, let's go up to the house." She handed the basket back to John, then started up the beach toward the boat shed. John followed cautiously, simultaneously seining the picnic basket and trying to step between the slippery seaweed covering the rocks.

At the house, John was immediately drawn to the black iron Sensible cook stove.

"My aunt had one of these in Provincetown, where I worked as a cook during the summers when I was going to college in Boston," he said. "Cooking on a woodstove is an art form—calculating the density and dryness of the wood and knowing where to place which pans. I got pretty good at it."

He tested the oven door, examined the firebox, tapped the thermometer gauge, and lovingly traced the chromed, flowered patterns with his fingers, like a small boy with a favorite toy.

"Yep," he said, stepping back admiringly, "just exactly like this one. Okay if I take a picture?"

"Go right ahead," Annie said, and then added, "It came around the Horn."

Annie poured coffee and sat at the table with Betsy while John inventoried the entire first floor: chairs, clocks, drapes, silverware.

"Mind if I look over the rest of the place?" John asked, poised near the bottom of the stairs. "This house is classic Northwest architecture." He leaned on the fir newel at the bottom of the stair, craning his neck to see upstairs.

"Not at all. Just watch your step in the attic."

John disappeared up the stairs.

"He has a reporter's nose," said Betsy, smiling. She sipped her coffee. "Do you live by yourself?"

"I am definitely alone out here," answered Annie, "but sometimes I feel I am just a bit player in a gothic novel, fighting the evil tax man and the grim reaper from atop my citadel by the sea. Throw in a latent identity crisis, and that's my life."

"You know," Betsy began slowly, "I do feel like I'm in a time-warp here, like Thoreau's Walden Pond. Nature and simplicity, surrounded by a society hooked up to video, constant communication, and instant gratification. It seems we have sold our souls for baubles and false security."

Annie was impressed.

"You must have been a literature or philosophy major in college."

"Guilty as charged," Betsy shook her head. "Double masters, romantic literature and mystical poets."

Annie decided she liked this woman who cut to the chase so quickly. John, the hyper, offset by Betsy, the philosopher. It seemed a good match.

Finished with his investigation, John came to the table and sat between the two women.

"Well, I'm ready for lunch. How about you two?"

He opened the picnic basket and spread out cold chicken, pesto pasta salad, and a cranberry and orange mélange. They washed it down with a red wine, which John had extracted himself from Oregon grapes.

When the meal was done, Betsy pulled out an aluminum springform pan from the bottom of the basket and set it on the table. She slipped the lug and unveiled her specialty: an eight-inch-round cheesecake.

"New York style—rich and heavy and delicious," John said, as Betsy sliced and delivered generous mounds to their plates.

Silently, they lifted their forks and ate reverently.

Annie said, "I am in the presence of greatness." Taking another bite, she pointed her fork at the cake. "Forget the spaghetti; do the cheesecake."

Betsy smiled, and John feigned a hangdog look.

"The flag is coming down as soon as we set sail," he promised, his mouth full of cheesecake. "Tell me more about your family."

A smile lit Annie's eyes.

"The Pippin maternal tree migrated from the Isle of Skye off the coast of Scotland. The family made their reputation growing apples and siring beautiful women with long red hair and temperaments to match. By the time they came to America, the name Pippin was already famous throughout Scotland for apples and the women who grew them."

Annie got up, walked across the room, and picked up a family picture in an etched silver frame.

"Here's a picture of Mom and all seven sisters, sitting on a swooping apple limb in our Sunday-best pinafore dresses." She handed it to John.

"Wow—you all look so much alike; it's as if you were the same person in graduated sizes," remarked Betsy, leaning toward John to view the photo.

Annie laughed.

"That's true. I wonder if Sarah's girls will look alike."

"So they know they will be girls?" asked Betsy.

"They didn't bother with an ultrasound, but chances are mighty good, even if the twins are not identical. For five hundred years, there has not been a single male descendant in this family. If the girls married, the married surname meant nothing. We girls belong to the maternal line."

Annie sat quietly thinking for a minute.

"You know, I swore I would never come back, but here I am, bound by that sorority of red hair and apple seeds. It's a bond that stretches back to 1660 when the family first landed on the shores of America, a time when America was in need of strong women and fruited plains. And now four generations of Pippins have been raised here on this island.

"Sometimes late at night, I swear I hear giggling and laughter in the hallways, stampeding feet, doors mysteriously opening and closing. Maybe it's just the wind, or maybe it's the leftover hormones of the generations of women who grew up here.

"I remember one time," Annie reflected while folding her napkin, "when I was in third grade and the school bully cut off one of my pigtails with his jackknife. The next day, my sisters and I jumped him on the trail to the schoolhouse and trimmed him up good with a couple of pairs of my mother's scissors. Sometimes we cut a little deep. There was a lot of howling and some blood drawn. When she found out, my mom made us do extra chores, but after that…if I gave somebody the stink-eye, they backed right off."

Betsy chuckled, "I wish I'd been one of your sisters. I think we called it the 'skunk-eye,' though."

"We always covered each other's back, although we did fight each other like alley cats often enough," Annie admitted.

Annie had one more piece of cake, as did John, who then collected the dishes. He immersed them in the pot of soapy dishwater that had been warming on the stove, dunked them into the pan of rinse water, and dried them with a red-and-white checkered dishcloth.

Betsy watched with amazement.

"He never washes a dish at home!"

John just smiled. He was reaching back into his childhood.

Annie decided to pick the wild chanterelle mushrooms she had checked before. They had begun to push through leaf mold, encouraged by the fall rains. She invited John and Betsy to accompany her. John brought his camera.

The steep, mossy trail was slick from the morning rain. Betsy struggled to follow Annie's lead, grabbing roots and tree limbs for support. After several minutes, she found a tree stump and sat down, exhausted.

"I'm feeling a little worn," she said. "I don't think that second bypass took as well as the first one. I guess I'm running out of decent spare parts."

She stood up, determined to press on. But Annie raised a hand.

"You rest here and just relax," she said kindly. "John and I will gather the mushrooms. We'll collect you on the way back."

Betsy smiled and agreed. John and Annie pressed on.

As they hiked, Annie said, "You know, I read an interesting article about using baboon parts in heart operations. Or maybe it was pigs."

"With that kind of replacement you might learn to sniff out truffles," John added.

After ten minutes' worth of wet branches slapping them in the face, John and Annie encountered a grove of eighty-year-old fir trees. Fallen vine maple leaves splashed vibrant yellow on a background of green pin-cushion moss. Annie showed John how to identify the telltale bulges in the moss, then use a knife to cut the stems of the buttercup-shaped mushroom.

"They smell like pumpkins," John marveled. "And there are so many of them."

John and Annie quickly filled two small gunnysacks with the gourmet treats, then made their way back down the slippery path to Betsy. As the three walked to the house, Annie pointed out the apple orchard.

"There are only about sixty bearing trees now, where there were hundreds when I was a girl. I had a childhood connection with almost every tree—from pruning to picking to fertilizing them in the spring with that god-awful horse-drawn wagon filled with smelly manure to harvesting the fruit in the fall.

"The trees left now are varieties not favored in the market these days. Overseas markets prefer the deep red color of the delicious or the Fuji and gala apples from New Zealand and Argentina with their long shelf life. Seven Sisters has the old apple trees: the pippins, the yellow transparents, the oversize king apples, and my favorite, the Gravenstein. At first, Gravensteins grew only in Germany. Their cultivation was a zealously guarded secret until someone smuggled out the first seedlings. Wars have been fought over less.

"To my mind, the red- and yellow-striped Gravensteins make the ultimate applesauce. My mother thought the transparents made the best pies. The zesty king makes apple juice that tradition dictates will 'knock your socks off or give you the trots.'"

Back at the house, Annie dusted the fir needles from the gills of the mushrooms with a small pastry brush. She saved half of the batch to can and gave the rest to John to take home.

"How about one more cup of coffee before you go?" she suggested.

As they sat and sipped the dark, savory brew, John enthused about the day's events and all the pictures he had taken.

"You'll be my lead story next weekend," promised John. His eyes wandered to Annie's stove, lingering there. "Hey, here's an idea. I don't know what you've got planned for Thanksgiving, but I'd be willing to spring for the entire feast for a chance to cook on that old wood stove."

"Someone else cooks the turkey? Sounds like a deal to me," Annie said. "My daughter, granddaughter, and her husband will be here. With your family too, it'll be like a real, old-fashioned Thanksgiving."

Betsy smiled her approval while she packed the picnic basket with the chanterelles.

Annie walked them down to the dock, where she helped shove out the launch. The sun had disappeared behind the mountains, and the whitecaps had started to whip up. A blue heron glided noiselessly down the shore. Once on board the good ship *Bon Appetit,* Betsy and

John waved goodbye. Annie watched the boat's red and green running lights disappear down the channel as it headed for its home in the Shilshole Marina, just north of Seattle.

Annie turned and started back to the house, Buddy trailing. Suddenly, she heard the siren go off in Port Gamble.

Someone was in trouble.

She looked south toward the mainland and spied the red flag flying from the post office.

Years ago, Annie's grandfather had arranged a warning system that worked two ways. When the island folk were in trouble, a red flag flying alerted the people of Port Gamble to come and help. The signal worked in reverse when the mainland had important news for the island.

The alarm was sounded only in dire circumstances.

Within moments, Annie's boat was cutting through the white caps as it sped across the water toward the Port Gamble Post Office.

# Chapter THREE

Postmistress Gladys McKnight hailed Annie as she ran into the general store, her words flowing out in a rush.

"Annie, Sarah has been taken to Tacoma General. The twins arrived early." She held out a key ring with just two keys on it. "Do you need to borrow my car?"

"Thanks," said Annie, grabbing the keys. She dashed out the worn, wooden screen door, letting it slam behind her.

Within minutes she was careening down the highway in grim determination. Sixty miles and three bridges later, she pulled up in front of Tacoma General, slamming on the brake as she double-parked at the hospital entrance. She vaulted out of the ancient Toyota and hurtled through the door. Her brain quickly shifted into crisis mode, her senses sharpened by the familiar smells of Lysol and sickness. Intuitively, she navigated the halls till she found the recovery room corridor. She stuck her nose into room after half-lit room until she spotted Sarah, lying perfectly flat, with attached intravenous tubes splayed out over pillows. Two nurses were hovering on either side.

At Annie's abrupt intrusion, they turned in unison.

"You can't come in here," they said, much like Tweedle Dee and Tweedle Dum.

"Bullshit," Annie said. "This is my granddaughter."

Though used to being in charge, the nurses stepped aside, watchful but yielding. Annie picked up the chart from the bed, scanned it, threw it back down, and put her hand on Sarah's forehead. The mothers, two generations apart, smiled at each other, one through C-section anesthetic, the other on full-alert.

"How do you feel, honey?" Annie asked.

"I can't raise my head up; it makes me nauseous. And I haven't even been able to go down to see the babies." Her eyes grew moist. "They said I probably won't be able to have any more children."

Annie wrung out a cold washrag, folded it, and put it on Sarah's forehead.

"Where are the babies?" she asked the closest nurse.

"Second floor," she said. "But you can't—"

Annie raised her eyebrow ever so slightly to terminate the nurse's admonition, then whirled out of the room and down the hall to the elevator where she met Calypso.

"Get the lead out, sweetheart," Annie goaded her daughter as she pounded on the elevator button. "We're going up to see the babies."

On the second floor, the neonatal nurses instructed the women to wash their hands and helped them slip into a hospital gown and slippers. Then they led grandmother and great-grandmother to the plastic-topped incubators.

They found Peter there, staring at his babies, transfixed. Annie walked over and wordlessly held him tight. She peered into the case and saw amid the sucking, whooshing, constantly beeping sounds of life-support machines two spindly replicas of humans. Their tiny faces were covered with tape that held giant tubes stuffed in their noses and down their throats, helping them to breathe. The monitor wires, hooked to toes and scrawny chests, made the two souls look as if they had been recovered from a Roswell site. At a little over two pounds apiece, they were too early for the world, but there they were.

Annie wanted to scream out, "Put them back. They're not done yet." The words stuck in her mouth. She stood there, motionless.

In elephant herds, it's been said the eldest matriarch leads. The power of the larger bulls is supplanted by the wisdom of the oldest female, shrewd in the ways of survival. Seeing the stunned look on Calypso's hard-lined face, Annie knew it was up to her to rally Peter.

"They are going to make it, they are going to make it," Annie said quietly like a chant. "They are of my blood, these are my great-grandchildren, and they will take their rightful place on the island!"

This was no entreaty found in any prayer book but written in a grandmother's love. It came from the fierce will to survive, passed down straight from one heart to another.

Peter grabbed Annie's hand and took up her mantra, mouthing the words with her, willing them to be true. As he stood with Annie, he felt the strength flowing out of them and directly to the little forms in the incubators.

Peter could hardly believe something so small could survive, but if Annie believed, he accepted it as fact. As he let the anxious tension flow out of him, Peter felt exhaustion take its place. He shuffled over to a rocker in the corner and plopped down unceremoniously, wearily surveying the twenty or so cubicles where newborns with lungs not yet ready to breathe the air of life fought for their lives.

"Let's get Sarah down here on a gurney," Annie said. She asked a nearby nurse, "Would that be all right?"

"If the mother wants to come to her babies, that's perfectly fine with me," answered the nurse in charge, an older woman. She recognized the powers of a fellow matriarch. She herself had willed the spirit of life into many infants over the years.

Twenty minutes later, Calypso wheeled Sarah into the neonatal unit and carefully maneuvered her to the side of the incubators. She rolled over and reached to touch the miniature hands of both children at the same time.

"They're so small. I never imagined they would be this small."

A nearby nurse asked, "How many weeks along were you?"

"Twenty-eight," Sarah said in apology.

"Don't worry," the nurse said with a knowing smile. "We bring them through everyday. It's just the lungs that are undeveloped. If they can't breathe on their own, we do it for them. Steroids and a mother's touch. Your twins will be going home on their due date or sooner. You have my word on it.

"Now, do we have names for these little sprouts?" she asked, ripping two pieces of tape from a roll. She smoothed the tape on the lid of each incubator with one hand and pulled out a permanent marker with the other. "What's it to be, Mom?"

"The girl is definitely 'Annie,' after her great-grandmother…"

Annie beamed.

"…and the boy is Zachary Peter, like his father."

It wasn't till that moment that Annie realized the significance of this birth.

"A boy," she said to herself. "A baby boy."

Generation after generation of girls, and now a boy. The very idea made her glow.

Peter rocked back in the chair. He smiled and even though he never smoked, he suddenly wished he had a cigar. He levered himself out of the chair and wandered down the hall to find one.

Annie and Calypso stayed at Sarah and Peter's house during that first critical week, journeying to the hospital several times each day. Together they shared the highs and lows as the twins progressed one day, lost ground the next, and sometimes the two women couldn't help but seek solace from one another. At the hospital the constant digital readings of heart rate and breathing coupled with the blood tests told the story: the twins were growing stronger. After a week, reluctantly, Annie headed get back to the island to prepare for the last market day of the season, and Calypso had to return to the bowling alley, but she was already planning a new tattoo to honor the twins.

When Annie made her way to the Saturday market—via the same horse-drawn carriage she'd shared with John three weeks before—she noticed a mood that seemed more high-energy than usual. Unfamiliar people smiled and waved and called out her name in greeting.

"What is going on?" Annie wondered.

Ivan came out of his shop, twirled around, and clapped his hands over his head in a floured greeting. A cloud of puffballs rose into the air.

"Annie, didn't you know that you're my hero? I proud like turkey vulture. A dingo ate my baby. May the force be with you!"

Annie smiled, still confused. She waved at Ivan and the scrum of people who surrounded the carriage. Why the sudden attention?

"Annie, this is your fifteen minutes of flame. I love you, you magenta bastard," Ivan continued.

John appeared out of the crowd and eased Annie out of the carriage and onto the cobbled street. He thrust the Sunday pictorial from the *Seattle Times* at her.

Even without her glasses, Annie recognized a picture of *The Ark* pounding the waves on the front page.

"There are more pictures inside, along with a story about the island and how the county is trying to tax you out or rezone it."

Annie laughed in delight but handed the paper back to John. All the hoopla would have to be dealt with later.

She put on her apron and arranged her goods. People immediately crowded in from all sides. They shoved pieces of paper at her for her autograph and thrust small children into her lap for photos. They asked her advice on pruning trees and making pie crust and inquired where she stood on the debate whether or not to eat the core. Two boys began a seed-spitting fight, and the crowd egged them on. Throughout it all, they continued to buy Annie's stores till there was nothing left.

John was sent to round up extra baskets and ribbons. Annie herself commandeered apples up and down the other market stalls, just to have something to sell. Still, the crowds kept coming. The afternoon shadows lengthened on the alley, and Annie grew weary and hungry, having had no chance to eat since breakfast.

It was Ivan who came to the rescue, pushing his way through the crowd.

"Move to downwind, please, this woman is too popped to poop," he said in his thick accent, putting his arm around Annie and shoving a piroshki in her hand. People laughed and allowed Annie to snack as they continued to buy her remaining inventory.

At the end of the day, a few stalls still held some baked goods, dried flower arrangements, whistles made out of clay, and tee shirts proclaiming, "In Seattle, You Don't Tan . . . You Rust." But, there were no apples anywhere in the market. Apple Annie had sold them all.

"You're the last of a breed, Annie," said John as they headed back to the boat in John's car.

Though Buddy was AWOL, Annie knew where to find him. She called his name, and he skidded out of the fire station door with a group of raucous firemen right behind him. The fire chief, a hefty bald man, yelled out to Annie as Buddy raced down the sidewalk onto the dock.

"We took him to be groomed at the Puppy Dog's Tale. He had the works."

As Buddy grew closer, Annie stared incredulously at her canine friend. The groomer had tied red, white, and blue ribbons to his ears, affixed five more bows down the length of his tail, and lacquered his toenails to match. He smelled like cheap perfume.

Buddy slunk aboard the boat sheepishly, as if to say, "They made me do it."

"Don't blame him, Annie. When we came back, they had given him #12, 'The Yankee Doodle Dandy Firecracker,'" yelled the fire chief.

Annie laughed.

"Oh, he's a dandy, all right."

She motioned Buddy aboard. He jumped into the boat and assumed his usual position, looking ridiculous. Annie kicked the engine over and turned the bow to the west. She waved to John then eased out of the slip into the bay and set a westerly course. The mountain peaks were holding up a thin horizontal band of purple clouds, backlit by the remains of a flaming red sunset on the Pacific Ocean.

Red sky at night, sailor's delight.

When she docked at home, the wake startled a great blue heron that gave an indignant, raspy, prehistoric honk. He took flight, gliding noiselessly on a five-foot wingspan down to the shoreline to continue wading for prey.

Unannounced, fall arrived to slap the unsuspecting and those in denial with a cold splash of reality, tsunami fashion. The first storm of the season boiled in from the Pacific. It pivoted around the southern peaks of the Olympic mountains, galloped across the foothills, and plunged headlong into the soft waters of the inland peninsulas. Gale-force winds and diagonal rains slammed into the island with a ferocity that left no doubt: Indian summer was over.

The wind ripped branches, uprooted trees, and forced gulls to huddle grimly behind logs and crouch in deserted buildings. No longer was it a land for sun worshippers, baseball games, or picnic baskets. Winter in the Northwest had begun.

The storm buried the island in record rainfall, forcing Annie to spend her days holed up, carving faces into apples. She dangled them, cannibal style, from wires hung over the stove, where they shriveled to wizened heads. As they shrunk, the knife lines became exaggerated, forming faces that ran the gamut from angelic to demonically possessed.

Annie sewed tiny gowns and outfits from the remains of well-worn work clothes that had been meticulously washed, folded, and saved over the years by her mother and sisters. Scrap piles had long since spilled out of the attic and into the stairwell, waiting patiently to be incorporated into an heirloom-quality braided rug or quilt, only to be relegated to life as a humble apple doll dress.

During a break in the storm, Annie took the boat to Port Gamble.

The small, picturesque mill town had once held the record for the oldest continually running sawmill in America. In their day, the Cape Cod homes of white siding and black roofs stood overshadowed by the mammoth virgin forests of the Pacific Northwest. Today, the gingerbread houses still stood in mute testimony to a culture of powerful men straining to harvest the resources of an untamed land.

Annie went into the store overlooking the landing dock to get the mail. The 150-year-old company store had never been renovated.

It stood unchanged, unpainted, and scruffy. Only a world-class sea-shell collection and the post office inside allowed it to survive.

Annie phoned Sarah.

"Zach and Little Annie are still on IVs and ventilators," Sarah said. "And they're kept under ultraviolet lights for warmth and to counteract their jaundice. If they don't start breathing on their own, we're going to have to give them that steroid shot. Right now they're being stimulated with caffeine." Sarah gave a nervous giggle. "Peter thought that meant a double caramel macchiato!"

Annie smiled as she put down the phone. She felt encouraged but knew the little ones were not out of the woods yet.

A southern wind was whipping up a mild whitecap stew as Annie headed back. An osprey hovered overhead then dove full tilt into the chop, trying to snag a salmon. Coming up empty, the bird banked into the wind and faded into a small dot against the cloudless eastern sky.

Nearing the island, Annie spotted a stiletto-shaped ski boat beached near the boat shed, the sides emblazoned with orange and green lightning bolts. She could make out two figures—one bent over as though searching for something, the other leaping from drift-wood log to stump.

Annie moored the boat while Buddy greeted the visitors. The jumping figure became a tall young man, sporting a smile and dark brown eyes. He gave Annie a quasi-military salute.

"Hi, I'm Justin Nelson." He gestured at the other figure. "I'm here with my Grammy." He knelt and gave Buddy a double noogie behind the ears.

Behind Justin a shivering woman with white hair remained dou-bled over. She was dressed in woven sandals, avocado capri pants, a red blouse, and a green jacket advertising "Mother Truckers Bowling Team" on the back. A thick, black, patent-leather belt cinched the outfit together, with an oval silver belt-buckle the size of a '57 Buick grill that read, "Damn, I'm good."

Annie took in this garish fashion statement and wondered if the belt buckle was holding the woman up or dragging her down.

"Annie Pippin, I know you," cackled the pretzeled figure, apparently speaking to the ground.

She approached with the help of her cane, then turned her head sideways to appraise Annie. The woman was a mass of wrinkles and white hair. On her chin she sported a classic mole, sprouting two hairs that curled like a Fu Manchu mustache.

The woman gave Annie a wide grin.

"Carol Ann Nelson, Snug Harbor, class of '29. I knew you when you were a baby. I went to school with some of your sisters. My parents owned the dairy farm near the high school. We had that two-headed calf we sold the Barnum and Bailey."

Annie remembered the cows—black-and-white Holsteins that sometimes ranged onto the football field during games, leaving deposits that the leather-helmeted freshman fourth-stringers had to shovel away during timeouts. And Carol Ann's sexual appetite had been carefully documented with crude letters carved into the nearby high school bathroom stalls that still showed through the paint when Annie had arrived at the same school years later.

Without thinking, Annie blurted out, "Why, Carol Ann, you haven't changed a bit."

The old woman emitted a hacking, gasping, choking sound and toppled sideways onto the soft beach sand. She rolled over, seemingly struggling for breath, gagged, and then let loose an enormous belly laugh. She kept it up till she began to gag once again.

Annie rushed to her side. The woman slowly rolled to her knees, planted her cane, and levered herself into her original twisted pose.

"You almost killed me with that one, Annie," she gasped. "Jesus, that was funny. Don't ever do that again," she said, stifling the impulse to begin laughing again. She wiped her mouth with the back of her hand and squatted on a nearby log, leaning forward with her black cane under her chin.

Annie sat beside her.

"Are you okay?"

Carol Ann reached into her pocket and extracted a cigarette and lighter. With palsied hands, she attempted to coordinate ignition without setting her hair afire.

"Blessed Virgin," she swore, as the Camel finally collided with the flame. She drew a deep breath of smoke, held it, and exhaled with slow satisfaction. Victorious, she drew a crumpled page from a newspaper out of her purse and handed it to Annie. It was the story John had written.

Carol Ann watched as the smoke from the cigarette curled skyward, apparently mesmerized at its formation.

"I saw that story about you, Annie," she rasped. "I'm involved with a hospice program, and we're looking for a retreat area. Some place secluded and peaceful. When I saw this piece in the *Times*, I remembered your oyster shacks. I got to wondering…are the shacks habitable?"

Annie pointed to the fallen roofs and broken windows of the shacks that stretched down the sandy hook from the island's body

"The shacks are a mess. No one has lived in them for twenty, maybe thirty, years. Look, why don't we go up to the house and talk about this? We can have some coffee."

Annie extended a hand to pull up Carol Ann. The gnarled old woman turned to her grandson.

"Justin, stay with the boat and let me know when the tide comes in again."

The two women walked up the path to the house. As they climbed, Carol Ann said, "I was here for a party once and met a gorgeous boy, the son of an oyster picker. We had some good times…"

Her voice trailed off in the wind. She sidestepped up the stairs, like a new skier working her way up the bunny hill. While Annie held the door, Carol Ann shuffled inside, sat down heavily in a chair, and again rested her chin on her cane to survey the scene.

The room seemed suspended in time, a smorgasbord of furniture styles—rose-colored, over-stuffed arm chairs with ottomans, embroidered Victorian couches with slim carved legs, Queen Anne tables, an elaborately carved hutch, and a square, rosewood piano. In the middle of the lower floor stood a long, brass telescope on a tripod, reportedly the property of a distant relative, a nineteenth-century whaling captain from Nantucket.

Annie bustled about the kitchen, returning with two mugs of coffee. Carol Ann accepted hers then launched into a monologue.

"Where have you been, Annie? I knew you'd come back. Eventually, we all do. I did. But not long after that my folks died, and my sister and I sold the family farm. I hated my childhood, tied to those idiot cows. I still hate dairy products. Maybe I should've drunk more milk, just to get even, but I didn't. Now I've got osteoporosis. So I guess those damn cows won after all.

"But I had some fun. Went to Vegas, became a showgirl, married a dealer. We worked there for a few years, then I convinced him to move to the Northwest. We were running a club in Seattle when he got the cancer. Because of him, I got involved in hospice. When he died, I just kept volunteering. I've been there the longest now of anybody, so I'm the one in charge.

"Course, I don't have much time to devote to it. My girlfriend and I have our own 900 number, 'Hot to Trot.'" Carol Ann winked. "That low, whiskey voice still sucks them in.

"Anyway, here's the deal: We can fix up the shacks, and people can come over for the day or whatever."

Annie rubbed her thighs with her hands and measured her words carefully. She didn't want to be rude, but she just didn't want to get involved.

"I don't have funds to fix up the shacks," she said.

"No matter. I have a handyman who belongs to the hospice group. He offered to come over to fix them up," Carol Ann answered. "We would buy the materials, and the labor would be free. I can have him here pronto. What do you think?"

Annie stalled.

"I don't know…I just don't want it to become a problem. What kind of people would come, anyway?"

"Who knows?" Carol Ann shrugged. "When people get ready to check out, sometimes they just want to find a peaceful place to hang out. I'd say you got that in abundance."

Annie felt exhaustion taking over. She couldn't think, and she knew she was no match for Carol Ann, who she remembered as having had a reputation of a pit bull when she set her mind to something.

Maybe it would do some good, she thought. She knew she had some extra lumber and rusted door knobs in the boat shed that could be put to use.

"All right," she sighed, "let's try it,"

"Good," Carol Ann said. She handed Annie a card that read, "*Hot to Trot. Phone 1-900-HOT-BABES.*" "You'll either get me or Vicki," she explained. "Just identify yourself; that way we'll keep in touch. I'll make sure it doesn't cost you a thing and you can even make a few shekels."

Annie stood up from the table, wondering if she had been bamboozled by this Snug Harbor Class of '29 alumna. Maybe those bathroom stalls were still fulfilling a prophecy.

Early the next morning, Annie was spooning coffee into the strainer when she heard a knock on the door. She clicked the lid back on and looked under the stove for Buddy, wondering why he had not detected the stranger. Buddy lay fast asleep under the stove, not a care in the world.

Annie opened the door to find a hulking male leaning against a crutch fashioned out of a tree limb. The man had the broad, flat forehead of a Viking, with a chevron scowl that led downward to one piercing blue eye. A black patch covered the other.

An assortment of screwdrivers and hammers hung off the crutch shank, each nestled in its own leather holster. A tattooed tiara of spouting whales, in tasteful but faded mauves and greens, encircled his bald head, and several thick gold, hoop earrings festooned each ear. As the man dipped his head in introduction, the earrings produced a sound reminiscent of distant sleigh bells.

Annie smiled inwardly, thinking that if this guy was suffering from ringing in his ears, she could probably diagnose a complete cure.

The man sported a scraggy gray beard that began at the cheekbones and straggled south to just above the brass strap buckles on his blue overalls. The red manufacturer's tag on the bib read, "Bubba Industries, Buzzard Roost, Alabama."

At his side stood a drooling, rawboned hound dog, with one hind leg missing and ears displaying the same pierced ear pattern as his owner. All signs pointed to rabies, hunger, or a disturbing sort of male-pattern bonding.

Annie caught the sound of cackling coming from the porch railing, where a one-legged Bantam rooster, sporting green and black tail plumage, leaned against a post. The bird also had one eye missing; the other cocked up, looking at Annie, a sort of James Dean sneer on his beak—a rooster with attitude.

Annie first thought was the man had washed ashore during the night. She wagered his first words would be "Arg, matey" or "Got a Bud Lite?"

Excuse me, ma'am," he said, in a deep, deferential, dulcet tone as sweet as any radio announcer. "My name is Moby. I am an associate of Carol Ann's. I'm the carpenter."

# Chapter FOUR

e gave a broad smile, and Annie could see he had perfect teeth. Annie always had a soft spot for sparkling dentition. She let the defensive scowl fall from her face. These were obviously harmless fools, literally on their last legs. She could outrun two of them, and Buddy could handle the third.

"Would you like to come in? I'm afraid you'll have to leave your animals outside."

The man motioned to the dog.

"Tripod, you stay."

The drooling dog turned around in a circle twice, tucked his remaining hind leg under him, and curled up with his muzzle against his paws. His darting brown eyes remained watchful.

Moby said nothing to the chicken.

The man hobbled into the kitchen and eased his 250-plus-pound frame into a frail-looking but sturdy spindle-backed chair.

"Coffee... Mr. Moby, is it?" called out Annie, walking to the stove.

"Yes ma'am. Moby, it is."

Annie stoked the stove and filled the coffeepot with water. To fill the silence, she asked, "Have you always been a carpenter?"

"No," Moby chuckled throatily. "You wouldn't know it to look at me now, but I started out as an actor." He pointed to his leg. "When I lost my leg and eye, I also lost my career.

"But that was in the late forties, just after the war. After I left Tinseltown, I migrated north, picking up carpentry jobs along the way. I had learned carpentry from my dad when I was just a kid growing up in Portland." Moby gave an appreciative shake of his tattooed noggin. "My dad was a hell of a craftsman. He could build anything. Always had a cigarette dangling from his lips. Said smoking made him think more clearly. My brother and I took up the habit in our teens and acquired the family legacy."

Annie looked at him uncertainly.

"Legacy?"

"Lung cancer. It took both my dad and brother, and eventually it's gonna take me too. But not just yet.

"I watched them carve up my brother and my dad, cutting out lungs, putting them through radiation, chemo. They still died within a year, withered and delirious, hog-tied to their hospital beds. That's not for me. I still feel healthy, though lately I've lost some weight. It may look like I'm handicapped, with the one leg and eye, but for the last forty years, I worked on high-end houses on Mercer Island, and I can do a fair amount of work yet."

He explained how he had met Carol Ann this summer at hospice.

"I'm tired of building trophy houses. I need to get back to banging nails. I grew up on the Columbia River, so I know my way around water. I rowed over in my rowboat. I wouldn't be a bother. I'd cook my own meals and such."

The entire swirling conversation came out as he concentrated on doctoring his coffee with milk and three teaspoons of sugar. Annie was surprised this pirate didn't drink his coffee black with rum.

Wasn't there some joke about a one-legged carpenter, or something about being busier than a one-legged fireman? Or was it bricklayer? Or banker? In any event, Annie felt the man was sincere. No one rows his boat filled with tools out to the island for exercise, and he did know Carol Ann.

Annie smiled.

"'Moby'…is that your first or last name?" she asked.

"I go by Moby Dick, my stage name, taken from my most, shall we say, acclaimed movie," he replied, stretching out a kink in his one good leg as if remembering a time when his body was whole. "I call my construction business *Moby Dick's*, with the logo like this on my forehead," he explained, pointing. His one eye twinkled. "Of course, when dealing with my more sensitive customers, I wear a hat or a bandana."

"You know, we have no electricity on the island," Annie said, "and what little lumber there is would be in the boat shed. Most of the materials would have to come from the beach. I don't have any money to sink into those cabins."

"I understand. I planned to camp out in the most waterproof shack and start working with hand tools, scrounging up what material I can. And Carol Ann gave me some money to buy what I need. But I'm here because I want to be. Whatever time I have left, I want to spend working with wood. The waterfront and the quiet here are big bonuses. This has nothing to do with making money."

Moby inquired whether there was another cup of coffee to be had. Annie brought the pot to the table, setting it down on an iron trivet shaped like an apple. She let him pour his own. It would be nice to fix up a few things around the farm. How much work he could do she would find out.

Over their second cup of coffee, they talked about family. Annie described the recent and dramatic expansion of the Perkins clan, and Moby owned up to having a globetrotting daughter he didn't see nearly as much as he liked.

An insistent crowing blew in from the front porch.

"He's got no class," said Moby. "He goes off as the spirit moves him—middle of the night, afternoon. The only time he is quiet is in the morning. Like rooster, like owner."

Annie laughed.

"I've got a clock like that," Annie said. "It's been in the family forever, but it never keeps the right time."

With that, Moby got up from the chair, excused himself, and hobbled out to the front porch. He scooped up his rooster with his free hand and called to Tripod. He stepped off the porch, then turned to face Annie.

"I'll just look around and get squared away. You needn't worry about me; I can take care of myself."

"It sounds good," Annie said. "I really didn't expect someone so soon."

"That's Carol Ann for you."

He gestured to the cast-iron tub with water overflowing into the stream.

"Is that the only fresh water?"

"Yes, there's a bucket here by the back door. Take some water with you, and I'll come down to check on you tomorrow."

Readjusting the rooster on his hip, Moby hobbled down the trail.

"What's the name of your rooster?" Annie called out.

"Ahab, Captain Ahab" was the answer as the trio disappeared down toward the water. They looked like leftovers from a battleground of the American Revolutionary War.

*Ahab. Of course the rooster is named Ahab.* Annie went back into the house thinking, *If only the rooster could play the piccolo and Moby carried a flag. They certainly had the limping part down pat.*

Another few days of drizzle and gray overcast followed. Gusty winds forced a majority of the leaves to pirouette from the red maples surrounding the orchard. The trumpet-vine flowers lay scattered in the wet, bent grass against the shingled boat shed. Soon the island landscape would take on the muddled grays and browns of a winter makeover.

Occasionally, Annie would see Moby prowling the beach, dressed in a rain slicker, in search of wood scraps, followed by Tripod. Sometimes, Ahab flew haphazardly after them. The smoke from the last shack, which Moby used for his headquarters, was a welcome sign of occupation to an otherwise depressing group of abandoned buildings whose best days had long since passed.

She busied herself stacking wood, cleaning leaves out of the gutters with a long ladder she knew she had no business climbing, searching through quilt books for a pattern for the twins, and fine-tuning her will, using a form her lawyer had provided.

One morning, when the sun bravely peeked through the thick clouds, Annie pulled on a navy pea coat and a pair of black fireman boots. Calling to Buddy, she splashed down the trail to the beach. She listened to the squishing sound of the gravel protesting as she made her way toward the last shack. As she neared, she heard a long streak of loud cursing, punctuated by hammer blows. Then more of the same, followed by another series of hammer blows, and finally a "Take that, you son of a bitch, you mother—"

Annie knocked loudly on the door. Seconds later, a sheepish Moby opened it and ushered Annie in.

"I like to put the fear of God in my work," he said, pointing to the board he'd been swearing at. "I threaten the wood into compliance and then nail with authority. It's taken a long time to develop this rapport." Good-naturedly, Moby gave the nail one last lick.

Annie had to admit the shack did look much improved. Moby pointed out the wood-paned window he had found in the boat shed and the pink door he'd rescued from a pile of driftwood, on which he'd affixed a crystal doorknob he'd brought with him. He had repaired both single beds and bent some metal he had found on the beach to replace the burned-out firebox in the stove. The tongue-and-groove cedar floors had been worn smooth by beach sand, and the walls made of knotty-pine shiplap had yellowed evenly with time—except for the odd lighter rectangle in the middle of the wall, evidence of a calendar or picture that had hung there long ago.

"It looks good," said Annie, peering into the firebox in the stove, then pulling open a drawer built into the tiny clothes closet jammed in the corner. The one-room space sometimes accommodated a family of five or six, sleeping in hammocks that hung overhead when it was too cold to sleep on the outside porch.

"Families wintered over when the demand for oysters was high in San Francisco during the gold rush of '49. Native oysters so sweet, they called them 'oyster dulce,' the sweet oyster. They say the sweetness has something to do with the chemicals or nutrients in the water surrounding the island. All I know is the family shipped them out by the ton on clipper ships and steamers heading down the coast."

Annie saw Moby shudder at the mention of oysters, and he quickly changed the subject.

"Yep, some stove pipe, a damper, and some replacement glass for the windows, and we've got her," he said, sitting in a chair.

"I'd like to invite you to dinner and to have you witness my will," Annie said, mentally taking oysters off the evening's menu.

"I'd be glad to come. I mostly just find my way around a can opener out here," Moby said. "I should probably work on my will too, although everything will go to my daughter. I sure don't want the feds to get a penny, if I can help it."

With Ahab on the porch rail announcing the sunset, Moby knocked promptly at 6 p.m. His eyes betraying his hunger, he quickly hobbled to the table.

The daylight hours waned quickly in the shorter days of autumn. An ancient kerosene lamp cast an eerie light in the gathering dusk. The "gloaming," Annie remembered someone called it.

Annie had laid out a fine, old linen tablecloth with matching napkins. Into the mismatched goblets, Annie poured some rhubarb wine she had bottled last year as an aperitif. Its pink blush matched the rose-patterned Spode china.

Annie's grandmother had cherished the dishes and silverware that survived the covered wagon journey west and said they were only to be used for a special occasion. For a hundred years they collected dust, never coming out of the cabinet—except for birthdays, baptisms, and weddings. Annie's mother vowed that, on her watch, things would be different. They celebrated with their grandmother's dishes the day after they laid her to rest in the orchard.

"Everyday is a special day," Annie's mother had said.

All of this history Annie painstakingly explained to the hungry man, who tried to look interested as he eagerly awaited a few scraps of home-cooked food.

"And when there is only one heirloom dish left, we will retire it to the buffet, and that dish truly will be special."

Moby was salivating like his dog by the time Annie finally brought out a big bowl of clam chowder and a cedar basket of baking powder biscuits, accompanied by homemade strawberry jam and a huge slab of butter and big mugs of coffee. Annie prattled on about the historical nature of the basket that had been woven by the "first people" on the island, but Moby couldn't hear anything above the sigh of contentment that occasionally escaped his mouth.

"Moby, I declare, you eat like a man with a hollow leg," said Annie without thinking.

Moby nodded approval, crumbs falling from his mouth in appreciation.

"That's a fact, ma'am."

"Call me 'Annie.'" She ladled another round of soup into his bowl.

"That's a fact, Annie," Moby repeated. He watched with anticipation as Annie took an apple pie out of the oven. It soon filled the warm room with the smell of cinnamon and cooked apples.

Afterward, they retreated to the living room, where Moby, fortified by the repast, signed the will where it said, "Witness states that Annie Pippin Perkins is of sound mind," and so forth. That done, they both yawned and sat sleepily in chairs till first Moby and then Annie fell asleep in front of the fire.

Annie woke first, dished up the pie, replenished the coffee, and brought the tray into the living room, waking Moby by shaking his shoulder. He looked up and gave her a little-boy smile.

"I make a great impression on a first date, don't I?" he laughed.

They ate the pie in silence, and then, stimulated by the coffee, Moby told of his life and his days in Hollywood.

He had been drafted out of high school in Portland for the Army Air Corps, which was looking for pilots and gunners. After three tours of duty, they made him a bombardier. The war ended and, like everyone else, he was unceremoniously dropped back into civilization and left to resume his life. He drifted south to California and Hollywood. He joined the stuntman union and, at six-foot-four, doubled for John Wayne, jumping off wagons and cliffs. One day, while he was working as an extra, a director spotted him, made a few inquiries, and invited him to shoot soft-porn flicks based on men in uniform.

"The one with me playing the periscope in the swimming pool, surrounded by showgirls in skimpy swimming suits, was called *Periscopes Up!* That's when they first used my stage name, Moby Dick, in the credits. In those days, there were no special effects or plastic surgery, so like Monroe and Jane Russell, if you had it, you flaunted it. I made films for five years. You understand, porn was pretty tame in those days.

"I became a celebrity of sorts and had some money, so I bought myself a new Cadillac convertible. I was docked by a guy running a red light in Santa Monica. My head hit the bullet-shaped horn in the middle of the steering wheel, and I lost my eye. There were no seat belts back then, of course, and my leg was completely severed by the door when I fell out onto the pavement. My career ended that night.

"The same thing happened to Sammy Davis Jr.'s eye, but at least he could sing and dance. I was washed up in films, so I headed back north, picking up carpentry jobs along the way, like I said, and ended up in Seattle. I had a wooden leg they made for me at the VA, but it hurts too much to wear it now. I married, had a child, got divorced, and built subdivisions in Seattle and Mercer Island.

"Every year, there is a film festival in this little town in Oklahoma named after me. The Moby Dick's Tavern and the Moby Dick's Private Parts Auto Store send me a plane ticket and pay me five thousand dollars just to introduce my films. The town fills up with all these little old ladies. I swear, ever year the thing just gets bigger." He winked. "The festival, that is."

Annie sat entranced. No prude, still she had never seen a porno flick much less met a porno star, and she found herself intrigued by Moby's story.

"I guess we all have our gifts."

"Like they say in Hollywood, 'I'm still big; it's just the pictures that got smaller.'" Moby set down his coffee cup. "Thanks, Annie, that was a great meal. Sorry about the snoring."

With that, Moby struggled to his feet and headed for the door. He stopped and turned.

"I thought I'd borrow *The Ark* to go to Port Townsend for some odds and ends tomorrow. If you're interested in going along, I'll stop by in the morning. Good night."

He turned on his flashlight and disappeared down the trail, the lone beam piercing the darkness.

Annie thought to herself, *Moby Dick—soldier, porn star, father, carpenter, cancer victim. No, not a victim, just someone like the rest of us, playing to our strengths and adapting to our challenges.* Intuitively, she knew he was a man worthy to live on the island. Her father and her grandfather would have called it an honor to be his friend.

Annie awoke to a cold and clammy house. A dense fog had parked on the water, and the symphony of foghorns created a confusing vertigo for man and bird alike. At night, the seagulls preferred the safety of the island, but this morning, they paced the beach, their black beady eyes searching for a crack in the fog to begin the day's foraging on the fall chum salmon.

In a salute to fall, Annie had lately gone to wearing three robes in the morning, one green with no belt, one a red and black plaid, and the third, a deep purple chenille. Together, they compensated for the overlapping deficiencies of their individual blown-out armpits, ripped shoulder seams, and torn collars. They were all cinched together nicely, with a cotton clothesline rope. The bulk made it impossible to bring her arms all the way down to her sides, but the effect was damn cozy. She hoped she would have the good grace not to be found dead wearing it. She imagined they would say: "The poor dear wasn't quite with it at the end, you know."

Nestled in her three robes and sitting in the Morris chair, with her feet sticking in the oven to warm them up—after the usual harrowing trip to the outhouse—she allowed herself to think that maybe if this hospice thing worked out, the island might be put on a paying basis. It was hard to imagine who would come to this primitive site when they could more easily live their remaining days in comfort surrounded by loved ones, but just in case, she vowed to see if she could rummage up any blankets, pillows, and quilts for the oyster shack clientele.

Mid-morning found her in the attic, poking through stacks of boxes, assorted humpback trunks, and leather-strapped suitcases. Clumps of clothing hung precariously on swaybacked ropes, and piles of fabrics lay stacked on top of dusty three-mirrored dressers. Portraits of relatives who hated each other, unwittingly forced face-to-face, watched in stony disapproval. Everything in the attic was laced together with dusty strands of cobwebs shimmering in the diffused light from the dust-glazed dormer windows. An army of dead flies littered the sills of the windows, along with the odd spider, legs folded neatly into little packages.

Annie unhooked the two fraying, black leather belts with brass buckles that bound an old steamer trunk. She depressed the brass shackle button, and the spring-loaded mechanism snapped open with authority, releasing the scent of Tennessee cedar shavings sprinkled over the contents to ward off hungry moths. Throwing the lid open, she saw the family quilts her mother had stored there.

Her mother, grandmothers, sisters, and aunts before her had chosen patterns out of books for the quilts they made—wedding ring, bear paws, tulips, or simple geometric patterns common in their day. But when it had come time for Annie to make a quilt, she had ambitiously chosen to replicate the entire island, filled with apple trees, the house, fields, boats, fishes—all anchored by the famous seven rocks. It had taken months to complete, but it was a work of art.

Annie lifted out the quilts one by one, holding each one first at arms' length, and then burying her face in the soft flannel backing, savoring the pungent scents of roses, lavender, musk, peppermint, cedar, and jasmine each aunt had added. The quilts also smelled musty, but she knew the stale smell would disappear when she aired them out on the porch rail. She decided it was time to put them to good use.

She closed the lid, gathered the quilts in her arms, and somehow managed to negotiate the two sets of stairs before setting her burden down on the kitchen table, just as Moby knocked on the door.

The excursion to Port Townsend was for stove parts, glass, and miscellaneous "gee gaws," as Moby called them. Annie helped load the two dogs in the boat and then sat back and enjoyed a leisurely ride as Moby piloted. They docked at the wharf on the Port Gamble side, where Moby kept his truck. The truck resembled its owner—take it or leave it. Either you enjoyed the joke or you didn't. It was one of those bulbous dump trucks from the '50s—rounded nose and fenders, ugly, utilitarian, built to last forever. It had served Moby well over the years.

Painted primer black with random patches of rust, the vehicle resembled an oxidized orca whale. With several pieces missing, the oval-shaped chrome grill looked like the mouth of a bottom feeder with dental problems. On each door, hand-painted in white letters, was the name, *Moby Dick Construction,* arched around a sperm whale shooting up water.

The *piece de resistance* was a hole in the ceiling of the cab roof through which Moby had run a hose, hooked up to a water reservoir and a hydraulic pump under the seat, suitable for spouting.

Belying the exterior, the interior of the truck had been newly revived with gray seats and—the only luxury option—a shiny chrome push-button radio.

"Gotta have my music," Moby informed her as he tuned in a classic station and the sound of "Pennsylvania 6-5000" filled the truck from another era.

Moby herded the truck north through the Chimacum Valley. The land was dotted with old farmhouses, interspersed by expedient mobile homes. Black-and-white Holstein cows grazed on the last of the grasses left by the Indian summer.

At one point the truck skidded to a gravelly halt at the only stop sign for eight miles. A group of kindergartners crossed the road, shepherded by two bored-looking sixth graders in yellow slickers carrying red flags.

Moby pumped the handle under the seat, and the truck blowhole sprayed ten feet into the morning air, splashing water on the hood and pavement, as the tiny troopers crossed like ducklings on parade.

The children laughed in glee and pumped their arms in the air for a repeat, so Moby spouted once more. (A number of parents were perplexed to see crude crayon drawings of spouting trucks hung on bulletin boards at the next open house.)

Rattling on, Moby and Annie suddenly found their nostrils twitching and burning under an aerial assault—the downwind stench of the town paper mill. Moby quickly rolled up his window, his one good eye already beginning to sting. Environmentalists periodically picketed the obnoxious odor-producing plant, but to no avail. To locals, the air smelled sweetly of money. Moby put pedal to the metal in an attempt to escape. Annie braced her legs against the dash and shrieked in alarm. Then suddenly, the peril was over—the air cleared, bluebirds trilled.

Annie readjusted her hat as the rooftops of Port Townsend Seaport flashed by her window. Stone towers, cupolas, elaborate fretwork, bay windows, and steep roofs lined the bluff, overlooking the single main street of town one block from the water.

Late in the 1800s, the town had over-speculated, determined to be the terminus of the transcontinental railroad. Architects and craftsmen came from San Francisco and Chicago to show the railroad the town was worthy of the status about to be bestowed on it. By the time the railroad decided to end in Tacoma, seventy-five miles to the south, Port Townsend was all dressed up in Victorian finery with no ball to attend.

For the next eighty years, the town with the fourteen-foot-high shop windows gathered dust. Then Port Townsend reinvented itself with year-round music festivals and boat shows. The railroad may have passed it by, but it became the terminus for sixties hippies, grass-rooters, artsy folks, and assorted oddballs, living in a contemporary, quasi-liberal time warp.

Moby coasted into a parking place in front of a store in the brick-building town center. Above the door, the transom window read "Pickles' Secondhand Store and Assorted Stuff." Next to the tall bay window stood a granite cornerstone: Hasting Building, 1886.

Annie noted the date.

*Probably the last time the windows were washed*, she thought.

A shopkeeper bell, mounted on top of the eight-foot-tall door, ding-a-linged their entry. They surveyed the dim interior, lit by a single pull-chain light bulb dangling from the ceiling. In the center of the room stood a small counter holding up a two-gallon jar full of mammoth pickles swimming in green juice. The surrounding floor space held pyramids of clothing, plumbing parts, ancient typewriters, electric tools, life preservers, shoes—apparently anything ever conceived of, manufactured, or dragged in from the sea. As far as the eye could see, the mounds disappeared into the shadows, as if they resided in the mist-shrouded depths of Angkor Wat.

A sign hung from the ceiling.

*Pickles' Place, Junk by the Pound...*

*If We Don't Have It, You Don't Need It.*

They heard a faint, scurrying sound from behind the counter. A small man with brown, beady eyes, cauliflower ears, and a huge pickle protruding from his mouth slowly emerged, looking left, then right, then straight at them. He shucked a black lace brassiere from his shoulders, took a bite from the end of the pickle, and tossed it back in the jar with a splash. As he came around the counter, they could see he wore a yellow tee shirt, brown jodhpurs, and gold, five-inch heels. A black riding crop, which he slapped, Patton-like, against his thigh, completed the ensemble.

He flashed a lightning-quick shopkeeper smile.

"May I help you?"

Despite the menacing crop, the man seemed friendly, if a tad off-center. Moby told him what he needed. The man kicked off of the shoes and motioned Moby to follow him to the back room, leaving

Annie to contemplate the jar full of violated pickles. Unable to ignore her curiosity, she leaning over the counter—only to be greeted by waves of lingerie billowing out of half-opened drawers.

Ten minutes later, the two men emerged from the back with a fully loaded wheelbarrow. Moby wrote a check, and he and Pickles loaded the truck.

They had traveled several miles up the road before Annie finally asked, "What was *that* all about?"

Moby grimaced.

"Annie, I don't think we want to talk about it."

Moby and Annie giggled, snickered, and shook their heads till Moby declared, "If we have to deal with weirdoes like that, we deserve a piece of pie and coffee at Mom's Café."

"Pot calling the kettle black," Annie said, as she stared straight ahead.

Pies were Mom's specialty. Farmers and loggers habitually hunkered over the generous portions of middle-America meat and potatoes in anticipation of dessert. If they cleaned their plates, they would be rewarded with the specialty of the house—lemon pie with meringue a full seven inches high.

"Two wedges of lemon pie and two coffees, please," Moby ordered confidently.

"That's what my grandpa does. Starts with dessert," the petit high school waitress said as she wrote down the order, looking as though she had never eaten a bite of pie in her life.

Between bites, Moby turned to Annie.

"Day after tomorrow, you're ready for business. Should have three shacks ready. I think you need to call them cabins now, kinda upgrade the program, you know."

Moby calibrated the entry of another bite, while watching to see how Annie would attack her piece. Wiping meringue from her nose, Annie decided to divide and conquer. She separated the filling from the fluff, speared the lemon first, and plunked it into her mouth. Freshly baked, warm, tart. She savored it on her tongue.

As *The Ark* neared Seven Sisters Island, Annie spotted a blue fiberglass rowboat stranded on the beach by the outgoing tide. Two men in suits, their cuffs rolled up to their thighs, were standing in mud up to their ankles, struggling to push the boat out to the water.

# Chapter FIVE

As Moby and Annie clumped down the beach toward them, the men looked at each other, panic in their eyes, as though they were considering swimming the mile back to the Port Gamble boat ramp rather than be caught defenseless.

"Ahoy," said Annie, standing on the gravel beach, avoiding the mud. "Can we help you?"

"Yes, well…we seem to be beached."

The taller man lumbered toward her and handed her his business card:

*Doug Beadle*
*Jefferson County Assessor's Office*

followed by one evidently introducing his partner:

*Jim Short*
*Assessor Technician*

Beadle, an average-sized man, wore a doughnut-ring fringe of hair around his polished pate. Two narrow rat-eyes stared down a skinny nose above a duster mustache that housed a piece of lint. His consort, Short, was just that. Plain-featured and rumpled, he too resembled some undesirable rodent.

*These two certainly look perfectly suited to their jobs*, thought Annie. But she put a smile on her face, as though pleased they had visited her island.

"Ah yes, assessors. I'm hoping to maintain my zoning status," Annie said warmly, hoping friendliness would count for something.

"We arrived a few hours ago and have been surveying the island," Beadle explained. "Unfortunately, our nautical skills seem to be lacking." Motioning his partner to join him, he pulled out his pad. "Since you're here, we have a few questions. Do you mind?"

When Annie shook her head, he launched into his inquisition.

"What is the building by the cemetery used for?"

"Nothing now. It once was a school for the children of the migrant workers and sometimes a church," Annie explained. "But now, as you see, the roof is practically gone."

"And how about these buildings on the sand spit here?" Short asked.

"They used to be shacks for oyster pickers, but they're pretty rundown these days."

"So then," Beadle continued, "your farm income is derived totally from the apple orchard and the oyster beds?"

"That's right," Annie said, trying to be helpful, believing honesty—but not too much—to be the best policy.

Moby leaned over his crutch, a practiced look of menace adorning his wrinkled forehead. He had learned over his building career that bureaucrats were not to be trusted. The less information they had, the better. He cleared his throat.

"Excuse me, Mr. Dung Beetle."

"That's Doug, Doug *Beadle*," the man corrected him.

"Whatever. Mr. Beetle, the tide is heading out fast, and unless you want to stick around for another twelve hours for the next high tide, it would be wise to get your ass…uh…boat in the water right now."

"But we have been trying," said Short, pointing to the mud plastered on the tassels of his formerly white loafers. "There is no way, short of a crane, that boat is going any further."

"Well, there is a way. Gym Shorts, is it?" Moby asked, innocently baiting the man.

"Short. The last name is *Short*," Jim said.

"Okay, Mr. Shorts. The method requires gathering rounded pieces of driftwood, throwing them under the boat, and rolling the boat down to the water. Here, let me show you how."

Moby hobbled to the shoreline, gathered several skinny logs, dropped them near the bow, and lifted up the front of the boat. He slid the logs under the bow and pushed.

"We are making a skid ramp. See, even a cripple can do it!"

The two men caught on. Despite Moby's insults, they were grateful for a means of escape. Moby exhorted them while he followed behind the stern, pushing. The men scurried back and forth, pitching logs before the boat, until finally it floated. They frantically piled aboard and began paddling, as if the island might explode any second.

"Whoa," Moby yelled out. "Here's your leather briefcase." He lofted it in the air, sending it pin-wheeling toward the boat. It landed on the back seat, near where Beetle was priming the outboard motor.

"Choke the motor—and be sure to put on your life preservers," Moby shouted.

The motor caught, and the men faced forward in the boat, no doubt with hopes of a brighter future on the eastern horizon. They were a hundred yards out into the channel when Annie heard two gun shots. She looked out to see smoke coming out of the motor and the men standing up in the boat, their yells indistinct but frantic. As the stern started to take on water, the men scrambled to the bow. One of them took off his sport jacket and waved it over his head to attract a passing pleasure boat. The boat pulled near to render assistance.

Annie looked over at Moby's shack, but the door was closing and all she saw was a rifle barrel retreating into the darkness. She thought she heard Moby's voice.

"Gut shot."

A few days later Annie looked out the window to see Moby going down the beach to meet two people in a rowboat. They were towing a large rubber raft covered with a tarp. By the time Annie was dressed, Moby had pulled both the raft and the boat ashore and was helping two women out of the boat. They were as alike as matching bookends: both diminutive with the same pixie haircut gray-hair, same brown eyes. Identical gold-rimmed glasses, perched on turned-up noses and hooked to neck chains, made them look like cloned school librarians. Closer inspection revealed the differences. If they had been books, one would have been described as a bit worn around the edges, probably left out in the rain occasionally, and never returned on the due-date; the other, crisp, straight, and unmarked, rarely checked out.

"You must be Annie," the more capricious-looking one began. "I'm North Carolina Storm. We have already met Moby. Here is our introductory letter from Carol Ann, and a check for six hundred dollars for accommodations." She paused to cast a quick glance around the island. "This place is wonderful. It reminds us of—"

"—our childhood farm on Cape Hatteras," said the clean binding, finishing the thought. "I am South Carolina Storm Caulkins. You can call us North and South. Everyone does." A look of concern crossed her brow. "Listen, one favor we need to ask…North coaches a soccer team. I was hoping to prevail on someone to ferry her back twice a week to practice and games. Perhaps you, Mr. Moby? For a fee, of course."

"We'll work something out, ladies," Moby said with a smile. "Would you like to choose a cabin? These first three are available. We'll get the baggage later. Please, follow me."

Annie sat on a driftwood stump, fished her glasses from her coat pocket, and read the letter.

*Dear Annie,*

*Hope you are doing well and getting along with Moby. He is not everyone's cup of tea, but he is a good worker. The two sisters, North and South, fight like cat and dog but are devoted to each other. North has ovarian cancer, with only months to live, and her sister will take care of her. They have money, so I told them to pay you $600 a month and to pay for extras, whatever they might be. They understand Seven Sisters is not a European spa.*

*Let me know if there is anything you need. I appreciate your help.*
*Carol Ann*

Swiveling around on the stump, Annie could see the sisters trailing after Moby, inspecting the cabins. She watched him proudly usher them in each door, pointing out his handiwork, and heard the genuine appreciation in their comments. They walked around each cabin, then stared across the water at the view. Soon, Moby was leading them triumphantly back to their boat.

"They picked the one with the pink door, except they'd like a porthole to look out of. I saw just the right one at Pickles' Place," Moby said proudly, as if he were a successful broker selling penthouses in a Manhattan high-rise overlooking Central Park. He turned to the sisters. "Let's get your luggage and move in before the tide changes."

"Good idea, Mr. Moby. We'll move our provisions in and be as swank as Martha's Vineyard," said North.

"No," countered South, "Catalina. "Martha's Vineyard is on the East Coast. We'll be as swank as Catalina."

"What do you know about Martha's Vineyard, or for that matter, Catalina? You've never been to either one. You don't know squat about anything, unless you see it on television," North shot back.

"Well, everything you know about Martha's Vineyard you read in that trashy *People* magazine. Just because John John spent summers there, you think it's so hot."

North bristled. Both sisters turned and leaned so close their noses almost touched, fogging each other's glasses.

"Ladies, ladies," Moby jumped in, his feelings mixed. A good catfight would be a welcome diversion. "Please."

Still facing down her sister, North eased back a tad. South continued glaring. The identical veins in their temples protruded, and they began to nod their heads up and down like two bobble dolls.

"Ladies, we need to unload the boat. There's a wheelbarrow leaning against the boat shed. I'll load, and you two can wheel."

The sisters shot glances at each other that promised they would finish this skirmish later, in private.

"That would be fine," South said graciously. "I could certainly use the help." Then she smiled sweetly at Moby, for her sister's benefit. Annie gratefully retreated to the house, leaving the two wildcats to Moby.

Annie sat in front of the stove, stocking feet in the oven, drinking chicken noodle soup. While her usually cold feet thawed, she imagined she was enjoying a "spa day." As usually happened during unguarded moments, she assessed her mortality.

It was good to have buffers, she thought. Three generations should be enough backup to keep the family going. The island was going to be in good hands. She closed her eyes and thought about Sarah and the babies. How wonderful to have the family growing again. Annie nestled into her blanket and gave a deep contented yawn. Her eyes sought a ten-inch-long bread pan on the wooden shelf above the stove. She struggled to her feet and took it down, turning it in her hand so she could better see the dogwood flowers her grandfather had scratched on its side with an awl.

She had heard the story of her mother's birth many times as she grew up.

Like the twins, Annie's mother had been born premature. The contractions signaling the baby's early arrival started one night during a storm. The family had been frantic. No way could they fetch the midwife in those tumultuous seas. After hours of difficult labor, a blue-gray child with a mop of red hair plastered to her head was born into her father's arms in a pool of blood.

Annie's grandfather held the doll-child on a towel, gently blowing into her nose, as he did with piglets born limp and still. The baby responded with shallow breaths, and then a loud wail. Next, he rubbed her with a coarse towel, the same way he would stimulate a newborn horse. The baby howled louder.

The tiny infant fit perfectly inside the bread pan, which they fitted with a mattress of dishtowels. They set her on the open oven door, under a linen towel canopy, next to the warm firebox, constantly rotating the pan before the flames. The older girls gathered on chairs around the stove, alternately sobbing and praying, pouring their love into their tiny sister throughout the night, until she was out of danger and strong enough to be brought to her mother's breast for nourishment. If it hadn't been for this bread pan, Annie thought, she herself would not be here today.

Annie put down the pan and smiled, filled with renewed hope for her great-grandbabies, safe in their incubator at Tacoma General. They had the best care available, and they came from strong stock.

Annie drifted into a nap by the stove. There would be time later to finish her chores.

It was late afternoon before Annie roused and headed to the beach to collect firewood. She noticed Moby going into the boat shed and whistled to get his attention.

"Moby, why don't you come to dinner tonight? Invite the Carolinas too, will you?"

Moby's mouth lapsed into a chewing motion when Annie mentioned the menu: vegetable stew, fresh rolls, and comstock apple pie.

Annie returned to the house, set out dishes, and prepared the dough for rolls, kneading till her wrists hurt. Then she shepherded the mass into a bowl to rise. At dusk, a clatter on the porch raised Buddy's hackles. Annie opened the door to find Moby and South removing muddy shoes.

"Just started to rain," said Moby, taking off his jean jacket. He took a red parka from South and hung both jackets behind the stove to dry.

"Where's North?" Annie asked, as she grabbed a potholder and maneuvered the large iron skillet, brimming with stew, to the table.

"All tuckered out. She just doesn't have the stamina anymore. She's been through so much surgery and chemo lately."

Moby poured water in the glasses and surveyed the table with delight.

"What kind of jam is this?" he asked, picking up the blackish-red, half-pint mason jar.

"Wild blackberry," answered Annie, tucking herself into the table. "From the wild berries that grow along the path in the spring. They're small and seedy, but oh so sweet."

Moby heaped a spoonful on his roll and stuffed the entire contents into his mouth, savoring the hot bread, butter, and jam all at once—as only a big man can. Annie ignored him but the move was not wasted on South, though she said nothing.

"I hope North can make it till spring. I'd like to make her a rhubarb pie out of those plants next to the orchard," South said.

"How did you get your names?" Moby leaned back in his chair, then eased it back down when Annie gave him a disapproving look.

"Carolina was split into two states during colonial times, and this never sat well with the relatives, especially General Ebenezer Storm of the Stonewall Brigade. He figured he had lost his arm in the war for no reason. He had hoped Carolina would become the cultural and political center of the fledgling nation, but split apart, its importance would dwindle. He was right, and he felt the great state of Carolina owed him. So in our family, everyone's middle name became Carolina. Then when twins arrived…well, you get the idea.

"North has good days and bad days. She absolutely refuses to be warehoused in a rest home or an apartment. She wants to smell the saltwater and listen to the gulls."

"Does she have any other family beside you?" asked Annie. "Someone who can help with her care?"

"She has two grown children, but they have lives of their own. I took care of them when North was in the hoosegow for a few years, a bum wrap with a bum boyfriend. They call us both 'Mom.' North has given me a chance to share in a life I never would have had, and I'm grateful to pay her back now. I won't tell you she doesn't have her faults. Lord, don't I know about that."

South looked down, as tears trickled down her cheeks. A muffled cry escaped her closed lips, then she shook her head resolutely and dried her face with an embroidered handkerchief tucked in the sleeve of her sweater.

"I don't know what I will do without her." She massaged her eyes with her fingers as if to rub away the pain, then asked in a small voice, "Do you think I could have some more coffee, please?"

Moby put his hand on South's shoulder as Annie filled her cup.

"We'll take good care of her," he said. "Don't you worry. We're all short-timers here."

North was not feeling up to a trip to the mainland, so Moby took South to coach North's soccer team in their game. After they'd been gone an hour, Annie traversed out to the Carolina cabin to check on North, carrying her ancient umbrella to ward off the drizzle.

She knocked softly, and when she received no response, she opened the door to the cabin. She found North sitting in a wicker rocking chair, huddled next to the fire and bundled in a green army blanket. She appeared to be sleeping—her eyes closed, her chin on her chest. But at Annie's entrance, North opened her eyes and rested them on Annie. She seemed far away, either in pain or thought, but she managed a wry smile.

"I brought a better quilt to keep you warm," Annie said, as she set it in her lap. "It was made by one of my aunts a long time ago."

She unfolded the blanket, exposing the blocks of yellow sunflowers and green leaves.

"How thoughtful of you," said North, "but I couldn't possibly take one of your heirlooms."

"You keep it as long as you need it," Annie said in an uncompromising voice. "How are you feeling today?"

"You know, I was just sitting here thinking of all those years that scooted by so fast. I learned to cook, drive a car, make love, balance a checkbook—when I had the money—and never once did I learn how to die.

"In some ways, I'm lucky. I can put things to rest, say the necessary goodbyes to my sister and my kids, look one more time at the sunset, watch the maple leaf seeds helicopter in the wind, listen to the silence of the fog. It has been a wonderful journey. I wish I had taken more time with the people I loved." Abruptly, North changed direction. "Do you think I'm going to hell, Annie?"

"I don't think there is a hell," Annie confessed. "I like to think if you tally all the people you have loved in your life, and the number is even one more than the line of people you wronged, you're okay. That should be the measure of a life. And if it isn't, let the chips fall where they may, I say."

"I like that." Looking down at the quilt, North's eyes filled with tears. "I get puddled up so easily these days. And…oh, I don't know… it seems like everything moves in slow motion.

"Yes," she said, patting the quilt, "it would be an honor to use this quilt." She snugged up the blanket against her chest and folded her hands on top of it.

The two women stared at the fire for a long time. The intense, throbbing, red heat in the middle of the fire gave way to yellow flames licking through a knothole in a white board, probably a piece of a picket fence once lost to a winter storm. They watched, mesmerized, as two small, black beetles climbed to the end of a branch, desperate to escape the searing heat, then perished, when one mistakenly headed the wrong way, into the fire, and the other one followed. The women witnessed this event as unbiased spectators, helplessly lost in their own history.

Eventually the chair stopped rocking and North slumped over, drifting off. Annie removed the quilt from North's lap and wrapped it around her like a barber might. She sat back in her chair and studied the sleeping woman. North's eyes were circled with pain, but the blanket's bright yellow sunflowers, always facing the sun, seemed symbolic of the full life she'd led.

*The Ark* hove into view around the sister rocks and disappeared into the boathouse. Annie went down to catch up on the news and collect the mail from Moby. South and Moby were both sporting gray baseball caps with lettering that read, "Awesome Possums." They were wearing grins from ear to ear—and smoking cigars.

"Those cigars could only mean you two just had great sex or your soccer team won," Annie quipped.

"Get your mind out of the gutter, old woman," Moby chided. "We waxed 'em, 4–0."

"Moby is teaching me the fine art of cigar smoking. Whaddya think?" South asked. She posed jauntily, her hand on her hip, cigar thrust in the air. "We're celebrating—the girls were hitting on all cylinders today." She turned, and jumping as high as a seventy-year-old woman can, gave Moby a high five, a low five, and then completed the ritual with a little tail bump and grind.

"I can see Moby is having an effect," Annie said.

"Those girls were playing up to Awesome Possum potential today." South turned to Moby. "How many did little Natalie score?"

"Three, I think. Yep, three. Remember that penalty kick in the upper right, over the goalie's head? Zoom, right in the net." Moby held up three fingers.

"They played their tails off today. Next weekend they've got a tournament. I hope North is well enough to take over her team."

South pulled Annie's mail from her purse. Moby blew smoke rings in the air.

"You know, I could never do that," South said in awe. "North could."

"Let's go practice by the fire. I'm getting cold," said Moby, heading down the beach. He stopped and leaned on his crutch. "Annie, my girl Christine is coming for Thanksgiving. Is that okay?"

South chimed in, "I think our kids are coming over, too."

Annie started counting mentally, then shrugged.

"No problem. I'll just have to alert John. We're gonna need a lot of turkey."

Sunday morning found Annie alone in the boat on her way to Port Gamble. She could hear church bells calling their flock from the little communities dotting the shoreline of Hood Canal.

Annie tied up *The Ark*. Buddy, having one of his arthritic days, declined to join the adventure and disappeared under the covered bow. At the top of the gangplank a pay phone awaited, surrounded by relics of long-distance calls: cigarette butts, chewing gum, broken clamshells, and a bloated phonebook exposed to the rain, looking as if it served Manhattan's millions rather than a rural community of fifteen hundred. The receiver smelled of rank cologne, the product of teenage, fifty-cent love trysts.

Fighting nausea, Annie held the phone as far away from her as she could and still carry on a conversation.

Sarah answered on the first ring with good news. The twins had gotten the magic bullet: a steroid to coat the inside of their lungs.

"Their little noses are full of tubes to help them breathe and to feed them," said Sarah. "Peter and I finally get to hold them in our laps, even though they're still all wired up, like little marionettes. But they're gaining weight."

Annie next phoned John and explained the growth in the island's population.

"With Moby and his daughter and the Carolinas and their two kids and their families, I think there will be at least ten more guests for Thanksgiving. We were thinking we would all help out with the side dishes if you would bring the turkeys."

John readily agreed. More chitchat, and finally, Annie hung up the phone. Outside the booth, she pulled up some wet grass and rubbed it on her offended ear to dilute "Love Potion Number Grind."

The day before Thanksgiving, Moby went to the mainland and picked up North's son and daughter. The son was what Sarah would have called "a hunk"—thirtyish, tall, with a yachtsman's tan and a chiseled face, crowned with thick, black hair and a well-trimmed beard. He looked as if he had just stepped out of an Eddie Bauer catalogue. His wife, a tall blonde, looked as if she had been ordered from the same catalogue—right after the page with the snug-fit jeans and just before the Holstein-print flannel nightgowns. They would have children only if they could preorder all the options.

North's daughter and her husband were, in police terms, of average build and average height, sandy brown hair, no distinguishable marks; no priors, and were probably voted most likely to be ignored. The three grandchildren also seemed unremarkable, except to the two women who had waited all morning for their arrival. South and North stormed out of their cabin, beaming. They enveloped the crowd in group hugs and slobbering mother- and aunt-kisses. They were a universe unto themselves.

The group withstood the other island introductions politely, and understanding this was a support group for their mom, the son and daughter thanked Moby and Annie effusively. That done, the Storm contingent adjourned to the cabin to bask in the combined force field of their love for one another.

Moby turned to Annie as they left, pointing down the channel to a white dot approaching from the east.

"Looks like the turkey is right on time."

Annie shivered in the cold wind, hunched over, and stuffed her hands in her pea coat pockets.

"That could be anyone."

"One way to tell. They probably have us in their binoculars," Moby said. He raised his hand in salutation. The boat answered with three long toots.

"It must be difficult to be right all the time," Annie said, playfully kicking Moby's crutch.

The *Bon Appetit* dropped anchor. The dinghy was loaded with John's children and their spouses and children. John proudly waved at the beach duo as the first assault hit the beach. They unloaded all manner of sleeping bags, suitcases, backpacks, and coolers. The children scattered like sand fleas, with mothers in hot pursuit. By the third trip, the beach was littered with baggage and people, standing around as if they were immigrants waiting to be processed at Ellis Island.

Annie worked herself through the crowd like a politician on election day. She shook the hands of young and old till she reached the shoreline, where the patriarch was laying the last of three plastic-wrapped turkeys into the wheelbarrow.

Pant cuffs rolled up, seaweed wrapped around his knobby knees, John happily stopped to acknowledge Annie. He lifted her up in the air with a crushing bear hug, then set her down gently on the gray, sand-dollar-littered beach.

"Annie, we have brought the guests of honor," he said, reaching over and slapping the birds one by one on their pimpled rumps. "Range-raised and grain-ripened." He reached into a brown shopping bag and pulled out a round bottle of tequila. He twirled it into the air, expertly catching it by the neck inches from the rocks.

"Two bottles per bird," he trilled. "Tomorrow we feast on the infamous Turkey Loco-ooooo."

# Chapter SIX

"Everyone, this is Annie," said John. "She is the mistress of this faire isle, and"—looking to Moby—"this would be her trusted aide de camp, Moby Dick, of stage and screen fame. We are in their debt." With that, he gave a sweeping bow.

A young man with jet-black hair slicked back into a fifties duck-tail stepped from the crowd. He had fine, patrician-like features, centered around an aristocratic nose and an obvious European air. He took Annie's two hands in his, held them to his face, and kissed them. With a thick accent, he introduced himself.

"I am John Paul. I am pleased to be here on your island, Madame."

John said, "Ah yes, this is John Paul, the pastry chef, on loan from Le Cirque in Paris. He is giving seminars. I did an article on him two weeks ago, and he has no family here. So I invited him along."

John Paul held up a sugar pumpkin the size of a soccer ball.

"I cook the classic American dish—the pumpkin pie, no?"

Betsy came up from behind and put her hand on Annie's shoulder.

"We appreciate your letting us invade your home. If there are any problems that arise, please don't hesitate to let us know."

"Don't worry," Annie reassured her. "This island has had its share of potlatches."

Suddenly, organ music wafted over the waves, and a tugboat steamed around the corner. Seventy feet long, the boat was painted nightshade black with creamy white trim. Its highly polished brass portholes beamed bright. It was the mighty *Pissant*, owned and operated by Joseph P. Woodson III, the heir to the pink urinal block empire and known as Pinky to friends, admirers, and sports fans throughout the planet who had often stared at his pink product while whizzing away their third beer, making room for the fourth.

Pinky had not rested on his founder grandfather's laurels but gone on to invent the solar-assisted honey bucket, with optional skylights, magazine rack, and musical toilet paper dispenser. Annie knew Pinky and his wife well. At his own expense, he often shipped portable toilets to far-flung lands, then got them to the most remote refugee camps by truck or donkey or helicopter. The motto on his business card read: *If you have the will, we have the way*. Or as Pinky more succinctly put it, "You dump it…we'll pump it."

Pinky and his wife, Dorie, had assumed the shape of their famous fixtures—short, round, and scrubbed pink. Both of them were shedding fur, as Pinky described the balding process. An even match, they were both blessed with a ribald sense of humor and lots of silver-spoon money.

Pinky had painstakingly installed a pipe organ throughout the hull of *The Pissant*, the keyboard residing in the wheelhouse. Dorie played the organ while Pinky, ever the showman, entertained with song and dance. The boat dropped anchor in the channel fifty feet off shore. Pinky leapt to the bow and stood on a small performance platform he had specially built in the bowsprit. He pointed to the steering house, and a rousing organ introduction warmed him up for his rendition of "New York, New York," which he sang full out, resplendent, with Sinatran suave and sky-grabbing fists.

Annie led the clapping, and the others joined in. Pinky swung into the Perry Como classic, "Seattle," with equal crooning verve. More applause, and "The Pink" bowed his acceptance of their appreciation. He grabbed a dangling rope hung from the smokestack and swung over the bow toward shore and vaulted into calf-high surf and waded ashore, reminiscent of Douglas McArthur in the Philippines.

The man would do anything to please a crowd.

Dorie lowered a dinghy and came ashore in a more reasonable fashion.

The couple shook hands with everyone till they got to Annie, who received a theatrical hug and a loud smack on the lips from Pinky.

"You didn't think we were going to make it, did you, Annie?" he asked.

"I'm glad you did. You two are always welcome." Annie spoke with affection, giving Dorie a hug.

"Annie, you say the word, and you've got the state of the art potties out here," Pinky said, eyeing the weather-beaten outhouses behind the oyster shacks, which the incessant south wind had slanted at a rakish angle. "Well, you can't beat the view from here. Except remember Nepal after the earthquake? Now that was a view to die for from every pit-toilet door. Mt. Everest, if you could find a clear day."

Annie laughed as the three went into the house.

Both Johns came scuttling in, engaged an animated discussion in front of the stove, then left in a hurry, still scheming the great turkey roast.

"Annie, would you like to come aboard for dinner?" asked Dorie. "Nothing special, just meatloaf and baked potatoes."

"If you're cooking, I'm eating," said Annie.

"There's no rush. We can just relax here and eat in an hour or so." Dorie watched Pinky get up and look out the window. "How's the boat doing, honey?"

"The boat's okay. But the beach sure looks like an ant nest out there. People, kids, dogs everywhere. Hell, somebody even brought a dysfunctional rooster. He just blasted off a minute ago."

They rowed out to the tug and Annie marveled at the gleaming polished brass and the immaculate planked decks. Inside the saloon, she drank in the luxurious appointments: the maroon carpet, golden-ribboned mahogany paneling, deep pin-cushioned leather sofas, and a black-marble fireplace. Annie's eye stopped on an oddly shaped clock. Closer inspection revealed it was a finely detailed wooden outhouse, with a clock in the door.

"It keeps regular time," Pinky said. "And over here"—he led Annie to an alcove—"is another keyboard for the organ."

He pressed a button and a fireplace flickered to life, just as Dorie brought in dinner and set it on the coffee table. They ate, drank coffee, and talked till ten, when Annie asked Pinky to row her back to shore. Although cloud cover made the night completely black, she made her way by rote up the well-worn path to the house, something she had done a thousand times in her youth. Ahab had crowed three times by the time she tumbled into bed. *Too late to wash up or brush my teeth*, she thought. Tomorrow would be a busy day.

No sooner had Annie washed her face the following morning than John and the entire holiday population began funneling into the kitchen for an organizational meeting. John read off the list he had constructed the night before.

"Dinner is between three and four," he began. "We will fine-tune when we enter the turkey-completion-zone."

Moby was in charge of transport. Sarah and Peter would be picked up early in the morning on the Seattle side and Moby's daughter was to be picked up at noon in Port Gamble. The Carolina sisters, with their southern roots, would do the yams and the sweet potato pie. Cranberry orange compote: Betsy. Fresh squeezed lemonade, a Thanksgiving tradition of the Pilgrims according to John, along with ice water and wine: John's offspring. Moby, with his daughter, would head the potato team. Pinky and Dorie had volunteered for homemade rolls, table setup, decoration, and condiments. Annie: apple and mincemeat pies. John and John Paul were in charge of the turkeys, dressing (with and without onions), the gravy, and the pumpkin pie. Sarah, Peter, and Calypso would fill in as necessary.

"Clean-up will be done by everyone, I repeat, everyone," John's voice rose above the rapidly dissipating, task-driven audience. "And people, people—be prepared for miscellaneous tasks." But his exhortation fell on an empty room.

Thanksgiving had begun on Seven Sisters.

John had helped Moby stoke two of the wood stoves in the cabins before the meeting. Now he stacked Annie's stove with fragrant logs of split Douglas fir and began to boil the giblets. The oven thermometer needle pegged at 500 degrees within the hour, as they began preparing the turkeys.

John and John Paul positioned huge sombreros on their heads—one black, with a silver-sequined cactus, the other red, with black bulls running around the brim. Together, the two Johns set about cutting up an entire crate of limes into quarters. The tangy smell of lime seeped into the stuffy room. Soon mounds of electric-green wedges drooled on the kitchen table.

Annie knew this would be no ordinary Thanksgiving.

John took out four shot-glasses. He filled each to the brim with tequila from one of the six bottles he had placed under the table for safekeeping.

"You girls want some of this action?" he challenged.

Annie and Betsy looked up from their projects and nodded. John pulled two more sombreros from a box, which the women dutifully donned. He pushed the shot glasses in front of the other three caballeros, handed each a lime, and poured sea salt into the web of their hands.

"I'll demonstrate," he said, in a patronizing tone.

"Allow me," Annie butted in. She sucked the lime, spit it out on the floor, licked the salt from her hand, and pounded down the tequila.

"I see we are in the presence of greatness," John said. He followed the same steps, then slammed his shot-glass upside down on the table. The others did likewise.

John explained, "Turkey Loco is a traditional dish with strict rules. Whenever the turkey is touched, the cooks must take a shot of tequila. *Muy importante.* We are now ready to move on in the tradition of the great Aztec chefs of Mexico."

John Paul watched wide-eyed while John took spring-loaded poultry shears and cut the turkey in half down the backbone. Then he carefully pushed down on each half till he could hear bones cracking. They dispatched the other two turkeys the same way. As the birds lay crumpled on the table, John declared another round of tequila.

There were now eight shot-glasses upside down on the table.

"Next, we pat the turkeys dry with a towel, squeeze the lime quarters onto the bird, and rub on the juice. Then we massage the turkey with a blend of oregano, salt, and pepper." John manipulated the turkey with the dexterity of a master masseuse.

"I think I'm getting jealous," said Betsy. "How come you don't rub me like that, John?"

"Woman, if you were a free-ranging turkey, you'd get the same treatment," John shot back. "This proud, twenty-two-pound Heritage turkey, harkening back to the days of the Pilgrims and well worth the eight bucks a pound, has lived its entire life in a pure state of grace and contentment on a farm in eastern Oregon."

"Well, I was a free-ranging chicken back in the sixties. I weighed 122 pounds. Come to think of it, you didn't mind oiling me down in those days," Betsy said.

John flushed momentarily, savoring the years of his youth. Without warning, he grabbed Betsy, bent her over the table—scattering the limes—and gave her a long, French kiss. Even the Frenchman, John Paul, clapped his hands in amazement.

"Oh la la!"

Bringing Betsy upright, John declared it time for another shot.

Looking at Betsy, he apologized. "I'm sorry, Madame. I will never let a turkey come between us again. Besides, I don't think relations with a turkey is legal in this state. A salmon—maybe."

By this time, Betsy was laughing hysterically—a combination of the tequila, the limes, and John's advances. She put an arm around Annie's shoulders for stability and laughed till she bent over gasping.

Having made his madcap move, John returned to the serious business of preparing Turkey Loco.

"Now we put the turkey in the oven and insert the meat thermometer into the thigh. We will take the turkey out when it reaches 165 degrees. No higher, no lower." He checked the chart and mumbled, "Eleven to fourteen pounds, two and a half to three hours or so . . ." He looked down at his watch. "It's noon, so we eat sometime between three or four . . . . "

John declared another shot all around. He and John Paul repeated the process with the two remaining turkeys and then hustled down the path to place them in two of the ovens that had been preheating in the cabins. When Annie went out on the porch to watch the two gauchos trail down the beach, she saw Moby and a tall, thirty-something young woman leaving the boat shed. She hailed the two as they approached the porch.

Moby's daughter cut quite a figure, with her long red skirt, a white ruffled blouse with a black bow at the neck, and black cloak with red piping. On her head she sported a red felt hat with a thin black feather slanted at a jaunty angle. Next to Moby's roguish pirate image, she looked like a captured princess.

Moby put his hand on the young woman's shoulder and smiled broadly.

"Everyone, this is my girl, Christine."

Christine's smile echoed her father's, as she stepped forward to shake Annie's hand.

"I'm so glad to meet you, Annie. Dad's told me all about you and your wonderful island. Thanks for inviting me."

Moby maneuvered up the steps and went into the kitchen. He took a deep breath and followed his nose to the stove.

"Mmmm. Smells like Turkey Day to me."

Christine discovered the piano, plunked the keys, and wrinkled her nose. She returned to Moby's cabin to get her piano tuning equipment. John and John Paul burst in the door, bolted past Moby, and poured themselves another drink. Moby eyed them.

"Looks like I've missed something here—but I'm 'swilling' to catch up."

John explained the time-honored tradition of Turkey Loco and its inherent contribution to international diplomacy.

Moby demanded a hat from the box and declared himself as loco as the next man. He poured two glasses of tequila, quaffed them, and sat down on one of the kitchen chairs looking like a Mexican pirate.

"Moby, we need those potatoes by three," Annie reminded him.

Moby stood up from the table and fired off a snappy salute beneath his brimmed hat.

"Poncho Tequila will meet that deadline, Ma'am." He had one more defiant drink and then tottered down the path to join his daughter.

Annie stood at the stove stirring the chutney sauce when Sarah came up and put her arm around Annie's waist.

"Whatcha building, Grandma?" she said, reaching for the stirring spoon Annie was holding.

Annie gave up the spoon willingly and put her arm on Sarah's shoulder. Sarah stirred, and silently Annie leaned against the new mother who was still waiting to bring her babies home. Soon Calypso came up on the other side and put her arm around Annie's waist.

"Look, I got that tattoo I was talking about."

Next to the mermaid was a freshly minted tattoo of a simple red heart with the names of her grandchildren: Zack and Annie.

Sarah, who had accepted her mother a long time ago, said, "It looks good, Mom."

Annie put her arm around her daughter's shoulder, and the three women just stood standing over the warmth of the stove for a long time watching Sarah stir the chutney.

Annie shuddered and closed her eyes and leaned her head back. She had not been physically this close to her daughter as far back as she could remember. Things were changing. She could feel a bond between these very different women.

Maybe it was Thanksgiving, maybe it was the babies, and maybe it was the warm stove, but Annie knew she would remember this moment the rest of her life.

John burst in.

"I need some allspice, Annie. Have you got some somewhere?"

The spell was broken. Annie backed away and reached into the spice cabinet. As she handed the spice to John she looked back at her "girls" still holding each other, and she knew the next generation would be in better hands.

From the farmhouse window, Annie could see people shuttling between cabins, sharing food tips, and coordinating the zero hour of the great feast. Near the cemetery, John's grandchildren were playing on resurrected swings. With their feet, they dug anew the old toe-dragging troughs beneath the swings, exposing the raw earth once again to the mud-puddle gods.

Finishing her apple and mincemeat pies, Annie trundled off to find a vacant stove. The smells, coming in aromatic waves from the main oven, were enough to give John a wide, goofy, distilled grin as he stuck a thermometer into the thigh and nodded approval. He, John Paul, and Moby poured another round and loudly argued who was to test the other birds of honor. John Paul won the contest. The test results came back affirmative and word spread that four o'clock was the hour of destiny.

John's daughter barged into the kitchen, dragging his mud-spattered granddaughter.

"Dad, did you tell Vicki she could play in the mud-puddles in her new shoes? Did you?"

John gave a sly, grandfather grin.

"I did tell her that, and I jumped in the puddle myself," he said, drawing up his pants to expose his mud-caked socks and shoes.

John's daughter put her hand on her hip.

"Dad, how could you? She's a mess!"

John's smile faded into a look of loving concern.

"Honey, when you kids were growing up, we always had lots of rules. Your mother and I were so afraid you wouldn't grow up to be responsible adults. And now your sixty-three-year-old father knows that we should have encouraged you to jump into more mud puddles. Call it the prerogative of a grandparent to right a wrong."

Exasperated but touched, John's daughter shook her head and laughed.

"All right, Dad, but that little grandfatherly wisdom will cost you a pair of Mary Janes."

John danced a jig and smiled at his granddaughter, grabbing her by both hands to join him in the little dance.

Vicki looked up at her grandfather with love and admiration. As far as she was concerned, grandfathers were gods.

"Shoo, now," said John, giving her a little swat, and she ran off to find another puddle.

He pulled out three jars—carefully labeled and wrapped tightly with newspaper for protection. He held each one to the light and read the names as if he were reading the results of a beauty pageant.

"Chili-Orange Glaze. Brown Sugar Crackle Glazing. Mango Chutney Sauce." He placed the jars reverently on the table, and whispered the final sacramental instructions to John Paul and Moby in turn. Armed, they silently slipped out the door to slather the last rites.

At 3:45 p.m., like an army of ants on the move, the inhabitants of the tiny island began to emerge, proudly carrying their offerings with potholders and making their way up the trail. The main table brimmed with bounty. The three turkeys stood at the ready, proud and golden. The table itself represented an elliptical triumph of engineering, built as it was with sawhorses, plywood, planks, and ironing boards. It stretched from the kitchen through the dining room, met the vanishing point in the living room, and made a sharp dogleg to left into the butler's pantry.

Steam rising from the many delectable dishes condensed into water droplets on the bottom of the candle-lit chandelier. Annie stood next to the men and caught the eye of everyone around the table, searching for inspiration in their respective gazes. Buddy and Tripod slithered in the door to take roost under the table.

Annie cleared her throat, and the crowd hushed.

"For over two hundred years this simple blessing has been given on great family occasions in the Pippin family. Please bow your heads.

"To all people under heaven, there is a time for all things. A time to be born, and a time to die, a time to plant and a time to sow, a time to weep and a time to laugh, and a time to mourn and a time to dance, a time to scatter stones and a time to gather them." Finished, Annie turned to the men. "Gentlemen, start your carving knives."

The table instantly came alive with clattering dishes, general oohs and aahs, demands that the gravy be passed, and satisfied grunts of feasting. The guests settled into concentrated indulgence followed by a renewed flurry of banter and requests for selective seconds. When North began arguing with her sister over the olives, South picked up a pimento-stuffed orb and bounced it off North's forehead. North retaliated with a hard roll to her sister's chest. No one seemed to mind or even notice.

Readjusting their belts and unhitching their skirts, people slowly pushed their chairs away from the table.

John said, "I think that went pretty well. I deem an hour's recess till dessert."

All grunted approval and went their respective ways, seeking relief. Moby retreated to his shack for a nap, while John Paul, newly initiated to the finer points of tequila and American melting-pot cuisine, made it just in time to the brush outside the back porch where he got to taste the meal again on its way back up.

South and North continued their feuding on the worn, green 1950's overstuffed sofa till they fell asleep, leaning against one another and snoring in unison. The children had taken lanterns and had gone back to swinging on the swings and skipping stones in the water. Peter and Sarah nestled into the love seat, clutching their photo album and content to wait till they could bring their own mud puddle jumpers to the island. The rest sat around campfires or lay distressed in bunks.

Of thirty original partygoers, only seventeen answered the dessert bell on the first ringing. The apple and mince pies were heaped with mounds of whipped cream. John Paul proudly passed out pumpkin pie, even though his countrymen thought the vegetable worthy only as pig fodder. This was America, the land of Porky Pig, with none of the sophisticated philosophies of the existential Camus or the erudite humor of that French-revered comedian, Jerry Lewis.

Some spurned dessert, returning instead to the kitchen to glean fragments of the main course, kept warm on the oven. Having long since finished tuning the piano, Christine played a few requests, then moved into music no one recognized, though they felt the power and beauty of her playing. A concert pianist, she deftly slipped from honky-tonk to jazz to Disneyania. Her virtuosity echoed across the lagoon. A flock of mallards, compelled by the primal song, paddled toward the sound.

North's daughter wondered aloud if Carolina had not been divided, would the two sisters have continued fighting the war of identity two hundred years later.

"Oil and water, those two, oil and water. Shake before using." Then she got up and picked through the desserts.

During a lull, Christine and Annie talked about traveling overseas. Still sitting at the table, cheeks pouched, John looked over a mound of dressing slathered with thick turkey gravy and warbled, "This is one of the best meals I've ever eaten." He suggested they polish off the day with another round of tequila. John Paul deferred by burying his face in a pillow to muffle his gagging.

The wind shifted to the north. By morning, the clouds had disappeared, and ice skimmed the top of the bucket of Moby's wash water. He splashed the freezing water onto his face. Shivering, he made his way to the fire by his shack and sat on a log in contemplation, sucking his teeth till he dislodged a remnant of yesterday's turkey. He identified it as from the chutney-and-mango ensemble. He grunted, watching the island slowly come awake. First came the mumbling from inside neighboring cabins, then the smoke billowing dark gray from each chimney and drifting skyward, then the shoeless dash to the outhouse.

Christine emerged from Moby's cabin in a lavender, ribbed, retro-1940s robe with blue morning glories embroidered across the shoulders. Moby couldn't help thinking she was the perfect cross of two misfits. She had inherited her mother's delicate, neurotic beauty—as Moby described his wife of two years—and her father's iron-willed constitution. He put his arm around her, and she snuggled up against him like a child. They sat silently staring into the flames. As if on cue, a blue heron landed in the cusp of the high tide and waded to his knees. The bird assumed a stoic stance, glaring intensely into the lapping waves, leaning forward to skillfully spear a six-inch perch. The fish flapped in the bird's slender bill before the heron tipped his head back and consumed his catch. The heron turned a beady eye toward the fire, as though he knew he was being tracked. With a characteristic honk, he rose into the air and glided down the beach.

"You know, Dad," said Christine as she adjusted her robe modestly over her knees, "I was wondering why you left town and moved out here. Is everything all right?"

"I just needed a break. The traffic is a killer over there."

She gave him her smile, but she knew a deft deflection when she heard one. He would tell her when he was ready—or he wouldn't.

Christine got up from the log and went around behind her father, where she squatted down and put her arms around him, resting her chin on his shoulder. Moby breathed in the faint competing scents of apricot and smoke in her hair. Father and daughter were motionless for a long time, then she stood up.

"Dad, I have to be in New Orleans tomorrow. Can you get the shower working for me?"

The moment over, Moby reluctantly got up and went into his shack. He stoked the fire and turned a series of bewildering handles and knobs. A galvanized pipe let water run from the top of the cabin into a metal barrel. A line fed through the firebox, then exited into another twisted mass of copper pipes and valves that supplied hot water to the shower in the back of the cabin, a Moby original.

He tapped the pipes with a hammer that dangled from a green nylon rope next to the stove. He gave an affirmative grunt as he heard the water gurgle from joint to joint.

"Shower will be ready in fifteen, twenty minutes," he said, still holding the hammer in his hand and listening intently to his creation hiss and moan. "I'll be back in an hour. Need to shuttle some people back to the mainland."

Moby was halfway down the beach when *The Pissant* hauled up anchor and began to steam away. On the bridge, Pinky belted out, "Somewhere, over the Rainbow," accompanied by Dorie on the organ. Thick black diesel smoke pouring out of the smokestack formed a backdrop to their finale.

Moby loaded the Carolina troops on *The Ark,* while the two sisters, grousing about something or other, wrapped a quilt around their bony shoulders. They huddled together until their family was out of hailing distance, a mere speck on the horizon.

Later in the afternoon, Christine caught Moby's shuttle. She wore hip-hugging Levis, an ivory-colored ruffled shirt, cowboy boots, and a black stockman's coat from Australia—topped off with a white Stetson.

Annie reflected to herself that Christine was every bit as dramatic as her father.

Before she sailed off, Christine managed to find a private moment with Annie while her father tinkered with the engine.

"Annie, this is a card from the foundation I work for. Call this number, and I can be here in twenty hours or less. They have a jet at our disposal. I know you don't have a phone on the island, but I would appreciate anything you can do. Dad would never send for me, but if the old pirate needs me for anything, just call." She gave Annie a hug. "Thank you for taking care of him; he's one of a kind. But you already know that."

Annie decided to check in with John and Betsy's brood, who had been segregated by age. One cabin was filled with teenagers engrossed in a noisy game of Monopoly. The other cabin had babies taking bottles and their parents sucking on coffee at the gate-legged table. Some of the youngsters sat dangling their feet from atop the bunks, their heads jammed against the dusty, cobweb-strewn, two-by-four roof rafters. Betsy sat in a rocking chair propped against the wall. Her eyes were closed, and she had a gray blanket on her lap.

Outside, John was fussing at the fireside grill in front of the cabin. He had loaded the grill with oysters and a blackened pan of drawn butter. He straightened as Annie approached.

"Something wrong with Betsy?" Annie asked, as she hunkered down on a log in front of the fire. She prodded an oyster with a fork to see if the shell had opened yet.

"She's been tired these last few days—probably a touch of the flu, or maybe stress," John answered. "She gets pretty excited at these family gatherings." With a hunting knife in one hand and a potholder in the other, he pried open an oyster. He threw the top shell away on the beach, then placed the other half back on the grill.

"It's probably nothing. Does she have a temperature?"

"No, she says she just feels tired. I think this one is ready."

John speared a perfectly grilled oyster with a fork and handed it to Annie. Annie dipped it in the butter, savored the nutty flavor, and wiped the errant juice rolling down her chin with the sleeve of her sweatshirt.

Tapping the shells with the handle of his knife, listening for the hollow thud of a cooked oyster, John looked up at Annie.

"It doesn't get any better than this, does it?"

The next morning, Moby fired up *The Ark* and took John's family back to their car on the mainland. He and John continued on to Port Townsend in the "Great Beluga," as Annie had dubbed Moby's white dump truck.

They rattled their way up the valley. Pickles was having a Thanksgiving Weekend Sale. He had slashed some of his slow movers by fifty percent. Surplus Army gas masks, unmarked cans of paint, and mismatched shoes represented just a few of the fabulous bargains. John noticed that the shoes came with curious marks on the toes.

Pickles himself was dressed in his version of Christmas attire—a court jester hat in red felt, tipped with white furry balls, and a red velveteen jumpsuit with frog-green river waders that reached to the crotch. He walked stiff-legged through the aisles as he and Moby gathered up the stove parts. John stood by the cash register, transfixed by the pickles, minus the ends, floating in the jar.

They put the stove parts on the floor scale near the counter. Pickles calculated the cost by the pound from a greasy, tattered sheet he kept next to the cash register. Before the transaction could be completed, the doorbell jingled. A boy dressed in black-and-white soccer togs strode confidently to the center of the room. He pulled a pair of red shoes from a brown paper bag and plunked them on the counter.

Pickles almost salivated as he examined the offering. Raging lipstick red leather Capezios—open-toed, six-inch stiletto heels, with a single slender strap to encircle the ankle. Simple, but oh so elegant. The hourglass shape of the undulating sole was beyond erotic. These shoes, with their unscuffed soles and an unstained leather innersole, were clearly virginal, or nearly so.

Pickles pulled the boy aside and the two engaged in an animated conversation until, obviously exasperated, Pickles opened the cash drawer and pulled out some loose bills from under the tray. The boy left, and Pickles retreated with the shoes to behind a pile of rubber rafts. He returned with an engaging smile that revealed a tinge of red on the cutting edge of his front incisors.

"All right, let's see what we have here," he said quickly.

With a raised brow, John tilted his chin to indicate to Moby what they had both witnessed. They paid Pickles. He loaded the parts into a wagon, pulled the merchandise to the street, and helped Moby put everything in the bed of the truck.

Hurriedly, he said to Moby, "Stop by anytime."

Then, he scurried sideways like a sand crab back to his shop, flipped the plastic sign that hung from a string in the middle of the window from "Open" to "Closed," and raked down the shade. Before they pulled away from the curb, John looked out the window to see the lights in the store go dark. Seconds later, a light shone from a small curtained window in the second story.

The two men vowed to deal in the obviously preferred Pickles commodity of women's shoes the next time they hit town. They headed straight for the dock, loaded the launch, and headed home in the failing light.

Halfway to the island, they came upon a flotilla of four rubber rafts, strung together like a spider web with strands of gray tape. Each of the rafts was stacked high. Piles of black garbage sacks, suitcases, coiled-up rugs, and the legs of chairs punctuated the night darkness. A woman dressed in a yellow rain slicker hunkered over the front of the lead raft, paddling furiously with a metal leaf rake.

The men pulled alongside. The woman looked up gratefully.

"Thank God, you've come. Can you men help me to get to Seven Sisters Island? The barometer is falling, and the winds are picking up from the west at ten to fifteen miles an hour, with gusts reaching thirty."

"We are going to Seven Sisters ourselves. We will be glad to take you with us. If you get in our boat, we can tow your rafts."

"Bless you. Do you need the report on the mountain passes? Or the road conditions on Interstate 405 or 90?"

"No, I think we'll try to get by on what you've already given us," John replied kindly.

He reached down and helped the small but surprisingly spry, white-haired woman into the boat while Moby tied a line to her raft and continued on their trip.

The woman explained that her name was Merriweather Snowbird, the former weather and traffic reporter for KRAK 101.4 FM. She had left the Angels of Mercy Rest Home because she didn't like clam chowder every Friday, because they never had any oyster crackers, and because she didn't believe there were any angels working there, except for Matt, the custodian, who always brought her a Milky Way with dark chocolate on Sundays.

"The place is full of crazy old people," she said.

John moved toward the back of the boat where Moby was holding on to the tiller.

"I think we've got a runaway tiger by the tail," he said. "She's a feisty one."

Moby smiled. "Balls the size of a weather balloon, I'd say."

Going slow, so as not to swamp the rafts, the boat and its trailing cargo finally rounded the rocks and eased toward the spit.

Moby took the soggy refugee into the kitchen, where she sat on a stool in front of the stove. Her teeth chattered, and she shook uncontrollably, clearly on the verge of hypothermia. Annie removed a plastic nametag pinned askew to her sweatshirt, where an orderly had misprinted her name as "Merywither S."

Rapidly, Annie undressed the woman down to her mismatched underwear. She surmised the bra—an underwire frame in mauve, two sizes too small—and the panties—several sizes too big—were the result of an impersonal communal underwear box sitting in a too-narrow hallway. Annie could picture that hallway, crowded with wheelchairs backed against the wall, filled with hopeless men and women who had no more to give, smelling of urine and rancid hair. The lives of the people in those wheelchairs revolved around staring at the floor and waiting, always waiting. Annie had seen it too many times.

She could not rescue them all, but she could certainly salvage those with the courage and strength to escape to freedom. She calmed the woman, drying her with a towel, and swaddling her with two layers of robes. She removed three oven-warmed bricks, wrapped them in dishtowels, and slipped them under the robes. A half-hour later, Annie sat with a cup of tea and listened to staccato snores that vibrated the dishwater on the stove.

Annie slept late. When she awoke she did not hurry to rise, but lay in bed listening to the rain.

The Eskimos may have a hundred words to describe snow, but their vocabulary pales when compared to locals describing precipitation in the Pacific Northwest. Today, it was not a drizzle, not intermittent or sporadic showers, not a squall or even a sprinkle, of which there are at least twenty kinds.

This morning the weather was definitely a light mist.

Annie looked out the window to see Merriweather standing in a yellow rain slicker under a cedar tree near the trail to the boat shed. The smoke from the Carolinas signaled they were up and moving. John and John Paul were loading the empty tequila bottles into the launch, and the rest of their supplies followed.

Annie slipped on her rubber boots, opened an umbrella, and went down to the beach to send them off. Betsy took one last look around and said, "I could stay here forever."

"You're welcome any time," said Annie, as she helped launch the skiff.

Merriweather came up to the group and looked at Annie.

"Is the bus always this late?"

Annie was taken by surprise, but recovered.

"I'm sorry, sometimes it is."

Taking the woman by the arm, she led her up the path and fed her lunch. Merriweather insisted on borrowing Annie's rake.

"If my bus doesn't come, I need to rake my leaves. I'll be collecting feathers in the afternoon," she informed Annie. "Busy, busy, busy!"

Moby unloaded Merriweather's rafts. He found what seemed to him to be expensive Chinese hand-woven rugs, along with unusual leopard-covered suitcases full of clothes. One raft had a load of split pea soup, an electric lawnmower, furniture, pictures, four cases of gray tape, and two cases of WD-40. Most puzzling were the eight garbage bags chock-full of silk leaves.

Moby had just finished his inventory and was making his way back to his cabin when, by chance, he spotted a tiny bright-red raft bobbing between the swells a good quarter mile from the spit. He grabbed the binoculars he kept hung on a nail just outside his door and focused them seaward. He could just make out the back of what looked like a penguin rowing with two tiny plastic oars. The boat was taking on incredible amounts of water as the waves broke over the side of the flimsy craft. Moby couldn't believe that the raft remained afloat.

He watched in despair, for he knew there was no way to rescue the rower. By the time he got *The Ark* out and rounded the island, the man would have been out of his sight for at least fifteen minutes. Helplessly, Moby watched the drama unfold, then gathered a backpack of blankets and a half bottle of wine left over from the night before. He stood at the edge of the beach following the boat's progress, nursing the wine, wondering whether he would be saving someone from drowning or officiating at a wake.

# Chapter SEVEN

The raft spun sideways, then almost capsized under the assault of an especially large wave. Defiantly, it bobbed upright, challenging the storm. Moby could see now its passenger was a man, his long white beard plastered to a black rain slicker. Something black poked out from the beard near the end of his nose.

A hundred yards from shore, the man made eye contact with Moby as the current helplessly spun him like a leaf in a whirlpool. He didn't have a look of desperation, but of "business as usual" as he leaned into the oars.

Moby sensed someone by his side. He looked down to see Merriweather standing with her rake cradled in one hand and a roll of gray tape in the other. Mantra-like, she mumbled, "Twenty to thirty-five miles an hour, small craft warnings. The inland waters are going to be treacherous out there today."

She handed Moby the rake with the tape spooled around the handle, wrapped the loose end around her waist three times, and waded out into the surf, searching the horizon for the raft. Fifty yards from shore, the waves began breaking over the hidden sand bar. The raft careened in one direction, the man the other. He could be seen thrashing, tumbling in the waist-high surf, unable to find purchase. Then he disappeared.

Merriweather fought through the breakers toward the last place she saw the man, the gray tape spinning out behind her, like a spider spinning her silk. She plunged into the water, grabbed the man by the hair, held his head up with one hand, and looked expectantly at Moby. He caught the signal and reeled the two of them in with the help of the surf. He waited for the tape to break, knowing when it did he would have to watch helplessly as the two of them were washed away.

But the tape held. Merriweather pushed the man toward shore, and they were soon in the shallows, where they both crawled on their knees and collapsed on the sandy beach. From a pocket of her raincoat, Merriweather pulled out a personal-size can of WD-40 and sprayed both of the man's ears and his eyes, then gave him a shot up the nose. She removed a mutilated cigar from his mouth, gave him another shot in his mouth, and when he started to protest, crammed the cigar back in.

With Moby's help, she dragged the man up the pebbled beach to John's still-smoldering fire and wrapped him in the blankets. The long, white beard, matted with seaweed and sand, and the ashen lips indicated that the man had been in the forty-degree water too long.

"He's hypothermic," pronounced Moby. He tried to pour the wine into the man's clenched lips, but it drained down his chin.

"Get him inside," Merriweather commanded.

Together, Merriweather and Moby dragged the man to an empty cabin and laid him on the bed.

"Now, help me get his clothes off,"

As she and Moby wrestled with the soggy clothes, the man turned a bluish tint and began to shake uncontrollably.

"We're going to lose him! Quickly, cut off his beard," Merriweather screamed at Moby.

She shucked her clothes and stood naked, waiting while Moby hacked through the thick beard with his pocketknife, throwing it to the floor, where it landed, a soggy albino rodent. As she crawled on the half-frozen carcass, Moby wondered how Merriweather's wafer-thin body would be able to offer any warmth to the bone-chilled mariner, who stared unblinking at the ceiling.

"Wrap the blankets around us and start a fire," she ordered.

Moby could see Merriweather's body recoil from the cold, clammy, would-be corpse, but he did as he was told. For a long time, the blanket heaved, while Merriweather clawed to stay aboard, sacrificing her body to appeal to the man's basic instinct to survive. It wasn't long before Merriweather began to shake too, their teeth chattering like twin Spanish castanets—a desperate dance of death played out in the darkness of the old shack.

Hours crept by until finally the man settled into a shallow, troubled sleep. Only then did Merriweather release her grip. She stood and wrapped a blanket around herself, then sat in a wooden chair by the roaring fire. Moby handed her a large mug of hot, black, three-day-old coffee. She greedily sucked it down.

"You saved that guy's life. Where in the world did you learn to do that?" Moby asked, as she handed him the mug and he poured another cup of sludge.

"My adopted family's people were from Nova Scotia," she answered between gulps. "My grandfather told me that was how his ancestors saved fishermen from hypothermia. If they found survivors on the beach, they would wrap two or three of the village girls around the fisherman, and if there was any chance, the men could be stirred back to the living. Legend says it was best to use virgins, but you gotta work with what you've got. My mother said sometimes that was the only way to meet someone from another village."

Merriweather shook the last dampness from her hair before the fire. Moby crumpled up an old newspaper and stuffed it into the man's soggy shoes to wick the heat into the inside. He set the shoes on the oven door to dry.

"Say, why didn't that tape break?"

"Special stuff. I don't buy it at the corner hardware store. I send away to Texas. Industrial strength, NASA stuff."

Moby marveled at the clear-eyed certainty at which this odd woman had handled a crisis. But by the time Moby returned from the boat shed with a suitcase of clothes for Merriweather, she had reverted to form.

"Are you still cold?" he asked, as Merriweather stood behind the stove, slipping into the clean clothes.

"There will be light rain tonight, turning to showers. Expect a drying trend into the first week of December, with chilly temperatures ranging into the low thirties at night, and the mid- to upperforties during the day. Chance of rain, 30 percent Sunday, 60 percent Monday, and 10 percent through Thursday. The roads will be filled with holiday shoppers on this busiest shopping weekend of the year, so be careful out there."

Moby suspected Alzheimer's. He had met people who could seemingly perform normally when necessary, or at least pretend to, and then slip back into a hazy fog. He smelled the odor of WD-40 once again, as Merriweather sprayed a cloud into the air and walked beneath the falling mist.

"Universal elixir of motion," she said. "Don't you just love it?"

Moby and Tripod stumped toward home.

"Tripod," Moby addressed his old friend, "this island is becoming a haven for some real oddballs." Tripod sneezed in apparent disgust, although Moby knew it probably had more to do with having lubricant sprayed up his nose.

Unaware of the drama, Annie saw smoke coming from the chimney at the cabin John and Betsy had used. That didn't make sense. Had they come back?

Annie wandered over to the cabin, knocked, and receiving no answer, pushed open the door. Stifling hot air race-horsed out the door. Wary, Annie left it open as she investigated the snoring lump in the corner.

It wasn't John.

The man lay face-up in bed. He had a red, bulbous nose, bushy white eyebrows, a thick soggy cigar still clenched tightly in his teeth, and a scraggy half-beard with seaweed strands clinging to it. He looked every bit the alcoholic elf, fallen from Santa's sleigh. Annie took his pulse, found it strong, and went through the wet clothes strewn on the floor. Written on the collar of a tee shirt in black pen was the name "A. Murphy 243."

Annie reached down and tried to extract the cigar, but the man's teeth held it in a death grip. Her fingers slipped off the gooey stump.

"Yuk," she said, wiping the cigar slime on the bed sheet. She put the wet clothes into a rain barrel outside the door to dilute the salt, built the fire back up, and closed the door. There was nothing more to do for the mystery man till he woke up.

The island now had two residents who had washed ashore and about whom Annie hadn't a clue. She assumed there was a Carol Ann connection somewhere.

She gathered up Merriweather from one of the shacks, and together they headed to the boat shed, where they began to sort through the weatherwoman's belongings. Annie recognized the leopard suitcases as a special edition of Louis Vuitton. She figured they must have cost eight to ten thousand just for the cases she could see.

Merriweather rummaged through the bags, then gave a little snort of triumph.

"This is all I need," she said, holding up a garbage bag in each hand. One was filled with bird feathers; the other with gray tape and lubricant. "Now, I've got to get back to my house."

When Annie left Merriweather back at her cabin, she was weaving a web-like hammock out of the gray tape. On her way home, Annie paid another visit to the mystery Murphy. As she opened the door, the man sprang upright in the bed and peered owlishly at her.

"Mercy me!" Annie gasped, startled. "How are you feeling? Better?"

"Who? I always buy Fords. Never had a Mercury. Horrible suspension, and the engines are pure crap," Murphy said, spitting out a piece of errant seaweed.

Annie came closer.

"No, where did you come from? How did you get here?" She spoke slowly, loudly, clearly.

"Who? Yes, I'm quite comfortable, thanks. And you're right, I don't hear too well."

Annie took a pencil and notepad from her apron pocket, kept there for when she wanted to jot down a thought.

"Who are you? Where did you come from?" she wrote.

Murphy took the page she offered, turned it upside down, and frowned.

"What is this? Can't see without my glasses. Lost them out in the water."

Annie took her glasses out of another apron pocket and handed them to the man, who put them on. He tilted his head sideways and frowned.

"These glasses don't work too well, and I'm sleepy," he said, handing them back. With that he slid under the covers and slipped into a doze.

Annie shook her head and headed back to the house. Passing by Moby, who a sat by a fire on the beach, she stopped and warmed her hands.

"Who's the new guy? Any idea?"

As Moby launched into the exciting story of Merriweather's rescue, a ski boat roared around the point and nosed into the gravel beach. Annie could see three heads bobbing in the boat, one of which was a middle-aged woman. She lowered herself into the knee-high water and waded ashore, careful to keep her large purse from getting wet.

"Are you Annie?" the woman asked, her face wrinkled with worry. "Is this Seven Sisters Island?"

Annie nodded.

"Thank God! Is my father here?"

Annie and Moby exchanged glances.

"Would that be someone by the name of 'A. Murphy'?" Annie asked.

"Yes! That's him!" The woman turned to the boat and motioned the two other people, children by the look of them, to come ashore. She turned back to Annie and Moby.

"You don't know how worried I've been. He just disappeared yesterday from the convalescent center in Seattle."

"Is he ill?" asked Annie.

"Not physically, but…well, sometimes he's not quite all there. He starts every conversation with 'Who.' I don't know why. They call him 'Owl' at the center."

Once the two young children made it to the beach, each wearing a backpack, Annie led the little procession to the cabin, with Moby bringing up the rear.

The woman moved to the bed, where she grabbed the man's hand with affection.

"Dad," she softly admonished, "you scared the crap out of us. Why did you leave without telling anyone?"

The man turned toward her but seemed at a loss.

"Who is it?" he asked crossly.

The woman took two hearing aids out of her pocket, stuffed them into the man's ears, then produced a pair of glasses, which she slipped on his nose. Immediately Murphy brightened.

"Hi, kids," he said, smiling at his grandchildren.

They smiled back. At least he had those two in his corner.

"Dad, you cannot just disappear like that without telling us. They're broadcasting an alert on television, telling everyone to look for you."

The woman's voice verged on the ragged edge of exasperation.

"Well, call off the dogs," Murphy scowled. "You found me, didn't you? Turkey loaf. That's what they fed us, turkey loaf. Do you know what's in that? Turkey asses, beaks, toenails—anything that falls on the floor at the packinghouse. And cranberries that look like Jell-O. I can't eat that crap, and I told them I was leaving."

The woman sighed.

"Dad, I told you we had to go to Jeff's parents for Thanksgiving, and you know you don't get along with them. We talked about it, remember? Are you trying to drive me crazy?"

The man folded his arms.

"I won't eat turkey loaf for Thanksgiving. You were never fed turkey loaf when you were a little girl. If your mother were alive, I wouldn't be in that home. You're just too busy for your old man, working at your fancy law firm."

The woman pursed her lips and looked at the ground.

"All right, Dad. We'll find you another place. Let's just go home."

"I've lived a good life," he began. "I'm an old dinosaur. I've logged the forests from Mt. Rainier to the Olympic Mountains, fished the waters from Portland to Kodiak. I've swum up the river like an old spawned-out salmon, and now I just want to lie on the bank and die."

"Dad, you're not even sick. I just can't take care of you at home. You're too cantankerous." The woman knelt down in front of the fire. "I don't understand why you keep going to those hospice meetings. There's nothing wrong with you. I—"

"There is too something wrong. They just can't find it. Besides, I don't want to be warehoused in a room the size of a dog kennel. I need to be free. I've lived my whole life outdoors. I hate the smell of diesel fumes, the sound of honking cars—and those old biddies are always bugging me to play canasta. I'd tell you more if my grandkids weren't here. Just give me a whiff of some good old-fashioned sewage, and I'll be a happy camper," he said, leaning out of the bed and unsuccessfully trying to light the waterlogged cigar in the fire.

The woman pulled the backpacks off her children and set them on the floor.

"I brought you some clothes, Dad. Please get dressed and then come outside and we'll talk."

She ushered her children out of the cabin, with Annie and Moby following. Behind them they heard the slide of a bolt followed by three loud clicks.

"Sure glad I installed those three doorknobs," remarked Moby.

The woman reached in her purse and pulled out a piece of paper.

"This is a note from Carol Ann. She runs the hospice."

"I know Carol Ann. Is that how you got the idea to look for you father out here?"

The woman nodded.

"She thinks there might be another runaway here."

"There is," Annie confirmed. "There must be an epidemic of turkey loaf in Seattle."

The woman gave Annie a withering look, one she no doubt employed often in the courtroom.

"Why don't you leave your dad here for a while?" Annie said. "He almost killed himself getting here. I'd hate to think it was all for nothing."

Annie turned to the note from Carol Ann.

*Dear Annie,*

*I fear there is an exodus descending on your tiny island. I mentioned the island in passing at a meeting, and I think some of them see it as a last-ditch effort to connect with their childhood or nature or whatever. You wouldn't believe the excitement it has caused. Be on the lookout for Merriweather Snowbird. She went missing yesterday morning. She has mild dementia and an inoperable aneurysm in her brain that could go at any time. She likes to wait for an imaginary bus that takes her to work and loves to rake leaves. Her collection of silk leaves is missing, as well as most everything in her mini-warehouse storage. She taped her door shut and escaped on a ladder made of tape down three stories. Remarkable really. She is a celebrity here in Seattle from when she was the weather lady on Channel 5 TV and on the radio. She has no relatives and no real means of support. If you see her, please contact me.*

*Carol Ann*

Annie smiled, folded the letter, and put it in her pocket. She admired these people. She bet there was more to their stories than anyone knew. She turned to the woman.

"You can tell Carol Ann that Merriweather is here with us, and we'll take care of her for now, as well as your father. He'll be safe here. Don't worry."

The woman scrutinized Annie's face. She must have liked what she saw for her manner softened.

"I'm sorry for not introducing myself. I'm Al's daughter, Julia. Julia Latham." She extended her hand to Annie and then Moby. "We placed my father in a very exclusive rest home on Lake Washington, near Madison Park. It's really lovely there. I don't know why he won't just stay put."

She reached into her purse, rummaged for a moment, then extracted a checkbook. After hastily scrawling her signature on the bottom of a check, she tore it out and handed it to Annie.

"Here's a blank check for food or whatever he needs. I run a successful law firm in Bellevue, so money is no problem. I have plenty of that; I just don't have much time right now." She shook her head ruefully, then cast a forlorn look around the rugged simplicity of Seven Sisters Island. "I don't mean to be rude, but I can't understand why he would leave the creature comforts of the home where we had him. I mean, that place was really beautiful."

"We have beauty here, too," said Annie, "but a different kind. The seashore, the birds, the solitude, the sunsets."

"What about the lack of amenities? You know—electricity, phones, shopping…not to mention emergency care?"

Moby answered this time.

"I can't speak for your dad, but I'm here to contemplate these last moments of my life. Not to live in a climate-controlled room, like a museum piece. Not to be entertained by someone else's life or Hollywood fantasies, but to feel the cold on my face from the morning wind and the heat from the belly of a stove fueled by wood gathered on the beach at dawn. To listen to the sounds of nature: the waves washing over the rocks in a storm, the rain beating on the wood shingles on the roof at night. To cook my own food and share the sound of a loon calling for his mate. And for one last time, to revel in my humanity, my time unfettered by the interruption of phones and salesmen. Connecting to a nature that is too often denied in search of comfort. To know in my heart what is pure and simple and timeless. And when my time on this earth is coming to an end, my friends will turn my face to the sky, and I will look into the clouds, and see the face of God, and die with dignity."

Moby did not think God had a face, and he had long ago given up on an afterlife, but what he'd said suddenly sounded so damn eloquent.

Julia stared at Moby, stunned, and then she recovered.

"Dad has always lived on the edge," she said after several moments. "When he was a boy, he worked for a logging company. He climbed trees three hundred feet high to run the cables that pulled the logs to the landing.

"He's a self-made man, very proud and independent. You've noticed he refuses to wear his hearing aids. My mother was the only person he ever listened to, and she died three years ago."

They heard three clicks and the sound of the bolt sliding back. The door creaked open, and Murphy emerged, smelling of tobacco and peppermint schnapps. Gray wool pants were stuffed into the tops of black logging boots, and a white tee shirt and thick red suspenders could be seen under an unbuttoned wool red-and-black-checked Filson jacket. He grinned around a new cigar.

"You forgot to tell her I managed the sewer system in Bremerton for thirty years, have a photographic memory, and that the old noodle is A-OK."

The children ran to their grandfather as if he were the Pied Piper. He bent low, scooped them into his arms, and kissed them both on their cheeks.

"I wouldn't trade you two for all the *mea culpas* and *pro bonos* in the world, and I don't ever want either of you to wear a suit. Do you hear me?"

He turned to his daughter. "Matter of fact, I'd like to have these little squirts come here and live with me full time. Whatcha think about that counselor?"

"Guess what, Dad? Grandparents have no standing in custody cases. That was affirmed in *Troxel v. Granville* that started here in Washington and went straight to the U. S. Supreme Court. Sandra Day O'Connor herself wrote the opinion," Julia said testily.

"Hah, you can bet your law firm of Dewey, Cheatem, and Howe would never keep me from my grandchildren, and I'll bet that bitch O'Connor would break down the door herself if she was kept away from her grandkids."

Al, Annie, and Moby all turned to the woman in defiance of authority.

Flustered, Julia realized she had slipped into legalese. What was she doing quoting legal precedent to the man who taught her to throw a baseball and showed her how to catch fireflies? She knew he was above the law and always would be.

Resigned, she turned to him with a kinder tone.

"Dad, could you be happy here?"

"There are trees and water and the sound of gulls on this island. I think I'll stay. It's a man's kind of place."

"That's funny, Dad, because it's called 'Seven *Sisters*,'" Julia said, but he had already begun pointing out a hermit crab to the youngsters.

"This place reminds me of a little island outside of Sitka, Alaska," said Al, picking up the crab and handing it to one of the children to hold. "We were logging spruce and yellow cedar growing on cliffs. Dangerous as hell. Your mother was only four at the time, but she loved it there."

He stood and took each child by the hand, then sauntered down the beach.

"You know, your mother had a pet raccoon and a tame wolf that followed her everywhere. That's the God's honest truth. If your grandmother were here, she'd back me up on this. One day, we thought your mom was lost, but…"

The wind stole the rest of his words as the old man and the two youngsters moved away.

Julia's gaze followed them.

"It's all true," she said, shaking her head. "I had a wonderful childhood." She turned to Annie. "Please take good care of him."

She walked down the spit, smiled at Moby who was keeping the boat from beaching itself on the outgoing tide, and collected the children from her father. Then, without warning, the senior law partner turned toward her father and gave him a bear hug. She let out a fierce growl, like she had done when she was a little girl. She was still her father's daughter. Al grinned in return.

"I'll be in touch, Dad. We'll bring some of your things. Stay away from that raft!"

She and the kids climbed over the boat transom and, with a rev of the engine, the speedboat lived up to its name, quickly disappearing over the horizon, hell-bent for Seattle.

Al turned to Annie.

"Where the hell are these seven cisterns everyone keeps talking about?"

During the next week, the winter winds and rain pelted the island inhabitants in a steady rhythm, drumming on the roofs, washboarding branches against windows. The foghorns blared their warning, piping aboard the winter doldrums.

Life settled into somewhat of a pattern on the island. Moby, with a new respect for Merriweather, took it upon himself to dump the silk leaves under the apple trees in the morning for her to gather. In the afternoons, Annie helped her sort through her yardage. It turned out that Merriweather was an excellent seamstress, even with just the island's ancient treadle machine to work with. Moby came in for a fitting for a yellow leisure suit, swearing he would wear it over the holidays.

The Carolinas continued feuding, stopping long enough to give piano lessons to Al, who said he preferred to be called "Owl," which seemed to sit just fine with everyone.

Moby finished the last cabin and started looking for new projects. He pined for an overstuffed sofa to put on the beach, on which he could sit and watch the tide go in and out. In the time-honored tradition of island salvage, the front seat of a vintage Cadillac beached itself fortuitously in front of his cabin one day, after floating on the high seas for God knows how long. Moby winched it into position in front of his fire and installed it under the porch overhang. He and Owl proclaimed it "sensually squishy" and never tired of singing the praises of its soft, Corinthian leather, whatever that was. There was no disputing it was large and ugly but delightfully serviceable.

Annie phoned Sarah mid-week on a trip to the store. Sarah sounded tired but upbeat. Everything on the baby watch was progressing smoothly.

"Did you know Mom took some time off and spent the week with us? She went to the hospital with us everyday, and we worked on the nursery together."

Annie smiled to hear that her daughter was making a real effort to bond with the twins.

"That's wonderful, dear. Keep me posted on any news, and we'll see you at Christmas if not before."

As Christmas approached, the shortened days tightened island camaraderie. The Carolinas organized a series of progressive potlucks, hopping from one hovel to the next. Moby and Owl were poor contributors, but the women allowed that what comes around goes around. That sounded okay to the "canned-good boys," who were the first to arrive and the last to leave the table.

Annie looked out one day to see John's boat arriving with the flags at half-mast. She went down to the beach and watched as John wrestled to put what appeared to be a huge stuffed sailfish from his boat into the dinghy.

As the small boat slid into the gravel, all he said was "She's gone."

"Oh, John," said Annie, and it seemed to be enough.

His shoulders slumped.

"She went quickly." Then lifting the huge stuffed fish, he said, "She asked that her ashes be brought to the island. I thought this sailfish would be a fitting resting place. We caught it on our honeymoon in Mazatlan thirty-six years ago.

"My first job in Boston, our first child, our second, and the third, the move to Seattle, the books, the spaghetti sauce—everything that mattered, she was a part of. No, she was the most important part of everything. And now . . ."

John blinked back the tears. The wordsmith did not know what to say.

That night, Owl, Moby, and John had their own private wake for Betsy following a long-standing male tradition: talking about their women—mothers, sisters, girlfriends, daughters, wives, and lovers—over countless bottles of wine and two bottles of peach schnapps. Their reminiscing was punctuated with long periods of brooding silence, till they could stand up only long enough to sing their lungs out in off-color, off-key songs with hamburgered lyrics.

When John took up residence in the same ten-foot-square cabin he and Betsy had shared at Thanksgiving, a slight renovation was needed to hang the twelve-foot-long sailfish. Moby cheerfully cut a hole through the cedar shingles on one side, allowing the fish's pointy sword to hang out in the weather. (After Owl nearly skewered himself walking between the cabins, Moby stuffed a buoy on the sword for safety.)

Owl skillfully cut a hole in the side of the fish, Moby hinged a small cabinet door for access, and John gently placed the urn inside.

After the remodel, John seemed to lose steam, spending days at a time hunkered in the dark cabin, sometimes not even bothering to build a fire. The islanders took turns staying with him, sometimes getting him to talk, sometimes just sitting quietly with him, staring into the fire.

To John's mind, it was Betsy alone, by sheer force of her smile, who had willed the universe into existence for the last thirty-six years. As far as he was concerned, she made sure the sun rose in the morning, the moon came out at night. All things bright and beautiful and everything in-between had relied on her.

He knew that, for a while, he had been the luckiest man on earth.

He also knew that Betsy would be disappointed in him if he gave up on life. It was a time to mourn.

It was during this period that Moby and Owl decided to build their mutual coffins in the flat-roofed shop behind Moby's cabin. They selected the wood from Pickles' and talked for hours, standing in curls of aromatic Alaskan cedar that spiraled out of their planes as they smoothed the coffins to a soft sheen. The two men understood each other perfectly. It seemed that Owl suffered from same disease that affects old dogs and husbands the world over: selective hearing—a survival tool and a defense mechanism that allows them to acknowledge only those sounds that are important to the male world.

Lying inside the coffin and staring at the ceiling as the rain reverberated off the rusted iron sheets of corrugated roofing, Owl yelled out to Moby, "I have always believed in reincarnation. I don't believe the life force can just disappear. The soul lives on forever." He ran his hand along the inside of the newly built box. "You know, I think I need some handhold here on the sides, in case I want to sit up quickly, in case I'm not really dead. Hey, Moby, look in here a minute, will you?"

Moby peered over the side.

"Handholds about here? What do you think?" asked Owl, putting his hand halfway up the side.

Moby considered the option out loud. "Handholds would be helpful inside and out. You can't be too careful," he said, pointing out where he thought they could attach them effectively.

"No, I mean about reincarnation. What do you think?" Owl asked, bobbing up and down from supine to sitting.

"Oh, well, I think when you're dead, you're gone. Kaput. The only thing left is what you set in motion before you die," Moby answered matter-of-factly. He usually tried to stay away from religious discussions, but today he let fly his pet theories. "Christians are arrogant souls. Everyone else on the planet believes in a long-suffering commitment to attain paradise, but Christians, they want it in one generation. I'm a bad ass for sixty years, and then for the last sixty seconds, I suddenly believe in Christ, and voila! I'm set for eternal life. It is just a little too self-serving for my taste. The rest of the world is out there, slugging it out for thousands of years, with no guarantees. Look at the Hindus and the Buddhists. They are in it for the long haul."

Owl shrugged his shoulders.

"Different strokes for different folks. Say, what do you think about a shelf for a flashlight? And the handholds—leather or iron?"

"What in the hell do you need a flashlight for?" asked Moby. "I thought you wanted to be buried at sea."

"I do, but I thought maybe if I somehow came back to life, I could find my way out of the casket. That's why, if I go first, I want you to throw in my tool-belt and make sure the chisels are in it. I was also thinking I would line it with some nice flannel, a pillow, and a life preserver—just in case, and maybe one of those air horns would be useful.

"You know, I was thinking we should test-drive this baby. Take it out in the bay and float it around a little, get the bugs out. That wouldn't be too weird, would it?" Al lay back in the casket, with his hands folded in on his stomach, and closed his eyes. "I just don't think I'm a satin kind of guy, you know?" he continued, as he folded his hands over his chest, practicing looking angelic.

Moby took his cigar out of his mouth.

"Hell no, that wouldn't be weird at all. Practice makes perfect. The bay is just full of guys out sailing their caskets. We could even start a Yacht Club, maybe have races on Wednesday nights. We'll call them "The Not-Dead-Yet Regattas.'"

"Now you're talkin'," agreed Al.

Moby laughed, then turned serious.

"You know, I was thinking it would be nice to have a church here on the island. Annie told me that the building with the caved-in roof at the end of the orchard used to be a schoolhouse. I think that would be an easy remodel for a couple of coots like us. Build a proper steeple with a bell and put a new roof on it."

Owl's eyes popped open, quickly jolted back from the dead.

"Yeah, that would be a great project. I'll bet we could all contribute time and money. I'm sure there's cedar on the island for roof shakes, and there are plenty of granite beach rocks to make a steeple. I love working with rocks." He climbed out of his casket excitedly.

Leaning on the workbench, Moby doodled a rough elevation on a piece of paper, showing the bell tower and arched windows down each side.

"If the place needs more light, we just put in a few dormers with windows in the roof."

Moby continued drawing, arrows showing the path of light and a cupola on top with a crude angel wind-vane. "Something in copper, I'm thinking."

"This is good shit," said Owl, giving the project his highest sewer commendation. He held the sketch at arm's length, in the direction where the building stood. "Let's drum up support."

The two men strapped on their raingear and trudged to the Carolinas' cabin, where the scent of fresh baked pies activated their salivary glands even before Merriweather, leaf rake in hand, opened the door. The pies stood perfectly browned on the stovetop as North basted a mixture of egg whites and sugar on the top.

"Gravenstein pies, boys," South said, sitting at the small, wooden gate-legged table, surrounded by fluffy white curtains, clean floors, and freshly made beds—the antithesis of the world Moby and Owl inhabited.

Moby was reminded that while he had spent most of his life building houses, it was the women who made them homes. He and Owl would return later to their scruffy headquarters with dirty dishes and cobwebbed ceilings, but for now, they had a vision to share. They spread Moby's elevations of the church on the table. The sisters and Merriweather hunched over the plans and stared at them for a long time.

"So, what is it?" demanded North.

"A church, here on the island, a remodel of the old schoolhouse," Owl explained.

A light must have turned on in the two Carolina heads simultaneously, for they became instantly animated.

"It looks like the church from back home," South said. "Ours had a stone steeple, a graveyard where all our relatives were buried, and the cutest white picket fence where they tied up the horses. Then one day—"

"—a hurricane came while we were visiting on the mainland," continued North, "and washed the church away, along with the entire town. It was built like a brick shithouse—"

"Excuse your French," interjected South. "All that was found was the steeple roof, floating out in the ocean. When they pulled it out of the water, the rope was still attached to the bell, which acted like an anchor. We could get that bell from the relatives and hang it in our church here."

The phrase "our church" did not escape Moby's attention, and he knew the Carolinas were on board.

"Let's pick up John and go talk to Annie," said South, wiping her hands on her apron then exchanging it for her coat. She took the leaf rake from Merriweather and put it behind the door. "Come on, dear," she said, as she pushed them all out the door.

"But...the pies," said Moby, throwing a wistful glance back at the stove. "What about the pies?"

"Later," South said. "We're doing the Lord's work first. Pies second."

Moby and Owl hesitated, unwilling to leave such perfection behind.

"All right, bring them along," North said. "We'll pick up the recluse on the way."

Moby the pirate led them down the path, trailed by North, South, Merriweather, and Owl in the rear, protecting the pies under dishtowels.

Courtesy of the ambiguities of the north wind, John had smelled the apple pies all morning. He let in the troupe at their first knock, and they explained their mission.

Looking over the plans spread on the table, he exclaimed, "Bravissimo! It would be a monument to Betsy. Do you suppose there would be a place for a sailfish on the wall?" he asked, absent-mindedly reaching across the table to break a piece of crust from one of the pies. He was summarily whacked on the knuckles with North's umbrella.

"There will be none of that," she said.

John grinned sheepishly and quickly pulled the tingling hand out of harm's way.

"Betsy would have loved it," he said, then slapped the table with gusto. "Let's do it. Money, time, whatever you need, I'm in."

He grabbed his recently resurrected college letterman's jacket and held open the door.

On the porch to the main house, the group could make out the sounds of two distinct snoring patterns. Moby peeked in the window. He saw Annie, sitting bundled in her quilt, feet sticking in the oven door, and Buddy playing dead dog under it.

They had almost decided to come back later when Buddy opened an eye then got to his feet. Seeing Moby's face, he began to beat his tail against Annie's leg, waking her. She looked down at him dazedly for a second, then realized that there was company on the porch. Struggling stiffly to her feet, she stifled a deep yawn, and opened the door. The motley group paraded in, looking like characters out of *The Wizard of Oz.*

The warm pies were set on the stove while Moby rolled out the sketches and explained approximate time lines and which materials could be gleaned from the island. Annie looked over the print approvingly but voiced a concern.

"It seems like such an ambitious project. Wouldn't it be better to wait till spring to start?"

"Who knows what will happen by spring, Annie," Moby said, as he sat down in the chair.

He adjusted his patch and looked across the table with his one good blue eye. Annie looked at Moby and thought how he had single-handedly brought the island back to life. Somewhere, drifting lazily in the back of her mind, a golden saffron-robed priest selected a sturdy branch the size of his leg and deliberately carried it across the smooth stone pavers of the monastery floor. Taking a mighty swing as he twisted on his heels, the monk struck the five-hundred-pound brass gong hanging on a massive oak frame embellished with carvings of fiercely writhing dragons and tigers. The rounded sound echoed down through the forested valleys and out into the ocean, sending chills of enlightenment through Annie's body.

The island was no longer in descent. Her mother and her aunts had presided over a long decline, and now a dead man walking was returning the island to the glory days.

Yes, she nodded, yes, the island is coming back.

"Yes," she said quietly, and then more loudly, "Yes. Now is the perfect time to get started."

Moby slammed his fist on the table, knocking over the salt shaker. Merriweather quickly grabbed a pinch and threw it over her shoulder.

"All right. That's settled. Now where's that pie?"

# Chapter EIGHT

The Carolinas served pie and coffee while the group jabbered about their separate contributions to building the church. South promised to contact the relative in Nag's Head who had the bell and arrange to have it shipped out; John planned to help split the cedar shakes for the roof; Owl had done some masonry work and, with help, thought he could handle a three-story steeple. It all came back to Moby to organize the army and make the renovation a success.

Owl tapped his spoon against a coffee cup, and all conversation stopped.

"I wish to make a presentation."

He stood and pulled a wooden plaque from a brown paper sack by his feet.

"This is to recognize one of our own for a truly heroic rescue."

He peered through his glasses to read the inscription on the plaque:

"'To Merriweather Snowbird Clarke. Thanks for saving an old fart.'"

Tacked underneath the ornately carved sentiment hung the remnant of his beard, neatly braided, a greasy leather thong at the bottom. He handed the plaque to Merriweather, as everyone loudly clapped.

"Fair and warmer," she said sweetly.

The December north wind brought a raw chill to the island by night and a cloudless sky by day. Sandwiched in between the two was a warmish afternoon temperature that lured the inhabitants out to bask in the luminous sun; like cold-blooded lizards, they stretched out on warm rocks.

John had transferred a portion of Betsy's ashes to a small pepper mill grinder with a stainless steel top. Slipping the shaker into his pocket and then out again, he demonstrated the maneuver to Moby and Owl, who were hard at work converting their caskets to satisfy their current whims.

"Easy transport, that's the key—and I can sprinkle her around in places she might like. Betsy always liked to travel," he said.

The men grunted and nodded in concurrence. John, thankful he had another week before returning to work, gave the shaker a reassuring pat, waved an offhand goodbye, and walked with the wind at his back to the Carolinas' cabin. The resident rooster ushered in the afternoon session from his perch on the sawhorse that supported Owl's casket.

When it came time for the island's inhabitants to pilgrimage to Tacoma General to see the twins, there was a great deal of hemming and hawing about transportation. Moby asserted that the bed of his dump truck was up to Winnebago standards.

"We'll just see about that," North said, climbing up the ladder to the back of the truck.

Moby had not lied. North surveyed the waterproof canopy, two vintage orange over-stuffed couches, and a coffee table bolted through a threadbare but serviceable shag carpet. A warm breeze came from the truck heater and mood music—a string quartet working through one of Mozart's finest—wafted from the front of the cab.

"Not too shabby," North said, helping her sister up and onto one of the elderly couches.

Merriweather swung her purse over the tailgate, peering inside before she committed herself. A smile danced on her lips.

"I'm impressed," she said. "I think someone has been watching a little too much television. Especially the one called 'Pimp Out My Dump Truck.'"

Annie agreed, but then she hadn't expected anything less from Moby.

It wasn't long before the group was sailing down the interstate, riding "married," as Annie called it: guys in the front, gals in the back. A rising G-force made her brace her feet on the coffee table.

"Hey! Go easy on those curves," she shouted to the driver.

Owl, Moby, and John didn't hear Annie. They had retreated to their own little world, careening down the highway perched in their catbird seats, the cab lit only by the speedometer and the smug glow of three cigars.

Moby parked right next to the entrance to the sign that said, quite ambiguously he thought:

"No Parking. Pick up and Delivery Only."

Moby reached behind his truck seat and pried out two orange cones stenciled "County Public Works Dept." John put one in the back of the truck, and Moby casually placed one by the front bumper. Then they followed the women through the glass-door entrance.

Owl and John had put out their cigars, but Moby had simply bogarted his behind his back. He strolled with excessive nonchalance past the receptionist.

"Hold it. I smell a cigar." Her clear green eyes focused unerringly on the offender. "Smoking is *not* allowed in the hospital. You'll have to go outside."

Her glower told Moby she wished she could do more than just banish him.

"Oh, sorry," said Moby, the picture of contrition, then he yelled to the fast disappearing group of which not one had looked back. "Don't worry. I'll catch up."

Head Nurse Doris Lakes had shepherded the flock at the neonatal unit for the last thirty-seven years. When she first began, the ward was a sad place where tiny souls born too soon had little chance of survival, where heartbreak, tears, and very few victories dominated the landscape. But over the years, with the help of science and technology, Doris had molded a taut unit of specialized nurses who prided themselves on making the impossible possible. They saw themselves as the chief advocates for these babies who came into their world, wielding the fierce power of their calling like a sword. Their leader enjoyed uncommon loyalty among the rank and file.

Doris and her team performed miracles. They inserted IVs into the tiny doll-size hands with fingers like matchsticks, evincing nary a cry. They walked more softly than Indian braves, because they knew that just the mere whisper of air from a passing uniform could tear into the tissue of preemies. They understood they worked in a place of angels and miracles and acted accordingly.

At sixty-five, Doris Lake still carried the cheekbones and carriage of the Hollywood starlet fated with good looks but no acting chops. She'd given Tinseltown a go, but when reality had hit, she'd drifted north, found her way into nursing, and then made care of premature babies her vocation. Ten-hour shifts and saving vulnerable souls created the fabric of her life.

Swing shift was Doris's turf, where she ruled without peer. She was at her happiest in her office going over charts, bullying doctors into doing their finest work, all the while keeping one eye on visitors to her kingdom.

The Annie Entourage shuffled up to the window.

"We're here to see Sarah and Peter's twins," Annie said.

Doris tipped her head and peered over the top of her glasses. "Only immediate family."

She returned to her paperwork.

"I'm the babies' great-grandmother," Annie said with aplomb. "Don't grandparents have rights?"

"Oh yes. We are all grandparents," Merriweather said.

Doris looked up again, annoyed at having her authority questioned. Just as she was about to throw them out, she noticed a man with a crutch rounding the corner. She stood up and slid open the window further.

"Richard?" she called out. "Is that you?"

Annie's crowd parted, and Moby filled in the gap.

"Doris! How the hell are you?"

Doris came rushing out through the office door to give Moby an affectionate hug.

"It's been a long time, big boy." She nodded her head toward the odd little group. "Are you with these characters?"

"Guilty as charged."

Doris gave him a wry smile.

"Come on, then," she said and waved Annie and her troop into the sterilizing area.

Annie showed them how to step on the foot bar to wash their hands and helped them slip into the sanitized gowns and booties, then led them into the nursery. Red digital readouts flashed in the room, dimly lit to soothe the babies.

Little Annie and Zach were resting comfortably, hooked up to a series of pumps and monitors. Annie smiled to see that Peter had plastered pictures to the tops of their incubators, facing inward: the Eiffel Tower, the Taj Mahal, and Peter's sewer plant.

"Never too early to be exposed to great architecture," Peter had always said.

The crew pressed their noses to the plastic domes.

"They're so small and dainty," South cooed over Annie and moved over to examine Zach.

"How big were they when they were born?" Merriweather asked.

"Two pounds, five ounces," Annie answered, still amazed something that small could survive. "They're doing just fine. Mostly they have to wait for their lungs to grow and to remember to breathe. Those are the two most important developmental problems. There can be other problems too, but the nurses tell me they have great success these days."

"Damn, they're small," Owl grunted as he eased himself into a rocking chair.

The Seven Sisters Island's Wise Men had come bearing odd gifts ,which they laid on the large windowsill next to the twins. A case of spaghetti sauce, two large containers of WD-40, six rolls of gray tape, and two dream catchers from rounded willow branches, with a spider web design of thin gray yarn with tiny green iridescent hummingbird feathers woven throughout.

"There, that ought to take care of all those bad dreams these babies must be having, being away from their mother and all," said Merriweather. Then she hung the dream catchers from the IV hook over the incubators.

Moby hobbled in. He looked in at the twins in turn and spotted Owl reading from a copy of Blake's *Songs of Innocence* that had been left beside the babies' incubators.

"'Tiger, Tiger, burning bright,'" said Owl.

"'There was a young lady from Lin,'" Moby began. "'Her legs were exceedingly thin. But she—'"

Whack. North cuffed Moby on the back of the head.

"I'll thank you to keep a civil tongue."

"Shhhhh," Annie whispered. "You need to be quiet."

Annie took up her position between the plastic isolettes that housed her great-grandchildren. At the invitation and with the guidance of the nurse in attendance, the rest of the clan gathered up the underweight crack babies and rocked them slowly, murmuring love songs.

Moby looked down at the tiny fuzzy dark-haired girl in a pink blanket he cuddled. He thought of his daughter Christine and how he might never see her again. And how short life is between the top of the mountain he'd once been on and the spare oyster shack he called home. He closed his eyes and wished it were Christmas and that his girl was coming to see him again.

Despite the inclement weather, the island hummed with activity. John and Al had built a tenuous scaffolding and were tearing mossy cedar shakes off the schoolhouse. Merriweather happily raked up the discards. The Carolinas trundled wheelbarrows to a fire on the beach that billowed slate-gray smoke.

Annie and Moby walked over to the school. Tripod trailed, head down.

Moby pulled out a dog-eared, folded paper and spread it out on a large rock. They all gathered round.

"It's forty feet high to the top," he said proudly. "And right here—" he pointed to the rounded open spot, just beneath the roof "—that's where the Carolinas' bell is going to take up residence. A real fire-and-brimstone steeple. Something that will be heard and seen up and down the channel."

"We can't climb up on that roof without killing ourselves," said Annie.

"Most of it we can fabricate on the ground," Moby answered.

John said, "Owl and I scouted an old-growth cedar log up on the hump of the island. We could use that for the roof, but we've got to get the sections down here somehow."

"We're going to need some help. I've got feelers out," Moby said. "By spring, we'll be ringing the brains out of that bell."

Annie sat back in the chair with her feet in the oven. She closed her eyes and dozed. When she awoke some time later, total darkness had descended. She got to her feet and lit the kerosene lamp, then went out onto the porch with Buddy, leaned against the rail, and inhaled the frozen winds of winter.

Annie worked her way down the beach, the wind forcing her to take refuge near the Carolinas' woodshed. Her scarf caught the wind and set sail. She chased after it, catching up when it snagged on the roots of a small birch tree that had beached itself on the outgoing tide. When she bent over to pick it up, she heard a scream of terror.

A voice yelled out, "I see the light, I see the light. No, I'm not ready yet."

A long wail followed.

Annie spun around, trying to identify the direction of the noise. A light radiated from the Carolina cabin. She staggered to their door and pounded furiously. Aided by the wind, the door flung open wide. She saw South sitting on the bed next to North, holding her and rocking her.

"What's the matter?" Annie called out, as the wind whipped through the tiny dwelling.

"It's all right, it's all right," South comforted her sister.

Annie sat down on a rocker by the stove.

North became calmer and let out a muffled chortle. Then she laughed in earnest till she began crying. She became quiet, then burst into giggles again. She looked over her sister's shoulder and tried to explain, sputtering. "Somehow, the flashlight under my pillow got turned on, and when I woke up, it was shining in my face. I thought it was the light at the end of the tunnel, calling to me." She guffawed loudly, and finally Annie and South felt free to join in, till they all had tears in their eyes.

"I'm not ready to go yet," North prattled nervously. "I want to be here for Christmas. And one of my former soccer players is playing in the women's college championship game in New Orleans next week. She sent me a ticket to come and bandage her ankle for good luck. I've been taping that girl since she injured her ankle in a Possum game as an eighth grader, all the way through high school, till she got a scholarship to Indiana. I see her every year at Christmas. She has blown out both knees, lost two seasons with rehab, but she still runs like a deer.

"Her name is Felicity Splett, but she's always been 'Lickity Split' to me.

"When we were kids, I never so much as got to bounce a basketball or wear shorts. These girls play football if they want, do wrestling, and play soccer full tilt. It's a wonderful time for women.

"I've put in my time," said North, leaning back on her pillow. "I've outlived most of my friends, and I've had a wonderful run, thanks to my sister and the children. I don't want a religious service, but I am not going till Moby finishes my casket. That man is the world's worst procrastinator. I paid him two hundred dollars, and he still hasn't measured me up. I've a good mind to go and wake him up right now."

"We'd let you go, dearie, but we don't trust you with a flashlight anymore," said South. "You damn near scared me into a heart attack."

Before the sisters could fire any more salvos, Annie excused herself. It had been a long night.

The next morning, Annie was awakened by muffled quacks. Thousands of ducks had landed in the lagoon. Their legs bicycling upside down, they dipped in the water and grazed on seaweed; they groomed and preened the feathers that would support them for the remaining flight: two thousand miles to California, Mexico, and beyond.

The "church crew," up early themselves, had already gathered the last vestiges of king apples in a wheelbarrow and deposited them in front of the cold-storage door. Annie wrapped each apple separately in newspaper, searching for bruises. She stacked them in wooden boxes, with the green "Seven Sisters" logo on the side.

Walking to the beach, Annie startled the ducks. They all lifted from the water in a single motion, banked left, and disappeared from sight. The rocky shore was littered with thousands of down feathers—floating on the calm seawater, suspended in huckleberry branches, and stacked against the leeside of logs. It was as if a gaggle of giggling children, wielding defective feather pillows, had fought a major battle.

The gulls, driven off by the sheer number of ducks, now reclaimed their ground. They worked for breakfast, bombarding the beach with hapless clams, which were defenseless against Newton's laws of physics.

By late afternoon, the church roof had been tarpapered and stapled down watertight. The crew celebrated with cups of hand-pressed hard cider that John had been percolating in his woodshed. As he poured the nectar, he reminded them that next week he would be going back to work.

"I'll be commuting four days a week, but back home here every night, so if you need anything from the mainland, just let me know."

Moby opened his mouth as if to comment about the cider but no words came out. He just held out his cup for another hit.

"It's good shit, man," Owl proclaimed.

The following Monday, John and Moby set out in *The Ark*, bound for Port Gamble.

The fog had settled above the waves, despite a stiff wind that snapped the canvas awning like a bullwhip. For a brief moment, the fog and clouds cleared to the west. In that small window of opportunity, the Olympic Mountains, bathed in sunlight, white and perfect, stood saw-toothed against a dark and angry storm system that promised to swat the island by nightfall. Over the roar of the engine, John could but gesture with his hand to attract Moby's attention, but before Moby could turn around, the clouds closed in. Like a momentary glimpse of a beautiful woman skimming through a crowd, the vision passed. John wondered whether he imagined it, or perhaps something extraordinary had passed his way.

Moby artfully swung the boat against the dock, and John climbed over the side. Moby lifted Tripod over onto the dock, where he stood, cold and trembling. Moby shook his head.

"He's been like this for a couple of weeks. I'm going to get the results from the vet this morning."

"He doesn't look good," John said, tying off the boat. "I'll catch the bus to the ferry and see you this evening."

Moby was glad to see that the gangplank leading up to the parking lot was almost flat, thanks to a winter high tide. Tripod and "Monopod" were no match for the slippery runway when it was slanted, even with the wooden cleats that served as traction. Tripod hunkered down and dug his nails in as best he could, but in his weakened condition, he skittered backward. Moby braced his foot behind the dog's back leg, helping him to the top. Embarrassed by his failure (and because Moby had pinned his ears up with a clothespin to keep them from dragging in the dirt), Tripod sulked all the way to the truck.

When they got to the vet's, Tripod refused to leave the truck, so Moby went in alone to get the result from the tests. As he signed in at the desk, he heard one of the technicians whispering to another.

"The pirate is back."

The vet was perfunctory in his diagnosis.

"There's nothing in the blood, and the urine is clear. He's probably just old." The dismissive attitude made Moby angry and he stormed out, vowing not to return. He pondered the problem as he left the clinic parking lot and headed to Mom's Diner, where he planned on meeting a carpenter with a team of draft horses to talk about dragging the cedar bolts down the hill and maybe helping do a little roofing.

The heavy smell of cooking sausage and fresh-brewed coffee hung in the air. Moby scanned the café until he spotted blue-flannel-shirted shoulders that looked like they could handle a brace of two-ton workhorses.

He slid into the booth and thrust out his hand.

"Moby. And you're Travis?"

Most people were taken aback by the ring of tattooed whales around the head, if the crutch or the patch didn't get them, but Travis simply shook Moby's hand.

"That'd be me."

Moby had ways of judging men who worked construction. If he couldn't observe them working, he wanted their hands to be strong, calloused, the nails slightly dirty. Scars were a plus, or at least a cloth band-aid protecting a recent injury. Plastic bandages signaled a rookie; gray tape earned extra points.

Moby was willing to take four out of five. He didn't believe in references, and he didn't trust looks. He had been burned by what he called pretty boys and flim-flam men—they littered the food chain of misfits that frequented the construction industry. Moby paid only when the job was done. There would be no retainer. Carpentry was a hands-on proposition; if your name was "Three-fingered Jake," he dismissed you on the spot. The fact that Moby himself could be considered handicapped and his appearance could be disturbing, factored not a whit. Right or wrong, that was what made Moby the boss and Travis the man for hire.

Moby explained the situation on the island, the church roof, and the local inhabitants. He reached under the seat beside him and handed Travis a shingle he had cut out of a log. It had a mahogany hue and its ridges were straight. Although the log had been earth-bound a hundred years, it gave off the pungent smell of fresh cedar.

"That's a good-looking piece of cedar," said Travis, as he ran his hand down the grooves, then held the shingle up to his nose.

Moby liked what he saw. There isn't a carpenter worth his salt who wouldn't be drawn to the sweet smell of fresh cedar.

Travis flashed the smile and face that had garnered him the "Robert Redford Look-Alike" award in the 1988 Senior Class Hall of fame at Port Townsend High School.

Moby hailed the waitress for a cup of coffee. She sashayed over to the table, shamelessly checking out the hunk.

"High octane?" she asked.

Moby nodded, and the coffee began falling out of the sky, slopping up the side of the cup.

"You in, Sundance?" she quizzed Travis.

He gave her the smile. She decided to ignore his dirty fingernails.

"Sure, fill 'er up," he said.

Moby swiveled around to see if Mom was in the kitchen. There was noise, but he couldn't see the frizzy red hair in the order window. He turned back to Travis.

"So, are you interested?"

Travis saved the smile and was all business.

"I can drag the bolts down to the beach by the church. You can help me split the shakes, and then I'll do the roof."

Moby nodded, looking over his cup.

"We can help, but we're working with geezer rookies here. Most of it would be up to you."

Suddenly, a sustained blast of cold air blew out of the kitchen. An unattended newspaper flew off the counter and landed spread-eagled against the window. The regulars at the counter turned their backs to the wind, bowed their necks, and gave protective cover to their food with their arms. The calendar chattered against the wall. From the kitchen came a muffled apology from Mom.

"Sorry, guys. It will be over in a minute."

"What the hell?" Moby swore, as he bent low to stop his eye patch from joining the newspaper.

"It's Mom," explained Travis, yelling over the howling wind. "Hot flashes. She got old Henry at the sawmill to put in a giant blower from the old fish-freezer plant. Cools her off, I guess. She trips a switch in the kitchen, and it's every man for himself."

Moby glanced sideways at the counter again as the wind whipped tears into his eye. No one seemed to take offense. An occasional icy blast was a small price to pay for the best breakfast in the state—and for the feeling that when no one else gave a shit, Mom would feed you. And when you left, your belly would be full, and you'd feel better about the world. There wasn't a bartender in the world that could hold a candle to Mom. And everyone knew it.

As quickly as the hurricane blew in, it blew out.

Travis took a long drink of coffee, then looked Moby right in his one good eye.

"When the draft horses are pulling the bolts to the beach, I charge four hundred a day. When I'm doing carpentry, that's twenty-five an hour."

Moby nodded. "If we can work out a swap of labor for the rest of the log, would you be interested?"

"That's a definite possibility, if the whole tree is as good as the sample," replied Travis. "I'm not available till Christmas vacation. I would be bringing my son with me, and it would be easier if we didn't have to commute. Is there a shelter for the horses?"

"No problem. We'll be looking for you after Christmas," said Moby. "How about if I draw up a contract?"

Travis shook his head. "If we need a contract, we shouldn't do business together. I'll be there after Christmas. See ya then," he said. He stood up, shook Moby's hand, dropped two dollars on the table, and walked out the door.

Moby was pleased. He finished his coffee slowly, watching Travis out the window. The man hopscotched a path through the puddle-pocked parking lot, started up his white pickup, and splashed his way to the highway. He quickly disappeared into a fast-approaching fog bank that rolled up the valley on its way to the ocean.

Moby dropped two more dollars on the table and made for the door. The waitress delivered plate-sized killer pancakes to two loggers and twirled to return to the kitchen. Moby gave her his best pirate smile as he opened the door, setting off the tingling bell.

"Bring your parrot next time," she called out. He closed the door, making the "Open" sign rock back and forth.

Rattling down the road, Moby mulled over the Tripod diagnosis, or lack thereof. Absentmindedly, he realized he had missed the turnoff to home. He took the next road that looked as if it would get him back on track, but instead the road changed from two lanes of blacktop with a faded yellow strip to one lane of gravel. The gravel road was flanked by barbed-wire fences and grassy ditches overflowing with runoff.

With no place to turn the truck around, Moby kept driving. He soon passed a series of signs hand-painted in black lettering on planks of white delaminating plywood. The signs hung at odd angles, each in its turn hanging from by a single nail hammered into a lichen-covered fence post. As he drove, he read, Burma-Shave style,

*If your pet . . .*
*Is feeling low . . .*
*We can give it . . .*
*Get up and go . . .*
And a hundred feet from the last sign . . .
*Pet Psychic/Herbalist, next right*

Most of his life Moby had been a hard-headed realist. While most people mellow over the years, Moby, to the discerning eye, had not. The change in his heart had come about slowly. The old Moby would have torn down the signs in defiance of a gift beyond his understanding and ripped giant ruts in the road in retreat. But the new Moby was beginning to embrace a tolerance for what he previously called "supernatural bullshit."

Moby turned down the road. It wound through more than a mile of spindly, too-closely-bunched fir trees with no commercial value, the kind of trees loggers call "peckerpoles."

The road ended abruptly in a field. A lone, silver, aluminum-riveted trailer perched on a grassy knoll in the middle of nowhere. There were no visible signs of life. Moby disgustedly chided himself and began to turn the truck around. Then he spotted a hand poking out of a window, waving a yellow scarf. He shook his head, cut the motor, and coaxed Tripod out of the front seat. He picked his way through the bunch grass to the trailer door. The door was flung open to reveal the scarf-waver: a petite, blonde woman with lively green eyes and an alligator smile.

# Chapter NINE

"Welcome, welcome," she announced, flourishing two scarves gaily, as if ushering a plane onto a flight deck.

Vertically challenged, Tripod had to be lifted into the trailer, followed by his equally gimpy owner. The woman, ignoring formality—and Moby—bent down and gathered Tripod's muzzle in her hands. She began talking directly into the dog's eyes, which were even more sorrowful than usual.

"We're going to make you all better. Don't you worry. You'll be baying like the hounds of Baskerville when I get done with you." She smoothed her hand across his head. "Yes, you will."

Looking up at Moby, she extended her hand.

"Lila Simpson."

Moby reached out to help the woman to her feet, then took off his stocking cap.

"Moby, ma'am. And this here is Tripod. Tripod has been feeling under the weather for the last three weeks or so. He won't eat. He sleeps a lot and has a definite hitch in his giddy-up."

"Hmmm...I can see he needs some help." She looked down at the index finger of her left hand where an ornate ring held the tiny face of a watch. "Let me make a phone call, then I will be right back. I was just on my way to Paris to help a middle-aged anteater with roughly the same symptoms. It might be menopause. Who knows for sure; anteaters can be so flaky. But a robust fellow like yours, we'll have him on his feet in no time."

Then, remembering the dog's—and his owner's—handicap, she laughed, a sound Moby found warm and heartening.

"No pun intended. I'll just be a minute." She waltzed down a short hallway, opened a door, and was gone.

Moby settled back into a rose-colored, overstuffed sofa while Tripod collapsed on the rug like a discarded beanie baby. One wall of the tiny waiting room was covered floor to ceiling with hundreds of pictures from adoring fans. Lila and alligators. Lila and elephants. Lila and gorillas. Lila surrounded by a flock of ostriches. The woman enjoyed a worldwide reputation for tapping into the psyches of critters, judging from the framed testimonial letters from pet owners and zoos ranging from Memphis to Milan to Moscow. Another wall featured hundreds of newspaper clippings.

Moby was just leaning over to examine one of the articles further when Lila burst back into the room. Her green eyes glittered.

"All ready. Just follow me."

She led the handicapped pair down the short hall into the only other room in the trailer. Moby saw no tables or chairs, only more photos and letters decorating the walls. After Lily closed the door, the room descended, like an elevator.

Moby wobbled a bit, caught off balance by this unanticipated movement. He looked at Lila, a startled question in his eyes.

Lila explained, "It's an old Nike missile base. My quarters are down sixty feet, in the underground silo, where the missiles were kept." The room came to a soft halt. "Here we are," she said.

The door opened onto a huge circular room, lavishly appointed, with thick rugs, and exquisite, hand-carved furniture. Moby looked up, guessed the ceiling to be forty feet high.

"It is so much easier to do my work here," Lila said, straightening the pillows on the sofa. "It's so quiet, completely removed from the frantic pace of the outside world. I only wish I could get the larger animals down here. The giraffes particularly are easily distracted. But even giraffes don't hold a candle to those South American leopard frogs. Everyone knows they don't have a thought in their heads."

She gazed fondly at Tripod.

"It is so nice to get a walk in-patient. Do sit down, Mr. Moby, while I sit here with Tripod."

"I was wondering about the fee," Moby said. "If you—"

"Mr. Moby," Lila interrupted, a crimson flush creeping up her neck, "we are talking about one of God's creatures. There will be no talk of money till there is a cure."

She reached into her pocket and pulled out a remote control. The lights dimmed. A four-foot, mauve, monolithic crystal rose from below the floor. A single laser light shot purplish shards of color throughout the room. Sitar music twanged somewhere in the darkness above.

Rarely chagrined and seldom rattled, Moby felt both. He settled back and let the woman work. He surveyed the circular room, estimating the diameter to be around sixty feet. He marveled that the tiny trailer, with no obvious road or power lines linking it to civilization, had so expertly camouflaged this deep, concrete hole.

Lila pulled the clothespins from Tripod's ears, letting his ears dangle naturally. Slowly, she ran her hands over his body, stopping occasionally, as if gathering data, then methodically moving on. At last, she put his head in her lap and bent her head low, apparently meditating.

This pose continued for twenty minutes, with Lila sometimes jerking her head back, as if struck by a blow to the forehead, like a penitent receiving salvation in a revival tent. Tripod too, convulsed at times, till finally Lila laid Tripod's limp head on the carpet, used the remote to lower the crystal back into its resting place, and moved to sit in a chair opposite Moby.

"There doesn't seem to be any one thing wrong with Tripod— more like a web of somewhat unrelated problems that have gradually worn him down. He still mourns the loss of his leg, never having accepted that. Pinning his ears on top his head embarrasses him. He is sexually repressed, sapping his confidence. Evidently some bird is stealing his food, which angers and upsets him. A bacterium in his large bowel is impeding his digestion; it needs to be flushed out. He came from a litter in which he was the runt, something he has always resented. And he finds 'Tripod' degrading, although he didn't particularly like 'Digger'—his first name—either. And one more thing, he doesn't like you to undress in front of him. The dragon on your butt freaks him out. His words, Mr. Moby, not mine."

Moby sat mute, taken aback by this litany of miseries his dog had suffered. Lila looked up at him, the reproachful look of a headmistress on her face.

"And when is the last time he had a meal of broccoli and carrots?"

"Uh, well…never, I guess."

"Yes, I thought as much.

"This is an extremely sensitive animal. Bloodhounds often wear their hearts on their sleeves. They are loyal and loving. Did you think he was born with those doleful eyes? No. This is a sick dog. He needs immediate treatment."

Touched as he was by the woman's obvious compassion, Moby wondered how much of what she said was true. Still, he couldn't deny her gift.

"I took him to the vet, and they ran some tests. But they just said he was getting old."

Lila waved her hand dismissively.

"Yes, well, that's medical treatment via the assembly line. I look at each animal as a sentient being. They should be revered as such."

Moby asked shyly, "Did he mention a name he would like?"

"He doesn't know for sure. Just a more action-packed name. A 'tripod' is just something that stands there, a crutch for a camera. He doesn't feel it represents his real persona. But he is worried, now that he has come out in the open with these complaints, that he will lose your respect."

She called Tripod to her side. Moby swore the dog looked up sheepishly at him.

"Oh, no, I'd never feel that way," said Moby, scratching the dog behind the ears and looking into his eyes. "I just want him to get better. He's a great dog. He and I make a good fit."

Tripod thumped his tail on the floor in gratitude and licked Lila's hand.

"I think he's feeling better already. So, where do we go from here?" Moby asked. His eyes strayed to a large projection of the solar system on the wall.

"I'd like to give him a mango colonic enema—that should put his large bowel in balance. And I will give you a list of food groups, breathing exercises, and possible name combinations. Physically, he has overcome his handicap nicely. It is just this excessive baggage that seems to have gotten him down," Lila said, scribbling furiously on a yellow pad. She rose and moved over to a mahogany credenza, where she opened first one drawer and extracted a large manila envelope, then a second drawer, from which she took a toothbrush.

"He does have a breath odor problem, you know," she said, placing both paper and toothbrush into the envelope. "I'm going to take him in for the enema. You'll be ready to go in half an hour."

Lila and Tripod disappeared into another room, while Moby sat on the sofa thumbing through a *National Geographic*. Before he could find the article on the tattooed women of Papua, New Guinea, he dozed off.

When Lila returned, Tripod seemed almost perky, his ears a full-inch off the ground.

"Wow," marveled Moby. "He looks like his old self."

All three rode the ascending room up to ground level. As they stepped out, Moby heard the distinctive thwack, thwack, thwack of rotary blades, which seemed to be coming from just outside the trailer. He looked at Lila, surprised once again by this unusual woman.

"Is…is that a helicopter?" he asked.

"Yes," said Lila, matter of factly. "My ride to the airport."

She picked up a well-worn satchel on the table and opened the door, only to be greeted by the copter's overpowering downdraft.

Lila's long scarf slapped Moby in the face as she lurched forward onto the porch.

"See you next week," shouted Lila over her shoulder. "We need to do a follow-up. Both of you, eat your greens. Remember, fiber is our friend and the gateway to a happy bowel."

Moby watched the helicopter swallow Lila, her scarves, and her medical bag. The helicopter rose, banked to the east, and disappeared down the valley.

John was huddled in his car with the motor running trying to stay warm near the Port Gamble post office when Moby pulled into the parking lot. Soon Moby had the boat's green and red running lights turned on, and the trio set off down the channel.

John sniffed the air.

"Do you smell mango?" he yelled over the roar of the engine.

Christmas was fast approaching. Moby and Owl, under the strict supervision of South, worked on their piano duet of "Angels We Have Heard on High." Their rendition was to be a surprise for Moby's daughter. If you knew what they were playing, you could almost pick out a note or two.

South could only shake her head at the carnage. She picked up Owl's sausage fingers.

"These are the fingers of a Polish ditch digger. You two are setting music back a thousand years. You no-talent louts will not embarrass me. I have a reputation, you know."

"Yeah, it's in the entertainment field all right, but it ain't legal in this state," said Owl.

South took the sheet music from the piano, rolled it up, and smacked each man on top his head.

"That would be my sister, you ruffians. Even so, you keep that flip mouth to yourself."

Annie called them in for coffee, hoping they'd get the hint that practice had gone on long enough for one night.

As the two men swaggered into the dining room, Moby elbowed his partner.

"Bet they'll be surprised at our encore."

"Encore, what encore?" South's eyes narrowed in suspicion.

"Just a little surprise we've cooked up," Moby mumbled cryptically.

"I should have gone with North. She's in no condition to make that trip on her own," South said wistfully. "But she's such an independent cuss."

"She'll have no trouble connecting with other soccer groupies, especially with all those medals and patches from World Cups on her jacket. Hell, she'll be lucky to get past the metal detector at the airport," said Moby, chocolate cookie crumbs falling from the corners of his mouth.

"She'll be all right," Annie said, sliding the cookie plate away from Moby.

"What?" asked Moby, feigning innocence.

"Trooper," South blurted. "That's a good name for a dog. I had a collie, born on VJ day, and that's what we called him."

A cold front had spilled out of the Arctic and crushed its way south, plowing through the coastal mountain ranges and the granite fjords of British Columbia and arriving at the doorstep of Seven Sisters without knocking. It scoured the clouds from the winter night, leaving a silver sparkle on every twig and leaf, buttering each beach stone. Only the sentinel moon and the twinkling stars witnessed the transformation, so silent did it creep.

Oblivious to the changes of nature, the venerable farmhouse generated hearty warmth and formed a translucent crescent moon on each windowpane against the thin wooden bars. Inside, the keepers of the island chatted in endless and wandering conversations between cookies and tea, whiskey, and cigars. They were sharing their most precious commodity—time.

There was a knock on the door. Merriweather stumbled in, rake in hand.

"I was lonely," she announced, pulling up a chair while Annie poured her a cup of tea.

"The weather has a cold death grip on us, I'm afraid," she said, stuffing most of a cookie in her mouth.

The crew stared out into the lengthening shadows of the afternoon and watched as the smoke from the chimney boiled out of the rusty chimney tops of the shacks as if liquefied. The high-pressure zone was still and heavy, causing the smoke to roll down the frosted cedar shingles and drop straight to the ground, puddling on the shoreline. When the puddles tumbled into the water, they vaporized and spiraled eerily skyward.

"Looks like some kinda swamp creature movie out there," Owl said.

"Reminds me of the *Creature of the Black Lagoon*," South said with a shudder.

They all jumped when Tripod began his instinctive bloodhound wail, as if on cue.

"Shit happens," Owl swore in his best plumbing voice.

The next morning, Moby threw open his door and roared a challenge into the silence. The sound of his loud voice ricocheted off the still water, disturbing the shivering seagulls standing mincingly at the end of the jetty, dreaming of an easy meal in a landfill.

Owl, still in his underwear and with his hand scratching below his waistband, stepped out of his own door and equaled Moby's blast, swearing at the cold.

"Goddamn, it's as cold as a well-digger's ass out here."

South opened her door in response to the yelling.

"You watch your mouth, you bastard," she chipped. "And for God's sake, get dressed."

Moby laughed and watched as Merriweather threw open her cabin door and sprayed WD-40 on her rake tines. Next, she pulled on a pair of red mittens, tied the velvet chinstrap of a purple hat with earflaps, and headed down to the orchard. Owl pulled his hand out of his shorts, quickly slipped on his boots, and hurried down the back way to the orchard to spread Merriweather's silk leaves on the ground.

"Top o' the morning, Merriweather," Owl greeted her minutes later, as he threw the now-empty burlap bag under a wheelbarrow used for gathering the apples.

"Clear and cold, clear and cold," she snapped, as if near-naked men standing in the orchard was an everyday occurrence. "The weather still has us in a death grip, I'm afraid." She stopped and leaned on her rake. "The leaves seem to be in one big clump today. The wind must have blown the rest away," she said. "Guess it will be a short day. I have Christmas presents to make, anyway. I'm working on a support bra out of gray tape for my niece and a nice belt for her husband. And judging by the cut of your jib, I'll need to make you a little something too, Owl. Maybe a jock strap."

In the middle of one night during the cold snap, Annie was startled out of a hard sleep. Only the bobbing light on the mast of a gill-netter and the far-off lights of a cargo ship pierced the dark. A figure stood in her room, just on the edge of the moonlight that streamed in the tower window.

"Annie, are you there?"

Annie put on her glasses. She could make out Merriweather, with Buddy sitting next to her.

"Are you okay?" Annie asked, struggling to sit up.

Merriweather sat on Annie's bed.

"I know I'm going downhill, and I can't do anything about it. I wanted to come to talk to you, before I disappear again.

"If I get bad, you know, really bad—where I don't recognize any-one for a long time—will you find a way to just…just do me in? I don't want to live like that. I worry about becoming a burden. I know the way my mother was. She lived for fifteen years in a nursing home.

She was always scared, wetting the bed. The nurses were mean to her, they laughed, made fun of her. I don't want that to happen to me.

"Can you help me, Annie? If I get bad?"

Annie took Merriweather by the hand and helped her into her bed, then climbed in on the other side. They lay, heads together on the single pillow, for a long time.

Annie turned to Merriweather and whispered into her ear.

"I don't want you to worry. I'll think of something."

"Thanks, Annie." Merriweather let out a long sigh. "I knew you would help. I feel better now."

She turned over and went to sleep, leaving Annie to stare at the ceiling of the darkened room while her friend peacefully snored away. Finally, Annie fell into a fitful sleep.

When she awoke in the morning, her bedmate had disappeared.

The temperature dropped quickly; the sun nestled between two crimson clouds that had crept in from the Pacific. The wind from the north whipped up divinity whitecaps.

Just five days till Christmas.

Moby took the boat to Port Gamble. North was waiting at the wharf when he arrived. Moby helped wrestle her suitcases aboard, and they headed back to the island, steaming past the iceberg-like deadhead logs that had broken loose from the beaches by the ferocity of the winter storms. The logs migrated with the tides, looking to do damage. Like alligator snouts, they belied their treachery, as their tails hung down twenty to thirty feet, waiting to eviscerate an unsuspecting craft.

South collected her sister from the launch and hustled her into the cabin. The cold wind had stimulated in North a hoarse, hacking cough—thanks to the stale airplane air, long afternoons at the stadium, and her own run-down condition. Despite her cough, North insisted that South get out the Christmas decorations and gathered everyone for eggnog and stories of the soccer tournament.

As she recounted the final game, she collapsed in a gagging fit. South looked over, worried, and poured her a cup of chamomile tea.

"Don't mind me," North said. "But now that I'm back, I want to know. Moby, when are you boys going to finish that coffin I paid you for?"

Owl and Moby couldn't look her in the eyes. They'd both felt finishing the coffin would finish North, that its completion would signal that her time had come.

"Tell you what," said Moby. "Owl and John and I will take you to Pickles' tomorrow for you to pick out exactly the right color of red for the box and the lining."

The next morning, North and the men were up early and soon on the road to Mom's Diner for a quick breakfast and then on to the business at hand. The bell on the door announced their entrance into a relatively quiet Mom's. Soon the four of them were inundated with mounds of sausage, eggs, and hash browns. They ate, and John left a ten-buck tip. They received the same send-off as the regulars.

"Thanks—and keep your powder dry out there."

John, Moby, Owl, and North crammed into the front seat of the dump truck. Five minutes down the road, John tapped his pocket.

"Hold it. I think Betsy's missing."

Moby slowed the truck while John checked every pocket.

"Head back to the restaurant."

"What do you mean, you left Betsy?" Moby asked, making a U-turn thanks to a school bus turn-around.

"Remember? I put some of her ashes in a pepper mill to sprinkle her out in places I think she'd enjoy, and I forgot to put it back in my pocket," John said, leaning forward on the dash, anxiously staring out the windshield.

They splashed into the parking lot and tumbled out of the truck. John made his way back to the furthest booth. Two huge, out-of-work loggers, looking as if they had joined a federal retraining program for sumo warrior tag-team wrestling, had moved from the counter to the comfort of the worn vinyl seats of the booth.

John stood closest to the larger of the two specimens. The man had forearms the size of honey-baked ham shanks. He had half-finished the biscuits and gravy in front of him and was meticulously wiping up spilled gravy with toast he had liberated from a recently vacated breakfast at the counter.

"Excuse me, could I have that pepper mill?" John asked, pointing to his grinder near the man's elbow.

"No problem. Hell, about broke my wrist grinding it, but look at the size of the chunks. That's coarsest ground pepper I've ever seen. Thing is, I still can't taste the pepper." The man leaned out into the aisle. "Suzie Q, what'd you do to this pepper shaker?"

"Don't get your tail in a knot, Lester. It's the same stuff we've always had," Susan replied, wiping the crumbs from the next table onto the floor.

John tried never to judge a man by his coveralls, but this time it seemed appropriate not to escalate an already precarious situation. He tried to grab the pepper mill and exchange it, but the diner was too quick.

"Let me give it one last try, and then you can have it." Lester gave the Betsy mill a quick circular motion and the gray-black grains peppered his remaining biscuit and gravy. "That's more like it." He smiled, handing the mill to John.

As John scuttled out the door, he heard the man say, with a full mouth, "Now, that's what I call pepper!"

When they reached the store, Pickles was navigating in a pair of golden in-line skates, a live Christmas tree strapped to his back, complete with electric lights. The tree was attached to a fifty-foot electric cord, which slowed his range of motion only slightly.

"Describe the color," he said.

North thought a moment, then answered, "Well, take a thin slice of cranberry jelly, the seedless kind. And look through the jelly, up against the sunlight. Now add a touch of red from a persimmon seed. That would be it."

Pickles closed his eyes, his mind apparently working at computer speed. He smiled in a Grinchy way.

"'Caribbean Madam' with a 'Mango Madness' base coat. I can whip it up in no time."

Trailing the electrical line, ornaments crashing into each other, Pickles skated to a far corner of the store, where he pulled off a canvas cover to reveal an ancient brass color mixer. He hummed as he spun the machine around, pulling levers and pumping colors into a bright tin one-gallon pail of paint for a good ten minutes.

Then he stopped. He thought for a split second and then pumped in a full measure of blue. He pounded the lid on with a rubber mallet, fumbled with a black felt pen, and wrote "North Carolina Red" in big square letters on the top. Expertly, he slopped the pail into the shaking machine. Five minutes later, Pickles had ushered them out the door with a sweep of his branches.

Tempers ran hot when it came time to choose the perfect Christmas tree from the meager supply on the island. The decorating brought an even more strenuous tug-of-war as Christmas traditions clashed. When the fracas came to a compromise only ornaments made from beachcombing were allowed to grace the fragrant Douglas fir that held court in the parlor. The branches were tethered with sequins glued onto seawhips, a seagull skull spray-painted gold, angels crudely fashioned out of cigar butts, highly polished sardine cans, white seagull and black crow feathers and pink Tampax rods glued into a cross, graced the top.

Moby could only stare at the finished product with pride.

"Ain't she a beaut!" he proclaimed.

The Carolinas had their own small tree outside their cabin, from which clam shells and sand dollars swayed in the winds. Merriweather had festooned her tree with bows of everlasting gray tape rolled in sparkles and feathers. Owl and Moby were under deadline to polish up their piano recital and hovered near the piano, as Annie "baked up a storm," as her mother would have said.

Moby left early in the morning to meet Christine. As he sat waiting on the Port Gamble dock, anxiously watching the minutes tick by, he thought of everything that could go wrong.

"She is flying in from Italy—some crazy Moslem could hijack the plane with some ridiculous demand. Heathrow or JFK could be snowed in. Worse, that damn London fog that camps on the ground for days on end could shut down the airport. Seattle should have built that third runway by now. Chicago. They wouldn't lay over in Chicago, would they? Those bozos better not. Everything ices up there—wings, runways. The traffic controllers are overworked. Whatever happened to that lobby for the thirty-hour week? They need to be fresh—especially at holiday time. Damn it, she should have stayed put; it's too dangerous this time of year."

The afternoon chill began to creep into his stubbed leg, and Moby was about to launch into his tirade for the hundredth time when a limousine pulled up. Christine yelled out the window, "Did you think I wasn't going to make it, Dad?"

Moby mustered a grin equal parts bravado and relief as Christine closed the window and gathered her suitcases from the trunk. He hoped she would not see the wet in his eyes, but she had caught him.

"I'm here, Dad," she said quietly, wiping a tear that had stubbornly stuck to his chin, giving him a kiss and hugging him around the neck. She took his arm, and they walked toward the boat.

They returned to the island to find that John's family had arrived on the *Bon Appetit* and stuffed themselves, like dressing in a Christmas goose, into one of the vacant cabins alongside another cabin filled with Owl's daughter and her family. Calypso, Sarah, and Peter had come over in the first wave of travelers the day before and taken refuge in the second story of the farm house. The Carolinas' people were coming Christmas Day, but Merriweather had no one, so she moved in with Annie to free up her place.

Owl and Moby had built a second outhouse to accommodate the holiday traffic and installed a stove in both outhouses. Gender-specific, one had a blue door, the other a red one. Moby had insisted on an elaborate ribbon-cutting ceremony the weekend before. He pointed out the new magazine rack and explained the elaborate system of pulling on a chain to raise a small flag that signaled the outhouse was "under deposit," as he put it.

They had also instituted a usage fee of sorts. Each person who used the facilities had to donate a stick of firewood to the woodpile outside each outhouse. Unfortunately, as nearby firewood became more and more scarce, a fair amount of petty pilfering took place between the two genders when under duress. But the system as a whole seemed to work fine.

By Christmas Eve, the cold snap had reached its tenth bone-chilling day. Lakes had frozen over, water pipes were bursting, the air hung heavy with inversion smog. County officials fretted publicly about the impending thaw, but on the island, the cabins were filled with warm relatives and goodwill. The fireplace at Annie's was decked with children's stockings. Anticipation seeped through the inhabitants awaiting the piano recital and their reward for attendance—mounds of desserts and confections that Annie and John had fussed over for weeks.

Annie dug through the attic and found a candlestick for the piano. Inspired, Merriweather left to search the collectibles in the leopard baggage that had migrated with her to the island and returned triumphant with a half-dozen sterling candelabra of her own. The lit candelabra were perched from stump to rock, on porch and rail, from outhouse to kitchen table, lighting the forest night like a thousand fireflies. As the pilgrims trudged up the trail, they likened it to a Buddhist shrine, a Catholic Church, and a peace vigil, all rolled into one.

The kitchen table was heaped with cookies, candy, and Moby's particular brand of fruitcake that had prospered for two months under a dishtowel, meticulously soaked with four jiggers of rum every other day.

Pots filled with hot cider and eggnog crowded the stove. After the Thanksgiving Day binge, Annie banned alcohol from the party. In response, Owl tended a speakeasy on the back porch, with a secret knock known only to those in need.

The windows steamed up, the rooms grew hot and noisy, sweaty children and adults chattered away. Wrapped in a quilt and sipping tea in a rocker near the kitchen stove, a seemingly frail and worn-out North sat quietly, barely rocking her chair.

"Is North feeling all right?" John asked South.

"I expect she's still frazzled from her trip," she answered. "She just needs some rest. She'll be all right."

When everyone had eaten his or her fill, South ushered cookie-crumbed parents and powdered-sugar-dusted children into the front room for the entertainment. Two of John's grandchildren, girls in junior high, played a flute duet. Owl's two grandchildren, accompanied by their mother on the piano, sang a medley of Christian songs, ending with "Joy to the World." An eight-year-old boy, hailing from the Carolinas' stable, stumbled through a presentation of *The Night before Christmas*, with the prompting of his mother.

The crowd sensed disaster as Moby and Owl took center-stage, dressed in tuxedos, top hats, and white gloves, all rented from Pickles. They bowed, sat down together on the bench, and went straight to work, playing a flawless "Angels We Have Heard on High," with extra flourishes. They stood to wild applause, then turned their backs, took off the hats, donned matching green eye patches, and played a lusty Three Dog Night version of Jerimiah Bullfrog's "Joy to the World"—the second time with crowd accompaniment. Begging off the stage, the two sweating men adjourned briefly to the back porch for libation during intermission. Then the recital resumed.

Christine, dressed in a white gown, flowed to the piano.

"You're a tough act to follow, Dad," she said.

She went to the piano and began to play, slowly at first, and then faster, leading them through the mysteries of music for the next half-hour. It was a performance usually reserved for kings and heads of state, but tonight Christine played for her father and his friends. When the last chord echoed across the lagoon, everyone knew they had experienced virtuosity. They sat in stunned silence for a moment, then clapped energetically, till Moby, Owl, and Christine put on eye patches and played the only encore all three knew: "Chopsticks." Annie led the group in Christmas carols as the candles burned low. When a small girl put a half-eaten cookie in front of his nose, Buddy, having gorged on crumbs and offerings, moaned and turned his head away.

Christmas morning, the inhabitants of each cabin opened their family gifts, then journeyed to Annie's for special gifts and a breakfast of blueberry muffins and sausage. North's son and daughter helped North get up the path, followed by the rest of the troops.

The first gift was for North. Moby and Owl unveiled her coffin. Owl caressed the lid and spoke much like a game-show emcee describing a contestant's prize.

"The outside has been coated with two coats of a hue dubbed 'North Carolina Red' and three coats of lacquer. The casket itself is built entirely of pine, with 'North Carolina' carved on the top."

They helped North up so she could survey the work.

Owl continued, "The bottom is contoured in foam and upholstered with a quilt, complete with North Carolina's state flower, the dogwood. And here on the inside of the lid, we carved 'Coach of the Awesome Possums.' And on this shelf—a little feature I like—is a place for a whistle and a flashlight. But wait, there's more!" He slid back a hidden panel. "You can put jewelry, or whatever you want, right back here."

North stood in amazement.

"It's more than I ever expected," she said. "I don't deserve it."

Moby held up a hand.

"Sorry, North, but we don't give refunds. Besides, who else do we know named 'North Carolina'?"

"It just tickles me to death, boys. And I mean that literally." And she leaned over and gave each one of them a kiss. "Now give me a boost in here. I want to try this baby on for size," she said, reaching into her dwindling reserves for her usual feisty nature.

Her son picked her up and gently deposited her in the casket. She snuggled down, rapped on the wood sides with her knuckles, then leaned over and smelled the fresh-planed pine.

"Yes, it's just right," she decided. "You boys may be slow, but you do good work. And just in the nick of time, too," she said. "You go on with Christmas. I'll think I'll just rest right here."

Merriweather brought a large basket filled with gray tape potholders, which she passed out to everyone. Then she presented the Carolina sisters with luxurious floor-length boas, made from feathers she had found on the beach. For Annie, she had made an intricate cape that echoed the black-and-white speckled neck feathers of the loon by skillfully weaving white seagull feathers that contrasted the blue-black feathers of the great blue heron. When Annie put it on, she looked as if she could fly.

"This is exquisite!" marveled Christine, caressing the cape. "Truly a work of art. In Paris, something like this would steal the show at a runway collection."

"It looks like something God would create if he had invented gray tape and found a little spare time and feathers," Owl's daughter commented.

Merriweather beamed.

North insisted on staying in her coffin, with the boa wrapped around her neck. Her family lifted the casket by the four handles and trundled her down to the cabin.

Gift-giving over, the women went to the kitchen, and the men migrated outside. Moby broke out a box of Havana cigars and offered them around. Soon the bluish smoke encircled the porch as they puffed away, their fingers delicately curled around the waist of one of the last vestiges of manhood in the twenty-first century. Even men who didn't smoke were willing to pucker up and coax the foul smoke that curled out of the butt end like a smoking gun.

"Yes, there is something about a cigar," Moby said.

The next morning, after Moby spread the leaves out for Merriweather, she held her rake in a Statue of Liberty pose, teeth into the wind, and predicted, "The weather is going to change to mild and warmer, with showers off and on for the next four days."

That afternoon, it began to rain, signaling the big thaw.

Moby and Owl dropped John in Port Gamble. At the same time, Travis and his son were leading two draft horses up the ramp of an old amphibious troop carrier called *The Rubber Ducky*, which operated in the summer as a land-and-lake tour boat in Seattle and did whatever work it could get in the winter. The carrier was stacked with bales of hay, bags of grain, two large Stihl chainsaws, and a boatload of miscellaneous hand tools.

Moby hailed Travis from the dock. When he went over to shake Travis' hand, he smiled to see a new bandage on the thumb. Moby offered his hand to Travis' skinny nine-year-old son.

"Moby's the name; piracy's the game."

"My name is Tate, Mr. Moby," the boy answered, businesslike. His face was a field of freckles capped off by a bowl-cut mass of brown hair. "Are you really a pirate?"

"I've been called a pirate, and worse, son, but to a working man like yourself, I'm just old Moby." He ruffled the boy's hair.

The horses' hooves made hollow, thud-like noises as the animals nervously stomped their feet on the deck. The sound reverberated against the the aluminum hull.

The ramp closed. Tate clawed his way up the side of the craft and poked his nose over the side for another look at his first pirate.

In the days that followed, North continued to get worse, refusing to leave the casket. The long years of hard living had taken their toll, and her systems were shutting down one by one. The heart began to fail, the kidneys went next. Fluid was building in her lungs, and her breathing became so irregular and sporadic that sometimes the family started sympathetic panting themselves. Annie gave her a shot of morphine. After that, she seemed less agitated but still on the edge of a coma.

"I'm afraid she can't last much longer, but she's a tough old bird," Annie said in private to the family, after staring down into the casket at the frail woman whose hands clutched the feather boa. The cabin itself seemed to shudder with the forced, shallow breaths that filled the otherwise silent room.

The family stood vigil.

Annie had watched death many times and was not completely surprised when North began to rally and her breathing became stronger and more regular. North yawned and sat up, as if awakening from a long sleep. She demanded a good, strong cup of coffee.

"I'm working my butt off here," she said, and then calmly plotted her burial arrangements. "Hell, I can't leave till the bell comes from home and is ringing in the steeple." Her daughter soothed her by explaining that the bell had left South Carolina.

"But the steeple is nowhere near ready," South said. "It will be months before they can install the bell."

"That's right," North snapped, "and what you're saying is I'm not going to make it. Don't worry, I've got it all figured out. I want to be frozen till the bell is installed; I don't want none of that cremation crap, and I won't be molested by strangers, all my fluids sucked out of me, squirted with antifreeze, and covered with grease like I was some old battlewagon in a Quick-E-Lube. If I wanted that treatment, I wouldn't have gone to the trouble of this casket.

"I want to be buried in the old cemetery, with my soccer ball—the one I got from my girls last year at the Possum Reunion. I want to be dressed in my flowered spring dress—you know, the green one with the daisies—'cause I expect it will be spring by the time the church is done. I want to wear my straw hat with the fake roses, my push-up velour bra—the purple one—and I have become rather partial to this boa. It makes a statement.

"Do you think you can handle all that?"

South could only nod yes. She was afraid she would break down if she tried to speak. The children stood grimly at the head of the casket.

"Come around where I can see you," North demanded, and they shuffled down the side of the casket near her feet.

"I'm leaving you children in good hands. See that you take care of South too. I've been foolish, but I did the best I could. You children were my best work.

"Now give the old mom a kiss. I need to get back to business here."

The adrenaline rush ended as quickly as it had come. The instructions completed, North lay back down, passing away silently during the night—without pain, with her family crowded around.

Ahab crowed as North's last breath escaped her lips. The tide was at ebb.

The next day, North's last request began to be honored in a most unusual way.

Checking to make sure the wharf was clear of prying eyes, Moby and Owl pulled North's casket out of the boat and onto a dock cart. They covered it with a gray canvas tarp and carried it down the dock, the wheels of the cart thumpety-thumping over the wood-planked pier. They reached Owl's pickup truck and hoisted the casket carefully into the bed, latching the tailgate with steel S hooks.

The pair drove cautiously over the back roads into Tacoma. Moby had a buddy there who ran a processing and freezer plant that packaged and froze everything from sturgeon to corn.

It was pitch-dark when they turned onto the gridded roads of the industrial park. They had rattled over half a dozen train tracks when they heard a siren behind them. In the rearview mirror, Moby could see a police car, lights flashing.

"Oh, shit," Moby said. "The cops."

# Chapter TEN

oby sat quietly, while the officer adjusted his hat, put on his coat, and finally ambled alongside the truck. Moby cranked down the window.

"Where you gentlemen headed?" the policeman asked, standing back and surveying the side of the truck.

"Just heading down to the processing plant, officer. A buddy of mine is the manager down there—Jim Reuf."

"Jim Reuf…" The policeman searched his memory bank. "Yeah, I talked to him a month ago about a problem with one of his truckers." His eyes traveled to the truck bed. "What's in the back here?"

He lifted up a corner of the tarp and spotted the wooden box.

"Rotting fish," Moby answered quickly. "We had a retirement party, and Jim sent over some king salmon that had already headed south. Don't get too close, or you'll get a whiff that will knock you to your knees. That stuff really stinks—can't get the smell of it out of your clothes, except maybe with lemon juice, and sometimes even that doesn't work. Why, I remember one time, working in the woods, a skunk got under the tool shed and—"

"Yeah, skunk squirt is the pits," cut in the officer. He had dealt with old folks like this before. Once they got started, they never shut up. He dropped the tarp and turned back to Moby.

"I stopped you because your left-hand turn signal isn't working. If you promise to get it fixed right away, I won't give you a ticket."

"Why sure, officer. Can't just take it down to the gas station, though. All they have is some pimply kid behind a cash register. Now, when I was a boy gas stations were 'full service.'" Moby shook his head regretfully. "It's all money today, the big oil companies are in cahoots with—"

"So, you'll you take care of it?" asked the officer as he backed away.

"Count on it, officer." Moby squinted with his one good eye. "You have a good night."

The patrolman escaped into his prowler. Moby and Owl grinned, looking straight ahead until the cruiser had moved on.

"Whew, that was close," said Owl. "Let's get the hell out of Dodge."

They pulled into the plant just as the afternoon shift started streaming out the front entrance. After asking a lunchbox-toting hard-hat for directions, they found the front office. Jim Reuf sat behind a glass cage, talking on the phone. He waved them past the secretary, hung up the phone, and greeted them in the hallway.

"Hi, Moby," he said, shaking hands. "This must be Owl. And... your friend?

"In the truck, resting comfortably under a tarp."

"I met Moby, gosh, must be twenty years ago," said Jim to Owl by way of explanation. "He built my deck, and it's still holding up great. So, Moby," Jim clapped a hand on the older man's shoulder, "I don't suppose you would be in the market for building a ski lodge up on Snoqualmie Pass this summer?"

Moby smiled faintly.

"I'm afraid I'll be taking the summers off from now on."

"Well, you had a long run. You deserve a rest. Anyway, the night shift will be processing black cod in another part of the plant, so we have the place to ourselves."

Owl backed the truck against the loading dock. The three men unloaded the casket and set it on a cart ordinarily used to wheel strawberries, raspberries, carrots, and peas into the freezing chambers. Reuf shrouded the cargo with the tarp, and they shuttled it through the warehouse, the floors still glistening wet from the sanitary hosing of the day crew.

They continued wheeling the cart down the fifty-yard corridor, their voices echoing off the aluminum walls. Taking a sharp left, they arrived at a large, barn-like door on tracks. Jim slid the door back to reveal another warehouse, as long and wide as a football field. The large room was empty, except for a forklift and a white-enameled machine the size of a single-car garage.

The machine was surrounded by conveyor belts leading into a cavernous mouth. Other conveyors waited in attendance at an equally intimidating orifice gaping from the back end. Sprawling pipes descended from the ceiling, feeding nitrogen gas into what looked to be a monster with a voracious appetite.

"There she is," Reuf said. "The Freeze Queen 5000."

The men wheeled their cargo up to the machine. Removing the tarp, Moby opened the casket and sorted through the keepsakes the family had placed next to North. Reverently, they removed her soccer ball and a Bible, a roll of gray tape and a can of WD-40—Merri-weather's parting gifts—pictures of the family, a coffee cup emblazoned with a smiling grandchild, and fifty dollars of traveling money in a metallic, beaded purse that North had won in a dance contest at a nightclub, the Spanish Castle in Seattle, just after the war.

The men placed her gently on the rubber conveyor belt, rearranged her dress (as instructed by Annie), and wrapped the boa over her chest.

The women had made her up, so she had a slight, rosy glow, and they had sprinkled Chanel No. 5 liberally—just in case.

Moby nodded to Jim, who stood in front of a circuit board. He fired up the machine, switching on the conveyor belt. It lurched forward, moving North closer to the poor man's cryogenic lab.

The room filled with the grinding sounds of industry.

"She will be dipped into a pool of liquid nitrogen of minus 300 degrees and then into a blast freezer for fifteen seconds," yelled Jim above the roar. "That will freeze her about three inches deep. Then she'll come out the other end of the machine, and we'll put her in cold storage to finish the process."

"You think that'll do it?" asked Moby.

"Sure. We did the same procedure on a seven-hundred-pound blue tuna three weeks ago that we shipped off to Japan."

North disappeared into the machine, while Moby and Owl wheeled the casket down to the other end of the freezer.

"Mr. Reuf! Mr. Reuf!"

Jim whipped around to face his secretary, who had somehow tracked him down.

"…glad…found you!"

Although the woman valiantly shouted her message, Jim still caught only every few words.

"…important call…truck overturned… sixty thousand pounds of shrimp…had to close the freeway…"

Jim took a wild stab and punched the panic button, bringing the machinery to a grinding halt. Moby and Al quickly closed ranks to obscure North's feet, which were just beginning to exit the canvas curtain.

"Uh…well…I…" Jim stuttered and stalled. "Tell them I'll get back to them in five minutes." He held up his right hand, all five fingers splayed, to make sure the woman understood.

The secretary nodded and quickly left the noisy warehouse, leaving the three men to exchange looks of nervous relief.

Jim started the machine again. North inched out in a frosty cloud and lay board-stiff on the conveyor belt. The woman who hated the cold and considered hell to be her idea of a vacation paradise would spend the next few months in an icy purgatory in Jim Reuf's private storage, under a tarp, waiting for spring and her sister's promise that she would hear the chapel bell of her childhood one more time.

When they returned to the island, Owl and Moby found that Travis and Tate had gone straight to work. They had already cleared a trail to the top of the island's ridge, and with a massive six-foot blade on his chain saw, Travis had cut into the ancient seven-hundred-year-old cedar. Huge, round slices tilted sideways, like a roll of shiny quarters. The matched set of Percherons, their feathered hooves caked with mud, pulled a handmade sled, filled with the wood coins, down next to the boat shed. There, with a single blow of his maul, Travis split them into manageable, pie-shaped wedges, two feet thick.

Then the woodsman grabbed a large wooden mallet, and in a perfect, measured cadence, proceeded to split off shingles with a sharp-edged froe. The shingles popped from the cants spring-loaded, as if awakened from a long slumber, having waited for release to another dimension.

The wooden sled was stacked tall with fragrant cedar shingles, and the giant horses strained at the harness, pulling the sled down the shore toward the church.

As the horses hauled their freight, Tate rode on their backs, jumping back and forth between them, his spindly frame little more than a flea's weight to the locomotive Percherons. It was not his size but agility and balance that allowed him to play this dangerous game. One false lunge and Tate would fall under the churning feathered hooves or be run over by the runners that sliced deep furrows in the moist earth. Yet, this game was a necessary step in the dance to manhood.

"That Travis is one hard-working son of a b," Moby told Owl, as they watched the interplay between man and horse.

At the end of the day, Travis and Tate curried and fed their horses. Then, in the darkness, they made their way to Annie's for dinner. Afterwards, they sat and swapped stories, first at one campfire, then another. Before retiring, they checked the horses one more time, then bunked in the cabin next to John.

A similar sequence was repeated for six days, till enough cedar for the church had been hauled down the ridge, where it lay in a single, aromatic pyramid of wooden shakes on a bed of cold, soggy grass, ready for the roof.

When his dad could spare him, Tate would spend time with Moby. The old pirate took the youngster to town in the boat, showed him how to wrap a hot rock in a towel to warm up his bed, and challenged Tate to spitting contests. Moby even allowed the boy to pop in his glass eye, after he had put a little Vaseline around the edges.

Travis, however, never eased up on his work. After he rebuilt the scaffolding, he pitched the bundles of cedar shakes onto the platform in loose stacks. Tate clambered up the scaffold and handed his father one shingle after the other. They worked across the roof, neatly nailing each shingle with galvanized nails an inch in from the sides, snug but not buried.

Merriweather declared roofing to be her field of expertise. She established a bunker, complete with a lawn chair and umbrella, just below the roof. Pointing with a walking stick, she orchestrated the process. Helping along with an occasional "Not there, young man" and the every-so-often "That looks good," she guided each shingle into place so the edges were perfectly staggered on the entire roof. It was a guarantee the roof would last well into the next generation.

Owl, Moby, and John made piles of rocks on the frame sled. Travis would hitch the horses and drag the rounded, granite boulders up the beach, staging them next to the church, where the inevitable rain would wash off the salt. Though the islanders had the will, building the steeple seemed daunting. North had been adamant that the steeple be built of rock, even though there was no record of a hurricane ever passing through the Pacific Northwest.

The island architects were not willing to compromise her dream. After all, promises had been made.

The days leading up to New Year's Day brought a somber mood to the island. Turning the corner of a new year would be especially difficult for John and South, knowing they would move forward without Betsy and North. The winter gloom vanished, however, when the day before New Year's *The Pissant* hove into view and dropped anchor next to the beach. With great ceremony, Pinky opened the cargo hold. Dorie guided the boom that lifted a wooden round barrel with an odd smokestack protruding out of the top onto the beach.

Moby leaned on his crutch and called out, "What the hell is that?"

"That, my good fellow," answered Pinky, as he stepped into a rope loop hooked to the boom and Dorie lowered him like Peter Pan onto the beach, "is a hot tub."

Opening a door to a firebox on the outside of the tub, he explained how the fire was built in the stove, which was submerged in the tub, which in turn heated the water.

"No electricity needed."

They hooked the tub to the draft horses and parked it between two stumps. Owl ran hundreds of feet of hose—which Pinky had thoughtfully brought along—to the spring. John built a fire in the stove. Moby primed the hose by sucking on the end to create a vacuum. He drew in air until dizzy and was finally rewarded with a slow trickle of water.

Two hours later, the tub had been filled, smoke poured out of the stack, and the water turned warm, then hot. The women insisted on a gender split for soaking hours and a schedule was drawn up. (Days later, after the men had left scattered wine bottles and cigar butts everywhere, strict clean-up rules were added.)

Near midnight, all rallied at Annie's, sampling Owl's smoked oysters and breaking into John's wine collection. Well over five hundred years of collective memory unknowingly slipped into a new year.

Eventually, each one wandered back to his or her cabin and Pinky and Doris to their boat. Not done with celebrating, Pinky wedged himself up in the crow's nest on *The Pissant* and limbered up his second favorite wind instrument, the bagpipes. The music haunted the night, as the fog slowly crept in to cover the island. A palpable apprehension seized the island, and still Pinky played on, exhorting them to remember the past and step up to the future. The strains of songs—"Amazing Grace," "Danny Boy," John Lennon's "Imagine," Elvis Presley's "I Can't Help Falling in Love with You," and Led Zeppelin's "Stairway to Heaven"—clung to the molecular fog, filtering through the cracks and crevices of their drafty shelters and creeping into the fortresses of their minds, as they lay in their beds, eyes wide open, searching the darkness, struggling for answers.

New Year's Day brought a potpourri of activity on the island. Annie, Dorie, and Pinky started the day with breakfast on *The Pissant*. Merriweather raked leaves, and South gathered firewood, chain-smoking and swearing. Travis and Tate turned the horses loose in the orchard. Moby and Owl dug clams, which John steamed right on the beach. Throughout the day, the island residents popped in and out of the hot tub.

When South deposited a load of wood next to the firebox on the hot tub, she complained, "God-damned firewood. It's all wet." She lit a cigarette with the still-burning butt end of another.

"South," Owl sung out from the hot tub, "you don't smoke."

"Mind your own frigging business, you slimy wart hog," South fired back, as she disappeared into her cabin.

"Did you notice," Owl asked Moby, "that South has begun to take on some of her sister's personality? You know, one day she is the old South, and the next day she becomes the old North—swearing, drinking, and smoking up a storm."

"Well that *is* her name: 'South Carolina Storm,'" observed Moby.

"Yeah, but she's not just a storm; she's turning into a full-blown hurricane."

Late in the morning Annie had just taken out a batch of chocolate chip oatmeal cookies when she heard a rap on the door. Without turning, she called out, "Come in, there's no lock on the door. Never was, never will be."

Moby pushed open the door and called to his dog lingering on the porch.

"C'mon, Trooper, it's all right. She won't hurt you."

The dog trotted in with authority, ears flailing. He nosed Buddy, who lay half-buried under the stove and couldn't be bothered to muster up a proper greeting. The newly renamed Tripod did not take offense. He slumped down, stuck his head under the stove, eyeballed his comrade, snorted a greeting, and conked out himself.

Annie continued mixing her cookie dough batter, by habit sifting the pre-sifted flour. She enjoyed watching the white powder float down into the bowl, forming a hollow-centered volcanic mountain, mimicking the eruptive blasts that had gutted the major peaks of the Cascades.

"A lost art, sifting," she said. "Very satisfying."

She turned the handle of the sifter slowly, watching the curved wire beater whisk against the round screen.

Annie twirled the wooden spoon over her head baton-like, deftly dolloping the dough into neatly spaced mounds on the cookie sheet. With a single fluid motion, she pulled down the oven door with her foot, whisked the sheet inside, closed the door, and wiped her hands on her apron. In the corner of her eye, she caught a furtive movement. With the vengeance of a samurai, she delivered a karate-chop to Moby's wrist. He backed away quickly—but not without a fistful of dough.

Annie grabbed her spoon and took an extra swipe at Moby for good measure, as the perpetrator retreated further from the stove. He flashed a crooked victory smile, then settled in at the table.

Annie poured two mugs of coffee. The two friends sat silently at the table, munching on the warm cookies. Moby pried out a single chocolate morsel.

"Simple pleasures are wasted on the young."

A long silence followed before Moby spoke again.

"Annie, remember I told you about my…um…retro film festival every year?"

Annie gave him a knowing smile.

"Who could forget a story like that?"

"Well, it's happening next week, and I was thinking… Would you like to accompany Owl and me?" Seeing Annie's raised eyebrows, he hastened to add, "All expenses paid, naturally." He winked with his good eye. "Oklahoma in the middle of winter—sound like a winner?"

Annie sat with a cookie poised on the edge of her teeth. She couldn't deny a certain exhilaration at the prospect of attending a porno film festival with the guest of honor.

Moby rattled off the particulars.

"We would fly out late Thursday or early Friday morning and come back Sunday night. Limo to and from the airport, deluxe digs, and me reliving the height, shall we say, of my career?"

"Works for me," Annie grinned, sampling another cookie.

After lunch, Annie set out for a walk. She found Merriweather in the orchard, raking her silk leaves into piles. Annie helped her fill the six threadbare burlap sacks and stack them into the wheelbarrow. Then she pushed the silken cargo toward the boathouse, but soon she set the wheelbarrow down, flexed her fingers, and grunted. She turned to Merriweather.

"Don't you ever get tired of raking leaves?"

"Oh no, I enjoy being out in the weather. Before, people would stop me in the street to complain about a drought or a snowstorm, like I was responsible, you know, since I was the weather person and all. But I loved it all. Still do.

"Here, let me take a turn on the wheelbarrow," she said, giving Annie a gentle shove to the side. "It's so very nice of Moby and Owl to sprinkle the leaves out for me each morning. It has certainly saved my back."

Annie gasped in astonishment.

"You mean, you know Moby and Owl are doing that?"

"Some days I do, and some days I don't. But don't ever tell them. It's really very sweet. Should we gather a few oysters to smoke over the fire? I could use an appetizer."

The two women grabbed a bucket near the boathouse, and Annie showed Merriweather how to select the single shells and stay away from the clusters.

"The clusters are too hard to cook, and it's more difficult to clean the sand off."

Annie dumped the pail of oysters into the shallows of the incoming tide, swishing the shells clean, and piling them back in the bucket. Both women grabbed the handle and straggled up the beach. They loaded the mass onto a grill over the outside fire pit. Annie rekindled the fire while Merriweather disappeared into the kitchen of the main house, returning with a small frying pan, half a pound of butter, and freshly minced garlic. She melted the mixture on the side of the grill. Soon the cooking oysters began opening their shells, exposing the meat. With a fork, Merriweather deftly pried each oyster from its jaws, dunked it in the butter-garlic mixture, and popped it into her mouth. Annie followed suit.

Attracted by the smell of garlic, Moby and Owl wandered over, their own forks in hand. They all sat around the fire, each posted on a tree stump, feasting on oysters. Moby broke out a cheap white wine, along with paper cups. But Merriweather insisted that no wine would pass their lips till she found her crystal wine glasses. Scurrying to her cabin, she emerged triumphant, handing a glittering goblet to each.

Owl drained his glass and poured another round for everyone.

"I wonder what the poor people are doing today."

Travis and Tate were rowing furiously, returning from emptying the crab pots they had set on the outgoing tide. The catch was their contribution to the potluck Annie was having in their honor tonight. The dark red Dungeness crabs scuttled across the oak ribs of the boat, hid under the anchor rope, and assumed a defensive posture. They stretched their claws as wide as possible and blew bubbles from their mouths. Their tiny eyes were defiant, even in defeat.

Father and son beached their boat. The wave of fog caught up with them and obscured the beach, less than a boat length away. Tate collected the combative crabs into a sack. He slung the sack over his shoulder and raced after his father, whose footprints had already filled with water and small crabs brought in by the rising tide.

After dinner, they adjourned to the drawing room. There, they lingered over coffee, John's mile-high lemon pie, the warmth of the fireplace, the faint glow of the candles, and the comfort of being with each other. Travis looked at each island inhabitant in turn.

"It's been a pleasure working on the island. Thank you for your hospitality." He lightly punched his son's shoulder. "Tate and I are lucky to have met you all. And we plan on coming back and helping to finish that steeple."

He turned to his boy, his voice taking on a softer tone.

"Let's go, son. We've still got stuff to pack. Even sixth graders have to show up at school on time."

"Aw, Dad."

As everyone stood up and shuffled out, Moby ruffled Tate's hair and gave him a noogie.

"Have a good trip home, Tate, and come back soon to visit an old pirate."

"Yes, sir."

Tate smiled up at Moby, remembering his first reaction to the burly pirate had been fear.

"Arg," he growled and then let out a world-class belch.

"You have learned well, my son," Moby said, cuffing the boy on the back of his neck.

Travis thought he would have to civilize the boy when they got home, but he also knew that Tate had spent the vacation in the company of men. It was a time that neither of them would ever forget.

Owl, Annie, and Moby set off for Oklahoma. South and John had elected to skip the Moby film festival, though there were repeated requests for corroboration—via actual photographic evidence—of "the Moby unit," as South called it.

After a short layover in the Oklahoma City airport, the three boarded a small, eight-passenger "puddle jumper." As the commuter Cessna landed, Annie looked out the bug-spattered window over the prop and surveyed the airport in the middle of a sagebrush and tumbleweed valley, wedged between two low, rocky buttes. The control tower was a geodesic dome painted camouflage-frog green, with a shredded windsock made of a pair of queen-size pantyhose. A rusty nail anchored a corroded metal sign.

"Welcome to Bedrock Airport."

In black felt-tip pen was written Yabba Dabba Doo.

# Chapter ELEVEN

Annie shivered as she sucked in the minus-ten-degree temperature. Near the dome, dozens of women, most light-years away from the power of the Wonder Bra, stood holding signs: "W-e-l-c-o-m-e J-o-h-n-n-y J-o-h-n-s-o-n"; "Johnny Johnson, Homo Erectus"; "The sun never sets on Johnny's Johnson."

Grinning ear-to-ear as he stepped from the plane, Moby was immediately engulfed in women. When he emerged from the crowd minutes later, he looked as if he had encountered the mother of all rashes, thanks to lipstick smears from ear to ear. Annie and Owl had been brushed aside like so much litter by a crush that now followed Moby to a waiting convertible.

He pushed through the crowd and beckoned his fellow islanders to hop in. With a screech of rubber, the car was soon bouncing over a liberally pot-holed road to town, leaving a trail of red dust to coat the fans.

Moby tried in vain to clean himself off with a handkerchief Annie handed him.

"As you can see, it's totally bananas here," he laughed, "and every year it gets worse."

"I had no idea you were *the* 'Johnny Johnson' of tee shirt and bumper-sticker fame," said Owl. "How come you never told me I was hanging with royalty, so to speak?"

"It's not like I get residuals, you know," said Moby. "This craziness only lasts for three days, and then it's back to normal."

Five minutes later, as they neared the outskirts of town, they found themselves in the center of an impromptu motorcade. Several cars flanked the flame-red fifties Cadillac convertible limo, with women hanging out car windows, sometimes flinging bras that occasionally stuck to the windshield and antennae. One topless woman swayed provocatively through the moon roof of a baby blue Volkswagen bug.

Moby's driver cursed as he swerved to avoid an electric-turquoise Barely Bra that tried to ring around the hood ornament.

"Jesus, these women are out of their gourds," said Owl, in awe. "You can tell by their nipples it's cold out there."

"It's just a festival to get rid of the post-holidays blues," said Moby. "Think of me as a sacrifice to the gods of winter."

The Cadillac careened around a corner and drove under a sign straddled between two telephone poles: "Seventeenth Anniversary/ Moby Dick Review and Festival/Bedrock Springs." The festival was the single most important fundraiser in the town and essential to its survival. The one-horse town sported three taverns, two cafés, a church, one gas station, a water tower, and a dilapidated theatre. The theatre stood, still proud, with Hepburn cheekbones and a renovated marquee proclaiming in neon: "Johnny Johnson Film Festival. January 15 to 18. His greatest films. On stage, in person."

The car came to rest in front of an extraordinarily long, aluminum, riveted, torpedo-shaped Airstream. Bored, wind-whipped cows looked on, huddled next to barbed wire and teetering mailboxes. Moby opened the car door and tested the frozen earth with his titanium "Hollywood" leg, stood up, and waved to the trailing entourage now bailing out of their cars.

He hustled into the trailer, with Annie and Owl following, just ahead of the crowd. Two blond, crew-cut bouncer types attempted to hold back the women, with predictable results. The women simply slipped under their muscled arms and pounded on the side of the trailer until Moby stepped outside and invited what Owl guessed were thirty or more fever-pitched women into the warmth of the trailer. The rest had to wait outside the door.

There was an awkward truce, as the sweating mob, having cornered their quarry, now seemed at a loss as to their next move. Moby met the challenge with charm and humility, shaking hands with several of his "guests," even claiming to remember the president of his fan club—a short, stocky woman with Buddy Holly glasses and a perfect figure (according to Owl) of 55-55-55.

Before leaving, Buddy Holly managed to launch herself at Moby and lay a lip-lock on him. Then she ran out the door, taking the rest of the herd with her.

"You certainly have a devoted fan base," observed Annie as she snapped open a can of beer and handed it to Moby to assuage his bruised lip.

When next morning dawned, the town was already abuzz, with horns honking and cars scrambling to park in a field usually reserved for critters. Booths sprang up along a makeshift avenue, touting a wide variety of necessary "aids": anatomically correct, inflatable Johnny dolls, adult charm bracelets, Johnny spoons, Johnny blankets, industrial-looking hand tools, condoms, oils by the ounce or barrel, and long, phallic pillows embroidered with the Johnny Johnson autograph to snuggle next to at night. People ready to buy almost anything collectable or sexual formed army-ant lines in front of supply trailers.

"My God, where did all these people come from?" asked Owl as they slipped out the back way and into the limousine for the trip down main street to the theater.

Moby, resplendent in his long-tailed tux, explained, "They come from all over the world. I'm still big—pardon the pun—in Japan and South America. A lot of them fly in and some of them drive RVs." He pointed to a flock of motor homes clustered together at the far end of the field. "Some people in town rent out rooms for the weekend. The rest of the partiers stay in nearby towns that have more accommodations."

Just then, a tour bus filled with ogling women roared past, covering the limo with a fine grade of Oklahoma dust. A poster flapped from its rear bumper: "Johnny Johnson or Bust."

The trio climbed the back steps to the theater and entered through a creaky door into the Green Room. It sported a threadbare carpet, buckets of Lone Star beer, and a small platter of mystery cold cuts and cheeses. Three men and a woman representing the town council presided over the offerings.

Moby strode across the room, his limp almost imperceptible, and schmoozed with the dignitaries. Meantime, Owl and Annie were escorted to front-row seats, where they waited for Moby to appear. Like teenagers at a Saturday matinee, the almost-all-female crowd stomped their feet in anticipation. Six guards posted themselves beneath the stage.

"John...ny! John...ny! John...ny!" they chanted, vibrating the old wooden walls. Crimson velvet curtains parted at last to reveal their idol, standing alone on stage. Annie had to admit, he did look handsome. The balcony erupted. A shower of underwear, shoes, mash letters, keys, and money landed at his feet. Women whose last libido-driven shrieks had faded away decades ago spoke in one reflective roar, honoring the black-and-white celluloid memory of another era. Moby reached for the microphone, and the crowd fell silent.

"I'd like to welcome you to the Seventeenth Annual Johnny Johnson Days here at Bedrock Springs. We come here every year not to honor me, but to remember a time when we were all young."

Cheers and hoots filled the theater for a good half-minute till Moby raised his hands for quiet. To Annie's surprise, Moby motioned for the crowd to join in singing. They followed the bouncing ball on screen.

Those were the days, my friend.
We thought they'd never end.

We'd sing and dance forever and a day.

We fought the fights we choose.

We'd fight and never lose.

Those were the days, oh, yes, those were the days.

The audience responded with lusty enthusiasm, swaying from side to side like believers at a Pentecostal revival. As the end of the song echoed through the rafters, Moby smiled down on all, then went on to explain that he would introduce each film with a short background piece. The marathon movie event would end with the blowout banquet Saturday night.

The first movie, *Ride the WAVES*, Moby explained, was made in a time before plastic surgery, implants, and special effects—a time of innocence.

The movie began with a brawl between marines and sub-mariners in a seedy waterfront Shanghai bar. A battered Moby is transported to the navy hospital where, although swathed from head-to-toe in bandages, he manages to rise to the occasion and bed every nurse on the floor. The head nurse, engaged to the base commander, comes in to upbraid him, but is so smitten with his manhood, she too succumbs, and the two fall into everlasting lust. The nurse and Johnny ride off into the sunset past the sentry gate on his chopper as the commander watches balefully through a window of his stark, government-issue office. The commander vows revenge, and a series of chase scenes on motorbikes and more brawls between the two services round out the vignette.

The house lights came on, and Moby stepped forward to introduce the next film.

*Periscopes Up!* featured Moby, a brave naval officer on holiday, soaking up the sun poolside, surrounded by bathing beauties. He is unexpectedly attacked by jealous marines, who throw him in the water, where he strips and flaunts his periscope seemingly the width of the pool, enticing one of the women at the edge of the pool to peel off her suit and disappear with Moby into the deep end, leaving only her head above water as she gasps and squeals in ecstasy. There follows the obligatory skirmishes between the marines and the navy, the marines and the townspeople, and the marines and street punks until the marines stagger back their ship and cruise off into the sunset, sated, but no wiser.

Again, the lights illuminated the dim theater, and Annie and Owl looked at each other in amazement. The movies, completely politically incorrect and laughable, were classic camp. Their innocence seemed almost comforting in the present age of cynicism and brutality.

"Who knew?" asked Owl.

Annie could only shake her head and smile. Moby finished his remarks about the next celluloid masterpiece and the lights faded to black.

Annie drifted off in the darkness, thinking of parallel lives. While Moby was cavorting on the back lots of Hollywood, Annie was hop-scotching the world battling for lives.

She no longer focused on the black-and-white grainy film in front of her as her own mental movie fast-forwarded. She saw herself coordinating airlifts into Bosnia, straining to hear the drone of planes bringing food and clothes to refugees in Somalia. Desert Storm, Biafra, Bangladesh, Zimbabwe, Peru. Floods, civil wars, HIV, cyclones, hurricanes. . .

The third movie ended to a standing ovation as the star stepped back onto the stage.

Annie blinked. How could her life have slipped by so quickly?

Moby declared an intermission for lunch and limped back to the Green Room, where Owl and Annie found him prying off the artificial leg, dropping it to the floor with a thick thud, and massaging his stump.

Owl picked up a rolled ham slice and popped it into his mouth.

"It certainly seems like the great private parts distributor in the sky does not create all men equal."

Moby looked up and smiled.

"We all have our burdens, grasshopper."

The festival continued that evening even as a Canadian arctic chill jumped the fence at the border, stampeded down the Rockies, and took the first left at the Texas panhandle, sending cattle and school children scuttling for shelter.

The next morning, frozen revelers took in their final two films, then cheered as Moby received the key to the city under the blinking lights of the old theater marquee. Annie, armed with reproduction posters of Moby's film epics, rescued him from the crowds.

"Let's go home, Mr. Johnson. Your chariot awaits."

Moby said a brief goodbye to the city fathers in the Green Room and collected his check. He beckoned to Owl, and the two men sauntered down the theater corridor like drunken sailors coming in last in a 4th of July three-legged race. Laughing, they collapsed in a heap in the back seat of the limousine.

Before they knew it, the three were exiting a taxi at the boat dock, drinking in the panoramic mountain view, inhaling the brisk salt air as they sped across the sound in *The Ark*, and counting to themselves, the seven rocks of home.

A warm spell settled into the late January weather pattern on the island. Bumblebees crawled out from under the tree bark—defying the laws of physics, they ambled through the air, desperately seeking the stillborn blossoms. Frogs began croaking and legions of ladybugs strutted along windowsills, basking in the warm rays that barely broke over the horizon.

John woke up inspired. With the unseasonably warm weather continuing, he plotted a formal luncheon for the women, seconded by Owl and groused at by Moby when they elected him to set the crab traps. He was still basking in the glow of his film fame.

"Crab cocktails—no, crab cakes, with a huckleberry-cranberry sauce, oyster shooters, a clam bisque, with popovers. You guys handle dessert—something chocolate. Check out my cookbooks. Two wines, a white, and a raspberry dessert wine with the chocolate finale.

"Moby, you'll be the maitre d', then the waiter. Can you wear the tux? And Owl can be the runner. I'll cook the main meal."

Moby nodded. Pivoting on his crutch, he went into his cabin to rob Trooper's canned dog food collection to use as crab bait. He carefully punctured the can with a knife and set off for the boat shed.

Under John's tutelage, Owl concentrated on penning the official invitations, requiring formal attire and an RSVP. He delivered the invitations with Trooper's help.

Moby and Owl, usually content to eat out of a can, began to indulge in an elaborate plan for dessert. They went into Port Gamble for provisions, buying a baker's brick of Swiss chocolate, orange extract, canned cherries, baker's flour, spices, and a quart of heavy cream. They weren't quite clear how they would pull it off, but the plan was to surprise every one with a to-die-for dessert.

Early on the morning of the luncheon, Owl met Moby in Annie's kitchen and they got down to work. Owl chopped the chocolate and Moby measured the ingredients.

"Follow the recipe exactly," Owl kept saying.

"I've never been a detail person," Moby sniffed defiantly, stopping to carefully stoke the fire, keeping an even heat. The cake cooked, and the cherry topping bubbled, and when the last bit of chocolate syrup was drizzled over the cherries, Moby held his breath at the wonder of it.

"Chocolate Suicide Cake with Brandied Cherry Topping. It's a killer."

The stylish, late-afternoon luncheon was served out on the tide flats. A long, wooden table had been laid with white linen tablecloth, a soft breeze barely flapping the overlapping tails. Matching napkins, Annie's Spode china, Merriweather's goblets, and a hodgepodge of antique silverware completed the ensemble. The women arrived dressed in long skirts, shawls, and feathered hats. The delicious food, staged out of

John's cabin, was carefully nested in layers of cloths, holding its heat as the unseasonably warm day began cooling into evening.

An obsequious waiter asked solicitously, "Would madame like this or would madame like that?" However, the waiter's attitude fell off a tad when Owl pried a cigar from Moby's clenched jaw as he, helpless to protest, held a large tureen of clam bisque.

"Don't blame me," Owl said, pointing at John.

Rows of hungry seagulls crowded close to the table, eyeballing the guests and hoping for scraps. When none came, they began a chorus of scolding, till Moby gave them his version of the "evil eye." They abated and stepped to the side, just out of kicking range, still watchful.

When time for dessert finally came, Owl and Moby presented their triumph. Moby proudly doled out ample portions, and Owl handed out the plates. John smacked his lips happily and conceded mastery.

As the islanders sipped the last of the raspberry wine, the women toasted the men, who stood lined up at attention, absorbing the praise.

"We could have waited till summer, you know," said South, slipping on a jacket as the wind piped up. A napkin fell from her lap onto the sand, where the tide had began creeping ever closer to the table.

Moby picked up the napkin and handed it to her.

"Some of us may never see another summer."

February had brought an early spring—crocus were poking through the cold earth, and the pussy willows had given way to leaf buds. Moby half-expected to see swallows buzzing the boat shed any day.

Then, without warning, a cold front from the Arctic plowed down the coast of British Columbia dumping two feet of moist snow on land from the Pacific to Cut Bank, Montana.

The Puget Sound islands rarely saw snowfall, and when they did get some, it usually measured only an inch or two and disappeared by the next day. Two feet called for celebrating. Moby coaxed South into making snow angels with him, bribing her with a stiff jag of peppermint schnapps in cocoa that Merriweather had brewed over the open fire.

"You have to admit it really does sweeten the breath."

South held out her cup for more.

"First the angel and then the second shot," insisted Moby.

South obliged by falling backward, spread-eagle in the white powder, and waving her arms up and down wildly to make wings and moving her legs back and forth to make a dress. Moby did the same. Little kids in a playground of white powder.

True to his promise, Moby reached into his pocket and took out the flask. He unscrewed the top and poured a shot into South's extended cup. They sat back and admired the heavenly figures they had etched into the snow.

Annie groused about the turn in the weather, which made a trip to Tacoma impossible. But for Moby, snow was akin to a religious experience. Its sheer power to disrupt the carefully laid plans of men proved to Moby that, while he did not believe in an afterlife, there was still a higher order in the universe.

That magical night, a roaring fire backlit the slow-circling flakes.

Moby and Merriweather sat listening to the sounds of Glen Miller on the radio. Moby accompanied Merriweather to the edge of the light. At her request, he stood, maypole-proud, on the sand dunes while Merriweather circled him with waltzes, four-steps, and swing dances. They stood clinging together for the last slow dance before disappearing into Moby's cabin.

Travis and Tate returned over the long Presidents' Day weekend to help finish the church. With the scaffolding in place, the work proceeded rapidly on the church steeple. Moby welcomed the work, glad to regain the momentum they'd had during Travis' last visit. He and Tate put rocks and buckets of mortar into a wire basket hooked to a rope pulley system that Travis pulled hand-over-hand up to the platform. Clearly they would need another technique to lift the Carolinas' bell, which weighed well over eight hundred pounds.

Travis and Tate agreed to hoist the bell up into the tower, help finish the roof, and do odd jobs that Moby just hadn't the strength for anymore, including bringing the bell over in the landing craft with the horses.

Much debate ensued over the design of the steeple roof, but Moby had the last word as the architect-in-residence. He decreed that it would be a simple, straight, steep pitch, covered with cedar shakes, topped by a traditional weather vane. Merriweather wanted a rooster on top, South wanted an angel blowing a horn, John thought a cross would make it look more like a church. Travis and Tate registered their votes for the traditional brass ball and arrow. And Annie just wanted her great-grandchildren safe at home.

Annie and Zack continued to grow stronger by the day. One more week and they would reach the Holy Grail for preemies: their original due date, the day when most early-born babies are physically ready to go home.

Annie went over to Sarah and Peter's house in West Seattle to assist in the final preparations for the babies' homecoming. Peter picked her up at the ferry. Sarah, who had spent the day at the hospital, had already returned home and greeted Annie with a hug and good news.

"Grams, do you remember that design of Peter's sewer plant that was up for an award? Well, guess what!"

"Um," stalled Annie, unwilling to aim too high, "it got honorable mention?"

"No, it won! Isn't that cool?"

Annie wrapped Peter and Sarah in a group hug.

"Well, I'm not surprised. He's very talented."

"But that's minor compared to Zach and Little Annie coming home," said Peter.

Sarah's eyes glowed with excitement.

"That's not all. There will be a big banquet and award ceremony this weekend in Spokane, and Peter has been invited as the guest of honor."

"I'd rather not go to Spokane in the winter to pick up a prize," said Peter.

"This is an important career step, honey," Sarah said. "Maybe we could both go and take my mom too. It's only a six-hour drive. We could scoot over Saturday morning and come back Sunday. Since the doctors want us to spend two nights at the hospital before the twins come home, we could do that Sunday and Monday nights, then bring the Zach and Annie home on Tuesday as planned."

"I guess that would work," Peter conceded. "We have the rest of our lives to spend with our twins."

The week prior to the twins' homecoming was a busy one, as the fledgling parents and the new grandma worked together to put the final touches on the nursery. They set up two cribs, with the proper spacing between the slats, even though they knew that for the first few months—at least until they could turn over—the babies would sleep together in one bed.

Sarah hung the mobiles and the diaper caddy and set up the monitors to hear them in every room. Calypso filled the little chiffonnier with layette items, pink and blue "onesies," socks, booties, blankets, and tiny size 0 outfits she held up in wonder. Peter had already wallpapered the twins' room with brightly colored animals entering Noah's Ark and built shelves over the changing table, which they filled with cotton balls and wipes and squeak toys.

Watching Peter work so cheerfully, Annie could not help but think what a good man he was and what a good dad he would be.

"He's a keeper," she said to Sarah with an affectionate smile.

Peter and Annie installed a God-awful, mustard-yellow carpet in the nursery at Sarah's request, who thought it extremely sensible and the right price. Peter knew the rug would become a family joke later, when the stakes weren't so high. On Annie's advice, he kept his mouth shut.

"New mothers are the fiercest animals in the jungle," Annie warned him.

On Thursday morning, Annie and Calypso took a refresher class at the hospital on CPR for preemies they had signed up for weeks before. They returned to Peter and Sarah's home to find Sarah not quite knowing what else to do.

"I can't believe they're finally coming home," Sarah kept saying, checking the room for the infant safety hazards she had studied in her new parent classes. The plugs were childproofed, the lamp cords taped to the wall. She knew the new rules: babies must be placed on their backs, not their stomachs; blankets could not have more than a half-inch of loft. A fire extinguisher by the door, a sledgehammer mounted near the window—just in case they had to battle their way through the wall in the event of a fire. So much to worry about. Sometimes Sarah thought she and Peter were all ready; the next minute, she wasn't sure.

Annie told her, "You are going to be a better mom than I ever was. You and your mother have learned the hard way what matters."

Sarah turned to her tenderly.

"That's all behind us now, Grams. Zach and Little Annie are your second chance."

On Friday, Annie headed home. Moby picked her up in *The Ark* near the ferry terminal. She'd stay on the island for the weekend while Sarah and Peter were in Spokane, then return again on Tuesday to help them bring the babies home.

As Annie and Moby stepped out of the boat and onto the sand, the wind shifted, swirling the ashes from Merriweather's fire.

"There's a brutal storm coming," Merriweather said. "Gale force winds by this evening, changing to gusts of thirty to forty knots in the straits. Small craft warnings and heavy rains. Look for six to twelve inches of snow on the mountain passes."

True to Merriweather's prediction, the north wind ratcheted to force five, smacking the clouds across the sky. The defiant sun reluctantly slunk behind the mountains, casting a distinct turquoise glow for one brief moment, and then darkness descended.

Annie was bustling about the kitchen when she heard the wind hit the house. The windows rattled and the boards creaked. The house tried to stabilize itself. A hollow sound escaped from the chimney, like a child blowing across the top of a pop bottle.

The rain pounded diagonally on the windows. Annie looked to see if Moby had gotten inside. She could see him slanted against the wind, taking shelter at Merriweather's.

Saturday brought a lull between two storms. The morning was sunny with blue skies. In honor of North, Moby took South and Merriweather to the Possum's championship soccer game in Port Townsend.

"Let's haul ass," South said, using her best North impression. Off they went, in Moby's truck, down the Chimicum Valley past Mom's Diner, through P-town, past Pickles'. At last, they nosed into a recently graveled parking lot at the Civic Field, where the disciplined pigtailed Possums were already warming up.

Moby planted a large red flag on the sidelines. His mortality, or lack thereof, was bothering him these days. He had only lately begun to give recognition to his disease, which was starting to cause a shortness of breath.

Doctors threw around technical terms such as "mesolophia," "alveoli oxygen exchange," and "fluid buildup," but they had given no prescribed time as to when the cancer would decide to take him. Cancer toyed with its victim, taking one thing away, giving it back, then attacking another part, like a chess game with the Grand Master, title never in doubt.

If they give you a year, cut it in half, was the prevailing wisdom. The bottom line was he was a one-legged man on a slippery slope.

He took a shallow breath, fumbled into his coat pocket, and extracted a cigar stub. He lit it and watched the players on the rain-soaked field.

The Possums played a fierce game in honor of their late coach, with Merriweather and South patrolling the sidelines yelling encouragement. The Sabrecats were outclassed and although they tripped, swore at, and spit on the Possums throughout the game, when the mud cleared, it was the Possums – 4, Sabrecats – 1.

When the Sabrecats refused the traditional handshakes and trash talked North at the end, the Possums lined up on the end line and mooned the 'Cats, who howled foul.

South had a Cheshire-cat grin. She knew her sister would have been proud of that obscene gesture by "her girls."

Because South liked to be off the road by dark, Moby made sure they got back to the dock at Port Gamble by early afternoon.

As Moby helped the women down from the truck, the store-owner, Mr. Wiggins, came walking slowly out of the store. A man never in a hurry, portly and friendly, Wiggins seemed more serious than usual.

"Moby, when you have a moment, I'd like a word with you," he said and walked back across the parking lot.

# Chapter TWELVE

Curious, Moby made his way onto the generous overhanging porch and opened the wooden door to the store. A bell above the transom announced his entrance. Lit to accommodate nineteenth century standards, the interior was dim, even gloomy.

Wiggins put his hands on the counter and leaned forward.

"I got a call from Sarah's neighbor. She drove Calypso, Sarah, and Peter to the airport to catch a flight to Spokane. Guess they were going to some shindig over there. Snoqualmie Pass was closed by avalanches, so they took one of those puddle-jumper planes. They got the last flight out before fog closed the airport in Seattle."

He stopped and dropped his gaze.

"Ah, shit, I hate to be the one to tell you."

Moby stared at the man in silence, fearing what he knew he would hear.

Wiggins raised misty eyes, not quite connecting with Moby's sober ones.

"The plane crashed into the mountains near a ski lift. It just exploded. There were no survivors, even though they got to the site of the crash in less than twenty minutes."

Moby froze for a moment, then shook his head vigorously from side to side.

"Shit! Goddammit to hell!"

He wished he could stomp the floor with the leg that had long since deserted him. Instead, he pounded his fist on the counter with such force that Wiggins jumped back.

"Shit, shit, shit, shit, SHIT!" he yelled. He fastened a menacing look on the poor messenger. "You sure? Maybe there's been a mistake. Maybe that wasn't their plane."

Wiggins cocked his head toward the television on the wall.

"Here's an update now, looks like," he said to Moby. He turned up the volume with his remote.

Moby looked up to see the image of a woman in a parka standing on a snow-blanketed slope, a burning wreckage in the background.

"This is Emily Sands reporting for KING News at Snoqualmie Lodge. We are looking at pictures from the KING copter, here at the Snoqualmie summit. You can see the impact area, where the last commuter plane that left from Sea-Tac this morning crashed against a rock face—fewer than three hundred feet from the top of the lift. There were no survivors.

"Witnesses heard an engine cutting in and out just before the crash. No one on the ground was injured, but this was a close call for the nearly six hundred skiers out here on one of the last ski days of the winter, marooned by the temporary pass closure."

"Ah shit," Moby exhaled. "Can I use your phone, Wig? I need to confirm this. Shit, shit, shit, shit, shit!"

Moby phoned a connection he had at the airline, gave the guy the names, waited for the airline's computers to talk to each other, then got the damning confirmation. He put the phone in the cradle and stood for a long time saying nothing.

How was he going to break the news to Annie?

"Wig, I need a drink."

Way ahead of him, the storekeeper slid the bottle of whiskey down the counter. Moby looked at the fifth.

"It's not enough," he said.

Courage would come only by the half gallon today.

A considerably sobered Merriweather, South, and Moby headed back to the island and sadly trudged up the hill to the main house.

It was Moby who broke the news to Annie.

Annie blinked once, hard, then rapidly several times. She looked deep into Moby's face for confirmation. Only then did she know it was true.

Annie let out a scream, one long, animal wail, and ran out of the house and toward the water, where she dropped to her knees. She pounded the beach with a ferocious fury, swearing, spitting, pounding holes into the sand with her fists.

Moby tried to pick her up by the shoulders, but she scratched and lashed out, a woman possessed. She lay prostrate on the ground, wailing, and clawing at the gravel. She pushed her face into the sand, as if she wanted to be swallowed by the earth. Moby could only stand by and wait. The storm broke, with heavy rain and wind pelting the beach. Moby dug a trough around Annie to channel the water away. Merriweather covered her with quilts, while South gathered wood and built a fire. Then the little group huddled together protectively, launching their umbrellas to shield their mentor.

The island inhabitants understood there was nothing they could do but silently witness Annie's primal pain.

At times, Annie would quiet. Then, without warning, she would rage again. They worried she would become dehydrated as her tears poured onto the rocks. Throughout the night they waited, shielding her with umbrellas and keeping the fires stoked. In the morning, she lay spent. Merriweather lay beside her for warmth and to give whatever comfort she could.

As Annie again descended through the layers of grief, she began shivering, face down in the pit. Small bits of gravel stabbed at her forehead, her arms ached from the relentless pounding of the shore. But overriding the physical pain was a sense of doom that came from knowing two generations had been lost, that everything—everything—rested on her shoulders now. The buffer that her daughter and granddaughter had given by helping her keep the farm going, letting her keep her deathbed vow to her sister, was destroyed. And then when every door was closed, Annie found a window of hope and looked through to see a dream and a promise.

The vision can only be described as impressionist. The colors were muted and muddied, faces indistinct, but the spiritual essence was captured to the fullest.

In a golden sunset, Annie strode purposefully down the middle of an endless meadow. She felt the swish of the long pasture grass against her slacks and the air swarmed with the lingering heat of summer. Annie squinted as she closed on an ancient maple whose canopy shaded several silhouettes in Sunday pinafore dresses, contrasted against the blue sky to the west. As she approached, Annie heard familiar laughter. She stopped abruptly and realized the figures were her six sisters. One of them walked over to Annie. Though a ribboned bonnet covered the person's face, Annie recognized her oldest sister, Ruth.

"Annie, I'm glad you have come to the family for help. The curse that we seven die during our seventy-seventh year doesn't allow for the tragedy you have suffered. Well, I want you to know that no one is happy about it, but the forces are there for a reason. So, we decided to vote about allowing you to stay a little longer. Oh, you never heard such a ruckus: the wailing, the arguing, the crying and swearing. I'm glad Mama wasn't around to hear it. Some wanted to change the cardinal rule, and some were simply jealous that you should have more time to raise the twins.

"The family by-laws didn't cover this situation. Not as far back as we could find records. Anyway, the vote was three to three. As the oldest, it became my decision. I can give you a little more time, but I can't hold them off forever. You're lucky, because we heard of a family in Iowa that had the same situation, and they kept the curse in place.

"I have to go back now. They think I might tell you some of the other secrets. So, good luck, Annie. Despite our split vote, we all will be there when you need us. Remember, you're not alone."

With a little nod of her head, Ruth left the wordless Annie and slowly made her way back to join her sisters under the maple.

Annie stared for a long time and then began walking back on the trail of bent grass.

She stopped only once to look back at her sisters still standing under the tree. When she turned to walk away, she felt the cold beach stones on her cheek.

Again, Annie heard voices. Hypothermic, soaked, and shivering uncontrollably, she knew in her heart that the conversation with her sister had been as real as any other truth she had encountered in her long life.

Annie cleared away the small pebbles in her mouth with her tongue and rolled over to see John and Merriweather hovering over her with their umbrellas. They helped her to her feet, John muttering something about hypothermia. They carried her into the house, where, despite her protests, they bathed her, cleansed her cuts, and forced her into bed, surrounded by hot rocks in towels and two hot water bottles at her feet.

Just before she fell asleep, she told Merriweather to find the almanac.

"The garden, I have to tend to the garden," she said.

Hours later Annie bolted upright in her bed, gasping for breath. Her teeth were chattering, her body chilled from bedclothes drenched in sweat. Exhausted, she looked around the room.

The harsh reality of the late afternoon sunlight slashed onto the burnished fir floor and the wallpaper of now-faded roses that her mother had bought in Seattle.

Annie fell back, blankly staring at the white tongue-and-groove wood ceiling. She felt like she had ventured to the jumping-off place, and yet she had not jumped.

Her mission was clear. Somehow she had to muster the time and strength to raise the twins.

She closed her eyes slept through to the next morning. When she woke, she found her fingers bandaged, and John standing vigil beside her bedside. Waving aside her protests, he ladled homemade chicken soup into her eager bird-like mouth from a bowl she held between the palms of her hands.

Between sips, Annie kept saying, "I've got to get to my babies."

Moby took Annie to the hospital to see the twins. The nurses had heard the terrible news of the young parents' deaths. They had fallen in love with Peter and Sarah, as well as their twins. They cried with Annie and held her tight.

A middle-aged woman wearing a tailored gray suit approached the nurses' station. Her tortoise-shell-rimmed glasses magnified small, humorless eyes, and her hair had been confined to a tight, perfectly round bun.

"Mrs. Perkins? I'm Miss Barlock, a social worker here with the neonatal unit," she said. "Would you please come with me for a few minutes?" Though pleasant, the woman made it clear her request was not optional.

She led Annie down the hall to a small, windowless, extremely tidy office, where she seated herself behind a highly polished oak desk. With a wave of her hand, she indicated a chair for Annie to take.

"As I understand it, you are the sole surviving relative," she said, opening the lone folder that sat atop her desk.

"Yes," said Annie, the sorrow in her voice just below the surface. "Peter was an only child whose parents died some time ago. "Sarah's mother…my only child…died in the crash as well, so I that makes me the twins' only surviving relative."

Miss Barlock pursed her lips and peered into the file at something she apparently found very disturbing. She lifted her unfriendly gaze once again to Annie.

"Mrs. Perkins, I have been trying to contact you for the last two days. Evidently you don't have a phone."

Annie's radar immediately went up.

"I live on the family homestead on an island," she said, forcing a smile. "We have never found the need for a phone. But a message can always be gotten to me in an emergency—that's how I knew when the twins were born."

"I see," said Miss Barlock, in a tone that clearly indicated that in fact she did not see.

"I suppose I could get a cell phone if—"

"That won't be necessary at this point," Miss Barlock cut in rudely. "We need to discuss putting the twins up for adoption. The agency we work with has several couples who have already expressed an interest, so I'd like to get the paperwork started as soon as possible. Of course, we will keep the twins here at the hospital until the arrangements are made."

Annie sat up as straight as she could and again made her mouth form the semblance of a smile.

"Thank you for your concern, but that won't be necessary. I will be raising the babies."

Miss Barlock took off her glasses and gave Annie her most steely stare. When Annie showed no sign of crumbling, she said, "Don't you think it would be wise, Mrs. Perkins, to have the children brought up by a young family who could offer love and support over the long haul?"

"Well, no, I think it's important that they be raised by their family members, which, as you said, I am the last remaining one. I'm all those babies have."

Suddenly, the reality of these harsh words sank in, and Annie stifled a sob. The social worker handed Annie a tissue and waited while she pulled herself together. Annie blew her nose then again commanded her spine to make her sit up straight. This was no time for tears.

"I know I won't be around forever, but I fully expect to be around for their formative years. Our family has a rich heritage they need to know about. They need to be told about their mother, their father, and their grandmother. About who they are and where they came from. No one else knows their story like I do."

Miss Barlock gave a slight shake of her head. Her next words, though no doubt meant to be sympathetic, came across as merely condescending.

"I am sorry for your loss, but your thinking is clouded right now. The sad fact is that you cannot raise these children to adulthood. They need parents who can give them not just a few years but a lifetime."

"I understand that they need support, but I think I could come up with a long-term solution, given time," Annie explained. She was trying not to scream out, "For Christ's sake, I may not be young, but I have some good years left!"

"I'm afraid that, if it is true that there are no other living relatives, the state will have to step in and make a decision about their future. This falls directly into the jurisdiction of Child Protective Services."

Annie could see the woman had already made up her mind. She fought for control.

"If someone wanted to adopt these children, what would be the procedure?"

"They'd have to have a background check, a home study, go through a psychological evaluation, and one to two months later, a decision would be made. But really, Mrs. Perkins, I'm quite sure the state would consider you an inadequate choice for children of this age."

Annie had dealt with bureaucrats most of her life. She knew that what they felt most comfortable with was forms.

"Could I have the forms, please—if you would just humor an old woman?"

"Well, I just don't think...," began Miss Barlock. One look at Annie must have told her it was not a good time to refuse a reasonable request, for she opened a file drawer and withdrew the necessary paperwork.

Annie visited the babies, checked their charts, spoke with the nurses. She woke a sleeping Moby in the waiting room, and they left to go back to the island.

The island inhabitants were still in shock, not knowing what to say or how to help. There was not enough gray tape, WD-40, profanity, dream catchers, prose, chocolate decadence, or ginkgo biloba in the world to change the fact that the future of the island had been altered forever.

In spite of her sorrow, Annie knew she had to take action. She fell back on the organization skills that had served her well in crises not nearly so close to home. She set up a blackboard in the kitchen and called a meeting to determine strategies. With colored chalk, she wrote on the blackboard the two most pressing concerns: the economic survival of the island and the babies' future. Before they could go any further, Merriweather insisted that Annie add a third issue: the grieving process. Though loath to confront it, Annie knew Merriweather was right. She could not ignore this sudden and terrible loss in her life. But she also knew there was no time now for self-indulgence. She would grieve later.

John and Moby offered to take on the business side of the island, including looking into a long-term solution, such as setting up trusts for the children. Throwing out a few ideas, John suggested the possibility of a government or private grant or a bailout by a foundation.

As she wrote down the various ideas, Annie felt energized. Her sisters had given her time, and now she had the support of her friends. They would not let her fail.

"The deaths are a terrible thing," John had said, trying to sum up the situation, "but the only option is not to give up. There is too much at stake."

That night, South and Merriweather came to Annie's door, holding a lit candle.

"We have come just to sit with you this evening," South explained.

Annie was grateful for their presence. She had held so many in grief, it was good to have someone willing to hold her.

The three women moved into the living room, where Merriweather placed the candle on the coffee table. Its small flame fought against the dark, flickering wispy shadows upon the walls as they sat in silence.

Over the next several days, Annie wrote letters to heads of state and CEOs of the organizations she had served, knowing they would give her glowing character recommendations. She sent in the four-hundred-dollar fee for a home study, signed up for a physical, completed her health record, and set up a driving schedule to get to Tacoma to visit the little pumpkins.

Still, Annie understood she had set sail in uncharted waters. She had to prove she was capable of nurturing young lives. There would be no cushion of time, no learning curve to overcome her inexperience. She would not to be allowed to gracefully ease in; instead, she had to charge straight into the most important battle of her life. Everything else had been practice.

In the weeks that followed, Annie built up an impressive portfolio of international references from heads of state, newsworthy celebrities, and close friends. Her medical physical revealed her to be in excellent health, with a tinge of arthritis, and her financial statement—while not overwhelming—showed she had the monetary resources to care for two children.

Annie had been notified by letter that a woman connected with Washington State Child Welfare would come to the island to conduct the home study, which would complete Annie's bid to raise her great-grandchildren. Annie hated to leave the children in limbo. She hoped a decision could be made soon. She covered her tracks by completing another application—to be a foster parent. According to all reports, foster parents were needed desperately.

Annie considered going to a lawyer, but she came to the same conclusion most people reach about lawyers: they are slow, they bog down the process in legal mumbo-jumbo, they rarely know the legalities of your specific problem, and they are incredibly expensive.

Annie had given John power of attorney to have the forensic remains from the crash cremated. He brought a box with three marked containers to the house one night after dark.

"I can stay with you, Annie, if you'd like," he offered.

Wordlessly, Annie just shook her head.

Annie slowly pulled the three containers from the box and placed them on the wooden table, the same place where they had all sat at Christmas, so full of promise, laughing, sharing, reveling in the security of ushering in a new generation: the twins. And now that promise had been reduced to these cylinders. This was not an impersonal event in a far-flung intellectual universe, but a tragedy in this galaxy, in this star system, on this planet, and on this particular island.

An uncontrollable anger swept through Annie's body, and she railed at an unseen and cruel deity.

"Why this brutal, unprovoked, assault on my life? Hell yes, I'm taking it personally. Where is justice? Where is the payback for a life devoted to easing the pain and suffering in this imperfect world? Do you want me to believe I lived my life for nothing? For some sickening game of 'Mother May I'? A cruel test of an old woman?"

The depth of her grief, her rage, her helplessness to right this wrong exhausted her. She sat transfixed at the table, contemplating the urns.

It's such a waste, such a waste, she thought wearily.

Then leaving the dirty dishes on the table, without brushing her teeth or washing her face, she crept up the stairs to her room, where she crawled into bed and slept the sleep of someone who had no more energy to think or feel.

The next morning, as John walked to the boathouse to shuttle to work, the island was toasted by a deep-throated blast of a tugboat whistle. *The Pissant* rounded the spit and dropped anchor with a crash that woke Annie from sleep. She rushed down to the beach, arriving just as Pinky feathered the oars and glided the dinghy into shore.

"Come on in," Annie said, helping Dorie out of the boat. "I've missed you two."

Annie poured mugs of thick black coffee and served slices of apple pie. With a sad sigh, she told them the awful news. Dorie's eyes welled with tears. She put a hand on Annie's shoulder.

"Oh, Annie, we had no idea. I am so sorry." She turned to her husband. "Pinky, we need to stay here and help straighten out this mess."

Pinky nodded his agreement. He understood his wife's commitment went beyond sympathy to action. They would stay at Seven Sisters for the long haul.

That night, Pinky wedged himself in the bowsprit and, in honor of Sarah and Peter and Calypso, played the bagpipes for an hour. The mournful sound mirrored the sentiments of every islander.

In preparation for the home study, Annie had insisted the island be spruced up. Moby and John collected their whiskey bottles and covered them with a tarp, Merriweather and South swept and dusted every inch of the house, and Annie and Owl cleaned up the garden and flower beds. Everyone promised to be on his or her best behavior. The night before the visit, Annie spent the night at Peter and Sarah's to finish the paperwork on the estate, pick up the last of the delivered mail, and check up on the babies at the hospital.

"I'll be back tomorrow at noon," she reminded Moby. "That'll give me a couple of hours to take care of any last-minute details. I don't want anything to go wrong with this home study."

Moby nodded agreement as Annie nosed the boat out into the channel. He scanned the uncluttered horizon, appreciative of this final transition of winter to full-blown spring. The bleak, gray necklace of the winter shoreline was accented by newly minted green leaves of the salmonberry and alder. The sky and water had melted into a bitter blue. And there was hope.

His daughter Christine came to mind. He missed his girl. He knew if he sent for her, she would come running. Not yet, he thought, but soon, very soon. He sighed. But what if he died today, before she could come? And then as quickly as he thought that, he became afraid. Even though he wasn't superstitious, he took it back.

"It's a good day to be alive," he said out loud. "A very good day!"

Early the next morning Owl and Moby sat by the fire sharing a bottle of Wild Turkey and enjoying cigars. So immersed were they in the moment, they were startled when they heard a voice address them crisply.

"I am here for a Mrs. Annie Perkins."

They looked up and saw a tall woman in a gray trench coat. Staring at them from the middle of her forehead was a large, blackish growth the size of a quarter. Charitably, the eruption could have been called a beauty mark, or maybe a mole, but to Moby, it was a wart, clear and simple.

Owl pointed to Annie's house, and the woman spun on her heel and headed up the spit.

"Annie's not there yet," Moby yelled after her.

The woman continued down the beach, passing by Dorie in the hot tub, who was playfully twirling her halter top over her head while Pinky and John hummed "The Stripper." The home study woman wrinkled her nose and sprinted past her, chased by Buddy and Trooper.

Moby hurried down to the dock as Annie pulled in.

"She's here," he said simply.

Instead of becoming flustered at this bit of unsettling news, Annie remained unflappable. She calmly walked up to the house, where the dogs had cornered the woman onto the porch.

"Hello," said Annie, shooing away the mutts. "I'm Annie Perkins."

"Wilma Walker-Biggs," the woman introduced herself, handing Annie a card. Annie smiled. She knew Moby would soon be nick-naming her "Wilma the Wart."

Annie ushered the home study expert inside.

"I'm sorry I wasn't here to greet you," she said. "I was told the appointment would be at two." Annie handed the woman two manila folders. "Why don't you take a look at these while I make us some coffee?"

Wilma leafed through the portfolios. The first held letter after letter from influential people giving Annie the most glowing of rec-ommendations. In the folder she found Annie's income statements and health records.

The woman looked up at Annie, surprise in her eyes.

"Very impressive. You certainly have good credentials." Annie placed two cups of coffee on the table and sat down across from the woman. "Shall we do the interview now?"

Although twice the woman's age, Annie feigned great respect for her interviewer and fielded the intrusive questions with charm and wit. When they came to the actual living conditions for the children, Annie explained that the island had no power, running water, or telephone. Wilma gazed down at her form in confusion, finding no line on which to chart such aberrations.

"How can you expect to raise children without these basic amenities?" Wilma asked, clearly incredulous that anyone would willingly live in such a primitive state. "What do you use for a bathroom?"

Annie stood up and walked over to the kitchen door, which she opened to reveal the outhouse a few yards away.

"Does it flush?" Wilma asked expectantly.

Annie resisted responding, "Only when it rains." She closed the door, and looked at Wilma directly.

"You know, seven generations of my family grew up on this farm. We all reached adulthood, healthy and well-adjusted, and even made contributions to the world we live in. I expect that my grandchildren will turn out the same way."

Wilma looked down and scribbled some notes quickly on her report.

"Well, that about covers it," she said abruptly, rising to leave. Annie escorted her out to her boat, passing by Moby and Owl. Wilma looked at the two men, appeared as though she wanted to say something, then evidently decided against it. After the woman climbed aboard, Annie shoved the boat away from the sandy shore.

"Have a safe trip home," she yelled with a wave, hoping she sounded warm and fuzzy. When she walked by Moby's cabin, Annie heard the sound of a bolt action jacking a cartridge into the breech. She saw the rifle barrel extend through a tear in the screen door.

"Put it away, Moby," was her only comment, as she started back up to the house. She felt a surge of satisfaction as she heard a stream of curses and the door close to Moby's shack.

The days were alternately foggy or clear, rainy or dry, windy or warm, as spring burst loose from winter's grip.

Annie, Dorie, and Pinky shoved off several times during the week to visit the twins. Moby felt restless. He remembered he owed Pickles a pair of shoes and decided that was a good excuse to get off the island. He and Owl set out in *The Ark* for the peninsula, and before long, Moby's dump truck once again rumbled through the countryside.

This trip, Pickles seemed taller and, at first sight, uncharacteristically underdressed—a gray sweatshirt accessorized with simple gold button earrings. Then he clumped from behind the counter to greet them, and Moby could see where the extra six inches of height came from. Pickles wore a pair of pink go-go boots with goldfish swimming in the plastic transparent soles.

He unwrapped Moby's custom wingtips with the care and deliberation of an archeologist on a dig. Standing back momentarily in the sheer awe of the experience, he took in their majesty. Then, with reverence, Pickles caressed the shoes, smelled the shoes, held them up to the light of a window to admire their lines—did everything but make love to the shoes. Then, with a sigh, he carefully placed them back in their box.

"Come on back to The Hermitage for brunch," he said, putting the "Closed" sign on the door.

The Hermitage, as Pickles called his apartment, was a voyeur's delight. A one-way mirrored glass wall jutted out over the harbor. Pickles enjoyed a 180-degree view up and down the bay.

His back to Moby and Owl, Pickles busied himself in his efficiency kitchen. But before Moby could mount a serious snooping offensive, Pickles returned with a plate of deli meats and cheeses along with apple and pear slices and flutes of champagne. Moby and Owl dug in.

"Damn, these shoes are killing me. They're so frigging heavy." Pickles pulled off one of the boots and undid a plastic plug in the side, dropping in some fish food. "Pain. The price of fashion, I guess." He flexed his toes as he set the boot on the floor.

"We could use some pews for a church we're building. Preferably clear fir, old, with some carving on the ends," Moby said, finishing off the deli plate.

Pickles smiled.

"That shouldn't be too hard to rustle up."

Moby and Owl got up to leave.

"Make sure you keep feeding those fish, and remember, we need those pews pretty damn quick."

Just before he and Owl hit the sidewalk, Moby threw an irresistible enticement over his shoulder. "By the way, did I mention I have a pair of Jimmy Choo sling-back sandals...in purple?"

Before leaving the dock at Port Gamble, Moby trekked into Wiggins' market for the mail. Back on the island, he found Annie in the orchard, pruning, and handed her the stack, knowing she wouldn't want to wait to open one particular piece.

"Oh, God," she said, holding up an official-looking envelope. "This one's from Child Protective Services."

"Open it," commanded Moby.

Annie stared at the envelope for a moment, then ripped it open. The letter read,

*Dear Sir or Madam,*

*Your application for adoption and/or foster parenting has been denied for the following reasons.*

Below these devastating sentences a list of possible reasons were given. Annie found X's next to two of them:

  X  *unsuitable home environment*

  X  *no visible means of employment*

At the bottom someone had handwritten,

*Request denied, due to the above and the age of applicant.*

Annie folded up the letter and put it into her pocket.
Time for Plan B.

The Annie of old emerged. The bureaucratic-bludgeoning *enfant terrible*, that rootin' tootin', in-your-face, Iditarod-mushing, take-no-prisoners, bitch-slapping field general was back. Look out world.

Annie marched up to her porch and rang the bell to assemble her troops. Up the path they came, the crippled, the theatrically challenged, the walking wounded. It was all the army she needed. She read the letter and explained her plan, passing out an outline. She made it clear that the plan had certain risks and would take time and care.

Conscription was unnecessary. A chorus of "I'm in, Annie"; "We're here for you"; "Anything to help"; "Hell yes, we'll screw the bastards! You just tells us where and when" completed the roll call. The mission was a go.

They were going to kidnap the twins.

# Chapter THIRTEEN

nnie, Dorie, and Pinky spent the next three days at the hospital with the twins, secretly doing reconnaissance. The death of the twins' parents and Annie's daughter gained Annie the sympathy of the nursing staff. It was easy to photograph the nursery and document shift changes while wandering around with the twins, visiting with other neonatal parents, sharing their triumphs and fears. Being close to coming out the other side as healthy babies, Annie and Zack were role models for rookie parents as their own babies passed through the emotional and physical stages of growth.

Late at night, the conspirators would meet back at Annie's house, poring over diagrams and pictures, studying time charts, looking for the best opportunity and escape routes.

"It looks simple," Moby said, summarizing the facts. "The nurses change shifts at seven o'clock and meet across the hall to exchange charts. All we need is a diversion. Then we snatch the babies...." He pawed through the papers on the table, looking for the floor plan. "There we are." He pointed to the stairway, no more than fifty feet down the second-story hall. "Down the stairway to the door that opens onto this alley leading to the side street. Piece of cake."

Everyone nodded in agreement.

"Then we need a safe place to stay," Moby insisted. "The first place they'll look is the island. We need a place that's not associated with Annie."

"How about *The Pissant*?" Pinky asked. "We could dock down in Tacoma. They'll be looking on the highways and bridges. We can motor right up the sound undetected. It's perfect." Pinky looked at Dorie to see if she was warming to the idea. She was on board with the plan, 200 percent.

There was just one drawback.

"Pinky, you have a conference in Hong Kong the first of next week," Dorie said.

"Shit, that's right," said Pinky, taking out a handkerchief to mop his shiny forehead. "Can you do this yourself?"

"Damn straight I can." Dorie pounded the table with her fist. "I'm all over it."

"So, it's a done deal," said Moby, his one eye glinting with mischief. "I'll drive the getaway rig. It's the only vehicle we can get everyone in."

"Don't you think they might recognize the truck?" asked John dubiously.

"Hell no. Since that first time, I never drive it in the hospital zone. We always park about three blocks away. I'll just scoot by with the tailgate down, we'll lower the ladder, and everyone will climb aboard. It'll work slicker than frog grease."

Only the characters for the inside vignette needed to be cast. The problem was, everybody wanted in. After hours of wrangling, like actors in a small town school play, each person was convinced he or she would play the most important part. But everyone eventually was given a role. Even Merriweather (who was, in South's words, "getting pretty flaky") earned the part of "lead lookout."

After the meeting, everyone left aglow in his or her assigned role, excited to be involved in helping put Annie and the babies together.

"This is the way it ought to be," Merriweather proclaimed. "Family should be with family."

John doubled back and lightly knocked on Annie's door. She opened the door to let him in.

"Annie, are you sure this is the only way to go about this? It seems risky. I don't know if we've thought this through enough."

"If I don't do something drastic—something that will get media attention—they'll give those children to someone else and sweep me under the carpet. I can't stand by and let that happen any more than you would if a friend needed you."

John knew that in any crisis, there was a small window in which to take action. Once that window closed, that opportunity was lost forever. His hand caressed his front pocket where he kept the pepper shaker. He knew Betsy would agree.

She never faltered in matters of the heart.

One day of rehearsal at the hospital, and one day to calm the nerves. Annie spent most of the third day caring for the babies herself, feeding them and talking to their innocent little faces. She knew someday she would tell them why it had been necessary for their great-grandmother to kidnap them and stow them away on a tugboat.

Annie and South were holding the twins, idly chatting to the parents of a new arrival, when Pinky, on cue, slipped into the closet at the end of the hall. The closet was stacked floor to ceiling with bedpans for expectant mothers. When Pinky deliberately fell against them, the clatter sounded like a battle royal between the Iron Chef and Martha Stewart accompanied by a Metallica concert gone wrong.

The nurses boiled out of the conference room and went running down the hall to investigate. They streamed the opposite direction from Annie and South, who scuttled down the stairway and onto the street with the twins swaddled in blankets.

Moby and Owl pulled up into the darkened alley and loaded up the "booty," as South kept calling the twins, pulling up the tailgate with a loud clank. Instead of going directly to the wharf, Moby took a left and started to circle the block. John opened up the sliding metal conversation door to the truck bed.

"We can't find Merriweather. She's disappeared."

The conversation door slammed shut just as Moby's headlights picked up Merriweather doing her granny-step shuffle down the sidewalk that cut through the park.

"There she is! Where the hell is she going?" Moby swore under his breath.

He jolted the truck to a stop while John jumped out and hoisted her into the cab.

"Step on a crack, you'll break your mother's back," she advised. "Step on a crack, you'll break your mother's back. Step on a crack—"

"Thanks, Merriweather," said John kindly. "Don't worry, I'll remember."

The plan back in motion, the dump truck rambled down the road, the jerky ride forcing Annie and South, each one cradling a baby, to wedge themselves into the corners. The conspirators stared at each other, as passing streetlights alternately illuminated the truck bed and plunged it into darkness. Annie lifted the corner of the blanket and looked down at Zack. Bright-eyed, he smiled at her.

For a second, she wondered if this was the best decision for the twins. Maybe she was driven by guilt. Probably, but before these children were given up as so much grist for the government mill, someone had to stand up for them. She reminded herself that she alone was their best advocate. And there was that old Jesuit saying that kept rambling through her head, "Give me a child for the first seven years, and I will give you the man." Surely with a little luck and help from her sisters, she could do seven years.

She could not afford doubts; there would no turning back. She wiggled a little further into the corner, her shoulders squared against the iron sides of the truck bed.

Moby negotiated the truck down to the wharf about the same time Pinky and Dorie squealed into the parking lot. The tailgate flapped down, and the women and the two precious bundles silently slipped down the gangplank onto the waiting tugboat. Pinky stayed in the shadows, on the lookout for witnesses, but it was too early in the spring for lovers, and the night people had not yet crawled out from under their rocks. He gave Dorie the "thumbs up" as she glanced from the wheel cabin and quietly pulled out into the harbor. The red and green running lights faded into the fog.

John checked into his apartment in Seattle, while Merriweather, Moby, and Owl streaked for home to practice looking innocent.

The tugboat churned north. By midnight they had snubbed their boat to the pier in LaConner, a quaint fishing village with antique shops, cutting-edge clothing, and melt-in-your-mouth pastries. None of these diversions interested the women, whose sole objective was to keep a low profile. They stayed off the dock and out of the windows. The twins found the rocking boat and the throb of the motors to their liking and slept long and hard.

By morning, their little faces, and those of their kidnappers', would be plastered on the front page of every newspaper in the state.

The refugees spent a restless night as they waited till morning to contact John at the newspaper with the cell phone he'd given them. At seven-thirty sharp, they checked in with their lifeline.

John acted quite the chipper bloke when he took their call.

"Front page, just like you planned it, Annie. Headline reads 'Great-grandmother Kidnaps Infants.' Right now, they assume you made your getaway in a car, and there are reports that you may be in Portland or Spokane, so that's good. How is everyone holding up?"

"Honestly, it is a bit nerve-racking. But we're stocked with food, formula, and diapers, so I imagine we can hold out quite a while. Did my lawyer get a hold of you yet?"

"Not yet. He probably hasn't even read the newspaper. Once he does, he'll be on the horn, lickety-split. When I hear something, I'll give you a call."

"Good luck, Annie."

"Thanks…I need it."

A police chopper landed on Seven Sisters at daybreak. A SWAT team quickly took positions surrounding the house then kicked in the front door. Moby could see them through the windows as they raced about the house, secured the building, and then fanned out to cover the spit.

Moby feigned dozing by the fire as they crept up on him.

"Keep your hands where we can see them," they greeted him.

Moby put his hands in the air and listened to their questions. He politely pointed to all the empty whiskey and beer bottles.

"Can I serve you boys a drink? Jack Daniels? Crackling Rose? Or maybe a little waddle of the Wild Turkey I got in a swap session last night?" When he received nothing but silent glares, he persisted cordially, "Sure you boys don't have time for a drink?"

The troopers hit every cabin in turn.

They found Merriweather in the orchard. As they asked their rapid-fire questions, she merely leaned on her rake and gave them a sweet look, pretending or possibly not knowing what they were talking about.

Finally, the police motioned for the men in the house to assemble near the helicopter. They boarded, rose straight up, banked left, and were gone.

By noon, John had fielded calls from newspapers, magazines, television stations, senior groups, women's groups, knitting societies, and someone who wanted Annie to endorse an herbal drink.

The one person he hadn't heard from was Annie's lawyer, the man who was supposed to be out front, fielding questions, and looking for political solutions. At three o'clock, the lawyer's secretary phoned. He was not prepared for the media blitz and had decided to bow out.

Just as John prepared to phone Annie with the news, he received a call from the American Association of Senior Citizens headquartered in New York. The CEO introduced himself and made his case.

"Son, I was just briefed on your case. If you can get a hold of Mrs. Perkins, we would greatly appreciate the opportunity to make this a test case to advance the rights of grandparents and their grandchildren. This is one of the issues on our agenda, and we could have our top lawyer, Max Manahan, out there tomorrow. No charge, of course, as long as you need help out there." He gave John his home phone and his cell phone. "Hope to hear from you, Mr. Hunt. This is the kind of dogfight we'd like to be involved in. And you can believe me when I say we intend on winning by bringing in the biggest dog. Good night, sir."

When John phoned Annie, he said, "I've got some bad news and some good news. First the bad news: Your lawyer quit. His secretary said—"

"That weasel Griswold dropped out? What did he think? This was going to be some kind of picnic?" Annie, who never slept well on boats, felt more than a little pissy after a difficult night.

"But here's the good news—the AASC called. They want to send their top lawyer out here to defend you."

"What's the ASAC?"

"AASC—the American Association of Senior Citizens. The guy sounded legit. I think it could be just the answer we've been praying for."

"Why do they want to defend *me*?" Annie asked, suspicion in her voice.

"The association wants to use your case to further their agenda, which is advocating for grandparents' rights." John stretched his neck from the tension. "The head guy says he's ready to send out some big-shot lawyer tomorrow."

Annie said nothing for a few moments.

"Could you get this guy up here without being followed?"

"*No problemo*," John assured her. "I'll send one of the college interns out to pick him up and put him in a cab. I won't be involved at all, so there shouldn't be a trace. I'll get on it right away."

John began to hum a song that had been running through his head, not realizing it as the theme from *Mission Impossible*.

John phoned Annie the next morning to confirm the arrival of the lawyer that evening.

Dorie, South, and Annie waited impatiently in a dense fog. The tug was darkened, with only the halos of the streetlights casting a grainy portrait of the dock entrance. Finally, through the fog, they could see the faint red glow of taillights out on the road, then the crackle of gravel under tires as it entered the parking lot. A dome light reflected through the rear window, followed by muffled voices and a door slamming shut. The car spun gravel as it maneuvered through the puddle-plagued parking lot, pulled a U-turn, and sped away in the darkness back towards town.

Annie waited a full minute, then signaled with the flashlight. The barely visible outline, briefcase dangling from one hand, small suitcase in the other, came through the open gate. Annie strained her ears till she heard the reassuring click as the gate shut. The figure easily navigated the slippery ramp, moving quickly down the floating concrete pier toward *The Pissant,* moored nearly a hundred yards away.

Suddenly three cars skidded into the parking lot. A spotlight pierced the thick fog and then abruptly disappeared. The women on the tugboat saw the bobbing of flashlights and heard the sound of running, men swearing, and shoes struggling for purchase on the unyielding galvanized cyclone fence that guarded the dock entry.

Annie yelled, "Run, Max, run!"

Dorie kicked the engine over, and South threw off the mooring lines wrapped around the dock cleats. The boat pulled away from the wharf, its running lights off. Max stopped, looked back, then with a sprinter's speed launched from the slippery dock, sailing over the four feet of open water and bouncing off the rubber tire dock bumper, landing in a convulsive heap on the deck.

The pursuers ran parallel along the dock, looking in vain for a ship's bow to bridge the gap or a loose rowboat but found none. The plainclothesmen swore with disgust. They stood, hands on hips, bent at the waist, winded and wheezing, watching helplessly as the boat cleared the breakwater and disappeared into the fog.

While they had slipped safely behind the shroud of rocks, Dorie knew she would have to navigate by Braille. She flipped on the radar, looking to blend into the blipping profile that provided an up-to-the-second map of all the shipping traffic on the inside waterways of Puget Sound. She knew that the Coast Guard would try to track her. Her only salvation was to run as close as possible to another ship, hoping their radar would indicate only the bigger vessel.

"I don't think they can see us from the air in this soup," she said to no one in particular, working her way toward what looked like a tug pulling a barge heading north. She shouted down into the galley. "You girls need to keep a sharp lookout for other boats. We don't have our running lights on, so they can't see us. I'm going to draft right behind this barge. Somebody check on Max and see if he's all right."

South left her post and looked down at the figure splattered on the deck, arms and legs jutting in every direction as if smashed by a giant fly swatter.

"You're some kind of lawyer," South said, bending down to flip Max over. "You run around here like Super Fly."

She looked into the face of the flying attorney and gasped.

"This is a *woman* attorney we've got here. Right on! Power to the people. Hey, Annie, give me a hand."

Annie and South helped the groggy Max into a bunk, where she closed her eyes. Annie put a cold washrag on her forehead.

"Rest easy, dear, we'll have you right in no time. Do you hurt any place in particular?"

"What do you suppose 'Max' is short for? Maxine?" asked South. "Or is it just a stage name?"

Dorie meanwhile had successfully slipped behind a cargo ship heading north. An hour later, she jumped off, near Frenchman's Cove, a long-armed fjord accessible only by boat.

"If I can just find the boathouse for the *Alaska Star*," she said, as she looked at the depth finder to stay in the middle of the narrow channel, "I'm sure they're up in Alaska fishing for pollock right now."

She turned on the halogen floodlight on the roof of the cabin and spotted the seventy-five-foot-long empty boathouse portside. Dorie hoped the tug would fit. Praying silently, she watched the rafters barely clear the smoke stack. Moving to the stern, she pulled on the rope that held the rolled-up canvas tarp and jumped back as it slammed down on the deck. The tugboat was safely secured, even if the fog lifted.

"There's no way they can spot us by air, and they'll have had a tough time tracking us. By morning, they'll figure we could be anywhere," Dorie said, with more conviction than she believed. The three women had gathered in the bunkroom, surveying their damaged lawyer, who sat up with a hung-over, owlish look.

"I didn't think the deck would be so slippery. I'm Max Manahan." She shook each woman's hand. "Which one of you is Mrs. Perkins?"

"That's me, dear," Annie said, guiding Max back into the bunk. "We'll talk in the morning. You get some rest." Max didn't have much fight left. She lay down, rolled over, and fell fast asleep.

The twins had slept through the entire adventure, but now little Annie began fussing and Zack, recognizing his opportunity, sympathetically joined in, till they were both crying. South frantically warmed the formula, which Annie and Dorie fed to the hungry infants.

"She's awfully young," said South a bit later, glancing over at a slumbering Max. "I don't see any wrinkles. Can you trust anyone without wrinkles?"

"If she had wrinkles, she wouldn't have made that spectacular leap from the dock," Dorie pointed out, putting Zack over her shoulder and coaxing a burp.

Annie put her namesake on her knee. She put her hand under the baby's chin and patted her back. "I like this technique better. At least you don't wind up with urp down your back."

"I consider it a privilege to wear a badge of sour urp," said Dorie.

Dorie and Pinky had motored up the inland passage toward Alaska several times with the owners of the *Alaska Star*. Dorie was sure they wouldn't mind if the group availed themselves of the more spacious accommodations of the nearby cabin.

She forced open the door and examined the interior. Built of time-ambered cedar logs and driftwood, the one-room cabin was unquestionably a male domain. Decades of dusty cobwebs hung from the rafters, while vintage girly magazines from the 1950s onward lay in sloppy stacks. Piles of rusted gear parts and crab traps separated the six beds.

South poked a stick at one of the gray bed pillows.

"I don't think anyone ever washed these pillowcases."

Annie stared at the largest piece of "furniture" in the cabin. Atop two sawhorses sat a huge, round saw blade, a good six feet in diameter, with teeth the size of a great white shark.

"Is that the dining table?" she said. "That thing looks dangerous."

Dorie laughed.

"Yeah, you don't want to pull your chair up too close. The owners salvaged that blade from an old sawmill that used to operate up at the head of the fjord."

Dorie attacked the most obvious filth with an old broom she found and soon had the potbellied stove radiating heat. After scrounging around in the propane fridge, she pulled out a couple of battered pans and minutes later the comforting smells of fresh coffee, fluffy scrambled eggs, and sizzling strips of bacon filled the room. Annie and South trundled the infants inside, spreading a clean blanket on a bed. The mattress swaybacked toward the middle, providing a roll-proof safe haven for babies.

Soon steaming food covered the saw-blade table. A slightly smoky haze from the burnt toast hung in the air. Just as they sat down to eat off ancient paper plates they'd found, a quick knock came at the door, which then opened quickly.

In marched Max.

Gone was the frail, battered figure who had lain on the bow of *The Pissant*. This woman strode with confidence and grace. Her dark hair had been pulled back ballerina taut, her make-up expertly applied, her smile revealing perfect white teeth.

Max never just entered a room. She took it by storm. Maybe it came from her being born in the wine cellar of the family's mansion in Florida during a hurricane. She was a fusion of old money, beauty, and entrepreneurial guts. Her trust fund could have easily supported her in any manner of luxury, but she prided herself on earning her money the old fashioned way—with exorbitant fees. She shunned "pro bono" as the refuge of lesser barristers.

Yet as she looked at the three older women in the room, she could see she was outclassed. Neither her considerable charm nor beauty nor wealth nor the thoroughbreds her father stabled in Virginia would matter to these women. It was she who was on trial this morning.

Max poured herself a cup of coffee before she sat down under the steady gaze of the appraising women.

"Honey, we've got to get some meat on those bones," Dorie said, passing her the scrambled eggs.

Max had coffee black, eggs, though not much, and bacon—three helpings.

"For the record, I think she'll survive," Annie said.

At the sound of rustling of blankets, Max put down her coffee cup and went over to the twins, who were just beginning to stretch and make small hungry noises. They quickly cranked the volume up to demand mode. Max picked up Annie and tried to make small talk, but the infant had moved well beyond social chitchat. Only her bottle would turn off the volume.

Dorie handed Max a warmed bottle and watched with interest to see the results. The room relaxed as the lawyer cradled Baby Annie into a feeding position, tested the bottle for temperature on her wrist, and plugged Annie in.

"Don't worry," Max said. "I was the oldest of four kids."

The infant looked up at Max with big eyes and scrunched up her button nose as she made a concerted effort to coordinate her feeding hum and sucking action, preferring a little music with her meal. She was definitely a GIGO (garbage in, garbage out) kind of girl. No sooner was she finished feeding and burping than she made contented little grunts as she filled her diaper.

"Over there," said Annie, pointed to the diaper stash.

Max grabbed a diaper and the baby wipes, handled the job with precision, then brought the suddenly very social little animal back to the table. The baby demanded eye contact with each person. Having charmed one, she moved on to the next.

Zack was a bottle-and-a-half man. One for the stomach, and the other half for projectile vomit launch just before his burp.

Max caught the full trajectory of the Zack's carefully plotted scheme, as he arched his back and sent a lethal, rainbowed blitzkrieg of sour milk running down the ribs of her new Eddie Bauer, cinnamon, cable-knit sweater to disappear into the pleat of her wool slacks.

Max just laughed at the attack.

"So much for the Northwest look. Yuck!"

She stuck out her tongue and reached for the dishtowel. The women smiled knowing that children were master psychologists and experts at baptizing the unwary.

"That was quite a jump onto the boat," Dorie said, breaking the silence.

"Varsity track. Four years of the high jump. Cleared six feet, two inches the last year. Long legs help, but the funny thing is, they never allowed me to compete in high heels while carrying a briefcase. That's what slowed me up. I ran right out of my red Chanels from Paris."

"That's an expensive shoe," Annie sympathized.

"They were elegant. Hard to find, too. But we should get down to business." Max reached into her leather briefcase and handed Annie her résumé. Annie scanned over the usual college credits, law school, law review, and went down to the experience. She recognized three or four cases of age discrimination where Max acted as lead attorney. A case of a drama teacher in Arkansas not wanting to step aside at the mandatory age of fifty-five, a doctor whose hospital refused privileges after he reached seventy, and several other high-profile cases where Max had been successful in maintaining the rights of seniors.

"Why seniors?" Annie asked.

"It's purely an emotional issue for me. My grandmother and great-aunt were a large part of my life growing up. I find nobility in older people. It makes me angry when society mandates that we throw away a living treasure of knowledge and experience just because of arbitrary age discrimination. Besides, putting people out to pasture, sometimes in their most productive years, just makes no sense. A throwaway society cannot sustain itself. We need to honor our elders' contribution and support them as long as they want to give."

"Some would say that as people age they become more difficult," observed South.

Max waved away this claim.

"Oh, I know, sometimes old people are cranky, and crusty, and impatient—but they hold the key to a society that values all its members, cradle to grave. Their mentoring can expedite the learning curve of their children's children. If we look to the past, we will find the future. No one has a better appreciation of the relationship of growth and progress in a field than someone who has successfully navigated life for sixty or seventy years."

Max gave them all a knowing smile.

As her eyes traveled around the table, she suddenly let out a musical little laugh.

"Sorry, I forgot I was preaching to the choir here. Didn't mean to go so heavy on the sound bites," she apologized. "I was pulling excerpts from an article I just wrote for a magazine called *Senior Maturity*. The name seems kind of redundant, don't you think?"

Annie gave a little nod.

"I think you'll do." Annie looked at the other women, whose heads bobbed in confirmation. "Yes, you'll do quite nicely. What's our next move?"

"I'd like to check in with John. He's in contact with the New York office. How we play this depends a lot on public sentiment." Max searched in the briefcase for her cell phone.

John was giddy with good news. His article about Annie's dilemma had been picked up by the national wire service and had garnered headlines from coast to coast. The latest escapade with the tugboat escaping the county sheriff had led to the press dubbing them the "Tugboat Grannies."

"I don't know how they got wind of your arrival, so don't tell me anything about your location. Maybe I'm being bugged. You need to remain anonymous. Seriously, we could have a communication leak.

"I'm inundated with phone calls, faxes, and letters from organizations from all over the country wanting to help. Whatever you do, just don't get caught while we're putting the pressure on. It looks like our fifteen minutes of fame might last a bit longer."

Max put down the phone looking pleased.

"I think you ladies have got it going here."

At the distant sound of a helicopter, the four women leapt out of their chairs and hurried over to the window. But with the overcast sky and a light rain, visibility was poor, and the stove's smoke merged into the general gray above.

"Well, if we can't see them, they can't see us. Besides," Dorie pointed out cheerfully, "those two big firs hanging out over the water camouflage the boathouse. If they had followed us on their radar to this cove, they would have been here a long time ago. The weather channel said this morning that this drizzly fog will be hanging around for at least the next three days. Good for the complexion, they say."

"And good for hiding out," added Max.

The twins had gone back to sleep while the women talked. It seemed a good time to putter about, cleaning the cabin and collecting firewood. South sat down to flip through the old magazines, and Max said she'd like to take a hike on the trail along the fjord.

"I need some quiet time to plot my strategy."

Max returned a little over an hour later, her face flushed from the chill air and exercise. After savoring a coffee, she climbed onto the double bed and nestled into the far side.

"You can sleep in the middle if you want," said Annie. "We have enough beds to go around."

"That's okay," Max answered drowsily. "I don't want to get in the habit of hogging the bed. Someday I'll find someone to fill the other half."

Moby's breathing had been growing shallower by the day. Cancer was an insidious enemy to a man who liked to take life head on. The last refuge he had was his mind. He hoped the cancer hadn't migrated that far yet. He didn't think it had, but then again, how would he know?

Still, he spent more time lately in his head, recalling vivid memories of his childhood when he was filled with the wonder of life to come. He would smile privately, wishing he could live life backward, with the perspective and wisdom of age—not to change the outcome, but to listen in and appreciate the complexities.

*Owl is right,* thought Moby. *What gives life its sweetness is that the time is short, like those Japanese paintings where the artist contemplates for hours first in the mind, and then executes swiftly and without thinking. The lines are so delicate that they cannot be changed. Perfect the first time. What was the name of that style? I wish I could remember. Shit, what does it matter anyway?*

Travis and Tate had brought the draft horses to pull more cedar bolts from the top of the island and to help Moby finish the last few feet of the tower. As the two men stood high on the scaffolding, Travis showed Moby a design. It was an elaborate framework of logs lashed together. A series of pulleys would hoist the Carolina bell up to the steeple. It would be a perilous task, even with a crane.

"I'll bet no one has lifted a bell like this with horses for a hundred years," Travis kept saying, obviously relishing the challenge.

Despite his father's warning, Tate had climbed up the scaffolding.

"Hey, Dad!" he called down, cocky, taunting. "Look where I am!"

"Tate, you get your butt back on the ground," Travis yelled back as sternly as a proud father can.

Slightly warmer weather heralded the coming of Easter, and its imminent arrival sparked an inspiration in Annie. She explained her idea to Max.

"What if we lived in the caves on Seven Sisters? No one alive knows of their existence except me. And then everyone would be home, all together again."

Max found herself intrigued. It appealed to her sense of mystery, and she liked Annie's in-your-face, aggressive take-charge style. Dorie had already told her confidentially that they couldn't hole up in the cabin indefinitely.

"There's only so much waterfront that can hold a good-size tugboat," she'd said. "They're bound to find us eventually if they really want to."

"Oh, I'm sure they want to find Annie badly," said Max. "The fact that she's slipped through their fingers must really stick in their craw."

*Craw. Was that another name for giblets? And what was a gizzard?* Max worried that she was picking up country phrases from these women at an alarming rate.

*The next thing you know,* Max thought, *I'll be saying, "Let's skedaddle on down to the island."*

*Back to the island. That seemed a good refuge, but how would they get there undetected?*

Max, Dorie, and Annie sat around the potbellied stove after dinner, feeding the babies, while South stood at the kitchen counter making oatmeal raisin cookies.

Max's phone rang.

"It's John," she said, then laughed.

John complained he couldn't find his desk under the piles of letters and memos and that his diet the last few days had consisted of any and all sources of caffeine and remnants of deli sandwiches. He was living on the edge and loving it, because he had a newspaperman's dream: an exclusive.

"We're still top fold," he informed Max. "Senior citizen groups are picketing courthouses all over the state. I think Annie could run for governor.

"The state and county legal eagles are bantering about 'kidnapping' and 'reckless endangerment' charges, but you mess with grandmothers, and your political future is in the toilet. I talked with our legal consultant here at the paper, and he thinks you could work a pretty good deal. Just don't let them catch you."

"John, call my home office," instructed Max. "Tell them we're getting ready to make a move."

# Chapter FOURTEEN

orie finished feeding Zack, consulted with Annie about a rash they decided needed lotrisone, wrapped his clean bottom in a diaper, and stuffed the yawning boy into his blue sleeper. Then Dorie folded herself in a green wicker chair near the pot-bellied stove. The red-hot metal sent shock waves of heat, converting the cold spring air into a summer sweat. South passed around what was left of the oatmeal cookies. The women nested in comfort.

The sleep patterns of all the women on the island had changed. They now slept in an instinctive maternal monitoring mode, alert to every grunt and burp. In the middle of the night, Annie saw Dorie get up, warm two bottles, give one to her, and then the two women each picked up a baby and sat snuggling and feeding, all the time singing softly their own separate songs.

The weather channel predicted a clearing trend for the end of the week. Max was taken with the poetic justice of taking refuge in a cave in these days so near Easter, but to make the two-hour trip undetected, they would have to travel at night in a less identifiable boat. Annie suggested they try Pickles.

"He's an odd duck, but Moby is sure he can be trusted. I know he has a small launch tied up at the dock outside his store."

After much dickering, a plan was hatched: send Max and Dorie into Port Townsend in The Pissant's kicker boat to make contact with Pickles then return that night to pick up the remaining crew and make a run for the island.

Three hours later, Dorie and Max steamed into port, docked, and crawled up the rock bulkhead that protected Pickles' place from the fierce north winds. It was early on a Friday morning, long before Pickle aficionados would be up and about. They had the store to themselves.

In a salute to Frogs' Day, Pickles had dressed following a theme. He wore a frog green bodysuit, flippers on his feet, and a green face-mask complete with snorkel. He jumped from behind a pile of gas masks to greet the women.

"Yikes!" screeched Max at her first encounter with the eccentric store owner. Then, recovering her sharp sense of humor, she gave Pickles the Star Trek hand sign. "Live long and prosper," she translated.

Dorie explained the caper to Pickles, who declared himself smitten with the entire plan. He had been following the news updates the last few days and wanted nothing more than to be part of Annie's crusade. He rubbed his felt green gloves together in obvious delight, like a frog eyeing a swarm of flies circling a sugar bowl.

"The whole scheme sounds delicious," he said, hyperventilating at the thought of the adventure ahead. "Come on back to my apartment."

Dorie and Max followed Pickles into the rear quarters, entering a spotlessly clean room with a fabulous water view. Sitting on the counter were the red shoes Max had catapulted out of back on the dock in LaConner.

"What?! Those...those are my shoes!" Max gasped. "How did you get them?" She checked the leather for damage. Other than a few small dents on the toes, the shoes seemed in perfect shape.

"I got them a few days ago from my buddy in the sheriff's office in LaConner. Would you like them back?"

Obeying an inner intuition, Max declined.

"No, not just now. Maybe later. I think I'd better stick with flats for a while. Never know when I'll have to make a run for it."

Pickles smiled and spirited the shoes under the cabinet.

He gestured toward the water, where the good ship *The Noble Cucumber* sat at anchor. It was a classic fifty-foot dreamboat from the 1930s, built on the shores of Lake Washington. Two strips of 3/4-inch cedar over oak ribs made her a stout and sturdy craft. The hull had been painted a deep, luxurious cucumber green.

"She's none too quick, but then neither am I," Pickles said. "We'll sail at dusk, I presume, under the cover of darkness,?"

"That would be wonderful," said Max, standing on his flippers and giving him a kiss on the forehead.

Pickles blushed and gave her a bullfrog grin.

"Remember, you have to kiss a lot of frogs to find a prince."

"I've done my share of that, trust me," Max said, shaking her head.

Dusk found *The Noble Cucumber* plowing her way to French-man's Cove, where Dorie and Max disembarked, then returned with Annie and South and babies and all the attendant infant gear. *The Pissant* would remain in its snug accommodations until they could safely bring it back.

Dressed in denim and pearls, Pickles greeted everyone warmly and ushered them into the cabin out of the wind. He dispensed hot chocolate, regular and high-octane—that latter fueled by peppermint schnapps—all the while manning the ship's wheel, charming the women, and keeping a sharp eye on the radar screen for any intrusion into the clandestine sortie.

Max took her mug out on the deck, where she leaned over the rail. Sipping the doctored chocolate, she listened to the water rush by the heavy displacement hull, in sync with the insistent throb of the diesel engines. Patchy clouds obscured the moon, so Pickles ran with only the residual light from the scattered shoreline homes. Surprised by the deep dark of the sky, Max stared up with wonder at the clarity of the stars twinkling in between the clouds. From her apartment in

Manhattan, the only twinkling she could see was the dying fluorescent bulbs on the theatre marquee.

Dorie slid open the cabin door and quietly joined Max at the rail.

Something big rose up off the bow and slammed into the water. Max straightened up and stared hard into the blackness. The huge hulk surfaced again, bringing with it a spray of cold water that slapped Max in the face.

"What the—!?" Max cried, spitting out the water that had found its way into her gaping mouth.

"Spy hopping," Dorie explained. "We've run into a pod of Orcas—killer whales. They're jumping out of the water to get a better look at us." She pointed into the water barely three boat-lengths away. "See those dorsal fins? See how some of them droop? That's how you can distinguish between individual whales."

Max gazed into the foaming sound. She saw whales everywhere, beautiful, tuxedo clad. The air rushed from their blowholes as they churned like steam engines through the water.

"There are three main pods in Puget Sound, each one led by an old matriarch. Contrary to their name, killer whales don't hurt people. Oh, look! There's a big mama spy hopping right now!" Dorie pointed behind the boat as a big whale seemingly stood on its tail and looked directly at Max with an eye the size of a saucer.

A chill ran down Max's neck that made her shiver. Later, she would swear that in that split second, a bond had been forged that she would forever consider a sacred connection between her and the Orca.

The whales veered north. Dorie, declaring it too cold for her, went back into the cabin.

Max stood alone at the rail and drank in the beauty of the night. This part of the country couldn't be more different than the bustling city in which she lived. She thought about the life she led in New York. Her apartment refrigerator, with its economy-sized box of baking soda—her mother's gift at the apartment warming; her spider plant, perpetually on life-support, probably dying a slow death on the window sill at this very moment; the apartment's view of a brick wall three feet away; and the not very funny gag gift—a blow-up, life-sized Burt Reynolds doll, with a '70s mustache and a lecherous smile, that stood half-deflated in the closet.

Max had spent the last ten years doing good work, fighting age discrimination across the country by filing briefs and citing academic case law. Now she was surrounded by women who didn't ask permission when they found a moral wrong but took control, pushing the envelope with their very lives. These gray-haired women, semi-proper and certainly more conservative than Max, had opened a door for this supposedly emancipated sister.

"Now walk through it," Max whispered fiercely.

Annie called out from the wheelhouse, "Look out for dead-heads," as if Max had a clue that she meant floating logs that could wreck the boat.

Dorie emerged from the cabin and helped guide the boat past the Sisters rocks and into the boathouse. The ensemble silently disembarked in the darkness and made a beeline up the path, pulling open the four-inch-thick cedar door that allowed access to the fruit cellar and the caves beneath the island. They stood for a moment in the darkness. Then Annie lit a kerosene lamp.

The air smelled musky-sweet as it escaped the island's bowels and mingled with the freedom-loving salt winds. The group paraded down a small walkway that opened up into a cavern the size of a small house, the sandstone walls filled with petroglyphs.

"This will do very nicely," Annie proclaimed. The sound of her voice echoed off the rock walls and down into the thousand fissures, dead-ending in bedrock basalt laid down a billion years before, comforting the island to its very core.

The queen of the island and her court were back.

Annie went back through the fruit cellar and into the house. She stripped the bedding, depositing it in an old sea bag, tucked in a small gas stove and coffee, then returned to the cellar.

After Max helped feed and put the babies down, she gathered up her things. She would leave with Pickles and begin negotiating a settlement in the morning. She hugged each woman in turn, saving the last hug for Annie.

"I won't let you down, Annie," she promised. "I'll be back when we get the best deal possible, or we'll go to trial. But I doubt it will go that far. I don't think they want to screw with the 'Tugboat Grannies.'"

Dorie followed them out, skulking down to John's cabin, but she found it empty. She surmised he was probably still in Seattle. She skipped Merriweather's place, knowing Moby would be upset if Merriweather heard the news first. She continued along the driftwood-littered shore till she got to Moby's. She gently knocked.

"Enter and show yourself" came the salty invitation as Moby sat up in bed.

Dorie sat on a stool by the bed, patiently explaining the events while Moby listened.

"Moby, Annie just wants you to make one trip to the cave tomorrow with food. We don't want to tip our hand, in case the island is under surveillance."

Toward the end of Dorie's narrative, Merriweather's head popped up from under the covers.

"Hi, Dorie. It's me," she said cheerily. "Looks like the weather is going to clear up. Fair and warmer, highs in the mid to upper sixties, with a 30 percent chance of rain. Beware of stiff winds on the inland waters."

Dorie's open mouth curved into a crooked smile.

"How come nobody tells me these things?"

The next morning, Max took a long, hot shower, donned casual clothes, and walked up the hill from Pickles' to the county courthouse. An imposing structure, the courthouse had been built a hundred years earlier of large, peculiar, brown- and black-marbled sandstone blocks carved from a quarry in the Cascade Mountains, then barged to the site and pulled up the hill by teams of oxen. Square and simple, the courthouse stood a full three stories and housed most of the county's office space.

"An overbuilt, pork-barrel fiasco," squawked the *Port Townsend Crier* at the time of the building's erection. "The citizens of this fair land will never need that much government." So, although the building commanded the harbor with its copper roof and bell tower, the top two floors stood unused for the first sixty years. Now, the county government filled the entire building as well as two auxiliary buildings nearby.

Max found the deputy prosecuting attorney sequestered in the coffee room with his pastry. Max introduced herself and informed him she was representing Annie.

"I have a list of demands," she said crisply, pulling out a sheet of paper from her briefcase and placing it before him.

The poor man choked on his cruller, then ran out into the hall, down two flights of stairs, and into the street to find his superior, who was standing in a latte line in the middle of town. When the two men burst back into the office, Max sat sedately, smugly impatient, as they scurried around like Keystone Cops, trying to pawn the litigation off on the state. The state would have none of it. The word was Governor Lockhead felt this should be taken care of at the local level. Translated that meant the issue was too hot, and the possible fallout too great for the governor, but if the Jefferson County boys could handle it, the governor would make it worth their while.

Resigned to his fate, the prosecuting attorney, his deputy hovering, invited Max to step into the outer office that looked out onto Washington Street, the main portal of Port Townsend commerce. A bevy of frightened underlings lingered in the shadows. Recharged with his triple-shot-skinny-grande-mocha-with-whipped, the prosecutor thrust out his hand. Before he could speak, Max leaned forward to scrutinize his brass nametag. Her brow furrowed for a moment, then cleared as though the light bulb had finally come on.

"Oh, I get it," she said.

"Excuse me?" asked the prosecutor, clearly thrown off by this comment.

"Your name tag. It's upside down. But I guess that's so *you* can read it," she said, smiling sweetly.

"Uh, Bob. Bob Barnes." The flustered man fumbled with his lapel with one hand while shaking Max's with the other.

"Nice to meet you, Bob. Maxine Manahan. Call me Max."

"Well, uh, Max," Barnes said, "we've consulted with Child Protective Services, the FBI, the county sheriff's office, and we've decided to charge Mrs. Perkins and her accomplices with only the lesser charge of reckless endangerment of children, instead of the federal charge of kidnapping. That is, if she gives up the children and turns herself in within the next twenty-four hours."

Max acted as though the man had not even spoken.

"I'll tell you what, gentlemen. I'm going to come back tomorrow, and if you haven't met my demands, we'll just have to wait this out."

"Miss Manahan," Barnes said, waving a report at her, "you—"

"'Max,'" said Max, waving an admonishing finger.

"Uh, Max...you may not be aware of the possible danger to those children. We have information that Mrs. Perkins is not fit to handle children of this age, and that she has engaged in questionable practices, not the least of which is an assault on a public figure."

"Assault on a public figure? A kindly grandmother? What did she do, hit him with her Maalox bottle?" Max gave him her sternest glare. "If you want to resolve this situation, you will accede to my demands without fail, by tomorrow at noon. Good day, gentlemen."

Max turned and walked out the door, humming, "Tomorrow, tomorrow, it's only a day away...."

Barnes skated out into the hall after her.

"It will only be a matter of time before we find the whole group!" Barnes raised his clenched fist, crumpling the list of demands into a tight ball. "And when we do, we'll press charges on the whole lot of those miscreants. We'll confiscate boats and houses and...and...," he sputtered, trying to think of other expensive items he could seize but came up short, "...and whatever else we need as evidence!"

Max turned back a moment.

"Bob, you have failed for five days to find those women. They could be anywhere. It's almost Easter. Perhaps you should start looking in caves, because when these women have a Second Coming, it will be your darkest day. Mark my words. Tomorrow, gentlemen."

Max bounced lightly down the stairs, past a janitor who was polishing the marble floors, and out the front doors, stopping at the same latte stand her adversary had. She leisurely sipped a tall-skinny-machiato-dense-foam-no-lid as she sat at a table facing the courthouse, reading the *Crier,* aware that the prosecutors were scrutinizing her through the windows of the courthouse. She knew Annie was winning in the loyal court of public opinion when she saw the headline, "Tugboat Grannies Still on the Loose."

The story chronicled the plane crash, the island, the escape in the dark at LaConner. There were interviews with locals who knew Annie, had known her family before her. At the top of the paper in a box, it read, "Tugboat Grannies Watch, Day 7."

When she phoned John to get the statewide and national perspective, she found him close to manic.

"Max, I've got television people on my case, day and night, and they've hired their own people to find Annie. Are you sure they're in a safe place? This whole thing could blow up in our face if we aren't careful."

"All we need is a few more days. I gave the list of demands to the prosecutor up here, a Bob Barnes, and I'll be meeting him again tomorrow. I think they'll come around. They don't have many options at this point."

"All right." John sounded relieved. "I'm going to get some rest. Be on the lookout for reporters. They'll be up there as soon as they get word you've surfaced. I'll talk to you tomorrow."

Maintaining a low profile never crossed Max's mind. She and Pickles went to dinner at the most expensive restaurant in town. Out the windows, they watched as TV helicopters landed on the football field north of the town center. By the time they stepped out into the street, they were met with a media frenzy of cameras, lights, and microphones.

Max put on her sunglasses and calmly fielded questions. She confirmed the babies' good health and affirmed that grandmothers have rights of access to their grandchildren. She laughed when someone asked if the women minded being called "The Tugboat Grannies."

"No, of course not. These women are heroes. They, not the state of Washington, are the true protectors of these children."

The wedge followed them down the street to the secondhand store, where Max slipped in through the door, and Pickles fended off the crowd, only to have them surround the building in cars, vans, and even a few boats.

Max had chosen casual clothes for her first visit to the courthouse, but the next day she was all business, tougher than a New York slumlord. She stunned the courthouse staff by wearing an elegant, navy-blue Armani suit, her resurrected Chanels, a perfectly matched necklace and bracelet of natural pearls—courtesy of Pickles' antique jewelry collection—a blue hat with black netting covering her face, and a killer smile.

Outside, the reporters and their cameramen had a field day. Beauty, style, and the Tugboat Grannies . . . theater in Victoriana.

His nametag righted, Bob Barnes sat opposite Max at a long conference table. His staff had swelled to an even dozen. One of the men looked suspiciously like the custodian Max had seen cleaning the foyer the day before. Hopelessly outclassed, his throat already parched, his lips nearly welded together, Barnes poured a glass of water and looked over the draft of Max's demands one more time.

He decided to start on a positive note, explaining that he was willing to grant amnesty to the two other grandmothers involved. There would be no seizing of property and the state would conduct another home study.

"I think you can see we are reasonable people here, Miss Manahan." Max did not insist on his using her first name today, feeling her upscale outfit demanded his deference. "Mrs. Perkins will relinquish the children to Child Protective Services and be restricted from visiting the dependent orphans."

Barnes seemed pleased with himself with this pronouncement.

"We may need to look into certain improprieties that have come to our attention. We'll handle the rest of the details from our end." He pushed the paper across the table to Max, and then coyly pulled it back. "But, if we find her before we complete our business here, all bets are off."

Max methodically worked her fingers from her gloves. For a split second, she was more than a little tempted to slap the gloves across the Barnes's smug little smile, but she was a guest in his fair city, so she put the gloves together and folded them into her Gucci bag.

Without looking at the piece of paper, she pushed it aside with disdain. She reached into her purse and unfolded a newspaper.

"Perhaps you would be interested in a preview of the Easter Edition of the *Seattle Times*."

The paper was a mock-up, sent over by John. The front page was blank, except for the words the *Seattle Times*, Easter Edition, and small rectangles for the proposed weekend highlights: NCAA basketball scores, "Roses, Roses, Roses" in the Garden Section, and in the third rectangle, the words, "Tugboat Grannies, pages 2, 3."

Bob opened the paper and spread it tentatively on the table. Pages two and three were devoted entirely to the Grannies. There was a color photo of Annie holding the twins, taken at the hospital, pictures of the island, a biography of Annie's work in the Red Cross, a history of tugboats on Puget Sound, biographies of Dorie and South, a reprint of a column, "Foster Care in Disarray in Washington State," and a moving editorial by John.

Barnes's twelve underlings clustered around their boss and scanned the articles. They scanned desperately for a ray of hope, but found none. After a hushed ten minutes, Barnes pushed the paper to the middle of the table and gave a weak smile.

"I see you have an ally in Seattle," Barnes began, "but that doesn't affect us much over here."

"Really." Max feigned surprise. " You think the case is about law, gentlemen. It is not. It is about politics. You don't need any bad publicity. I thought your economy here depended primarily on tourism. Let's look out the window and see what kind of press is out there." She scooted her chair back, got up, and walked to the window. Three television trucks sat parked at the curb with satellite dishes fanned out, two helicopters hovered over the harbor, and a gathering crowd was working its way up the hill.

"It's a beautiful day in the neighborhood, isn't it, Mr. Barnes? I'm sure all of this attention is directed at the upcoming quilt show this weekend."

Max sat down at the library table and took a duplicate list of demands from her purse and then gave the group a measured smile. She drummed her coral French cut nails on the leather table top.

"Gentlemen, these are some of God's favorite people…grandmothers and babies. This may just come down to a matter of the heart. We will have our day in court sir. And the children will be living with their grandmother at the end of the day. Mark my words." Max dismissed them by methodically gathering up the newspaper.

She retrieved the gloves, took her time slipping them back on, then closed the clasp of her purse with an emphatic snap.

"I'll be at Pickles' Secondhand Store if you need me."

Before anyone could object, she put on her sunglasses, walked out the door, down the steps, and on to the sidewalk to work her charm on the waiting cameras.

Meanwhile, back at the island, Moby patrolled the spit, routing reporters trying to storm the beach. He would shoot off a round from his rifle into the air as the spirit moved him, just to keep every one guessing.

Annie remained insulated from all the action, sequestered away in their mole-like underworld, where there was nothing but the sound of dripping water from a spring and the smell of the earth. The twins were content and the women stayed busy cleaning the cavern and inventorying the shelves that held primarily books and newspapers.

Travis and Tate, unaffected by the hoopla, completed the framework for lifting the bell. The horses skidded the bell into position from the beach. Father and son repositioned the pulleys, threading the wire cable and clearing a path to allow a smooth, steady pull from the team of workhorses.

Merriweather had stopped making trails through the woods. She spent her days combing the beach for feathers and the nights roving the sheets with Moby—a happy time for her.

Back at Pickles' store, Max and Pickles rooted through his racks of clothes, like veteran shoppers at a flea market. Max was amazed at the range and sophistication of what she assumed was his own wardrobe. Pickles was tickled to have her try on combinations, allowing him to critique them with a practiced eye.

"Nothing trashy," he said, shaking his head. "We want to maintain a sophisticated elegance of professionalism."

Max slipped on an antique vanilla-custard silk blouse and a pleated black skirt and preened in front of the mirror.

"I haven't worn that for years," Pickles confessed, standing back, hand on hip with a pincushion around his wrist and a measuring tape over his shoulder. He made a few swift marks on the skirt with garment chalk. Max stepped behind a screen and slipped off the skirt. Pickles sat down at the sewing machine for a few minutes, then dashed over to his ironing board and meticulously ironed the pleats. He handed the garment back over the screen.

Max reappeared and won Pickles' approval.

"A perfect fit. But what shoes to wear? At first, I thought espadrilles." He pulled shoes from boxes as he talked. "What was I thinking? Joan of Arc? Get a grip, man.

"How about these?" Pickles lovingly unwrapped tissue paper to reveal a pair of periwinkle-blue Italian leather sandals. "You like? Too springish? Too *Three Coins in the Fountain*?" Out of another box, he pulled a cardigan sweater almost the same color as the blouse, with the same periwinkle blue flowers. "From Germany," he said. "Try it on."

As Max did so, Pickles held up a delicate, silver-chained necklace, with tiny amethyst beads.

"I don't know," said Max. "Do you think this look is a little too 'school girlish'?"

"I say no," Pickles said, without hesitation, and then he gave a wistful grin thinking about school girls and starched collars. "You said you kicked the shit out of them today with that New York look. Tomorrow, we go less hard, more feminine. Keep 'em off balance.

"I just wish I could wear clothes like this, but you—you're beautiful, and everything fits so perfectly. It's like dressing a Vargas girl. No, no, no, no. A Breck girl. That's it. The 'All-American Girl' they used in magazines to sell shampoo."

Max stared at him, and Pickles saw her eyes go misty.

"That's what my dad used to call me, 'The Breck Girl.'"

Max had shared clothes with girlfriends, but she had never had anyone like Pickles—the greatest clotheshorse in the history of girlfriends—to borrow clothes from. Most everything fit, and what didn't he quickly altered. And he had a genius for pulling the most unusual combinations together and making them work.

"You know, this is fun, but I wonder if we're taking the focus away from Annie and the kids." Max looked at the boxes spread on the rug around her. "It's about them, not me."

"Nonsense. You're making a statement. You are focusing their attention on what you're saying. Don't worry, you can't upstage babies and grandmothers. They're at the top of the food chain.

"Next, we go retro. The forties—Garbo in *Grand Hotel*, Ingrid Bergman in *Casablanca*. I've got some great stuff. We can talk about it tomorrow."

The next morning, Max did feel a little like Doris Day, decked out in her "good girl" outfit as she politely talked to the reporters on the courthouse steps. When she entered the conference room, she found Bob Barnes conferring with his staff.

"Good morning," she said cordially, looking down the table and smiling. No one smiled back except a man on the end with glasses, and his smile turned to a grimace when his neighbor laid an elbow into his ribs.

Cranky lot, Max thought to herself. Things must be going better than I realized.

"Ahhhemmm."

Prosecutor Bob cleared his voice, signaling the beginning of the meeting.

"We can agree with most of your minor points, but we have three provisions that we will not compromise." He ticked them off on his fingers. "One, the state wants the children turned over to foster parents. Two, we consider Mrs. Perkins to be a flight risk and want her under surveillance. And three, if there is agreement, we request that, instead of a jury trial, a superior court judge consider the evidence and make a ruling."

Max knew she was on shaky ground. Annie couldn't hide out forever. The state ordinarily would put forth a custody battle for the twins with no interference from anyone. That they were capitulating on any points was a sign they felt blackmailed, desperate, and crowded into a corner.

And that's one way to set a precedent, Max thought.

She had thought long and hard whether to trust a jury or a judge to make this decision. She and Annie had decided the best they could do was joint-custody between Annie and the state-mandated adoptive or foster parents.

There had been many discussions at the cabin, and they had decided a judge would probably be older, with aging parents. That would be a plus. Also, a judge would have a better grasp of the options available and be able to find a way to make a more complex decision than a jury. Possibly an older judge could see him- or herself in the same position some day, cut off from grandchildren.

Mentally, Max played devil's advocate. Then again, juries were very emotional. Annie cut a compelling figure, a victim who had lost her only daughter and granddaughter, the little guy fighting city hall, a reluctant celebrity. Celebrities as a rule did well with juries, who sometimes looked for heroes to award with their approval. But juries were also notoriously unpredictable. Given the right circumstances, a hung jury would put the twins in limbo even longer.

"To the third point, judge or jury, you can make the call," Max said, tossing Barnes a bone. "To the first point, I suggest a health professional visit every other day with Mrs. Perkins during the trial, to confirm the good health of the infants and the excellent care they are receiving. But the children will stay with their great-grandmother until custody is established, one way or the other."

"To the second point, well,..." Max shook her head. "Really, no great-grandmother is going to go on the lam with two infants, leaving behind the family farm and any hope of a normal life for the children. This woman has spent her life working for the good of others. There is no risk here. And I want the island proclaimed a safe zone to keep the public and the press away."

Barnes sat up straight, and Max thought she actually saw a gleam in his eye.

"We would like to check with the State Child Protective Services before any agreement is reached. Could we have a half-hour recess?"

"Fine with me."

One of the two assistant attorneys, a petite brunette in her late twenties, stood by while Max organized her briefcase.

"I like your outfit. Did you get it in New York?"

"Everything I'm wearing came from Pickles' Secondhand Store, right down the street," Max said. She hoped her honesty wouldn't start a run on the Pickles' inventory—at least before she was done with it.

Max slowly tried to work the conversation to her advantage.

"Do you ever get this kind of media attention up here?"

"Never. They don't even know we exist, unless there's a murder or road slides during a heavy rain. Like the train, everybody passes us by. It's a wonderful little town for kids to grow up in, but when they grow up and leave, they usually don't come back. Small-town America is full of old people, hippies, and starving artists.

"And it's hard to make a living up here. A few factory jobs at the mill, that's about it." She looked like she was about to say more when Bob Barnes walked into the room and gave her a disapproving look.

"Uh oh, caught fraternizing with the enemy." She put her hand on Max's arm. "We'll talk later."

For the first time in the negotiations, Barnes actually seemed cheerful.

"We don't appreciate being held hostage, but we are trying to resolve this matter judiciously. We will accept all of your points, and we think the proper venue would be for a superior court judge to make the ruling, after hearing all the evidence.

"The next available judge would be Strom Livingston. Court will convene Monday morning in the chambers on the second floor."

Barnes looked around triumphantly, although Max felt the victory belonged to her.

"Please bring a final copy of the concession points to Pickles' Secondhand Store this afternoon for my signature," she said. "We'll be ready for trial Monday."

"Well, that's all for today," Barnes said, getting up and beckoning his people to do the same.

"Yes," Max smiled sincerely. "Happy Easter, everyone."

Pickles had prepared freshly roasted red peppers and tuna sandwiches for lunch. He had also worked out a matrix of several possible clothes combinations for the coming week. Never quite settling into lunch, he would take a bite, pop up, and disappear upstairs, returning several minutes later carrying clothes on his back like a camel. Then he sorted blouses, skirts, dresses, and coats in separate piles on the back of the sofa. On the floor, he neatly arranged shoes, purses, and accessories.

On one run he brought down rain gear, raincoats, and boots.

"*De rigueur* up here," he grunted,

Max heard the counter bell from the storefront that Pickles had neglected all afternoon. When she went out front, she recognized the woman from the meeting earlier.

"I've brought over that paperwork," she said, self-consciously brushing her hair back behind her ear. "Do you have time to look it over now? If not, I could come back later."

"Now's good. Let's adjourn to the next room." Max held out her hand. "You know my name, but I don't know yours."

"Claudia Correll," said the woman, giving Max a warm hand to shake.

Max took Claudia back to the kitchen, poured her a glass of wine, cut a tuna sandwich in half, and put it on a plate.

"Pickle?" Max questioned as she left the room and burrowed into the jar by the counter, hoping to find one without a gnawed end.

"Sure. My mom always packed a pickle in my lunch with tuna," chirped Claudia. "A tuna sandwich without a pickle is a sad sight."

As they ate, Max peppered Claudia with questions about the judge, Strom Livingston. Between bites, Claudia volunteered that he was "by the book."

"They call him Sergeant Friday after that guy on the old TV show *Dragnet*. 'Just the facts, ma'am.' He lives in town and doesn't seem to have much of a sense of humor. He takes himself pretty seriously. Can I please have another pickle?"

Later that afternoon, Pickles ferried Max back to the island with the news. Annie and her troops surfaced, squinting mole-like in the bright sunshine. John, having heard earlier from Max, had brought three big Copper River king salmon for what he called a "Tugboat Granny Victory Dinner" on the beach. Pinky, Travis, and Tate had collected *The Pissant* from its hiding place.

The ecstatic group engaged in several rounds of hugs and back-slaps.

Annie and her babies were to have their day in court.

During dessert, John told of the thousands of letters, telegrams, faxes, and phone calls he had received in the last week. There were also six sacks of mail from the Port Gamble post office—filled with money, advice, and prayers.

That night, the islanders slept in peace for the first time since the plane crash. Each slept with his and her days numbered, each with individual hopes and fears, some innocent in the eyes of God and some guilty in the eyes of man. In the turbulent churning of civilization, the court case would be a small event, a test of tribal law, long since forgotten in America: the rights of a family versus the rights of the state. Some said, "Grandparents have no rights," and some said, "Where would we be without them?"

A pebble had fallen into a tidal pool, sending ripples across the ocean, gently washing continents as far away as China. Even as Seven Sisters Island slept, the ripples were beginning to return.

As a boy, Strom Livingston had been a collector—rocks, baseball cards, comic books, just about anything. But even more than collecting, he liked to organize and label, to categorize, box, sort, and stack. In a disorganized world, he longed to bring order. A simple mission, to be sure, but one that clearly needed to be taken on, and he was just the man to do it.

From the time he was young, Strom had planned every event in his life with methodic precision. A staunch Catholic, he had finished college in four years, graduate school in two, married the year after that, practiced law for fifteen years, and then had become a judge, bringing justice to his old hometown. After he had achieved financial stability, he and his wife had two children spaced three years apart—first a boy and then a girl. All according to the Strom lifetime plan.

He loved the law. There was precedent, there was truth, and there was retribution.

Strom knew his nickname. He had heard the whispered "Sergeant Friday" as he walked the courthouse halls. Instead of being insulted, he considered the moniker an honor.

"Lady Justice is blind for a reason," he would often remark. "She need only weigh the facts to find the truth. And that's all there is to it!"

Max woke to the smell of coffee and fresh bread, the sound of seagulls squawking, a rooster crowing, and babies crying. She cleaned a peek hole in the dusty window with the hem of her nightgown and drank in the view. The boards creaked under her bare feet as she went sleepily down the stairs.

"Cup of coffee, young lady?" Annie asked, without looking up from the stove.

"Please," Max said, looking around for the twins.

"Help yourself. The cups are on the table, and the coffee is here on the stove." Annie pulled a loaf of bread from the oven and slid it into the warming ovens above the stove. She plucked two bottles and made a beeline for the living room, where Dorie had a double handful of babies.

"Can I feed one?" Max asked.

*This is what it's all about,* she thought. *Babies, grandmothers, and an unbroken string of love.*

She knew it was up to her to keep it going.

Dorie tested a bottle and handed both baby and bottle to Max. Little Annie went right to work, her bright brown eyes studying the woman who was feeding her.

*What was it about babies,* Max wondered. *They are so intense, so commanding.*

Breakfast consisted of oatmeal with brown sugar and cream.

"It makes you regular," Annie said, in the belief that just saying it would make it true.

Max thought oatmeal sounded wonderfully earthy, unlike her usual bagel-on-the-fly in New York City.

Max played with the twins on the floor till their nap. Then she went outside to sample the island. She recognized Moby gathering firewood and could see *The Pissant* anchored in the lagoon. Down through the pasture came two of the largest horses she had ever seen, dragging a pile of logs. The draft horses in parades pulling beer wagons seemed like poodles at a dog show compared to the horses that drew nearer. She could see the sweat on their flanks, the mud caked on their leather harness, and the huge interlaced, knotted haunches, straining against the load. Her eye followed the skid line across the pasture—an ugly, dirty scar of muddied earth that split the pasture into perfect pear halves of spring green.

On the far side of the brace, under the deep chests of the horses, Max could see a pair of tall black leather boots. The boot tops looked brand-new, but from the ankles down, the leather was slashed and bruised by the underbrush. A thorny string of blackberry vine was jammed between one of the laces.

Max glimpsed the head of dark blond hair dipping between the animals. The man wore denim pants, the bottoms of the cuff purposefully shredded in neat strips to avoid the disaster of catching on roots or limbs in the woods. The strips dangled freely, barely clearing the boot tops.

"All right, easy now. I just want to untangle this strap," Max heard him say. His tone was conversational, as if he were adjusting the strap on his wife's dress before an evening out. His one hand curled around the chest harness for balance in the mud; the other untangled an unseen line. Abruptly, the man stood up, and with the same soft brown eyes of his horses, noticed Max for the first time. He gave a quick smile.

"Hi there" was all he said, as his hand tenderly explored down the horse's withers to the ankle. Standing up, the man swatted the flank. With a well-placed heel to shackle, he released the logs from the harness.

# Chapter FIFTEEN

**M**ax smiled to herself, wondering how the Manhattan Hunt Club would find a jacket to fit those shoulders. She had seen the tiny jockeys spring into their saddles, the trainers, the grooms, and the horse whisperers—they all talked to the horses. But their relationship to the animals seemed remote compared to what she had just witnessed. Here no space separated man and horse; they were of one mind, one pace, comfortable and connected.

The horses surged forward and drank deeply from an old cast-iron bathtub filled with spring water. The beads of water clung to their whiskers like pussy willows. Travis reached into a wooden box and pulled out two carrots, the leafy tops lying limp. The horses sucked them in with their limber lips and chewed with relish.

Max was not used to being ignored. Unloved maybe, but never ignored.

"I could use a little roughage myself," she said, punctuating her statement with a New York-minute smile.

"As you wish." Travis handed her a carrot, as a steward might proffer a fine bottle of wine. "You would be Lady Max, from the Big Apple. I would be Travis, keeper of the livestock. And if I may take this opportunity—"

He never finished. Tate threw open the boathouse door, and with a war hoop, sprinted down the path and jumped on his dad's back. He clung like a monkey, complete with a goofy grin, peering over his dad's shoulder at Max. The man obviously had a lot of admirers.

Four sets of brown eyes and two heads of blond hair. Max considered the ante raised. Both were obviously well-adapted to their environment and full of spirit, if slightly unkempt around the edges.

Max wondered if anyone had taken on the care and feeding of the horse handler and his son.

"This is Tate." Travis presented his son by flipping him over his shoulder and setting him squarely on his feet in front of her. Tate reached out to take Max's outstretched hand.

"Pleased to meet you, Tate. I'm Max. That was quite the dramatic entrance you made there."

Tate shrugged his shoulders.

"Dad, can I go see if Moby's up yet? I'm going to help put his fake eye in again today."

His dad nodded, and with the same reckless abandon in which he had entered the picture, Tate let out another holler, jumped over a log, and rounded the boathouse out of sight. Max could hear him yelling all the way to Moby's.

Travis pulled a thermos bottle from behind a log and offered some coffee to Max.

"Sure," she said, even though she was coffeed out.

Travis cleansed the cup by swirling fresh coffee in the mug, and dumping the liquid on the ground. As he poured steaming coffee into what apparently passed for a clean cup in these parts, Max could see that Travis, too, could be cleaned up into what passed for boyishly handsome. He looked to be close to her own age. She guessed that he probably didn't own a computer, much less a laptop or a BlackBerry, which cut him away from the herd of men she had been dating for the last five years.

Max felt her antennae go up. She would have to get more details from Annie and the other women.

Max spent the rest of the day acquainting herself with Annie's résumé, taking pictures of the island and its inhabitants, and listening to Annie recount tales of her childhood. She wanted personal reflections to add a human side to the guardianship dilemma of the twins. Annie and her daughter had been at odds for years, but her glowing reminiscences of Sarah as a young woman proved that the maternal bond had been reforged.

Next came marshalling arguments against age discrimination. Max had trotted them out numerous times over the years. Most of the laws were the product of social prejudice against older people. Often arbitrary, these laws were easily constitutionally challenged.

Since there was no electricity on the island, Max had to row out to *The Pissant* to recharge her laptop batteries. In the first rowing instruction session with Travis, she completely drenched him as she struggled to keep the oars in the water. But by the end of the week, Max had mastered the technique enough to solo.

Max and Travis began to form a begrudging friendship. Although close in age, they came from different worlds. She, who didn't drive a car in Manhattan, had become enthralled with the feeling of self-propulsion a boat gave her. And Travis had gamely fought his way through her woodstove-cooked dinner of burned stew and hockey puck biscuits. After the dinner, she had insisted on taking Travis and his son to Port Gamble for dessert. Flustered, she had rowed in circles at first, but they had laughed all the way to town. Travis rowed them all home.

On Saturday afternoon a boat Annie recognized as a captain's gig motored into the cove and dropped anchor. A rowboat was expertly lowered from the deck. A tall, straight-backed man in a military uniform, medals hanging off his chest, and cords dropping from shoulder to sash stood in the stern, while six synchronized rowers nosed the launch into the gravel shore.

Anne had identified the man simply by his posture. She greeted him with a hug, brought him up to the house, and introduced him to Max as Alberto Emilio Garcia, Argentinean ambassador to the US.

Schooled at Stanford University, the man spoke impeccable English. When he took off his jacket and hung it on the back of a chair, it promptly tipped over. Alberto calmly picked it up, laughing.

"Perhaps I will give some of my medals to the Vice Premier when I get home."

He told Annie that he had been in San Francisco, visiting his son, a graduate student in political science at U.C. Berkeley, when he heard of Annie's plight.

"You are in need of help, and I am here to offer whatever humble assistance I can render. Even now, ten years later, people in the mountain villages in the Andes talk about you and what you did for us after the earthquake. I want to repay you for your kindness.

"I have read the newspaper articles and heard reports on television. What can I do?"

Max jumped in. "If you have the time, you would be a wonderful character witness."

"I will make the time. My ship is in Port Townsend. If necessary, I will stay behind, and fly to the next port." Alberto smiled at Annie. "You have the heart of a lion, dear lady. It would be my honor if you and your friends would be my guests for dinner on our ship."

Annie fussed first, then accepted.

"What should we wear?"

"It is a simple shipboard dinner," Alberto explained. "We will be eating with the sailors on the ship."

Within the hour they had boarded the gig and were heading north to Port Townsend.

Anchored close to the city shoreline was the pride of the Argentinean Navy, the tall ship *Condor*. Considered by sailing enthusiasts to be one of the most beautiful sailing ships in the world, this traditional, full-masted, steel sailing ship was one hundred and sixty feet of pure white elegance.

Now used primarily as a training tool for young naval cadets, the *Condor* plied the waters of the world as a goodwill ambassador, showcasing Argentinean pride, giving onboard tours, and entertaining visitors with performances by the marching band.

As they neared the *Condor*, Dorie asked Alberto, "Is that your ship?"

Alberto bowed at the waist. "It belongs to the Argentine people and those who serve them."

Befitting an ambassador, Alberto was piped aboard. The ship's company, in dress whites, stood at attention.

He introduced the island residents to the captain, who turned to his men and in Spanish explained that Annie had administered aid to their countrymen after the famous earthquake in the Andes.

There had been talk among the sailors when their ship made this unscheduled stop in a carefully planned itinerary. And now they knew why. Although the ship was constantly visited by foreign dignitaries, none were as admired as this ordinary-looking older woman, dressed simply in black slacks and a green sweater, someone who had come to their country's aid purely out of love and concern. They clapped long and hard in welcome.

The supper was typically Latin American, starting at dusk and served by a squadron of cadets. They began in measured cadence to adorn the creamy embroidered tablecloth with *picadas*—appetizers of Argentinean cheeses, marinated vegetables, and cold cuts. The wine was a delicate Chardonnay from the rolling highlands, separating the scissor-sharp peaks of the Andes from the sprawling grasslands of the Pampas. Next came silver platters piled high with *empanadas* wrapped around lamb, raisins, scallions, and garlic.

As darkness descended, candelabra were lit and the pace quickened. Crude slabs of still-sizzling *bife de chorizo* were hoisted from the grill to the *platos de madera* in front of the guests, each wooden plate grooved to catch the juices. A dollop of garlic mashed potatoes and a tangle of Swiss chard with prosciutto completed the fare, as a robust Argentinean red from the Mendoza Valley spilled from pitchers held high above islanders' heads. The libation sloshed carelessly into the crystal goblets, leaving crimson stains on the cloth.

Annie and her army attempted to rough-ride up the San Juan mounds of beef and sausage. By the time they fought their way through a dessert called "One Thousand Leaves of Dulce de Leche," made with a thousand layers of phyllo laced with caramel sauce and butter, they were defeated. Grease spots, dark red blotches, and half-eaten plates of food littered the gastronomic battlefield. Overwhelmed, Annie threw up her hands in surrender.

"*No mas*," she said.

Apparently that was the signal for the ship's band, which had been providing pleasant background music, to swing into a tango. Three cadets dressed in black, skin-tight trousers and silver-encrusted jackets leaped out of the night and began a provocative stallion strut across the schooner's deck. Merriweather was pulled from the table into the moment. She swayed to the explosion of Latin testosterone till she collapsed back into her chair.

Alberto Emilio clasped Annie's hand in an invitation to join in the dance on the deck. Annie demurred.

"This is too much for my aging heart," she pleaded. "We have a big day tomorrow."

The ambassador smiled and gallantly relented. The islanders gratefully retreated.

It was midnight before they returned home, sated and exhilarated by the whole delicious experience.

In the morning, Moby moved about lethargically as he and Merriweather hid Easter eggs for John's grandchildren and Tate. That evening, after a modest Easter meal of roast lamb, sautéed asparagus, and rosemaried potatoes à la John, the island readied for the firestorm about to unfold in the courtroom.

"Don't be fooled; the state has its teeth into this case," Max warned them. "They won't give up their hold easily."

Monday, the twins charmed the public health nurse, Mrs. Camper, with belly laughs and burps. Her associate, the deputy health inspector, having heard rumors of Moby's previous assault on the Beedle motor launch, nervously paced back and forth on the beach, guarding his boat. His apprehension was not helped by the furtive looks put on him by Moby and John.

"These youngsters have certainly progressed," Mrs. Camper said cheerfully, going over the reports from the hospital. She rolled the twins around on the blanket and listened to their hearts. "It's amazing what modern medicine can do for preemies. They look like healthy, happy youngsters to me." She put her stethoscope back in her bag. "Do you mind if I nose around a bit? I'm going to have to testify at the trial this week about how the twins seem physically and mentally. Who is going to watch the babies during the trial?"

"They will be under the supervision of another grandmother. Would you like to meet her?"

"If it wouldn't be too much trouble. Just for the record. I need to cover the bases."

Annie took her down to South's cabin. South shook Mrs. Camper's hand, while Annie explained the situation. Mrs. Camper asked if South knew CPR. South showed the woman her certification card and answered all questions politely.

"Well, I think everything looks in order here." Mrs. Camper shook South's hand. "Will you escort us to the boat, Annie? I don't think I need to see any more."

The stubble-faced boat tender steadied the boat as the nurse made her way to the front of the bow.

"Good luck at the trial, Annie," Mrs. Camper sang out, as the boat swung out into the cove with the deputy looking back over his shoulder toward the beach.

Annie looked toward Moby's shack, just to be sure he hadn't heard a call to arms.

Sunset spread crimson into the cloud furrows as Max and Travis curried the horses in the makeshift shed next to the boathouses. The ever-invading trumpet vine, fresh green leaves just beginning to uncurl, considered its summer battle plan: to pry loose another season's worth of roof shingles and knot-holed siding from the ancient boathouse with the destructive, relentless, wandering tendrils.

Annie had always loved the orange-trumpeted blossom, but today she was angered at its malignant aggression. She tugged hard at one of the vines, tearing it loose from the roof and stepping on it as it lay on the path. She knew it would find its way back; it had its own destiny to fulfill. She also knew her anger was not about the vine; it was about Moby.

Annie could hear Max and Travis' laughter as they stroked the horses. She walked down the spit to the last cabin, where Moby lay recovering from the procedure that had sucked out two quarts of fluid from his lungs. The end game was near. Annie stopped on the slanted porch and leaned on a makeshift driftwood handrail lined with a collection of nearly a dozen drying cigar stubs of random lengths.

She listened. Hearing no sound, she sat on the car seat and lit one of the stubs, not smoking, but mesmerized, watching the burn of the ash lengthen. She remembered hearing that during a rival lawyer's summation, Clarence Darrow had once stuck a piano wire in his cigar and let the distracting ash capture the attention of the jury as it dangled precipitously, defying gravity but never falling.

She shook her head, acknowledging a fear that so many of her experiences had become obsolete. Could an old dog guide two pups into the future with skills three generations old? And she hadn't done much right the one and only chance she'd had. Listening to her heart, she heard another voice: She could not abandon these children And how could she face her sisters' wrath if she didn't at least try?

"Who the hell is smoking my cigars?" Moby shouted from the darkness.

Annie pushed open the door and leaned on the frame. Hand on her hip, the cigar wedged in the side of her mouth, she gave her best Mae West impersonation.

"It's me, bub. What are you gonna to do about it?"

Moby smiled from his bed. "Well, don't just stand there, close the door. I've got a sick man in here."

Annie came in, kindled the fire, and then moved into the chair next to the bed.

"How're you feeling?"

"Like shit." Moby pulled the covers up to his neck. "My whole body aches, but I expect to be up and around tomorrow."

"I need to get a hold of your daughter," Annie said gently, pulling a full bottle of whiskey from her pocket and setting it on the table. "She needs to know."

"For Christ's sake, Annie, let it go. At least till after the trial. Let her live her life. I don't want her around here. This shit is eating me up. At night I can hear it gnawing away at my guts."

Annie unscrewed the bottle top and handed the whiskey to Moby. He took three swigs and handed it back, expecting Annie to indulge. Annie hated whiskey, but in the spirit of the battle, she took a long drink and shuddered as she brought the bottle down. She stuck her tongue out and breathed the fire out of her throat.

Moby laughed out loud. "You can't smoke cigars—or drink whiskey."

"Is there anything I can get you?" Annie asked.

"I could use some pot to relax me. Short of that, I hope there are leftovers from dinner. I'm going to be hungry."

Annie was happy to hear the spunk, even if it was forced. She decided to wait a few days before phoning Moby's daughter. Moby had earned the right to call the shots.

As she walked by the boathouse on the way to the trail, she saw a suspiciously lumpy haystack.

There was plenty of moon to guide Annie home.

Travis unbuttoned Maxine's scratchy new blue jeans. She gave a sly, private smile and pulled him down on top of her. The hands that had guided the nearly two tons of horseflesh that afternoon, patiently probed her last defense. She surrendered to the smell of leather harnesses, the barbed edges of timothy grasses gently sawing into her naked back, and the taste of a man who lived far from the maze of New York concrete and forged steel.

Generations of scoundrels, saints, and sinners, in long strings of sturdy Conestoga wagons, took six months or more to ford rivers and battle hostile Indians to come to the fertile valleys of the West. Maxine Manahan, late arriving pioneer, made the journey in a single night in April. She crossed the Mississippi River, lingered momentarily in the high altitude of the Rocky Mountains of Colorado, and finally lay whipped, wet, and winded, her back resting on the cold wet earth of an island on the Pacific Coast.

She would never go back to rescue her spider plant, the balloon man in the closet, or the box of baking soda in the refrigerator.

In the wee hours of the morning, Max slipped out from under the shared horse blanket and looked fondly at a still-sleeping Travis. Balancing on one foot, she struggled into her clothes, damp from the heavy night air.

Hearing the sound of helicopters, she squinted into a rising sun and spotted three local television copters hovering a few hundred yards from the beach. She pulled her sweatshirt down defensively, tripped through the wet grass, and made her way to Annie's house.

In the guest bedroom, Max leaned on an old dressing table with an oval mirror, looking into a suddenly unfamiliar face, pulling straw from her hair and flicking with her finger some kind of little yellow seeds from her navel. She wondered if those were the wild oats she had been searching for. She lectured herself in the mirror.

"Girl, you better pull your bony ass together. This is the most important case in your life."

She straightened up.

"I can handle it," she said aloud. "This and more."

Annie woke early that morning. She had seen Max coming up the path. Having wrestled with the decision all night, she was convinced that the twins needed to attend the court hearing. Noisy, hungry, crying children and messy diaper changes be damned—in her eyes, the children were the focus, not age, sexism, or the state's right to find parents for her great-grandchildren. Max agreed with her, as she and Annie fed the twins and ate oatmeal together in the kitchen.

Only Moby, Merriweather, the dogs, and Ahab were to be left on the island. The rest were loaded onto *The Pissant* for the hour transport to Port Townsend. A small flotilla of well-wishers and reporters ushered them up the coast. Some waved and gave an encouraging "thumbs up."

"This is like the Macy's parade in New York," Max said excitedly, "without the balloons."

She leaned toward Annie.

"You've created a lot of interest, Annie," she yelled over the roar of the powerful twin 500 horsepower Ford diesels that belched forth a thick, black smoke from the smokestack of the tug, creating a ribbon that floated slowly north toward Canada.

As *The Pissant* entered the harbor, the *Condor* band struck up American march music. A banner strung from the mainsail said, "Argentina Ama Annie." Lined up along the docks and beaches, a crowd of women gave a huge roar as the tug steamed into the dock.

Pickles had been to Woodstock, the Academy Awards, and the World Series, but this was something else. The town bulged with hundreds of women. He could see that Annie and entourage would have difficulty navigating the crowds. He sprang into action with a flatbed truck loaded with hay bales for seating, staged for the Queen and her Court from the town's upcoming Rhododendron Festival. The crowd surged forward as Annie and the babies were hoisted aboard.

The street was a sea of heads, women of many ages and many backgrounds, but of a single unwavering voice when it came to family and children. They were angry and ready to defend a tradition, not rules made by men behind closed doors in legislatures and bureaucratic offices. They represented an older, unwritten law that lived not in any doctrine but deep in their hearts.

The strength of family would not be trampled without their voices being heard loud and clear.

From behind one of the hay bales, Pickles brought out a portable megaphone. He quickly realized he was in over his head. He shrugged his shoulders and handed the megaphone to Max.

"They're your people. You're going to have to talk to them."

Overwhelmed by the size of the crowd and their passion, Max shook her head. These were Annie's soldiers. She handed the megaphone to Annie, who held up her hand for quiet, and then yelled into the megaphone.

"These are *my* great-grandchildren."

She handed the mouthpiece back to Max and took the twins from Dorie and South, cradling both in her arms.

The crowd erupted into a roar that echoed down Main Street, past the city limits, and into the winding country roads, where the ripple effect of honking horns could be heard for miles in either direction as the crowd followed Annie and the twins up the hill to the courthouse. The sisters were coming.

Strom stopped with his cereal spoon halfway to his mouth. He cocked his head, listening intently.

"What is that noise?"

His perks in life had allowed him to build his dream home on a hill overlooking the city. He felt, in a fatherly kind of way, that the house echoed his life's calling. He opened the French doors to the patio and saw the backed-up cars blaring their horns.

"Ridiculous," he said. He closed the door and poured himself another bowl of cereal.

Down in the streets below, Clancy O'Neil, third-generation deputy sheriff for the county, stayed in his patrol car and just watched. When asked what happened, he would sensibly explain to the newspaper later that day, "What was I supposed to do? Arrest my wife, my mother, and my grandmother? There are times when you don't incite a crowd, and this was one of those times." Such instincts would allow him to run successfully for sheriff three years later.

Finished with breakfast, Strom walked the six blocks to the courthouse that morning, as was his regimen, rain or shine. He dodged the pockets of women in the courthouse alley and mounted the ivy-covered iron steps two at a time till he reached the second floor platform.

*You've still got it, Strom,* he congratulated himself, as he opened his private office door, put his sweater on an ancient oak hall tree, and sat down at the roll-top desk his father had used at his job at the ferry terminal.

The desk brought him a good deal of comfort and a feeling of continuity. It remained almost exactly as his father had left it. Some of the drawers still had ferry schedules going back twenty-five years. He opened the top drawer where his father had kept his watch.

His father had been a World War II vet, wounded in war. He had treasured this timepiece above all other possessions and carried it with him everyday until the day he died. Strom wound the stem clockwise exactly ten times and set it face up in the drawer. It had once chimed "God Bless America" twice a day, at noon and midnight, but no more. The watch had been crushed in his father's vest pocket at his death, and despite the best efforts of various European watch-makers over the last few decades, the music had died. Although it still kept perfect time, Strom would have given a small fortune to hear it play Kate Smith's signature song just one more time.

He quickly closed the drawer. There would be no time for wishful thinking today. He needed to be at the top of his game with this big city lawyer coming into town. He had heard how she'd bullied that prosecuting attorney, and he did not want to suffer the same fate.

Strom eased himself out of the confines of his office chair and tipped aside a replica of Gilbert's unfinished portrait of George Washington. Strom thought that the Numero Uno deserved a better likeness, but the president did double duty, adorning the wall and covering up a handy peephole to the courtroom below. Drilled through the paneling, the secret of the hole had been passed down from jurist to jurist. Its value far surpassed that of the key to the executive washroom that housed a balky toilet and its best friend, the toilet plunger. The hole allowed him to evaluate the field of battle, to identify and observe the main characters and bit players. He prided himself in this detective work that some might arguably have called a private invasion of rights. He felt it gave him a more candid glimpse before dispensing justice.

It was impossible to study the courtroom from the bench, where he sometimes felt his only purpose was to look like a wise owl.

He picked out Annie carrying what looked to be a sewing basket, but he didn't recognize the two women holding the babies next to her at the table. He knew babies. He'd had two of them himself. They didn't belong in a courtroom, and he made a "Note to self" that they would not last long should they decide to disrupt his court. He approved of the lawyer from New York. She looked to be a sensible, well-kept young woman—not the usual cut that graced his presence.

The courtroom crowd overflowed into the hallway, but everything seemed to be in order. In the back of the room, he thought he saw his mother, but the horde was still filing in and the woman vanished.

He slid the picture back into place, waited a discreet five minutes, straightened his robe, and entered at his customary time of nine o'clock.

"All rise for the Honorable Strom Livingston, superior court judge for the fifth district of Washington," the clerk announced in his best official voice.

The bailiff read the docket. "Annie Pippin Perkins versus the State of Washington."

Strom turned them loose. The county prosecutor, Bob Barnes, started by saying that neither the Child Protective Services nor the great State of Washington had any wish to impugn senior citizens. Within that context, he outlined the government position.

"We have found Mrs. Perkins's situation at this time to be not in the best interests of the children. There have been allegations of illicit drug use, illegal cockfights, pit bulls, alcoholism, prostitution, poor sanitation, and a dwelling with neither electricity nor running water. Her house is void of smoke detectors, has no safety glass in the windows, and we are concerned about possible lead paint on the walls of the house. In short, a poor habitat for children.

"Furthermore, polluted water surrounds the island, and Mrs. Perkins has shown to be a risk for flight from the authorities. In addition, there is the question of the age of Mrs. Perkins in relationship to an adoption of infants. Thank you, Your Honor."

Max rose slowly, and stood in front of the table near Annie.

"By the end of this proceeding, the court will find the character of Mrs. Annie Perkins to be above reproach. The prosecution's allegations are completely unfounded. More important, Annie Perkins is the sole living relative to these children, from a family who has had deep roots here in the Pacific Northwest for over 150 years. Thank you, Your Honor."

Strom commended the two lawyers. "You have both made succinct opening statements, and I think this matter can be handled judicially, expediently, and without undue emotion."

Strom was dead wrong. This was to be one of the most fiercely contested trials he would ever adjudicate.

# Chapter SIXTEEN

"Mr. Barnes, you may proceed with your case."

Barnes gestured to his assistant, Claudia. She put a map of the island on an easel so the audience and the judge could see its profile.

Barnes took a pointer. "We will begin with the island itself. As is evident, it is accessible only by boat or plane. I don't need to tell the court that, in case of an emergency to one of the infants, help would be slow in coming, if at all. Now to the water quality itself, samples taken from these three spots in the cove showed excessive amounts of nitrates and bacteria, almost certainly a product of the pit toilets on the spit. In other words, the water surrounding the island is polluted. I would ask that Mr. Snodgrass, the Assistant Director of Public Health, take the stand."

A round, pudgy man, dressed in a dark suit shiny from years of wear, rose and strode diffidently to the stand where, with some helpful prompting from the bailiff, he took the oath.

"Mr. Snodgrass," Barnes began, "can you tell us where these samples were taken?"

"I dunno exactly," he said, sweat emerging from his multiple pores, "but where you pointed out seems pretty dang close."

"And just what tests did you perform on these water samples?"

Snodgrass scratched his chin with fingernails that should have been quarantined and waxed eloquent about the various department procedures.

Snodgrass, former owner of Le Sewer Rat septic service, embodied the look of his former company, with close-set, squinty eyes and a long pointed nose. Nepotism befell him upon marriage to the mayor's wife's distant black sheep cousin, twice removed.

"All I know is that them oyster beds is polluted," finished Snodgrass pawing his crotch. "Most likely from them shit cans on the beach."

Wilma Walker-Briggs, the certified Home Study Representative, took the stand next. She sat ramrod-stiff in the witness chair, looking severely at Annie, as she gave a rambling account of the events at the island, including her narrow escape from vicious dogs. She had transformed her hair to sweep across her forehead and camouflage the wart. But as she began to perspire and gesture wildly in her passionate performance, the hair parted naturally over the volcanic event, allowing the audience to fixate on the blemish. The crowd dissolved into murmuring and snickering, with much elbowing to one other. Even Max, who had started out listening intently, became distracted. She thought about Clarence Darrow and the cigar ash.

Annie sat passively, sewing the satin edge back on Zack's blue baby blanket. Occasionally, Barnes would prompt Walker-Briggs, but for the most part, the witness eagerly recounted the events of that afternoon at the island, if with a trace of disdain.

Max stifled a yawn and impatiently doodled a stick-figure hangman of the woman on her legal yellow pad.

Max had no sooner flipped the page on her pad than the babies cried in tandem. Strom frowned and looked at the clock on the wall. He was a half-hour short of his usual 11:50 deadline. Babies did not belong in movie theatres or in courtrooms. Still, perhaps it was time for flexibility, he told himself.

"We will adjourn until one o'clock."

The twins continued to fuss even louder. Annie and Dorie scrambled to take the hungry babies from the courtroom and feed them.

In his chamber, Strom slipped out of his robe and quickly mustered out a side door, walking to his mother's for his lunch.

Strom opened the door, expecting that lunch would be far from ready, but there it sat on a yellow placemat. His mother asked about the trial, and he played along, pretending that he hadn't seen her in the courthouse. He quickly changed the subject and turned his attention to a seed catalog touting blightless tomatoes. He didn't like to think about cases during recesses. To his mind, it tainted the process of waiting till all the evidence was in.

It should be a simple case, he reminded himself. There was no judicial precedence granting any kind of custody, or visitation, to grandparents, or to any relatives beyond the parents. Strom had no intention of pioneering new turf.

A local deli had provided a picnic lunch for the defendants, saving them from the relentless press. It would be bad enough at the end of the day. Outside, the crowds camped on the courthouse lawn. As the spirit moved them, they left sentinels and foraged the one-stoplight town till there was nothing left but a half vat of lentil soup at Safeway. By the end of the day, even the soup was gone.

Fifty tee shirts stenciled with *Apple Annie for President*, and 110 shirts that said *Tugboat grannies rule,* sold out during the lunch break.

Court reconvened. This was Strom's favorite time on the bench. Adversarial tones were moderated; most everyone was busy digesting their lunch. The end of the workday seemed imminent.

Wilma Walker-Briggs had been grilled on the witness stand before. She sat up straight, haughtily confident, no chink in her armor showing. Max strode to the box. In the back of her mind, a song played, "You're a mean one, Mr. Grinch..."

"You said there were pit bulls on the island. Is that correct?"

"I believe so." Wilma nodded, striking a defiant pose.

"These are photos of the entire dog population on the island." Max opened a large manila envelope and drew out the photos. "Can you identify the pit bulls that attacked you?"

Wilma scrutinized the pictures. "I think this one...and, yes, this one—these are the dogs that chased me."

Max looked at the photos. "I'd like these photos to be held as evidence. One of these dogs is an aging golden retriever farm dog. The other is a three-legged bloodhound."

The courtroom laughed.

"Well, they were very ferocious," Wilma sputtered. "I felt like a whole herd had cornered me."

"I believe the term is 'pack,' Ms. Walker-Briggs, but this is no pack. You see, I know these dogs personally"—Max flashed the dog pictures towards the audience—"and I agree you might have been in danger." Max turned to face her audience. "In danger of being *licked* to death."

Again the crowd responded with a wave of contagious giggles.

Barnes jumped to his feet. "I object!"

"Objection sustained."

"Let's revisit the sanitation issue," Max went on. "Your concern is that there is no running water and that everyone on the island uses a pit toilet, an outhouse. Is that correct?"

"Exactly," Wilma said emphatically. "Outhouses are simply not used anymore in America."

"Are you aware"—Max read from a United Nations bulletin she had introduced into evidence—"that two-thirds of the population on the earth does not have access to flush toilets?"

"That may be true, but this is America," said Wilma.

"Yes, we are fortunate to have the convenience, but surely the other two-thirds are managing to survive, even prosper without the automatic flush," Max said tartly.

"Let's look into the cock-fighting allegation." Max pulled more photos from her envelope. "Is this the rooster you saw?" Max handed her a picture of Ahab.

"That certainly looks like the one," Wilma said.

"Actually, you can see by these three photos that this rooster is missing an eye and a leg, the result of an attack by a dog many years ago. He was nursed back to health by his owner, who does carpentry work on the island. Now, do you think a one-eyed, one-legged rooster would be much of a fighter, Ms. Walker-Briggs?"

Walker-Briggs looked doubtful. "I...don't know."

"Would you bet on a one-eyed, one-legged rooster in a cock fight, Ms. Walker-Briggs?"

Shock shot across the woman's face.

"I would *never* gamble!"

"Yes, sorry, my mistake. Let me put it this way," said Max evenly, then she raised her voice to convey irony of the situation. "Do you think *anyone* would be stupid enough to enter a one-eyed, one-legged rooster in a cockfight, Ms. Walker-Briggs?"

The woman shrank back into her chair.

"Well...I guess not," she mumbled.

"I would like to look now into the allegation of prostitution and nudity. Can you identify from these pictures the woman or women you saw engaging in prostitution or nudity?" Max handed her the photos of everyone on the island. Walker-Briggs shuffled through the photos and handed her the photo of Dorie.

"This is the woman you saw nude, soliciting money for sex?"

"I most certainly did," Walker-Briggs said with authority. "The woman was twirling her bra over her head and behaving provocatively in the hot tub, while two men on the beach were waving money. I couldn't tell how much."

Max held up the 8-by-10 photo for the courtroom and the judge to see.

"Ms. Walker-Briggs, you have picked out a woman named Dorie Dawkins. She is a seventy-three-old woman with six children and fourteen grandchildren. I have her net worth here." Max returned to her table and picked a paper out of a loose-leaf folder. "She and her husband are owners of Dawkins International, a privately held company, with a net worth of sixty-four million dollars, as of January this year.

"I'd like to enter these files into evidence."

The courtroom snickered in devilish delight. Wilma's faced turned beet-red.

"How was I supposed to know? She looked like a hooker to me."

Seeing the futility of his witness' testimony, Barnes, jumped to his feet.

"Judge, I object to this mockery of my witness. She had but a few hours on the island to make her evaluation. She can make only educated guesses as to what she saw. Clearly, the situation there is out of the ordinary, and she had an obligation to protect these children from an unhealthy environment."

Strom looked down his glasses at the witness.

"Stick to the facts, Ms. Walker-Briggs. That's the only interest here in this court."

It was precisely four-thirty when Strom gaveled the court to a close.

Pickles had backed the truck up through the crowd, right against the courthouse steps allowing Annie and her entourage easy exit. Annie refused. Putting the twins in a double stroller, Annie began her march to the sea, much like Gandhi defying the salt tax in India. Her followers lined the streets, shouting encouragement and stuffing money into a diaper bag passed through the crowd.

Annie waved and smiled at her supporters, occasionally looking back for Max, who had remained at the courthouse to try the case in the court of public opinion. Television reporters elbowed through the crowd, thrusting microphones under her nose.

A short, dark, Russian yelled, "Power to the people. Right arm. Remember the Alamo." Annie looked into the passing crowd and spotted Ivan from the piroshky bakery, waving his arms. Next to him stood Madeline from the Adult Lotion Shoppe. Annie smiled and waved, touched by the support.

She felt a surge of both pride and humility. She was honored to carry society's banner for older, second-time-around mothers. Battle-tested and world-weary, many of these women had interrupted child-hood fantasies to first raise their own children. When they finally arrived at a time to take their own dreams down from secret shelves, they were conscripted once again to raise their children's children. There would be no glory, no medals, no champagne breakfasts with strawberries. They would do what women have done for thousands of years: gather their chicks around them and begin again.

They might die with the job half-done, but it would be well-started.

By the time Annie and her troop had worked their way through the well-wishers, Max had caught up. Pinky sat at the keyboard on the truck, playing "When the Saints Go Marching In." Annie looked back at the people crowded together on the dock. They would be there to support their champion for as long as it took.

The courtroom crew returned to the island and gave Moby a full report. When he heard about Snodgrass' testimony, he stomped around on his one foot and swore a blue streak. Then he gathered Owl into his confidence and disappeared down the canal with the launch.

Owl (a fellow sewer rat of sorts) schooled Moby about the slippery trapping of Snodgrass and company. Snodgrass lived close to the head of the Health Department; neither mentor nor accomplice had septic tanks, but drained their sewage directly onto the beach. That made them vulnerable to blackmail.

Moby and Owl slunk into the brush, waiting till Snodgrass ate dinner and made his way out to the annex bus, where he performed the illegal side jobs of falsifying official health department records for unscrupulous contractors that kept him supplied with his toys—jet skis and sports cars. Moby and Owl saw the light flip on in the back of the bus office. They entered stealthily and made their way down the aisle, wading through official Health Department documents, strewn like sawdust on the floor.

Snodgrass, with a rodent's sense of danger, turned to face the men as they came into the light, his mustache twitching nervously.

"Who the hell are you? Get your asses off my property!" Snodgrass shouted, the half can of beer in his hand raised as if ready to defend his turf.

"I'll do the talking, Snotgrass." Moby leveled a sawed-off shotgun at the ample potbelly spilling below a grimy tee shirt. "There is a little matter of you lying in court today," Moby began.

"I spoke the truth," he sneered, but his eyes darted wildly,.

"I really don't have time for this, Snotgrass." Moby moved in closer and placed the gun barrel on his prosthetic wingtip.

"He's a crazy mother; don't mess with him," Owl said, playing his part.

Moby pulled the trigger—the gun exploded with a flash, and the front part of Moby's shoe disappeared into the fresh hole blasted in the floor of the bus. Blood trickled out of the remaining part of the shoe onto the ground below. Without batting an eye, Moby put the muzzle on the Snodgrass sneaker. "Now it's your turn."

Snodgrass looked down at the hole in the floor. The foam of fear gathered at the corners of his mouth, and he began babbling.

"Listen up, Snodgrass. I want a handwritten statement that those water samples you claim came from Seven Sisters were a mistake, and that the water around the island is definitely not contaminated.

"Write it now. My trigger finger is getting itchy."

It took Snodgrass three tries to get a legible copy, but finally Moby was satisfied.

"All right, rodent. Get your butt out of here, and don't leave your house till tomorrow morning, when I will see you at the courthouse. And tell your Health Department buddy that we have videotapes of both your septic tanks emptying onto the beach and will be happy to turn it over to the TV reporters. Are we clear, rodent?"

Snodgrass nodded nervously, looking down at the hole in the bus floor. He ran out of the bus.

"That catsup in the shoe was a good trick, eh what?" Moby congratulated himself.

"Capital, my good fellow," said Owl.

The two men adjourned to the launch, celebrated at the Whistling Oyster Tavern till closing time, then spent the better part of the early morning weaving the launch across the bay, looking for home.

With Dorie at the tug's controls the next morning, the island loaded up once again for the courthouse. The flotilla grew ever larger, joined by tour boats filled with fans out of Seattle and Everett.

On-the-spot interviews at congested road intersections found carloads of cheerful women filled with the zeal of their cause, happy to be included in the movement. Political figures, anxious to be seen—and, more important, heard—had scuttled their legislative committees, chartered their own boats, and jammed the harbor, barely allowing room for *The Pissant* to navigate to the dock.

Pickles, ever creative, had commandeered the vintage car club to escort the islanders to the courthouse. Annie, holding the two babies, led the parade, sitting in the rumble seat of a black Model A. She was followed by shiny roadsters and touring classics, as a misty rain fell on the parade.

Strom heard the noise of the crowd as it advanced, and soon the courtroom had filled to overflowing. The fire marshal tried unsuccessfully to clear the aisles, finally giving up, as more people crowded through the mahogany doors of justice and lined the walls, shoulder-to-shoulder.

At nine sharp, Strom entered and nodded toward the two lawyers. He scanned the room for his mother.

Barnes sheepishly approached the bench, looking like a dog that had piddled on his owner's shoes, and entered into hushed tones with Strom.

The bailiff called Snodgrass back to the stand.

Snodgrass entered the witness box and quietly explained a mix-up had been made in the samples taken. He pronounced the water surrounding Seven Sisters to be free from contamination.

"And," he continued in a much louder voice, inspired by the shotgun blast, "I think it is safe to assume that those waters will be pristine for a long time to come."

Max, who had been briefed by a soused, thick-tongued Moby on the tugboat, where he and his drinking partner were sleeping off the remains of the previous night's celebration, had no questions.

Barnes stood at his table waving a thick folder of papers.

"I have in my possession, Your Honor, death certificates for Annie Perkins' six sisters who preceded her, proving the existence of the 'Seven Sisters' Legacy.' It shows that every one of her six sisters died in her seventy-seventh year. This is Annie Perkins's seventy-sixth year, and, although she is in good health at this time, there is every reason to believe she has an unusual genetic predisposition that cannot be disputed."

The courtroom grew very quiet, and Strom leaned over the bench, waiting for Max to object, but she sat busily writing in her notebook.

Surprised he hadn't been challenged, Barnes gave the papers to the bailiff.

Strom beckoned over his glasses at Max.

"Your turn, Miss Manhattan...er, I mean, Miss Manahan."

For her look today, Max and Pickles had settled on an Italian white linen pantsuit, accented with a subtle red, blue, and yellow French Hermes scarf swirled around her neck. The colors of the scarf brought out the sky-blue in her eyes and the mahogany of her shoulder-length hair. All eyes were riveted on her as she walked up to the front.

Max called to the stand the ambassador from Argentina, Alberto Emilio Garcia. The stout, jet-black-haired man informed the court that Annie Perkins was an American hero in several mountain communities on the east slopes of the Andes. He gave a spirited description of the 1995 8.3 earthquake in the Andean mountain village of St. Sharon. A crippled economy, 2,000 percent inflation, and an unstable government had not deterred Annie. Late one night, she flew into Buenos Aires with supplies; by the next morning, she had somehow managed to cajole a team of private helicopters and small planes to land with the supplies on a soccer field adjacent to an airport runway. Steam was still rising from the cracks and fissures in the concrete.

Growing more animated, Señor Garcia bounced up and down in his seat, acting out how Annie had driven a bus herself down the broken roads from the soccer field into the town square. He told how she backed down corrupt local officials who insisted they would be in charge of the dispersal of food and clothing.

The ambassador opened a small blue velvet box and dangled a fist-sized cross, encrusted with diamonds and amethyst, easily seen from the back rows.

"This medal," he announced with solemn pride, "is the Cross of the Andes, given for meritorious service. It is my nation's highest award for service to the Argentinean people. I have the honor to present it today."

He left the witness box and lowered the gleaming medal around Annie's neck with great ceremony. He bussed her on both cheeks and leaned down to whisper in her ear, "It is my wife's heirloom jewelry. Pretty quick thinking, no?"

He straightened and, with Latin gravity, raised his hands above his head and began to clap, till the audience joined the touching tribute.

It would have surprised no one if he had gathered Annie up on his shoulders and marched her around the room, singing the Argentinean National Anthem.

The judge clapped his gavel and called the room to order.

Max thought they were off to a good start. "An American hero" was a nice touch she hadn't expected. She next presented two women who had raised grandchildren.

Barbara Morris was a black woman whose daughter-in-law had abandoned her two children as infants.

"I was workin' as a night watchman at a marina in Seattle. When my son died in a car accident and their mother disappeared, I was the only family those young 'uns had. I growed them babies up as my own. We never had a house we could call our own, because I housesat boats for people."

She chuckled. "When they was little, they had a hard time walking at first, 'cause they had these big ol' life preservers on them. They would kinda weave down the dock in their diapers and Mae Wests, but they was good kids.

"We had some hard times, but we always had just enough to scrape by. Marshall is twenty-three today, and Juliet is twenty-two. They both go to college in Seattle and still help me out. In fact, we all housesit boats now and get together once a week for supper.

"This was not my dream to raise these kids, but I never regretted growing 'em. It kept me young. And they turned out fine." A big smile revealed perfect white teeth. "Better than fine!"

Max asked that Barbara's two young adults stand up. Two attractive and well-dressed twenty-somethings in the second row got to their feat, beaming at Barbara. Several people in the room clapped.

"The courtroom will remain quiet," Strom admonished the room in general.

Barnes knew he must tread lightly.

"Ms. Morris, how old were you when you began raising these children?"

"I gave birth to my son when I was only eighteen, and he had the children when he was in his early thirties, give or take a few years  So, lessee, I was about fifty or so, and the babies were one and two when I took 'em over." Barbara recited the facts slowly, trying to remember the dates. "I think it was something like that. I was never much good at numbers."

Doing the math, Barnes asked, "Do you think you could raise Marshall and Juliet as children at your present age? You are about Mrs. Perkins's age now, correct?"

"A lady never tells her age, but I suppose so. You know I won't lie to you," Barbara said, earnestly leaning forward. "I wouldn't want to take that responsibility if I didn't have to, but if I was the only one, you bet, in a heartbeat, I'd be all over them young 'uns if they needed me. I'm what you call 'experienced.' I even have my own skateboard."

"But you had help, right?" Barnes continued to probe.

"We had lots of help. You know that saying, 'It takes a village to raise a chil'.' Well, that's the God's awful truth. We got reduced lunches, we had food stamps sometimes, and the kids, they got odd jobs, you know, pullin' weeds, washin' cars, stuff like that, when they was just little. Didn't hurt them none to do some work. Made 'em proud of themselves, self-reliant. And both went to college with work-study scholarships. It ain't easy, but it can be done. We never seemed to have extra, but we had enough."

Barbara sat back, and folded her hands in her lap.

Seeing he could do nothing to help his cause, Barnes declined to ask Barbara any further questions. Mrs. Patterson, a skinny, schoolmarmish kind of woman with thin lips, a gray bun, and kindly brown eyes, was called to the stand.

"How old are you, Mrs. Patterson?" Max asked.

"I'm eighty-four years young," Mrs. Patterson answered, looking proudly around the room. "And that's a long time, young lady."

"How old are your children?" Max asked, looking out at the audience.

"Well, let me see. Audrey is seventeen, Jackie is eighteen, and Stewart is nineteen last month," Mrs. Patterson answered calmly.

"Where did these children come from?" Max studied her note cards.

"These are my great-grandnieces and nephews. I never had children of my own. My Petey and I were never blessed. All of the children's relatives died when a drunk broadsided their van on the way to a funeral. It was a terrible tragedy.

"Luckily, the children had gone to a babysitter. I was the last one left in both families, so I took them in. I was sixty-seven at the time. My husband Petey had died the year before, and I was still in shock. But when those children came into my life, my life started over. I taught them to throw a baseball, make a bed, and cook. You know, I don't think anyone teaches their children to cook anymore. Even the youngest one could put together a good dinner, including dessert, by the time she was ten." She smiled.

"At your age, don't you find it hard to keep up with active children?" Max led the next question.

Mrs. Patterson looked her straight in the eye.

"I never raised children before, but I can tell you, I don't think anyone can keep up with children. They're too full of beans. I just follow behind and keep them safe, feed them, and tuck them in at night."

"I see." Max walked back to her chair. "And what would have happened to these children if you didn't raise them?"

"The children would have been placed in foster care. A woman at the agency told me it's unlikely they would have stayed together."

"Thank you, Mrs. Patterson." Max smiled and returned to the table, where Annie was feeding Little Annie a bottle. Then suddenly she turned.

"Mrs. Patterson," she said, "let me ask you a couple more questions. Who would you rather have make the choice in raising those children? The state or yourself?"

"I would have wanted to be the one to make that decision," she said. "Without question."

"And did you officially adopt them?"

"Heavens, no. It would have been too expensive. I saw I was needed. I took them home and just started raising those children like they were my own," Mrs. Patterson answered.

"Thank you." Max returned to her table.

Barnes smiled at the witness, and she smiled back. Then he began his questioning.

"Did the children mind being raised by someone who is older than the parents of their peers? Wouldn't it be hard for them to relate to someone old enough to be their grandmother?"

"You'd have to ask them yourself, but loving a child is not a question of age, but of desire," Mrs. Patterson stated, not seeming to take offense.

"But don't you think that if you had died when they were youngsters, they would have been traumatized? Wouldn't it be better to be raised by parents who have a greater probability to raise them to adulthood and after?"

"In a perfect world, that might have happened." Mrs. Patterson pushed a stray strand of white hair back over her ear. "But a sense of family, where your relatives came from, and why you have a sense of humor or why you are allergic to milk or why your little toe is crookety—these are important questions for children to have answered. That can only be passed down by a member of the family."

Barnes took off his glasses and looked directly at the witness.

"Is 'crookety' a word, Mrs. Patterson?"

Before Max could object, he moved on.

"Come now, Mrs. Patterson, couldn't they just get the family information from doctors' records or friends of the family?"

"Do you have children, Mr. Barnes?"

"That's irrelevant. You are the one in the witness box."

"It's okay," Mrs. Patterson baited him. "You can tell the truth without being sworn in."

The court audience erupted and Strom banged his gavel.

"Order!" he ordered, but when the guffaws died down, he turned a sympathetic eye on the witness. With a look of controlled amusement, the judge gestured with a nod for the prosecuting attorney to answer.

"I don't have children as yet, but I had a rooster for a pet," Barnes offered.

The courtroom laughed out loud. Strom stifled a laugh with a fake cough.

"I think living with animals is a good way to learn about relationships." Barnes tried to correct himself. "They take a lot of care."

The courtroom erupted again. Someone in the back yelled, "Relations with a chicken ain't legal in this state, is it, Judge?"

Again, Strom banged his gavel.

"This courtroom will come to order. Mr. Barnes, do you have any more questions?"

Barnes threw up his hands in surrender.

Strom looked at his watch and declared the court adjourned until one o'clock.

Most everyday, Strom walked to his mother's home for lunch. Over the years this schedule had worked well for them both, and it gave him a good excuse to make sure she had what she needed. As usual, he found her in her studio, painting. Flowers were her specialty, but she was constantly taking classes to learn new techniques, especially in landscape painting. The walls of the house were filled with her art. She refused to sell any of her work but would give it away freely if someone admired a piece. At seventy-four, she still swam with the grandchildren at the pool, drove down to Reno with her childhood friends every spring, and did crossword puzzles in her spare time, of which there was little.

"Hi, Mom," Strom greeted her. "Still getting ready for your next art walk? Don't you have enough flower pictures?"

"The day I stop painting flowers is the day they can plant me," she fired back. "Your sandwiches are in the fridge."

"I thought I saw you in court today." Strom ventured walking into the kitchen.

"You already know my thoughts about this case. And you know I would never influence your decisions just because I think family is more important than Democracy, the judicial system, or anything else. And that is all I have to say about that," she concluded, entering the kitchen from the studio.

Strom pursed his lips. "Oh brother," he muttered under his breath

As he sat down at the table, she began washing dishes in the kitchen sink as he ate. A comfortable silence settled between them as Strom reread the morning paper and his mother watched the news on a small kitchen television Strom had installed under the overhead cabinet.

After lunch, he kissed her goodbye. A light rain fell as he walked undetected the four blocks to the courthouse, dodging gaggles of chattering women, their umbrellas making a colorful mosaic against the soft grey skies. The courtroom steps overflowed, with the balance of the crowd spilling onto the lawn and down the street. The bay hosted more boats than when the town held its wooden boat festival. Parking was both a nightmare and a boon. Residents tore down fences around their lawns to create instant parking lots, their handmade signs tacked onto tree trunks: "$10 All Day."

As he climbed the back steps, Strom thought of the town's store-owners; he hoped they were happy with all the publicity. He bounded up the steps and into his office.

Catching his breath, he sat in his father's old oak rocker, feeling the smooth coolness of the wooden arms as he gripped the down-turned ends with his fingers. He leaned back, closed his eyes, and took a moment to gather himself. A few minutes later, his respite over, he tore off his jacket, threw it on his couch, and slipped into his judicial robe. He marched past George Washington, opened the door, and eased himself into the brown leather recliner that overlooked the courtroom.

Everyone stood as he entered. Strom acknowledged the room with a quick smile and a nod, and then slammed his gavel smartly on the desk.

"The courtroom will now come to order."

No one doubted who was in charge.

Max approached the bench with a folder.

"Your Honor, this document contains the certified names of 173 men and women and the names of their grandchildren, great-grand-children and even a dozen great-great-grandchildren—children they raised as their own, when their parents were unable to do so. We gathered this list just from the crowds outside the courtroom this morning. Forty-two percent of these children were not formally adopted by their grandparents but were simply taken in as family. And the official U.S. Census of 1996 states that at least four million children live with their grandparents and a third of these children, 1.4 million, are raised solely by their grandparents who are between forty-five and sixty-four years old. Data also shows that approximately three hundred thousand children are raised by grandparents over the age of sixty-five."

Barnes jumped to his feet. "I object, Your Honor. This list is irrelevant and suspect in its accuracy. This is not evidence. This is pandering to the court of public opinion. I submit, Your Honor, that the list is not an accurate document but merely represents a disgruntled group of disenfranchised citizens doing a de facto job of raising their grandchildren. You know as well as I that the state patently ignores the rights of grandparents by not allowing any sort of custody arrangement. Furthermore—"

Strom cut him short.

"I'm well acquainted with the law, Mr. Barnes. And I don't need a lesson from you on point of fact.

"All right, Miss Manahan. I will allow the lists to be entered into evidence. And I need the documents from the U.S. census bureau as well."

Max, who had gone back to her table during the tirade, now rose with her fingers in a thick book.

"I have here, Your Honor, the actuarial tables from *The New York Times Almanac*. I refer to page 379, 'Life Expectancy.' A white female, seventy-six years old, has an average of 8.3 years left to live. Other charts I have in evidence show an average of between 7.9 and 10.2 average remaining years."

She handed the book to Barnes, who scanned the page and handed it back to Max. His dour expression told the story.

Max handed the book and papers to the clerk, who handed them to Strom, who perused the pages while Max conferred with Annie.

"At this time, Your Honor, the defense would like to call to the stand Annie Perkins."

Annie was sworn in, and Max did her best to lead her testimony.

"Mrs. Perkins, would you please tell the court about your family's long association here in the Northwest, particularly the history of Seven Sisters Island?"

Max stepped back and gave the room to Annie. In the tradition of the ancient storytellers sitting round a fire, Annie wove a romantic tapestry of myth and magic, of her family's connection to the people, the land, and the sea. Her words recalled a time when the land and the people were inseparable.

When she finished, everyone in the room knew of the love Annie held for family and the love affair she had resumed when she reconnected with her island. They also knew of the wasted years and the guilt that plagued her.

Annie filled the next fifteen minutes with stories of her work overseas, the stormy relationship with her daughter, and the beginnings of their reconciliation. And she told of her love of her granddaughter Sarah and the difficulty of her pregnanacy and how Sarah had loved the island and the farm even as a little girl. Then she told of the tragedy and how the state refused to grant her even a small part in the twin's lives.

"I ask you, what is a great-grandmother to do when the chain is broken and babies are left to the state to provide them a home? We have never been a family that watches events, but one that makes things happen. These children are our best hope for the future."

Max rose from her desk and walked toward the witness stand.

"The physical for the home study showed you to be in perfect health for your age. Is that true, Mrs. Perkins?"

"I am in remarkably good health, according to the doctors—except for the arthritis in my feet that bothers me sometimes. I always thought it was an old wives' tale, but thanks to my rheumatism, I can predict the weather better than any weatherman."

"Did you, at any time, feel you were putting your twin great-grandchildren in harm's way during your flight from the hospital?"

"Heavens no." Annie sounded indignant. "I would never take a chance with those children, and that's all there is to it!"

"Thank you, Mrs. Perkins." Max stood in front of the witness box, shielding Annie from the audience. "I think you make a good case that you need to be included in your great-grandchildren's lives for as long as possible."

As if on cue, the twins woke up after a long afternoon nap, loudly voicing their concurrence. Max asked for a half-hour recess, smiling sweetly—as if Dorie hadn't jostled the twins awake at that precise right moment.

Strom suspected he'd been bamboozled by babies and grand-mothers, but he granted the request and retreated to his chambers. He had a splitting headache and remembered he had a bottle of aspirin stowed in his top drawer. He pushed aside his father's watch, shook three aspirin from the bottle, and downed them.

Barnes knew he had to treat Annie with kid gloves on cross-examination. No one liked to see anyone's grandmother grilled and a great-grandmother was in an elite league of her own. He also knew the streets were full of grannies these days. His own mother had warned him against going after Annie, but he thought the fugitive granny could be confused if he just kept firing questions at her. When court reconvened, Barnes believed he knew how to bait his trap.

"You are aware, no doubt, Mrs. Perkins, that the state provides no custody standing for grandparents."

"That's true. And you can call me Annie. It sounds less stuffy," Annie said. She had decided she would dictate the pace.

Barnes looked to Strom for help. Finding none, he decided to bow to the old woman's wishes.

"Then, Annie, how is it that you feel compelled to take the law into your own hands? Hasn't the state provided ample rules for these events?"

"There are God's rules, and there are the rules of men. But when it comes to children, there is a higher authority, and that would be a mother's love."

"Mother's rules? Mother's rules?" Barnes repeated, incredulously. "Are you putting yourself above our legislature? Do you put yourself above God's rules?"

"Throughout the world, the word God can mean many things, but a mother's authority, in my estimation, is absolute. It cuts across all cultural boundaries. In the absence of a mother, the torch is passed down the line in the family. In this case, these are my children. My responsibility."

"So then, the Supreme Law of the land, in your view, would be a mother. Don't mothers ever make mistakes? Aren't they sometimes crazy or just plain stupid?" Barnes badgered.

"That's why we're here—to decide if I have the children's best interest at heart or the state has a better interest."

"Where does state and federal law fall into your hierarchy then, Mrs. Perkins?"

Annie saw Barnes trying to tighten the noose tighter, but she was too smart for that trap,

"Let me put it to you like this," Annie said, leaning forward. "If your mother told you not to play in the street, but the state didn't have a specific rule to stop children from playing in the street, who would you hope the child would obey? Who has the authority? That's what we're talking about here, Mr. Barnes. We are talking, not about the rule of law, but about moral authority. You say the state has regulations and the legal authority to guide children, and I say, mothers and families are the highest moral authority."

Barnes turned to Strom. "Judge, I—"

"Mr. Barnes," Strom said, shaking his head, "you asked, she answered."

Barnes turned to the actuarial charts that Max had provided.

"It says here that once a woman reaches seventy-six, there is a fifty/fifty chance she will live to be eighty-three years old. Do you think you can beat those odds, Mrs. Perkins?"

"I'm certainly going to try," Annie replied, pursing her lips.

"Well, are you or aren't you going to be around to raise these children?" Barnes challenged.

Annie remained silent, but she locked her eyes on her tormentor.

"Answer the question, Mrs. Perkins. It is a simple yes or no," Barnes badgered.

Maybe Annie hadn't gotten enough sleep lately. Maybe she hadn't properly grieved her losses. Maybe she'd had one too many days in the unending weeks of uncertainty and pressure. Or maybe the biggest and most fearsome cat in the jungle, cornered and fearing for the lives of her young, had finally had enough.

Because Annie snapped and let erupt a round of fiery retorts.

"*VAYA AL INFIERNO!*"

"*KISH MINE TUCES!*"

"RAT BASTARD!" she screamed down on Barnes, shaking her finger.

The courtroom was stunned into silence.

Then in a controlled, great-grandmotherly voice, she said, "Your statistics be damned."

No one had been more surprised than Annie with the outburst. But before she could apologize, someone in the back of the room yelled, "You tell 'em, Annie!" And then a crescendo, building upon the quietness of her last reply, began and filled the courtroom, wrapping around everyone within earshot: "Annie, ANNIE, *ANNIE!*"

Mercifully Strom banged down the gavel and declared, "Court adjourned."

The gloves had come off, and the fight was on!

Strom walked up the hill to his house, where his wife greeted him with a hug. He looked over her shoulder to see his two children in the family room, watching Nickelodeon. He went into the den, where he turned on the five o'clock news.

Annie had been the lead story for two weeks, and today was no different. Groups of women shouting slogans and footage of Max talking to reporters pranced across his screen. Strom sighed and headed for the kitchen where his wife stood at the stove.

After dinner, the family followed the usual routine of homework, baths, and the *Late News* as though this day were not different than any other. Strom retired soon after his children went to bed, feeling the effects of a long and dramatic day.

At three in the morning he sat up in bed, wide awake.

# Chapter SEVENTEEN

hree a.m. It didn't make sense. Usually, he was a hit-the-pillow, gone-till-dawn type of guy. But tonight his head throbbed. He threw on his bathrobe, took two aspirin, and looked out the dining room window overlooking the harbor. He could see the lights on the dock playing in the water and the glow of Seattle on the east horizon. It was just the way he had imagined it when he had the house built.

He and his wife had climbed the hill with a picnic, complete with wine. They had christened the lot by making love, and afterward, buried the bottle and cork under a huge maple that dominated the hilltop.

The house was their dream house, although, Strom smiled to himself, with this view, he would have been content to live in a bus. The shadows played across the lawn in the wind, and he thought of the fifty-some years he had lived in the woodland community of his youth. He yawned and went back to bed.

Sometime between his early morning prowl and daylight, Strom had a dream. He was walking along a beach in a fog so dense it muffled the outside world into a cotton silence. He had no idea where he was, but he felt a comforting familiarity. He could taste the salt in the fog as it beaded on his cheeks then ran into the corners of his mouth.

The beach path skirted the shoreline, turned a blind corner, and then widened. A pocket of driftwood logs half-straddled the beach, their tails disappearing into the murky water. Three startled seagulls nervously sidestepped into the lapping surf and disappeared into the fog, leaving him alone. Strom heard someone call his name.

"Strom, come on over here, boy. I want to show you how to build a fire."

It was his father, no more than thirty, dressed in a pale green jacket, a brown, wide-brimmed hat atop his head. He was obviously much younger than Strom, who remained his current age in the dream, but neither man seemed to notice. Strom sat on a log watching his father shave thin curls of wood from a branch, using a bone-handled pocketknife.

"Cedar," his father said. "I always like to use cedar to start a fire. It cuts thin and has pitch pockets that ignite quickly." Strom's father arranged the slender strips of wood teepee-style, then struck a wooden match on his jacket zipper. He cradled the flame in his hand to shield out the wind, and it lit his face as he carefully maneuvered closer to the tinder. The stacked cedar strips caught instantly. "This is the critical part. Are you watching, Strom? You take a small handful of dry grasses and chips that come in with the high tide and sprinkle them on top. They have a low kindling temperature. Then you add the bigger sticks, and so on." He stopped to look at his handiwork.

"Building a fire is a lost art these days. Here, take the knife and practice making shavings." Strom pushed the blade through the cedar stick and managed to create a respectable pile of shavings. On one awkward stroke, the knife accidentally slipped, folding the blade onto his index finger, cutting his knuckle. Strom looked at the blood, but he didn't feel any pain.

"Let me see that cut," his father said, grabbing the hand. He inspected the wound carefully. "It's not too bad. You have to be careful with pocketknives—they can be dangerous." Strom's father uncrossed his legs. Two bloodstains showed through the wool pants below his right pocket.

Following Strom's eyes, he explained, "Two pieces of shrapnel. Got them in France when I was with Patton. The funny thing is, the wounds never healed. Suppose because there's a bit of metal still in there. That's what they tell me. No matter. Just bothers your mother sometimes."

He added more wood to the fire, and soon Strom could feel the heat on his face.

"You know," his father began after a moment's silence, "I've noticed you are a lot like me—a head man. Always thinking, always planning the next move. That's good. Now your mother is all heart. I guess most women are. I only went with my heart twice. Once when I married your mother, the other time after I was hit with that shrapnel. It made me mad that their machine gun nest was killing my buddies, and they had tried to kill me. I continued to crawl across that field hiding behind trees, dead bodies, and boulders till I got close enough, and I lobbed a grenade into that nest.

"They say I saved the whole battalion. I got a Purple Heart for my wound and a Silver Cross too. They called me a hero, but skirmishes like that probably happened a thousand times a day on the field of battle.

"What I'm saying is that the choices I'm most proud of and that made the most difference were when I went with my heart. I can't tell you how your life is going to turn out, Strom, but try to remember to make some decisions with your heart. Will you give it a try, son?"

Strom stuck his cut finger in his mouth and nodded that he understood.

Strom's alarm clock went off at 6:30 a.m., just as it had for the last eighteen years. He stared up at the ceiling alone in the bed. Must have been snoring, he thought. He rolled over and noticed blood on the pillow. Immediately, his eyes went to his hand, where he discovered the cut on his knuckle. At first, he tried to remember how he had cut himself the day before, and then the more he thought about it, the more he remembered about the discussion with his father.

The dream felt like a cherished memory from childhood. So vivid. So clear. He remembered the pale green of his father's coat, the brown cattails, the yellow heat of the fire. That in itself was unusual: Strom rarely dreamed in color; in fact, he rarely remembered any of his dreams. In his world of calculations and planning, this dream didn't fit, but it felt true and right.

He had talked to his father who had been dead nearly forty years.

Strom threw on his bathrobe and went downstairs. There was a note from his wife, saying she had gone with the children to her sister's in Seattle, that she hadn't wanted to wake him, and she would call later. Strom read the note and looked in the fridge for food. He heated some leftover oatmeal in the microwave and buttered two pieces of whole-wheat toast his mother had made in the new bread-baking machine he'd gotten her for Valentine's Day. Halfway through breakfast, he felt light-headed and disoriented. The cut on his hand began to bleed again. Wrapping a paper napkin around his knuckle, he pawed through the medicine cabinet, looking for a simple, dignified, plain plastic Band-Aid. He had to settle for something with black witches and orange pumpkins.

Strom went back to his room and sat on the edge of the bed, fighting the growing reality he couldn't preside in court that day. In the midst of the proceedings for what looked to be his most celebrated decision, he had an important mission today. He needed time to think.

He phoned the clerk's office and assured them he was all right and would be there the next day. The woman clucked sympathetically when he told her of his splitting headache and restless night. Strom didn't bother to explain further because he wasn't sure of the reason himself.

He strode down the stairs and found the police cruiser waiting to take him to the courthouse as it did every day. Today, however, the driver raised his eyebrows when Strom directed him instead to the ferry terminal. Jumping from the car, he ran down the steel ramp and onto the ferry's car deck.

"Whoo-whee, you're cutting her pretty close there, Judge," the deckhand said, as he casually uncoiled the three-inch hawser from the wharf cleat with a practiced flip of his arm.

"I thought you and the Tugboat Grannies were in court today," a second deckhand shouted over the noise of the horn, as the boat slipped away from the dock.

Strom merely nodded and smiled. It was good to be back on the water again. His childhood was magnetically connected to the moon-driven tides and the ferry schedules, which he had known by heart long before his multiplication tables. With his father monitoring the dock, as a child Strom had been on a first-name basis with all the captains and crew. He'd descended ladders deep into the boat's steel belly, where the pungent oil burned and diesel engines throbbed. He had watched as grimy men carrying oil cans and rags coaxed the engines to life, swearing wonderful oaths to the churning goddess who powered the commerce of chicken farmers, loggers, and fisherman.

This morning Strom climbed the tall steps up into the ferry's cabin. The ferry had come from the Chesapeake Bay area on the East Coast in 1947. Released into the Puget Sound and renamed the *Rhododendron*, she had darted across the waters for the next sixty years. The white body and the evergreen trim accented the long line of round portholes in her cabin like the speckled dots on the sides of a rainbow trout. Strom touched the brass plaque at the head of the stairs. *Rhododendron*. She was the last of the steel ladies that had plied the waters during his father's legacy. Her passenger saloon retained the elegance of mahogany woodwork, her doors highlighted by brass knobs and handrails kept bright by the hard-working crew.

He wondered why he hadn't ridden the ferry lately. His youth had been waiting patiently for him, no more than a skipping stone's throw from the center of town.

Thirty minutes later, the *Rhododendron* wedged herself between the pilings of Whidbey Island. The "walk-ons" surged off the boat deck, while the cars sat restrained, relegated to an unusual second-class status. Strom camouflaged himself in the crowd, eased himself down the rock bulkhead, and carefully picked his way across the top of the slippery, seaweed-covered boulders down to the sandy beach. As he vaulted down the last rock, the back of his hand brushed against a patch of razor-sharp barnacles. The shallow cuts began to bleed. He sucked the back of his hand and tasted the melding of his blood with the sea salt.

Strom walked to the edge of the water and swished his hand in the incoming tide till the bleeding stopped. The healing properties of the seawater were already working their magic.

Walking along the beach, Strom could see the profile of the tiny fishing village rising at the end of the dunes. Red-winged blackbirds darted from the willows. Migrating ducks and geese quacked and honked in conversational tones. They waddled with their broods between fresh and salt water, as though they had joined an exclusive spa. From experience, Strom knew that, given the difficulty of walking in soft sand, it would take him at least half an hour before he could even think about lunch.

Undistracted, he began to filter through the events of the last few days. He thought about the testimony in the courtroom and his conversation with his father. Strom was not planning on an afterlife as such, but the dream—the colors, the smells, the sound of his father's voice—were so alive, it was as if he had entered—what was the term?—a parallel universe, or maybe a spiritual Star Trek Vulcan mind-meld. He shook his head at his lame attempt at a metaphor, but he could not deny that the experience rang true. It was so like his father. The discussion in front of the fire had been totally in character, unsolicited, and out of the blue.

He looked down at the bandage on his finger and pursed his lips. He allowed only facts, corroborated and verified from several sources when he gathered information. He never rushed to judgment. He read three newspapers each morning to get a well-balanced perspective. An informed opinion: that's what made him a good judge. The cut, the dream, did not make sense.

Thirty minutes later, Strom left the beach and crossed to the narrow road that led to the forty or so summer and retirement houses that formed the loose community of the Oysterville-Strawberry flats. The village sat on the extreme southern tip of the large island, buffeted by fierce south winds. A natural hook physically divided the town in two. The north side, with its long sloping beaches, made a perfect home for oysters; the south side, with its long sloping hillside, gave shelter and sustenance to strawberry plants by the thousands. Only a handful of expendable cruising boats sat tethered to the pier, waiting for the inevitable summer crush of tourists that provided the town—with the exception of the Strawberry Festival in June and the Oyster Festival in November—with its only real economic adrenaline.

Strom had formulated an itinerary. He would breakfast at the Oysterville Restaurant, get a latte at the marina, and spend the day on the Harbormaster's porch, hunkered in a Cape Cod chair overlooking the hook. He'd catch dinner at the Strawberry Café and then, because the tide would still be high that evening, Strom would follow the road back to the ferry dock.

When he approached the restaurant, he looked with surprise at the sign on the lawn in front: "Oysterville Bed and Breakfast." The two-story Victorian had been painted and polished, its new image a far cry from the weather-beaten ghost house he remembered.

Must have had a change of owners, Strom decided as he opened the door. A bell above the door tinkled his arrival.

Two older couples sat at small, linen-draped tables, eating breakfast. Strom scooted into a bay window corner that commanded a view of the room. He nodded in the affirmative when a woman slightly older than himself poured him a cup of coffee—fresh ground by the smell of it—and handed him a menu.

"Have you been to our town before?" she inquired, attempting to engage Strom in polite conversation.

"I used to come here a lot, but it's been a while," Strom said, looking through the sparse menu. He liked the sound of the orange walnut scone with seasonal fruit, and when it came, he was not disappointed.

He left cash for his meal on the table next to the vase with the single white rose, then exited out the way he'd come in, closing the door softly behind him. He stood momentarily on the porch, surveying the familiar scene before walking the hundred yards to the vacant bungalow that served as the headquarters of the summer Harbormaster, not yet in residence. He found the anticipated lounge chair under the protective wing of the veranda. It protested mightily, groaning tiny foghorn sounds, as if he had disturbed it from a winter slumber.

Strom slid into the seat and positioned his feet on the porch rail.

A black-belted kingfisher, his spiky crest looking dapper, perched motionless on an electrical line that swooped out over the water, supplying power to the boat dock—an excellent site for observing a passing meal. The bird eyed Strom warily.

Pulling his stocking cap over his head, Strom snuggled into his sweatshirt for warmth. He took out his cell phone to check one last time with the world he had left behind. First he phoned the clerk's office and assured Jackie, the shared secretary who split her time among the three superior court judges, that he would definitely be in court Friday. He tried to get a hold of his wife, but her sister answered the phone and told him that his wife and children had left for the Woodland Park Zoo, and yes, she would pass along the information he was alive and doing fine.

By the time Strom had finished, the kingfisher had moved on, and the chair was in the shadows. He repositioned the chair and settled in once again.

Strom understood he was responsible for applying the law of the land equally and with justice for all. Strong words to live by, but he had proven to be more than up to the task, having earned the distinction that his rulings had never been overturned on legal grounds.

Strom closed his eyes for just a second as the midday sun heated the back of his neck. An hour later, he slowly opened them. He leaned back and forced himself to address the subject of the custody case of the great-grandmother and her deceased granddaughter's children. There is no law on the books that grants grandparents, much less great-grandparents, custody or even visitation. He mentally listed the mitigating circumstances: the babies' parents are dead, their grand-parents are dead, they have no aunts and uncles on either side, and the sole surviving family member is an older woman with a question-able lifestyle, though unquestionably compassionate and honorable.

The state had jurisdiction in these matters.

Decision was a no-brainer—the children are best served as wards of the state and adopted out as infants. They're famous and would be easy to place. Verdict rendered and case closed, barring last-minute evidence.

The kingfisher was back. Strom wondered if his son could iden-tify a kingfisher. If he would recognize the blue-black plumage. If he knew how these grouchy solitary birds divided up the waterfront, coming together only briefly to mate and scurry back to their strong-hold. These days, children could certainly identify cartoon charac-ters and Hollywood celebrities and were whizzes on the Internet. But more and more, Strom realized he was failing his children by not getting them out into nature.

He and his father had often camped and hiked in the mountains, as hard as it was on his father to walk long distances. Strom gave a deep sigh. His mind turned to the dream of his father. Strom never gave much credibility to dreams. He felt that dreams were overana-lyzed. A dream should have less impact than an everyday, factual event, which dreams weren't, in his opinion. But Strom had felt the rain on his cheek and the heat of the fire on his face. He had reveled to hear once again his father's voice and watch his mannerisms, as his dad taught him that particular technique of building a fire. The foghorns had sounded so real. Why had he never dreamed in color before? Why did he remember the color of the cattails, his father's jacket, and the hat? And his finger—that fresh cut where none had been before. What could account for that? Stigmata? Wish fulfillment?

Why was the dream so disturbing?

Suddenly, the kingfisher jumped up from the wire and hovered over the water making a churring battle sound before diving headfirst into the water and emerging with a small baitfish wriggling from his beak. With a powerful upward thrust of his wings, the kingfisher seemed to jump from the water and made a beeline for an overhanging fir tree near an oyster barge.

Strom leaned back and felt the warmth of the wooden chair melt into his body. That it had been a long winter was his last cognizant thought as he fell asleep.

The afternoon shadows rotated across the deck. The sun hung low on the horizon, the rays reflecting off the water forcing him to squint at his watch. He'd slept for two hours. He glanced at the power line, but the kingfisher had gone, and he had forgotten to get his latte.

Strom frowned. His father's suggestion about looking more into his heart probably had merit, and he would revisit the wisdom when he had more time. Time for dinner.

Strom slid the chair back against the wall and strolled down to the Strawberry Field Diner, a clapboard, squarish building with peeling white paint. A sign on one side of the door said, "Open." Another in the opposite window said, "Closed." No upgrade here, he thought, opening the screenless screen door and entering. The living-room-size area was dominated by a full-length eating bar, with a faded red counter and chrome spinner stools. The few tables looked to be salvaged. Their faux-walnut-grain Formica tops, chipped and cigarette-burned, were surrounded by white vinyl chairs.

The place appealed to Strom. He knew from experience that the lack of effort in decor often channeled inversely into the food—great milkshakes, hand-cut fries, or mile-high pies. One could hope. The owner, a large, round man with hammy fists and a "Don't screw with me" attitude, stood next to his short, rotund wife. Her chin barely cleared the counter top. Neither one smiled nor greeted him.

Strom felt exposed. He considered making a dash for the door, but, as the only patron, he was already committed. He stepped over a sleeping orange cat, walked across the room, and bellied up to the bar.

"What's good today?"

"Breakfast. That's all we do, is breakfast," the unsmiling man said, without moving his lips. "Breakfast for breakfast, breakfast for lunch, and breakfast for dinner, and if you want dessert—"

"Breakfast," the woman chimed in, just in case Strom didn't get the theme.

Strom cocked his head as he took in the information. He wondered if the wife was a ventriloquist or maybe the man suffered from Bell's Palsy. That would account for the lack of lip action. Or maybe he didn't have any teeth. Strom had run into that over the years. People afraid of dentists or pain or both. Embarrassed to open their mouths.

Strom countered with a cheerful, "I'm glad you were open. Breakfast is my favorite meal. Is there a menu? I'm starving." The woman shuffled over and handed him a menu. Strom quickly scanned it. The woman stood, pencil poised, as though he were about to dictate an important edict.

"I'll have the waffle with strawberries and whipped cream, and a side of sausage, in memory of the Strawberry Festival Court of 1967." Strom gave a nod to the picture of the same adorning the wall. There was a familiar look about the queen that year. Something about the drive-in movie theater in Port Townsend, the back seat of a '57 Chevy and...

The woman took a deep breath and bellowed into the order window.

"Rob, listen up. Strawberry waffle and pig, double it."

Rob delivered a mountainous pile of whipped cream and freshly sliced strawberries on two golden waffles and two saucer-sized patties of the best-tasting sausage Strom could ever remember eating. He finished the first waffle and gamely began plowing through the second while Rob and his wife leaned on the counter and watched him eat.

Finally, he gave a plaintive sigh and set down his fork. He paid the bill and as he walked to the door, gave one last look at the Strawberry Festival Court of 1967. Suddenly he felt very full, very old, and very grateful.

The forty-minute walk back to the ferry dock along the road was illuminated by the rising moon and sparkling canopy of stars. Strom saw three shooting stars, and by the time he reached the pier, he felt a deep contentment about his day. He phoned his wife and listened first to his son who complained that someone twelve years old should not be forced to go to the zoo with his sister, and then to his daughter, who wanted to tell him about the peacock feather she found on the sidewalk. It sounded like the Livingstons had had a good day all around.

The 9:15 was the last ferry westbound to Port Townsend. Strom paid his money and pocketed his receipt. He couldn't help but be annoyed at the mechanical ticketing that had been installed. In his father's day, the ticket sellers had to carry big rolls of multi-colored tickets, and make change with a stainless steel changer, both attached to their belts. Then, further down the dock, another ferry employee would take a paper punch to your ticket.

Things weren't as efficient in those days, Strom mused. But somehow it seemed more personal.

Port Townsend twinkled in the darkness, and Strom felt the warm wind of a spring Chinook whipping across his face.

Strom was first down the ramp as the ferry docked for the night. He hustled past Pickles' store and churned up the hill to the court-house. He hesitated only a second at the bottom of the unlit stairs to his office. Unlocking the door, he turned on the light, pulled a soda from the pint-sized refrigerator, and settled in at his desk to scan the case study.

An hour later, he was still leaning back in his reclining office chair when the faint sound of bells interrupted his concentration. At first he thought "ice cream truck," but that did not make sense at this hour. Putting down his papers, he realized the sound was coming from his top drawer. He had a fleeting thought of a timing device on a bomb, but curiosity won over caution as he eased open the drawer.

His father's watch was chiming the midnight hour. Strom listened, rapt, to every tinny twang of "God Bless America." The last note reverberated through his brain. Stunned, he carefully picked up the watch. He felt the heft and cool of the brass case, trying to understand what had changed. What had caused the watch, after nearly forty years, suddenly to play again?

His mind raced though the possibilities. Someone had dropped the watch. An earthquake had jolted its juices. Maybe the watch had worked all along. He was hallucinating. The music had come from somewhere else.

Each attempt to solve this mystery became more ridiculous. In a practical world, events like this just don't happen. It's not natural. It might happen to other people, but not to Strom Livingston.

He sat for a long time staring at the watch till he finally closed the drawer and walked up the street to his mother's.

The old brick house was completely dark, but he walked down the alley, climbed on a garbage can, and looked over the six-foot wooden fence into the back yard, where his father had built an all-glass art studio in the middle of the flower garden. Sure enough, in the dim light, he could see his mother's small, gray-haired figure bent over an easel.

Strom felt along the fence in the dark for the wooden dowel attached to a rope that would release the gate latch. He found it, gave it a yank, and the gate swung open. He maneuvered his way through the garden, dodging overgrown rhododendrons that obscured the stone path. Slapped in the face by a wet branch, Strom wondered why his mother never pruned anything back.

Probably waiting for her son to do it, he thought guiltily.

He eased open the half glass–half wood Dutch door. On the glass she had painted:

The Fortress
Be amazed all ye that enter
There are fairies about.

Strom preferred his mother not publicize her belief in fairies, angels, and leprechauns, and he had decided to admonish her for not locking the door, as he snuck up behind her. The room was heavy with the smell of brewing coffee and oil paint. He could see she was painting a still life of trillium in a clump of moss. He approached within arm's length to give her a proper scare.

"Hello, dear. Did you have a good day over on the island?"

"How did you know it was me and not some criminal, Mother?"

"You know you can't sneak up on me. I have my guardians looking out for me."

"Shouldn't you be in bed by now?" Strom admonished, determined somehow to best her tonight. It was a game they often played, but he never came out on top. Maybe he dreaded the day when he would win.

"I was waiting for you. I was worried," she said, mixing the oils on her palette to find the perfect shade of purple. "Did you know that trilliums turn purple just before they die? I wonder why?"

Strom refused to get sucked into a floral discussion. He wanted to talk about the dream he'd had of his father.

"Have you ever spoken to Dad?"

"Sure, lots of times. We were married, you know."

"I mean, did you ever talk to him in a dream after he died?" Strom decided to wade in over his head. Did he really want to know?

She put down her palette and looked up at the ceiling, as if looking for her husband.

"I've had a few dreams, and sometimes, if the wind is right, or the room is too quiet, I think I hear him talking to me. I never get to talk back. I guess he's trying to get even for all those years.

"Why, have you talked to him lately?" she quizzed him. "Is he still wearing that ratty green coat and ugly old brown hat? And I suspect he's still smoking on the sly."

"How do you know about the green jacket and the hat?" Strom was bewildered by her casual attitude.

"I don't know where he picked up the jacket, or the hat, either, for that matter. I threw them out years ago. I don't dress the man anymore.

"What did he say to you?"

"He showed me how to build a fire and told me to try and make more decisions with my heart. And when I woke up, I had a cut on my knuckle where I had cut it in the dream." He paused and then took the plunge. "And then tonight...at midnight, his...his watch started to play 'God Bless America.' You know it hasn't done that since he died.

"What do you think? Am I going out of my mind?"

His mother sat on her trusty, paint-spattered piano stool, the sound of her brush stokes a whisper in the silence.

"I think this is an important case. Your father is trying to help you make the right decision. Like the time you insisted you knew how to ride a bike, and he kept holding on to the fender all the way down the block. He pulled you back, just as you were about to ram a picket fence full tilt. You panicked, but your dad was there to save you."

Strom chuckled, then kissed his mother on the forehead.

"Good night, Mother. See you at lunch tomorrow." He headed toward the door, and paused. "Mother, you haven't talked to Dad lately, have you? You don't have some sort of constant communication going, do you?"

His mother waved her hand. "Sleep tight, don't let the bed bugs bite dear. I'll see you tomorrow."

As the early morning fog lifted, the tugboat contingent entered the harbor with the same rollicking fanfare of previous days, only to learn the judge had taken the day off. Max couldn't determine whether a day's recess was to their advantage or not.

"The babies could use a rest," Annie said philosophically.

But that's not what Pickles, the self-appointed campaign promoter, had in mind. He cajoled Annie into holding court to greet her admirers in person.

"I know it would be a long day, Annie, but these people have come from all over to support you and your cause."

Pickles whisked her off in a horse-drawn carriage. In pied-piper fashion, they led the crowd to the football stadium, where Pickles had set up lawn chairs for the principal players and a tent to house the babies. A line quickly formed around the track, the bleachers filled to capacity, and still they funneled in through the field entrance.

There were tears and hugs and photo opportunities. Donations of cash and checks soon spilled out of Annie's apron pockets and finally had to be put into a wicker laundry basket.

The babies wore imprints of every hue of lipstick, stunk of perfume both cheap and expensive, and were admired and fussed over, even as they slept or ate. The public changing of diapers was a community event that inspired applause. Goodwill flowed through the standing crowd, and those merely in their seventies gave up bench seats to their elders. The small country stadium was a breakfast bowl of warm, steaming whole grain love, a celebration of life.

Later, people carried home empty soda bottles, cans, and wrinkled wrappers to be tucked into drawers and pulled out years hence as proof of attendance. Tens of thousands would claim to have packed a stadium that could hold no more than three thousand—but in spirit, they had all been there.

Evening found Annie exhausted, soggy, and rumpled. There had been no time for strategy sessions, lunch had been but a quick bite, and by five o'clock even Pickles had just wanted the day to end. That night, they all stayed at Pickles' place. Tomorrow would decide the twins' destiny.

Strom didn't sleep well. He lay awake, worried he would have another dream and worried he wouldn't. Running through his mind was what his father had said, what his mother alluded to, and the oath he took to uphold the laws of the State of Washington. When he finally drifted off, his slumber brought no rest.

The town was packed as Annie and her troops marched in to take their places in the courtroom. Strom looked out into the gathered assembly, and his eyes locked briefly on Annie. He asked first Max, and then Barnes, if either had any more witnesses, and they said they were ready for summation.

Strom slammed down the gavel and demanded quiet from the gallery. He barely listened to the professionally impassioned closing arguments of the respective lawyers, instead focusing on Annie, who continued to mend the blanket and watch the twins gurgling by her side. When the arguments ended, a great feeling of relief washed over him. He called for a brief recess, and retired to his chambers.

After removing his robes, he did not retire to his expensive leather chair but began to pace the floor. His father's voice came back to him.

"Make some decisions with your heart. Will you give it a try, son?"

The adrenaline flowing, he began muttering under his breath, formulating his ruling. He grabbed a piece of paper, scribbling catch phrases in explanations that might be used in an appeal down the road. Finally, he lined up his decision simply, with no room for ambiguity or misinterpretation.

Without waiting to be announced, he reentered the courtroom, leaving everyone to scramble for a seat. Strom waited patiently, nodding to the principals as they looked to him for guidance. He spoke without his notes.

"I have lived in this community for fifty-three years; my father died in town working as a dispatcher at the ferry dock years ago. I miss him everyday, but my mother lives here in town, and she has been a great comfort to my family and me over the years.

"I take my oath as a judge seriously, in accordance with the laws of this state and this great nation. Throughout my tenure, I have studiously followed my mandate not to make the law but to interpret the law. However, today I am making a decision from my heart. I am searching not just to follow the letter of the law but the spirit, to find true justice and see that it is imposed. It is this justice that seems to have been misplaced in this time of mandatory sentences and political correctness."

Strom paused and looked out over the courtroom.

"In this matter before me today, I hold in my hands the future of two children, the last of a long and proud line of pioneers in this region. I have ample reason to believe Annie Perkins, the great-grandmother of these children, is the best judge as to their future, and therefore grant her full custody and the right to adopt these children as she sees fit. She shall have the right to use the expertise and any and all of the state-supported agencies involved with the welfare of these children or she may use private agencies to raise these children to adulthood.

"That is my ruling. We're done here."

Strom brought the gavel down hard three times.

Before the crowd could react, a small, gray-haired woman seated in the second row jumped out into the aisle, raised her hand in triumph, and yelled, "That's my boy. Way to go, Strom!"

Strom looked down, and smiled broadly. He brought the gavel down three more times, as hard as he could.

"The court will come to order. Mother, will you please sit down." He brought his gavel down one more time. "Court dismissed."

The courtroom erupted in laughter, and then a triumphant roar spread from the courtroom, out the door, down the steps of the courthouse and into the streets.

The last Strom saw of his mother, she was being surrounded by reporters. He knew she could handle the media—she was Strom Livingston's mother, the keeper of the fortress.

Strom jumped into a waiting patrol car. He had done his part. The hard work would be done by Annie Perkins.

Surprised and overjoyed by the verdict, Max gave Annie a heart-felt hug. She had been willing to accept joint custody, visitation rights, or merely some way Annie could have consulted with the state adoption agency. But a total victory—that had been beyond Max's wildest dreams, and while she questioned the legal grounds of the decision, she was pleased with its direction. She had to believe that this case had been tried in the court of public opinion.

Annie left the courtroom with babies in tow, climbed on the bed of Pickles' flatbed truck, and rode through the town like a victorious gladiator.

Before they left Port Townsend the following morning, Annie phoned the foundation that would contact Moby's daughter, telling her to come home. Wherever she was in the world, she would know instantly that her father was dying.

# Chapter
## EIGHTEEN

nnie's days were filled with interviews and pitchmen offering contracts for her to advertise everything from baby food to adult diapers. The television people wanted her to come to New York and Los Angeles for late night talk shows. Annie decided to filter all offers through Pickles, who reveled in the wheeling and dealing, while Max kept a sharp eye on negotiations.

But right now, all of it could wait. She needed to tend to her friend.

As soon as she got back, Annie went immediately out to the furthest cabin on the spit. When the light from the open door penetrated the darkened cabin, Annie could see Moby propped up on his bed. She closed the door and allowed her eyes to adjust to the feeble firelight.

Moby held out his hand as Annie approached. Sitting down on the chair next to the bed, she held his hand in her lap. Trooper had climbed up beside him and gave Annie his most worried, hound dog look. He knew Moby was in trouble.

"I've sent for your girl," Annie said. "It'll probably be a few days before she gets here."

"Good. It's getting close to time. She's a good girl to her old man. It'll be wonderful to see her again.

"I was thinking that maybe we could go to the hospital to get this lung drained before she gets here. I don't want her to see me like this." Moby wheezed and closed his eyes. "Annie? You know I wanted to be there for you."

Annie smiled bravely. Having spent most of her life in the trenches of catastrophe, she had developed a foxhole litmus test of who she would want with her if she were dug in against the enemy and the missiles of war were whizzing about her head. The list was a short one, and Moby, this half-man with the heart of a lion, had made the cut.

"You were there for me more than anyone. You're responsible for this place coming alive again."

Moby gave a weak smile, but for the life of him, couldn't muster an "Arg…"

Annie worried that Moby might become dehydrated. Sometimes when you're drowning in your own fluids, you forget to take in any.

"Are you drinking much water?" she asked, moving toward the bottles on the table.

"I could use a drink. Is there any peppermint schnapps left? At least my breath will smell better."

"You'll drink water, mister, and like it!" Annie knew that a little tough love would be better than letting Moby call the shots, at least for now. But right away, she softened. "We'll get you to the hospital tomorrow. I'll get Owl and John to help."

"Just let me gargle with it. I promise not to drink it," Moby slyly pleaded his case.

"Like I was born yesterday," Annie countered.

Annie gave Moby a glass of water. She watched half of it roll down his chest as a shaky hand attempted to steer the glass toward his mouth. She cleaned him up with a towel.

"You're going to have to do better than this when Christine gets here. And for Christ's sake, don't you dare croak before she gets here."

Moby smiled weakly.

"I'll suck it up. Just help me get this fluid out of my lungs." He closed his eyes. "I think I'll just lie here and think about Christine coming home. It seems like it's been a long time…"

Annie kindled the fire and straightened up the room. Opening the door to leave, she stopped.

"I don't know where I'm going to get the strength to raise those babies, but I'm going to give it one hell of a try. You get some rest, and I'll check on you later. How about if I get John to whip you up some chicken soup?"

"This ain't exactly a cold, you know. This stuff is terminal." Moby's mouth curved upward, and though still closed, his eyes crinkled. "But I think that might taste good. Thanks."

Annie placed a string in his hand. "This is attached to an air horn. If you need anything at all, just pull on the string."

"Yeah, I always like to have my hand on a G-string."

"Don't you be sassing me now, big boy. You're in no condition."

"Annie…could you give my pumpkin starts a little drink? Just some of that worm tea, if you could."

Annie nodded and went out the door to Moby's greenhouse.

The next morning, Owl and John helped get Moby to the doctor in Port Townsend. The internist took Annie aside.

"He hasn't got much time left." He handed Annie a small brown bag. "I've given you some morphine to keep him comfortable. If he gets really bad, bring him right back in. That's all we can do for him now."

Annie nodded, taking the sack. "Let's go home, boys."

When they reached Seven Sisters late in the afternoon, the entire island had mobilized to find Merriweather, who had been gone since early morning. In just the last month, she had taken to extremes—at times wandering off and at others afraid to leave her cabin for days. She had mixed her hearing aids in with the dog food, and sometimes she would take off her clothes and stand naked in the surf till someone rescued her. It would be hard to give up one of their own, but everyone knew she could no longer live on the island.

Moby took the lead.

"Let's find her. Tomorrow, we'll have to take her back to the mainland."

They found Merriweather standing on a maple stump near the top of the island wearing not a stitch of clothing. John wrapped her in a blanket and trundled her back to Moby's cabin, where she spent her last night on the island with Moby and Trooper.

In the morning, Moby and Owl took Merriweather on the boat, then borrowed John's car to drive her to Tacoma to the convalescent center from which she had escaped. They settled her into a room. The entry smelled of urine, and long scratches on the walls told of countless wheelchairs scraping their way down the halls to nowhere. To call her room "barren" would have been charitable—no curtains, no plants, not even a throw rug to temper the cold of the floor in the middle of the night.

Looking frightened, Merriweather didn't resist but began to cry as they eased her into a bed.

"That's no problem," the attendant said. "We'll give her a sedative for a few days, and then she'll fit in right proper."

Moby gave him a look that smoldered with fury. Though bent with pain, he somehow stretched himself to his full height and looked the attendant straight in the eye.

"This woman was an important celebrity on radio and television before you were even thought of. There will be fans coming to see her, once they know she is here, and there is family living in the area. We expect her to be well taken care of."

The attendant stifled a yawn as Moby turned his back.

"That's what they all say," he mumbled under his breath. And it was a sucker's bet that anyone would be coming.

Moby knelt at the edge of the bed and looked into Merriweather's face. She stopped crying as she watched Moby open her suitcase and plug in a radio turned to the twenty-four-hour weather station.

"Excuse me, sir." The attendant stepped forward and put his hand on the radio. "The patients are not allowed to have electronic equipment in their rooms. Safety, you know."

Moby glared at him, and the young man backed off.

Moby next pulled out two of Merriweather's most cherished feathered hats. They would have made Dr. Seuss envious. He placed them on the table next to the radio. Last, he handed Merriweather one of his Hollywood glamour photos in a brass frame. She smiled and clutched it to her chest.

Moby touched her cheek and gave her a kiss.

"I'll be back, sweetheart. Meantime, just hold on to that picture, and you'll be all right. Do you understand?"

Maybe it was just an involuntary motion, but Merriweather nodded yes.

As Moby and Owl walked to the door, Merriweather watched with growing apprehension. Moby looked back one last time, quickly wiping his eyes to keep her from seeing the tears. Then he walked back into the room and pressed the button on top of the radio.

*Expect fair to moderate winds south to southwest in the evening, with the barometer falling . . . .*

Merriweather immediately parroted, "Expect fair to moderate winds south to southwest in the…"

"Remember, I'll be back for you soon," Moby said gently, but Merriweather was busy with the weather prediction.

In the hallway, Moby collapsed against the wall. It had been a fine performance, but he could no longer support the façade. Tears blurring the little vision he had, Moby let Owl help him to the car.

Two hours later, Moby and Owl pulled into the parking lot of the public dock in John's car. Moby struggled upright from where he lay in the back seat and saw what his heart most desired: Christine, dressed as if she were going to a garden party, holding on to her wide-brimmed hat with one hand and trying to preserve her modesty with the other as the wind billowed her long, print dress.

The impractical outfit had been bought by her father a few years ago. Christine knew Moby fancied his life, as well as his daughter's, as sort of a Hollywood production of a story torn from the pages of a romantic Gothic novel.

Catching sight of the two men as they emerged from John's car, Christine sprinted down the dock and threw herself into her father's arms. She could feel his backbone almost cutting into her hand and felt the bloat of his belly. Her father had always been physically powerful, able to do more work than most men who had no disability. She knew, without a doubt, this would be her last trip home.

Sensing her concern, Moby closed his eyes and held on tight, trying to silence his daughter's unspoken fears and his own. He had few regrets, but one of them was that he would be leaving his little girl alone in the world. Between father and daughter, time and distance meant nothing. He had always been her protector, and it was a role he wanted to play as long as possible.

Owl carried the suitcases as "Johnson and Johnson," joined at the hip, followed him to the boat. Moby insisted Christine wear his coat for the trip to the island, over her protest.

South met them at the boathouse. She took one look at Christine and shook her head.

"Girl, you are one gorgeous piece of work, but we best be getting you into some serious clothing if you're going to stay here long. Tomorrow I'm going to grab your daddy by his ear, and we are going into town for some down-home glad rags. No more of those open-toed sandals around here." She handed Christine an orange and avocado tie-dyed sweatshirt. "This will keep you warm, but you've got to go up to Pickles' tomorrow and get some decent threads."

Even though it hurt to laugh, Moby chuckled out loud.

"I don't care what you're wearing, honey. You look great to me. I'm just glad you're here.

"Come on, help me in my greenhouse. I need to cultivate around my pumpkins. Let's go do a scratching out in the patch. I'm playing a Jerry Lee Lewis medley for them today. That should stimulate the root ball of fire."

The next morning, Moby, Christine, and Annie headed to Port Townsend. Max had been bunking with Pickles to field the continuing clamor for interviews and endorsements. She and Pickles were still weighing the previous day's offers for endorsements when the gang in the truck rumbled in.

Pickles absolutely bubbled over when he saw Christine.

"Shuck my oysters and grab the salami, Mommy. Where did this goddess come from, and why is she wearing these rags? Jerry's dead; let the man rest in peace. Come in. Come in. Come in." As he talked, he shepherded them into the front room overlooking the bay and poured them coffee.

Moby introduced Christine to Max and Pickles. Pickles held out his hand.

"Come, dear, we will shop."

Pickles led her upstairs and through the labyrinth of his empire, stopping only to sort through bundles and ask Christine about her life, then surprised her as he anticipated her exact sizes and preferences. He stopped midway on the second flight of stairs.

"Christine Johnson? Is that your stage name?"

She nodded.

Pickles lit up. "Yes. I remember hearing you play at the Mountreaux Jazz Festival in Switzerland. Vivaldi, I think—'92, was it?"

Christine stared at him, stunned.

"Actually, the Vivaldi was in '94. Were you really there?"

"You were wonderful. Perfection."

He disappeared behind a stack of sweaters and returned with an armload. They bundled the clothes into a dumb waiter that terminated at the main floor dressing room.

Christine changed into jeans, a sweater, and a pair of running shoes. She selected a number of outfits, and then packed the psychedelic sweatshirt into a paper bag to return to South.

Max walked them out to the truck. She confided to Annie that, even though she felt the case had been decided on somewhat faulty grounds, she hadn't heard any rumbling from the county prosecutor or the state. She was sure the "powers that be" had decided that to revisit the case was political suicide.

Moby started up the truck motor. Pickles followed them out, trying to get in the last word.

"Annie, have you considered writing a book? Strike while the iron is hot. Think about it, Annie. Destiny is upon you."

Annie laughed. "I'm afraid my fifteen minutes of fame are over. Thanks, anyway."

Moby hit the waterspout. Pickles backed off as the water splashed off the truck's hood and splattered his pea coat. Laughing, Pickles ran back to the safety of the store awning.

Since Christine's arrival, Moby had rallied. He walked taller, stood straighter, and his face had more color. Together, they spent hours on their hands and knees working the soil, watering and talking to his giant pumpkin starts. Moby had built an elaborate greenhouse on the side of his cabin and hooked up water pipes that traveled through the wood stove to deliver heat to the soil just beneath the starts.

"I'm getting a jump on everyone this year," Moby proclaimed.

He set up a lawn chair in the center of the patch and read aloud jokes from an old paperback, tidbits from the newspaper, limericks, and occasionally applicable verses from the Bible, especially the parts about all the begetting, which he liked.

"You need to create a bond with your plants. They need to trust you in order to feel comfortable," he told Christine. Moby had finished as high as third at the annual Great Northwest Pumpkin Festival in Portland. He was always trying to figure out what would get him into the Winner's Circle.

This year, he was like a man possessed. He collected rain water and hauled in bags of chicken manure so he could make his famous chicken manure stew, into which he stirred pinches of a secret blend of minerals to stimulate the plants and make it easier for the roots to absorb nutrients.

His biggest hope lay in a gallon of breast-enhancing hormone formula that he had found advertised in the back pages of *Mercenary Soldier* magazine. He carefully spritzed the purple juice onto the leaves just after sundown, while Christine held a flashlight.

"Dad, this stuff doesn't even work on people. Why do you think it will work on pumpkins?"

"It's science," Moby patiently explained. "I cross-referenced the ingredients, and they help the photosynthesis process, which in turn hyper-stimulates the growth of the blossoms. It's like using steroids for bodybuilding. It's not illegal, but it's not foolproof either."

Christine looked at him with great affection.

"Dad, you're nuts, but I love you." Then, because he looked like he might cry, she added, "I'm gonna have to give you a noogie." And before he could protest, she dropped her flashlight, ran behind him, and began rubbing her knuckles on his bald scalp.

After the pumpkin juicing, as Moby called it, father and daughter sat by the open fire in front of his cabin. She told him story after story—about the many concerts she'd given, the cities she had visited around the globe, and the oddball characters who dwelt in the art world.

They continued this ritual night after night. As he listened contentedly, Moby would lean back in his car seat and slowly drift asleep. Then Christine would throw a sleeping bag over him, tuck in the edges, and sit silently by the fire, listening to the tide, the occasional squawk of a startled blue heron, or the sound of her father's snoring.

One afternoon, Moby led Christine to the shed next to the cabin. There he showed her his casket, sitting on two sawhorses. He had fastened a padlock to the side. He gave Christine the key.

"Everything I own is in this box," he said, thumping the top with his fist. "Leave it closed till I'm gone, and then open it. There are instructions and phone numbers about the estate and details on how I want the funeral arrangements handled. I've taken care of everything. It's all in there.

"I don't want to waste a single second going over any of it. I just want to spend the rest of my time being with you, trying to hang on just a while longer."

Christine bowed her head and began to cry softly. Moby took her into his once-powerful arms and stroked her hair.

"Don't worry, we can do this. I'm just glad you could make it back home for the old man."

The building of the church had finally finished. Only two more additions would make it complete. Pickles took care of one, sending over two dozen old fir pews he'd found in a derelict Pentecostal church in a small coastal lumber town. And Travis and Tate delivered the final but perhaps most important touch when their draft horses hoisted the bell into the steeple with the help of Travis' ingenious pulley system.

Over the next few months, everyone on the island or connected with it seemed to have gone through some transformation, some in small ways, some in grand style. Max's change was the most noticeable. She decided that the high-powered, corporate lawyer was no longer who she was. She quit her law firm in New York, and she secured a position in a Port Townsend firm that allowed her to adopt the relaxed lifestyle of the Pacific Northwest. She took to wearing long peasant dresses and Birkenstocks. She did Tai Chi in the early mornings. And her romance with Travis progressed at a steady but slow pace that put no pressure on her. She was happier than she had ever been in her life.

Pickles had come to a meeting of the minds with Annie about publicity and chose an ad agency in Seattle to filter through the hundreds of offers.

John's chronicles of the island had earned him national recognition. He had been offered a one-hour, weekly, syndicated radio talk show dedicated to issues of aging. He wished Betsy were there to share the triumph.

Strom refused to talk to reporters about the specifics of the Tugboat Granny case. But he started to go to church with his family and was chosen Grand Marshall of the Strawberry Festival—provided he could round up his own convertible.

Annie had changed in subtle ways, though unaware of her metamorphosis until one morning, she came eyeball-to-eyeball with the progeny of her archenemy, the dreaded outhouse spider. Instead of the usual threats of bug bombs and broom attacks, she went about her business calmly. She and the spider maintained a civilized but safe distance from each other, purposefully not intruding on the other's personal space.

Annie couldn't speak for the spider, but she felt she had grown over the last year.

Doted on, bathed, and fussed over by willing hands of experience, the babies adapted well to their island. Little Annie rolled over first, and Zack, as if he knew his manhood was on the line, strained to flip over in an effort to catch up with his sister.

Though Moby's spirit remained whole and well, his body was being consumed at an alarming rate. Annie began to give him morphine when the pain was too great. Sometimes in the morning he would wake up in a pool of blood. Christine came each morning to fix him breakfast but, rarely hungry, he hid the food under the bed when she wasn't looking.

One morning, as they sat at the fire after breakfast, Moby said, "I have business in town today."

"I can do whatever you need done, Dad," Christine offered.

"No, Annie and I have to go in alone." Moby spoke too loudly, scaring Christine. "We have private business to attend to. Just the two of us."

Though Christine didn't understand, she put up no protest and soon went back up to the house. Minutes later, Annie came down to the campfire.

"Moby, what's this business we have to do?" She surveyed her friend, concern etched in the lines of her face. "You look tired. Why don't you just rest today? John can pick up whatever you need tomorrow."

"No. We need to do this today. Right now."

Annie didn't press him further but went to put on her "goin'-to-town clothes."

It took both women to get him into the boat. Once docked on the other side, Moby insisted they go to the hospital to drain the fluid from his lung.

"But we don't have an appointment," Annie protested.

Moby lay back on the headrest with his eyes closed.

"Please, let's just do it."

The woman manning the check-in desk balked when Annie made the request.

"We can't just have people showing up here whenever they want and demanding attention," she sniffed.

"Really?" said Annie, her tone deceptively sweet. "Well, we could just walk around to the emergency entrance, I suppose. But then, I don't think your administrators would appreciate having two elderly people wailing loudly about how this heartless, greedy hospital made a dying man suffer needlessly."

The woman pursed her lips, typed something in staccato on her keyboard, and nodded toward the waiting area.

"Take a seat," she said curtly, trying to sound as though she and not Annie had made the decision.

When Moby finally lay on the gurney, hooked up to the magical tube that evacuated his lungs, the attendant stared at the quickly filling bag in amazement.

"Three quarts?" He shook his head. "That's a lot of fluid, and you know it's just going to flood right back in there. You need to check into the hospital right now."

The draining done, Moby struggled up from the chair and put on his coat. He reached out and shook the startled man's hand.

"Thanks, I appreciate your concern, but I'm running out of time. I need to be moving on," he whispered, his husky voice betraying his ever-present pain. He leaned on Annie, and they slowly made their way out the door into the parking lot.

"Annie, I want to go see Merriweather." At Annie's startled look, he added, "I know it's a two-hour drive to Tacoma, and I'm sorry to make you do it, but I have promises to keep."

Annie answered softly, "Of course, Moby." She'd do anything for this man.

Down the road a bit, Annie pulled in at a "stop and go" gas station and ran in to get sandwiches for them both. When she came back to the car, though, Moby was sound asleep. He snored all the way to Tacoma.

When they arrived at the convalescent center, Annie shook him lightly. He blinked owl-like and then groaned.

"God, I hurt. Just give me a minute." He lay back, laboring to breathe.

Minutes passed. Then he pulled open the car door and slowly maneuvered himself out of the seat and onto the parking lot. He reached back in and pulled out his crutch.

"I'll be back in twenty minutes. Just stay here."

"But, I wanted to go too."

Moby silenced her with a shake of his head.

"No, I need to go alone."

Moby went in the back entrance of the facility, past attendants who were too intent on their smoking and jokes to notice just another old man. The urine smell twitched in Moby's nose, bringing urgency to his mission and a quickening of his step. He quickly found Merriweather's room. South had put up curtains she'd sewn from flowered bed sheets; other than that, the room was just as he had left it—festooned with the feathered hats and the radio playing its never-ending forecasts.

Moby closed the door and turned on the bed lamp. Merriweather lay on top of her bed, staring up at the ceiling, reciting the forecast for Dallas/Fort Worth.

"Highs in the 80s with a chance of afternoon thundershowers lasting into the evening. Winds…"

Her nightgown was pulled up to her waist, exposing the diapers that had fallen open. She had unknowingly scratched the red, oozing bed sores that covered her hips

Moby closed the curtain over the window, turned off the lamp, and leaned against the door, angry and defeated. Just barely a man and just barely alive, he knew his options were limited to the next few minutes. Moby's eyes adjusted to the somber darkness of the room.

Wiping away the tears with his sleeve, he made his way to her bed. He pulled the covers up to her waist and lay down beside her.

Even as their bodies lay close, Merriweather gave no indication of sensing his presence. They lay like that for a long time. Moby smiled in the dark as he reflected on Merriweather's spunk: paddling for the island in her life raft, hell-bent for glory, not willing to be warehoused another minute; and then later her wading into the surf to drag Owl to safety.

Yes, she was one of the special ones.

Moby leaned on his elbow, looking into Merriweather's eyes for any recognition. There was nothing. He pushed her hair back from her face and kissed her on the lips. She immediately threw a bear hug around his neck with surprising strength and pressed her dry chapped lips into his as if he were her new beau on a porch swing.

Moby slowly extracted himself and looked again into her eyes. A single tear ran down her cheek. Moby, now sure that he must keep his promise, calmly covered her nose and mouth with his hand and pushed down gently, careful not to hurt her. There was no struggle. She stopped breathing and wilted on the bed.

Moby closed her eyes, threw the diaper in the corner, and pulled her nightgown down to cover her knees. He looked at her one last time, trying to imagine how such a powerful spirit could be extinguished so easily. He turned off the radio and left the room, skirting the hallway and out the door, where the same men ignored his crutched gait as he disappeared into the darkness.

Slowly, agonizingly, Moby climbed back into the car.

"Well, how is she?" Annie asked.

"She'll be all right now," Moby answered, leaning back into the seat and closing his eyes. "Drive."

Annie cracked the side window to clear the foggy windshield and drove silently for a time. Suddenly it struck her why Moby had made the trip alone.

She pulled the car over to the side of the road and wept on Moby's shoulder. He put his arm around her. Annie looked up at Moby; she was crying so hard that when she tried to speak, she merely honked. Moby laughed aloud, and then Annie laughed, too. The fear of death, no match for laughter, slipped out the window and vanished.

Annie said slowly, "She made me promise to take care of her, but I just couldn't do it. She must have known she needed a back-up."

An ache lodged deep in Moby's throat, but he knew how to fix it. "Head to the nearest liquor store. I need a drink."

"I'm buying," Annie said, shifting into gear. "I owe you one."

When Moby and Annie made their way up to Moby's cabin late that night, Christine scolded them like a mother hen. Annie asked anxiously about the babies, but Christine insisted she and South had things well in hand. Reassured, Annie collapsed onto the bed, and Moby crashed on a stuffed chair.

Christine carefully wrapped quilts over each of the whiskey-soaked travelers, then stoked the fire and made herself comfortable in the rocking chair.

In the morning, even before Ahab voiced another false alarm, Annie got up and went toward the house. Moby slept late. When he finally awoke, the sun was slicing in through the cabin window.

"What time is it?" he asked.

"Ten a.m., Dad. You celebrated a little too hard last night."

"Then why is it so dark in here?" He attempted to sit up but fell back on the bed, knocking his head on the cabin wall. "Light the candle by the stove," he demanded, his tone uncharacteristically impatient.

"But, Dad…the sun has been up for hours," Christine protested. "We don't need any candles."

And then Moby knew. The insidious disease had crawled up out of his lungs and lodged in his brain. It would take him slowly, attacking his senses one by one.

Shaken, Christine helped her father out to the car seat. Sitting in the full sunshine, Moby turned his head eastward to absorb the heat. Trooper instinctually moved in to protect his master. Moby felt him near and put his hand on the animal's head.

"Bring me a cigar, Daughter," Moby shouted in defiance of the darkness.

As he smoked his cigar, he talked with Christine about his boyhood in Oregon. He asked her to guide him to the pumpkin plants. Had she had watered them lately? Did she remember to put the "super sauce" on the leaves?

"The plants are looking good, Dad," lied Christine, trying not to choke on her tears. "The leaves are dropping a little from the stems, so I think I'll try a little Roy Orbison later on this afternoon."

"That should stimulate those sons of bitches. Tomorrow, let's go for Little Richard. You can't beat that early rock stuff. 'Good golly, Miss Molly…'"

The next day, Moby couldn't taste the bittersweet flavor of the Cuban cigar, but he never let on. He jammed it in his mouth anyway and sat on the ground exhorting his plants, most reduced to bare stalks. That night, he was too dizzy even to sit on the edge of the bed. Christine lay beside him, chattering nervously, as he slipped in and out of consciousness.

Annie came and stayed to maintain a vigil and comfort Christine. Moby's breathing became so shallow that Annie needed to put her hand on his chest to feel movement. As she washed the top of Moby's head, she noticed that even the color seemed to have faded from the tattooed crown of whales.

"I don't have any magic words to make this easier," she said to Christine. "But I want you to know that your father, more than most men, lived life on his own terms. He doesn't seem to be in any pain right now. That's a blessing.

"There's something else you should know, Christine. This man…" Annie had to stop a moment. Now was not the time to indulge in her grief. She waited until she could speak in a voice both strong and uncompromising—just like the man who lay before her. "Moby single-handedly brought this island back to life."

Annie stood up and laid her hand on Christine's shoulder.

"He always lit up when he talked about you, Christine. He was… is…so proud of you. The cancer could have taken him long ago, but he refused to let it. He was waiting for you to come home."

Early the next morning, Annie was awakened by Trooper's howling, and she knew that Moby was gone. She let the tears run down her face, thinking how lucky she had been to run into a spirit like his when she so desperately needed help.

When she could cry no more, Annie checked on the twins and found them gurgling in the crib. She slipped on her robe, walked down to the cabin, led Christine back to the main house, and put her to bed.

Then Annie returned to the cabin to clean up Moby one last time. But first she needed to quiet Trooper and soothe the old hound's pain. She stroked his head as he laid it in her lap. Finally, he let out a long moan, followed by a deep sigh fluttering from his big floppy lips.

On a sheet of lined paper they found in the casket, Moby had, as promised, written down very specific guidelines. He wanted his remains to be burned on the beach in a plain pinewood box, saving the elaborate hand-made coffin for the burial of his ashes. That evening, Pinky, Travis, and Owl eased his body into a simple wooden casket, took it to the beach, and surrounded it with a huge pile of driftwood. At dark, they gathered round and lit the funeral pyre. Sparks and flames shot into the sky as the casket fueled a fire seen for miles from every surrounding shoreline.

In the morning, Christine and Owl scooped through the ashes, carefully sorting the bones into two canvas bags as instructed. The one sack would serve as his remains for the memorial service; the other was to be delivered to a pyrotechnic engineer Moby had commissioned to create a huge fireworks rocket.

With Moby's death, it was as though the heart had been cut out of the island. Even with the babies there, the energy that drove the island seemed to ebb, and the collective spirit of the island sank into the doldrums. Ahab and his overachieving crowing program disappeared the night Moby died. Now there was no one to exhort to "Seize the day, seize the day," over and over.

Several days after Moby's cremation, Owl and Christine went to survey the pumpkin patch. They stood looking in dismay over what was left of the drooping stalks.

"I'd say they were goners," Owl said, after digging up one of the plants and examining the roots. "It can happen when you push the envelope, but that's what champions do. Sometimes it works, sometimes it doesn't."

Hunkered down on one knee, he scanned the rest of the crop, shaking his head sorrowfully. Having lost interest, Christine walked over next to the woodpile. Suddenly, she saw something strange: a single wayward pumpkin vine that had been, until then, obscured by the tall grasses. She leaned over the waist-high pile of wood and parted the grass on the other side with a stick.

"Hi there, little fellow," she said. "Hey, Owl, look here." She crouched down and pointed the plant out to him.

"A rogue plant," said Owl. "And being right next to the cabin like that? It got the benefit of the heat transferred through the thin cabin wall."

"A rogue plant," Christine echoed. Of course, she thought, how else would her father come back to her?

"Do you think I should I leave it here?" she asked. "Or should I transplant it into the patch?"

"I'd leave it right here," Owl said. "It seems to have a mind of its own."

"It certainly does, doesn't it?" Christine agreed, kissing him on the cheek. "Yes, yes, yes. It certainly does seem to have a mind of its own." Giddy with joy, she grabbed Owl and launched into an impromptu dance. Never missing a beat, Owl matched her step for step.

Later that day, Christine repositioned the radio behind the woodpile and put in one of Moby's favorite CDs, a retrospective of Buddy Holly tunes. She gave the plant a long drink of tempered water and sifted a few of her father's ashes around the base.

She could have sworn the plant turned its leaves ever so slightly toward her in thanks.

Annie felt the palpable letdown of the islanders after the deaths of the island's "Founding Pioneers," as John called Moby and Merriweather. The antidote was to plan a gala event that sent the island into scurry mode—the dedication of the church combined with the memorial services.

Christine sent an express letter to the foundation, requesting the use of the grand piano she had traveled with for the last nine years. She hoped they would agree to let the Centennial Edition Steinway come to the island from the Japanese Consulate in France where she had left it. Three days later, she received word: The piano would be waiting for her at Sea-Tac Airport by the end of the week, awaiting her directions. The CEO added a private note expressing his condolences and adding that he hoped he and his wife would be allowed to attend the memorial.

Travis volunteered to take *The Ark* back and forth to ferry people and supplies to the island. Pickles, always the party animal, caught wind of the festivities and insisted on organizing as well as catering at least part of the feast.

With the bell in place and the church ready to be dedicated, it was time to go get North.

# Chapter NINETEEN

**N**orth's service would be held on the island with the two others on the Monday afternoon of Memorial Day weekend. The Saturday before the holiday—when all the cold storage plant workers would be off—would be the perfect pick-up time. All they needed was transportation. Once again, Pickles came to the rescue, this time with a lime-and-purple tie-dye-design Volkswagen van with vista windows and a peace sign hand-painted on the spare tire cover

"Kinda flashy, don't ya think?" John offered as he traced the peace sign with his finger tip.

"Naw, it's simply high-profile—just what you need for under-cover work," Pickles nodded in the affirmative.

Taking in Pickles' gold lamé Elvis suit, capped with a bauble lighted halo and paratrooper boots with a dozen shiny buckles, Owl shrugged philosophically.

"I see what you mean." He opened the driver's door and climbed in. "Let's get this popsicle wagon on the road."

Other than a few friendly honks from passing cars, Owl and John enjoyed an uneventful trip to the processing plant in Tacoma. With the help of the plant manager running a forklift, they chiseled the casket loose from the mountains of frozen containers of snap peas, corn cobs, brussel sprouts, and cauliflower stacked to the ceiling.

Gently, they deposited North in the back of the Volkswagen van, lashing the coffin to the sidewalls. John opened up the lid of the frosty red coffin and looked in. He tapped North on her forehead with his knuckles, as sheets of fog rolled from her body.

"Shit, she's as solid as a rock. Maybe we should have taken her out of the freezer a little sooner. I'm afraid if I hit a bump, she'll bust into a thousand pieces."

"At Thanksgiving, I used to fill up one side of the sink with cold water and immerse the turkey to hurry along the thawing process," Owl suggested helpfully.

John tried to remember the thawing times of turkeys, thinking out loud.

"A twenty-five-pound turkey takes at least a day to a day and a half in the open air. Doing the math, I estimate North at 120 pounds, so that would be..."

"Eight days, give or take," Owl interjected. "But we've only got two."

"Let's just get a move on and try to figure out something on the fly."

The two men swung north toward the freeway. As they left the outskirts of town, John spotted a huge neon pink elephant presiding over a do-it-yourself car wash.

Inspiration struck.

"What if we sprayed her down with hot water? All we need is to thaw out the surface. There's a plug at the bottom of the coffin, so the water could drain out. If we leave the top off and open up the windows, she can drip-dry all the way back."

Owl turned into a bay. He and John quickly slid the coffin halfway out of the truck. Owl shoved a handful of quarters into the machine and set the dial to "Presoak." John grabbed the wand and pointed it at North. Hot water pulsated out of the nozzle, and North began to give off a satisfying steam.

Suddenly soapy water filled the coffin.

"Hey! What happened?" John shouted over at Owl. "I've got soap all over the place. Push the rinse button."

"This dial seems to have a mind of its own," Owl fretted, twisting the indicator back from "Soap" to "Presoak."

Ten quarters and fifteen minutes later, John looked into the coffin and smiled at the result. North seemed to be thawing out nicely, at least around the face. A camper pulled into the stall next to them, and John looked up to see the wide-eyed faces of three kids pressed against the glass.

"Turn off the machine," John yelled. "We've got to get out of here!"

Unfortunately, in his haste, Al turned the knob to wax, and before John knew it, a white wax covered the body from head to toe. He threw the wand down and both men shoved the coffin back into the van under the stricken gaze of the children. The two men slammed the rear doors shut, jumped into the van, and peeled rubber making their getaway.

While Owl drove, John climbed aft to open all the back van windows. He had just settled into his seat when they heard the siren of a Washington State Patrol car that had slipped in behind them.

"Ah, shit. So much for Pickles' strategy," Owl said, pulling over to the side of the freeway. The officer eased himself out of his car and came toward them. He slid his hand along the side of the bus as he approached, looking in the side window at the coffin.

"Mind if I see your driver's license?" he asked Owl, who had already extracted it from his wallet.

Glancing at the card, he looked at Owl and John.

"I'm sure you know you weren't speeding in this rig." He smiled, showing even white teeth shadowed by a broad mustache. "Where you going this morning?"

Owl thought fast and bluffed.

"Car show up in Port Townsend. This is a classic, you know."

"I know. My dad has one of these." The officer stood back admiringly. "It never leaves his garage. Doesn't have the paint job you've got here, but it does have the peace sign on the spare tire cover in the front.

"The reason I stopped you is that I got a call that some kids said they saw a coffin with a body in it back at a car wash."

Owl pounded the steering wheel and let out a whoop of laughter.

"Told ya," he said to John, then turned to the officer. "We just left the car wash—had to clean up the rig. The coffin is just a prop, for the car show—the whole hippie, Grateful Dead theme and all. We pulled out the fake casket just to let the kids see it—you know, to give 'em a thrill." Owl chortled again. "I knew they fell for it."

The patrolman peered in through the window at the red casket.

"Yeah, it looks real enough to me." He handed Owl his license then bobbed his head knowingly. "When I heard the car they saw was one of these old buses, I figured it was something like that, but I wanted to check out the report myself. My dad will be glad to hear about your rig." He poked his nose in the window. "Got seat belts?"

"Oh yeah. We even had shoulder straps added," Owl said, slipping the license into his wallet.

"Looks good," the officer said and gave the tinny door an affectionate thump. "You're good to go."

It was a good ten minutes down the road before either man spoke.

"That was friggin' close," John shuddered. "'Scuze me, while I kiss the sky…'"

Almost involuntarily, Owl started tapping out a beat on the dashboard, belting out, "'Bye, bye, Miss American Pie. Drove my Chevy to the levee, but the levee was dry. And good ol' boys were drinking whiskey and rye…'"

Memorial Day in the Pacific Northwest is often greeted by gray, sullen weather, cool temperatures, or even a storm sashaying over the mountains to rumba on the parade. But not this year. The weather was gorgeous—firecracker hot, with shimmering blue skies, light, fluffy clouds, tantalizing breezes playing on the water, and clear, crisp shadows that would haunt a groundhog.

Earlier in the week, Pickles had picked up Christine's piano in the flatbed truck and delivered it to the boat pier. Ever so gently, he moved it in a wheeled cradle, clickity-clacking it over the wooden timbers, down the ramp, and onto the landing barge. Once on the island, he enlisted the help of Travis' roofing crew. The men sweated and swore, managing to ease the nearly thousand-pound piano onto a spindly board path laid across the beach gravel. The draft horses, cajoled by Travis, did the grunt work.

The men levered the piano in through the double doorway at the entrance of the church, bolted the legs back on, and eased it into position. Only when the piano stood in place did Christine reveal that it was valued in excess of five million dollars.

"Whew," said Travis. "What kind of wood is that! Petrified?"

Christine caressed the keyboard. "You probably couldn't replace it even if you wanted to. They made only seven of them."

Christine propped open the shiny black lid and took her time tuning the treasure. Satisfied, she positioned herself on the stool and began to play. The church reverberated with an impossibly rich sound, as if every piece of wood were harmonically connected to the piano. Spellbound, the men stood stock-still. When Christine stopped playing, the music seemed to have seeped into the building itself, adding a new dimension, a sacredness to the space.

Travis took his first run of the morning with *The Ark* to pick up the delivery of salmon, straight from the Columbia River. The fish had been iced and piled in plastic tubs. In addition to the fish, Travis was surprised to find a dozen people waiting expectantly at the wharf, hailing him as though he were the captain of the Jungle Cruise. Immediately, they began to climb uninvited into the boat.

"Who...who are you people?" Travis asked, at a loss as to the proper protocol.

"I'm here for the funeral," said one forthright dowager.

"Me too," echoed a young man, adorned with tattoos and dreadlocks.

A chorus echoed these statements. Travis took a quick head count.

"Well, I guess we'll all fit, as long as you make room for the fish. I'll cart these salmon on board, and we'll cast off."

As Travis glanced back over the boat's wake, he straightened in alarm. Groups of people in twos and threes walked from the parking lot to wait on the pier—presumably for his return trip. At the island, while the boat emptied, Travis found Annie and asked his questions rapid-fire.

"It's six hours till the memorial, and it looks like there are more mourners than we anticipated. No telling how many. Do you want me to bring them over? What are we going to do with them?"

Annie was surprised the word had got out. She looked for inspiration—first to the north, then to the south. It was blue as far as the eye could see, and the water was dead calm, reflecting the few wispy clouds that would make for a beautiful sunset.

"Bring them all over," she said, with a cavalier wave of her hand. "Today is the proudest day we've had on Seven Sisters in the last fifty years. We'll celebrate with anyone who wants to come."

Bouquets of wild flowers from the pasture festooned the church. A new rope stood slack at its entrance, hooked to the polished brass bell set to ring for the first time on the West Coast. The graveyard fence had been propped up, and the ancient golden delicious tree, judicially pruned the previous fall, now had its branches twined with long, golden tinsel—ribbons that fluttered gaily over the old gravesites.

Early afternoon found nearly three hundred souls roaming the orchard, lounging on the grass, leaning on tree trunks. Some wore Sunday best, some proudly sported Possum soccer uniforms, some came adorned in the most casual of attire. Strangers struck up conversations, while children did what they'd done for hundreds of years on the island—they found a way to have some fun.

Christine opened up the church windows and filled the air with music usually reserved for the great halls of Europe. From her hands, the old masters' notes mingled with the sounds of crying gulls and delighted children scampering in the grass. Christine surpassed the mechanics of execution and interpretation and played with a passion driven by the most fragile yet powerful flight of the psyche. She played out of love.

A freedom had come to Christine in the last few days. She had decided to stay on the island till fall, to nurture the single rogue pumpkin that reminded her of her father. Maybe it was time to plant her own roots.

The three champions lay in state at the altar, allowing small bands of mourners time to approach, to reflect, and to comfort one another. Next to Moby's hand-crafted coffin, his nail apron sat casually off the altar rail, as if he had simply stopped to take lunch and would be back to finish his work for the day.

At the base of the steps was a collection of hammers left by his devotees—some new, with the price tag still on, others with heads scratched and worn, handles taped and split. There was one box of his favorite Cubans and a new pair of steel-toed boots—right and left. Wherever Moby had gone, whoever left this tribute trusted he would be whole again in his new life.

Next to the workman's accouterments was a pile of items even more out of place in a place of worship. Moby's fans had rallied from all quarters of the world to pay their final respects. Leopard-print thongs, red-hot brassieres, and other reminders of Moby's movie days left no doubt about the attraction he had held among his devoted fans.

South decided upon an open casket to commemorate her sister. She stood by North's colorful coffin, smiling sweetly and sadly as soccer players—young and not-so-young—passed by, took off their jerseys, and piled them on top of the casket.

South had borrowed Pickles' scarlet macaw nail polish for her sister's manicure, which set off North's elegant fingers quite nicely. Some went away wondering where that new car smell had come from and remarked how her face seemed so shiny and smooth, with hardly any wrinkles at all.

With Carol Ann's help, Annie had managed to secure Merriweather's ashes from the mortuary, since Merriweather had no relatives. Rummaging through Merriweather's luggage, Annie had found an elaborate feathered hat and a Seattle newspaper article telling how Merriweather had a cult-like following: she had been a type of fertility guru, using prayers and dream catchers with feathers to help those in need. There were several moving testimonials from women who had tried everything, turned to Merriweather, and had success. Annie folded the article and put it in her apron. The hat, she decided, would decorate the Merriweather urn.

All too soon, it was time to move the remains to the island cemetery. First, Moby. The nail belt, along with the tools and cigars, were placed in the casket with his ashes. The extra weight of hammers, wrenches, and crowbars left as offerings staggered the six pallbearers who, led by Christine, carried him to the old graveyard.

Travis rang the bell once for each of Moby's eighty years.

The casket was slowly lowered with ropes. A simple wooden cross graced the hole. A long trail of admirers, each in turn, threw a spade-full of dirt into the hole. A bottle of fifty-year-old scotch was nestled in the center of the mound. Two cases of Wild Turkey on either side of the grave would be consumed later in communal swigging, one last round with a great and a good man.

North was carried by her players in solemn dignity while Dairy Queen coupons were passed among the masses for an unstructured ice cream get-together the following Sunday.

Travis tolled the bell sixty-five times.

Soccer in Port Townsend would never be the same.

Next came Merriweather. Members of the dream-catcher crowd formed a long line and handed the urn, followed by the feathered hat, from one set of hands to the next, till the urn reached the small hole dug near the base of an apple tree.

Travis rang the bell seventy-two times.

Two little girls filled in the hole and patted the tiny mound, leaving behind their small overlapping handprints in the fresh earth—a fitting decoration that would have brought Merriweather to tears. The hat was hung in the tree. Merriweather's followers scoured the beach for feathers, which they poked in the fresh dirt.

The mourners sensed that this odd group of unlikely comrades proved the oft-repeated Moby saying, "There are no strangers in death." United by their sense of loss, people commingled in unusual groupings. They shook hands or hugged in commiseration—rough workmen embraced young mothers, soccer girls in ponytails grabbing cigarette-stained hands. The ceremonies and burials over, John guided everyone to the long tables, where the islanders served up salmon in hot, steaming slabs, accompanied by macaroni and vegetable salads and huge trays of apple pan dowdy mounded with whipped cream.

Late that night, after all guests had gone, Annie bundled up the babies and together with Dory, Pinky, Travis and Tate, Owl, South, John, Wisteria, and Christine took *The Ark* and headed toward the east side of the island towing a fireworks barge purloined by Pickles.

In sight of the Seattle skyline, Annie stopped the barge and pressed the remote trigger. One solitary rocket blazed skyward, explosive powder intermingled with Moby's ashes. It began with a vertical glacial blue comet trail punctuated three times by explosives far louder than anyone had ever heard on Puget Sound, each report louder than the one before. The final explosion was a thundering blast of white lightning, momentarily cradled in the basin between the Cascade Range and the Olympic Mountains. Several house windows on Seattle's tony Magnolia bluff shattered, and the news that night talked of a possible meteor falling to earth. It was the last echo of a favorite son…illegal as all hell.

Finally the monumental events of the last few weeks came crashing in on Annie. She struggled to stand in the middle of the boat, wine bottle in hand.

"I am happy to have my twins to raise, but today, I have buried three of my dearest friends. Everyone, please, take a drink from this bottle in their honor."

She passed the bottle around, then sat down and cried. She shed tears of joy, of sorrow, of great loss and great gain. But mostly she cried for those who would never weep again.

Early one morning the following week, Annie decided, with a heavy heart, it was time to stop procrastinating and to finish sorting the last of the junk mail taken from the roll-top desk at Sarah and Peter's. She sighed and pulled the shoebox from behind the sofa and began to rifle through the letters offering credit cards and promotions. Then she came across an unopened greeting card, postmarked almost two years ago.

Annie slit the sealed envelope and pulled out a birthday card. A blue feather drifted onto the table. She opened the card.

"Hi, Sarah…Kinda forgot your birthday, but not totally. I got this feather from a bag lady who claims she can cure infertility with a prayer and a feather. She had a whole bunch of baby pictures that she said were part of her 'life's work,' as she put it! She wanted ten bucks so I gave her a twenty and said, 'How about…twins!!!!!' Ha ha…anyway… for the woman who has tried everything to get preggers…like basting your insides and standing on your head to $20,000 high-tech mumbo jumbo…somehow this seemed right. Now it seems kinda lame…but do I at least get points for trying??? Love ya! YBGF, Penny."

Annie held the card in her hand and looked unseeing out the window for a long time, overcome at the connection to Merriweather. She knew in her heart that Merriweather had worked her magic. It defied logic, but Annie knew there were stronger bonds at play than mere science.

She shook her head and tucked the feather into the envelope along with the card and put it above the bread pan that had held her grandmother so long ago.

A week later, Annie got on the boat for her usual mainland shopping run. Somewhat distracted, she wandered into the post office and sorted her mail.

One letter was from Carol Ann.

*Dear Annie,*

*Sorry couldn't make the funerals. Hope things have settled down for you. Think I have found someone to handle your church. Sister Mary Catherine, the nun I was telling you about, is interested. She's into harmonic therapy—bells, gongs, harps, and tuning forks.*

*Her heart is bad, but she has a strong constitution, should be a good fit for the island.*

*There is also a university professor of astrology from Chicago who wanders around with the mummified remains of a space alien he claims died in the Mt. St. Helen's blast. Check out his web site some time.*

*www.Sthelensalien.com*

*He is in the terminal stages of AIDS and may be heading your way.*

*You and your island are famous, of course, and I have a glut of "normals" clamoring to come out, but I've hand-selected a couple of compatible nuts for your special brand of fruitcake out there. No offense. Gotta go.*

*Carol Ann*

Annie tucked the letter in her pocket and looked up to see the unmistakable outline of a nun's habit wandering up the dock. Annie approached her from behind.

The woman seemed very small. She was dressed in the traditional, long, black robe, with a white, flared hood and wimple.

"Sister Mary Catherine?"

The woman quickly spun around. A cigarette dangled from her lips. Her pixie face was yellowed and wrinkled, but her eyes were haunting, clear, and searching.

"Who wants to know?"

"I'm Annie, from the island. Carol Ann told me to be on the lookout."

Sister Mary Catherine nodded, snapped the stub of her cigarette to the ground, and stepped on it with a vengeful toe. She fumbled through her side pockets, pulled out a pack of Camels, lit the new cigarette with a Bic lighter, and squinted up at Annie.

"What's the matter? Never seen a nun smoke before?"

Taking a long drag, she closed her eyes and let the smoke curl out of her nose. She opened her eyes wider and looked lovingly at the cigarette in her hand.

"I gave the Lord the first seventy years of my life, and I told him if he gave me any more time, it belonged to me. Camel straights. How I love them. I was afraid with all the candy-ass legislation, they would have banned these bad boys by now, but God is just to his children.

"I got the news about your island. I thought maybe I'd help you with your church. I've had some experience."

Annie backtracked. She wasn't sure that this is who she had in mind for the church.

"We haven't really decided on a direction. We only dedicated it last week."

Sister Mary Catherine put her hand on her hip and flared her cigarette hand in the air à la Betty Davis.

"Sweetie, I'm not taking over your church. I don't have time. I do need a place to run my harmonic cure workshops, but with baking and distributing muffins to the navy boys, my Tai Chi lessons, my salsa lessons, and singing folk songs at three rest homes, I simply don't have the time to run a church. Help maybe, but not run the whole thing."

"I'm sorry. Smoke?" She tilted the pack toward Annie.

"No thanks," and then Annie ventured. " Have you ever heard the saying: Give me a child till the age of seven and I will show you the man?"

Mary Catherine took a deep drag. "I use that saying all the time. It's an old Jesuit saying, and I'm pretty sure I coined the phrase myself."

"Really," Annie said skeptically. "I suppose you are also responsible for the saying: Have a nice day. You know, the one with the smiley face?"

"Nope, not mine," the nun picked a stray bit of tobacco from the tip of her tongue.

"Everyone knows that came from Forest Gump," she said emphatically.

"Not Al Gore?" Annie countered with a twinkle.

As she blew smoke from the side of her mouth, Mary Catherine deadpanned, "Whatever."

Annie gave a deep introspective smile. She pointed to *The Ark*. "We'll be leaving in about fifteen minutes."

Sister Mary Catherine looked over at *The Ark*, then grabbed her two bags and dipped her head in agreement.

Before returning, Annie wanted to go over to the small Farmer's Saturday Market next to the dock. She was sure she had heard a rooster crowing. Following the cackling, she found two children sitting on folding canvas chairs with a cardboard box at their feet. "Chicken 4 Sale" was scrawled on the top. A purple crayon sat squashed into the pavement.

"Good morning," Annie said. "Do you have a rooster in there?"

The boy was about to speak when the girl, her carrot-red pigtails bouncing, slugged him on the shoulder.

"Mom said I was in charge."

The boy's mouth curled as if he wanted to cry, but he held it in and rubbed his shoulder.

"We sure do, and a hen too." The girl turned sweetly to Annie. "Wanna see 'em?"

"I need a good rooster," said Annie, giving away the high bargaining ground.

The boy reached into the box and pulled out a handsome bantam rooster with an iridescent green tail and beautifully rusted neck feathers. The bird gave a protesting squawk as he cocked his head and looked up at Annie. "My sister is afraid to pick up the rooster."

"I am *not* afraid." The girl looked ready to hit him again, but the boy was too quick, jumping out of the chair. "Show her the other side, squirt," the sister challenged.

"The neighbor's dog almost killed him," the boy explained. "My mom says we have to get rid of him 'cause he's crowing all the time and bothering the neighbors."

"What's his name?" Annie crouched down for a better look.

"I'm not allowed to say what my mom calls him," the sister jumped in. "We just call him 'the rooster.' Here's the other one."

She pulled out no-nonsense, down-to-business looking, brown speckled hen. "We call her Sacagawea, after the Indian guide for Lewis and Clark. My mom says we can give away the rooster, but we should sell the hen for five dollars."

The girl looked up hopefully.

"I've been looking for two chickens exactly like this." Digging through her purse, Annie put two twenty-dollar bills on top of the box.

The boy grinned and reached out to grab the money, but his sister pushed him back.

"That's too much," she said.

Annie's eyes were beginning to tear up.

"It would be disrespectful not to pay more than full price for these handsome birds, and you would be doing me a great favor."

The two siblings did some serious soul-searching for about a second, then hastily stuffed the chickens back into the box, grabbed the two bills, and scrambled back through the crowd, tipping over both chairs in their haste to share their good fortune with their mom.

Sister Mary Catherine had found her way to the boat. Annie cast off the lines, and soon they were skimming over the water to the island.

With her hand still on the tiller, Annie listened as the chicken trilled and clucked on her lap. She closed her eyes and leaned back to let the late afternoon sun warm her neck. She turned her face toward the wind, and took a deep breath and smelled the salt air. She knew she had been given a second chance, and that the best part of her life was just over the horizon.

# Recipes

## Three Rubs, Two Chutneys, One Glaze

Chinese Five-Spice Rub. In a small bowl, mix equal parts ground anise, black peppercorn, ground cinnamon, ground cloves and fennel seeds in blender or pepper mill. Makes about two tablespoons.

Jamaican Jerk Rub. In small bowl, mix 2 tsp. ground ginger; 1 tsp each ground allspice, dried thyme, cayenne, and pepper; and 2 tsp. onion powder. Makes two tablespoons.

Provencal Rub. In a small bowl, mix 2 tsp. each crushed dried rosemary and dried thyme and 1 tsp. each dried rubbed sage and dried lavender. Makes two tablespoons.

Cranberry-Apricot Chutney. Prep and cook time: 20 minutes, plus one hour to cool. 12 oz. fresh cranberries, 1 cup sugar, 1/3 cup coarsely chopped dried apricots, 1/3 cup dried currants, 1/3 cup golden raisins, 2 T balsamic vinegar, 2 tangerines and 1 cup chopped pecans.

Sort cranberries. In a 3-quart pan over medium high heat, bring 1 cup of water, cranberries, sugar, currants, apricots, raisins and vinegar to a boil, stirring often. Reduce heat and simmer, stirring occasionally, until cranberries begin to pop, about 5 to 8 minutes. Meanwhile, pull off peel and white membrane from tangerines and chop coarsely, discarding seeds. Add to mixture and simmer for 2 to 3 minutes. Stir in pecans and allow to slake. Serve.

Fresh Pomegranate Chutney. Prep and cook time 30 minutes.

Chill 1 cup of pomegranate seeds overnight.

Add 1 cup red currant jelly, 1/3 cup finely chopped green onions including tops, 1 cup pomegranate seeds, 1 T minced fresh ginger, 1 T fresh jalapeno chili, 1 T lemon juice, salt and pepper.

Warm currant jelly in 2-cup glass measure, stir in ingredients and salt and pepper to taste.

Let stand for 20 minutes.

<u>Tonsil-searing Chili Sage Glaze.</u> Prep time 10 minutes.

3 T habanero or Scotch bonnet chili marmalade or other hot red pepper or chili jelly, 3 T orange marmalade, 4 tsp. ground sage, salt.

In a glass measuring cup, mix the habanero marmalade and orange marmalade. Gently heat, stirring once. Stir in sage. Baste entire turkey with glaze when thermometer read 135 degrees, spread marmalade glaze over turkey while singing "Ave Maria," and continue to cook.

## Seven Sisters Chocolate Floating Island

Cream together:   1 cup white sugar
                  1 T butter
Sift together:    1 cup flour
                  1 teaspoon baking powder
                  ¼ tsp. salt
                  1 T cocoa

Alternate dry mixture into first mixture along with 2 cups milk, put into buttered 9-inch cake pan sprinkle with walnuts.

In another bowl mix:   2 cups of brown sugar
                       1 cup white sugar
                       4 T Cocoa

Spread this evenly over mix in pan. Pour 1 ½ cups boiling water over top and bake 30 minutes @ 350 degrees. Turn upside down on large plate.

Alternative: You could splash a dollop of whipped cream, drizzle with huckleberry sauce and garnish with a mint leaf, but why would you bother?

## Merriweather's Cream of Chaneterelle Mushroom Soup

(From a foggy memory from a long good bye)

    1 cup chopped chanterelle mushrooms

    2 T. minced onions

    2 T butter

    1 blue-grey feather from a Great Blue Heron

    2 T white flour

    2 cups chicken or beef broth

    1 cup light cream

    ¼ tsp. salt

    ¼ tsp. pepper

    ½ tsp. fresh ground nutmeg

Cook mushrooms, onions, and butter in a large pan. Blend in flour, add broth, and stir till slightly thickened. Cool slightly, then add cream and seasonings. Ladle into bowls.

Disclaimer: Feather optional....save it to make a dream catcher.

## Annie's Apple Crisp

6 to 8 Gravenstein apples or any tart apple, peeped, cored and sliced

1 tsp. ground cinnamon

Pinch of ground nutmeg

small handful of white sugar

heaping handful of all-purpose flour

heaping handful of dark-brown sugar

heaping handful of old fashioned oats

1/3 to ½ lb. butter cut into small chunks

handful of chopped pecans or walnuts, depending on mood

Put four fir logs into firebox to heat oven to 350 degrees. Put apples into the large yellow Pyrex bowl. Add spices and sugar and mix together with wooden spoon. Place in a large buttered baking dish approximately 11 by 7 inch, or use the yellow bowl. I do.

Combine flour, brown sugar, and oatmeal into the medium green Pyrex bowl. Cut in butter with fork or pastry cutter till evenly distributed. Stir in pecans. Spoon over fruit to cover.

Bake until juices bubble and topping is golden brown, 35 to 45 minutes. Cool and eat with spoon. Set remainder in warming oven above wood stove. Good for the next five days, if it lasts that long.

## Moby's Oyster Stew

Prep and cook time: 20 to 25 minutes.

Chef urged to garble with swig of Wild Turkey, swallow half and spit rest into the wind.

    1 lb. pancetta or bacon

    2 leek (only the white parts, sans root) or 3 medium sweet onions

    2 heads (3 to 4 inches wide) fennel

    1 teaspoon crushed fennel seed

    6 cups half and half cream

    30 ounces of freshly shucked oysters and their liquor (approx 4 cups total)

    ½ cup Italian parsley

    1 T Pernod or Sambuca

    fresh ground pepper and salt

    2 to 4 T butter

Trim pancetta or bacon into ¼ inch dices and put into a 6-quart pan. Chop leek, trim and discard root end and bruised spots from fennel, then rinse and chop; Add leeks, fennel seed to pancetta and stir often over medium heat until limp but not browned, approximately 5 to 6 minutes.

Add cream, oysters and liquor and turn heat to medium high. Stir often until soup is hot, but not boiling. I repeat: Do not allow soup to boil.

Stir in ¼ cup parsley, liquor, and pepper and salt to taste.

Ladle into bowls and sprinkle with remaining parsley. Add a dollop of butter to each serving.